ALSO BY E

THE WORLD OF THE GATEWAY

The Gateway Trilogy (Series 1)
Spirit Legacy
Spirit Prophecy
Spirit Ascendancy
The Gateway Trackers (Series 2)
Whispers of the Walker
Plague of the Shattered
Awakening of the Seer
Portraits of the Forsaken
Heart of the Rebellion
Soul of the Sentinel
Gift of the Darkness
Tales from the Gateway

THE RIFTMAGIC SAGA

What the Lady's Maid Knew
The Rebel Beneath the Stairs
The Girl at the Heart of the Storm

THE REBEL BENEATH THE STAIRS

THE REBEL
BENEATH THE
STAIRS

The Riftmagic Saga Book 2

E.E. HOLMES

Lily Faire Publishing
Townsend, MA

www.lilyfairepublishing.com
www.eeholmes.com

ISBN 978-1-7339352-9-6 (Print edition)
ISBN 978-1-7339352-8-9 (Digital edition)

Publisher's note: This is a work of fiction. Names, characters, places and incidents are either the product of the author's imagination or are used fictitiously.

Cover design by James T. Egan of Bookfly Design LLC
Author photography by Cydney Scott Photography

For Joe.

If this last year has taught me one thing, it's that I would never want to do this life without you. Hands full, hearts full, side by side, you and me.

PROLOGUE

T HE POUNDING OF SULLY'S HEART echoed the pounding upon the door. She fought to untangle herself, both from her blankets and from the disorienting tendrils of sleep still wound stubbornly around her consciousness. Slowly, clarity seeped back into her—a gradual remembering of where she was and who she was. She slid out of bed, her bare feet upon the cold floor sending a secondary shock through her sleep-addled brain. She threw a dressing robe over her shoulders and lit the candle beside her bed with shaking fingers as the frantic knocking continued downstairs. In the flare and crackle of the flame, her own pale and frightened face was illuminated in the looking glass hanging on her wall. Sully stared into her own eyes and whispered to herself.

"Steady on, old girl."

She hurried down the stairs, hair flying like a ragged flag behind her. On the landing, a small face was peering out through the crack of a door with owlish, frightened eyes.

"Into the trap door you go, boy, and be quick about it," Sully hissed. The little face vanished as the door creaked shut.

As Sully reached the bottom of the stairs, Louise stood in the doorway to the kitchen, clad in a white nightgown, a lacy cap, and the same frozen, wide-eyed expression as one might find on a woodland creature who has just scented a hunter. Sully put a finger to her lips and pointed back toward the kitchen. It took several seconds and a sharp snap of Sully's fingers before her meaning could penetrate Louise's panic, and the woman scurried through the kitchen door, closing it with a squeak. Sully prayed she would have the good sense to get back into her bed and pretend to be asleep.

Behind the closed door, against which someone was still hammering insistently, Sully arranged her face into what she fervently hoped was a sleepy and bemused expression, and pulled the handle.

"What do you mean by—?" she began, the question shriveling to dust on her tongue as her eyes focused through the downpour on the two figures standing there.

A woman, draped in a black cloak, her face chalky white and twisted with fear. A small boy, shoulders hunched against the cold, shivered beside her, clinging to the folds of the woman's cloak.

"I'm looking for Lila Sullivan. Please, it's very important that I see her."

"Lucky for you then, that she's standing right in front of you," Sully replied. She tried not to let the wariness she felt creep into her tone. She did not recognize the woman.

The emotions shuddered across the woman's face so quickly that Sully barely had time to process them before her features settled back into grim lines of fear. She cleared her throat and said, "I've brought the boy to you, as Mr. Davies instructed."

Sully had to work hard to stop her jaw from hitting the floor. It took her a moment to find her voice again.

"I don't know what you—"

"Please, there's no time! Mr. Davies told me to—"

"Whatever Mr. Davies told you means nothing now. He's been arrested. The Lamplighters Confederacy is shut down, disbanded."

The woman blinked. "What do you—*arrested*?"

"Yes."

"When?"

"Three days ago. He... no one told you?"

The woman shook her head. Beside her, the boy gave a little whimper and the woman squeezed him against her side, shushing him.

"Look, I don't know where the mix-up has come in, but you can't just leave him here. You'll have to sneak him back to wherever he's come from and wait for us to send you word, or..."

"It's too late for that!" the woman cried out, her voice sharp. "I can't bring him back, he's in too much danger there."

"Where—" Sully began, and then she saw, as the woman shifted an arm around the child, a flash of gold and red livery from beneath her cloak and let out a gasp. "Are you... is this boy from an Elder family?"

2

The woman bit her lip and nodded. "Yes," she whispered.

"And he's..."

"Yes. Riftborn."

Sully peered down at the boy, fascinated in spite of herself. The woman had had the sense to change him into a ragged set of clothing, so that he looked very much at first glance like any other guttersnipe populating the Barrens. But a closer look revealed all the telltale signs of a child who had been well-cared for—a clean face, neatly trimmed hair, a full-cheeked moon of a face that had certainly never known the pinch of a hungry belly. Her heart swelled with pity for the child, who looked terrified. He couldn't be much older than three. The pity must have made its way from her heart to her face because the servant woman renewed her pleas with a sudden hopeful burst of enthusiasm.

"Surely you understand why I can't take him back, Davies or no Davies. But he's a good boy—obedient and old enough to understand what's at stake. He won't give you any trouble. Please, can't you just take him and see that he makes it out of the country?"

"You're not hearing me," Sully said. "With Davies in custody, the entire system has broken down. I can't get him out of the country. Blast it, I probably won't be able to move him out of this house!"

"Miss Sullivan, please. Please. I can't bring him back there, I just can't." She dropped her voice to a whisper so that the boy wouldn't hear. "You know what they'll do to him. What they do to all of them."

Sully looked down at the boy again. He was trying to peer past her into the darkened corridor beyond, pupils dilated with fear. He didn't want to be there any more than she wanted him to be there. He glanced up and, finding her gaze upon him, raised his little pointed chin defiantly and threw back his shoulders, as though daring her to call him frightened.

She softened in spite of herself. He was brave, this one.

Sully returned her gaze to the woman, who met it steadily. "I can't promise he will be safe here," she stated baldly. There was no space for empty platitudes here, no room for anything but the naked truth.

"I understand that. If the last few months have taught me anything, it is that nothing—nothing at all—is promised. But I had no choice. Please help him."

Sully sighed, running a hand through her wild nest of sleep-matted hair. "The Resistance is in shambles. I won't be able to protect you either if you're caught, or..."

3

"I know. I have accepted it."

"I'll need your word that you won't give us up if you're caught."

"You have it, I swear to you. Please, just help him."

The two women stared into each other's eyes, and Sully found in those wide grey eyes a reflection of her own steely determination.

"Well, that settles it, I suppose."

With a resigned sigh, she reached out for the boy's hand, and the boy, after a moment's hesitation, took it.

A Riftborn Child's Prayer (from the *Riftborn Children's Primer*, 3rd Edition, published 1826)

And now the sun has gone to bed,
And now to sleep, I lay my head.
And as I dream, I hope and pray
The Creator takes my sin away.
For in my heart the weakness dwells
And in my soul, temptation swells,
And though I fight the Path to stay
I fear to magic I may stray.
So strengthen me, Creator true
And I'll devote my life to You.
Amen.

ONE

T HE PRAYER OF THE RIFTBORN had barely begun and already Eliza's hands were shaking. Her palms, as she pressed them together in prayer, were slick with sweat. All around her, the Riftborn manor servants were rocking, swaying, crying, and moaning. The air was thick with their reverently murmured words and their cloying shame. It took every ounce of Eliza's resolve not to scream a warning, to let it reverberate up into the furthest reaches of the Sacrarium.

It's a lie. It's all a lie. Don't drink the Riftmead.

The golden chalices floated down the aisles, held aloft in the hands of the High Elder's white-robed attendants. The light from the many candles glinted off the metal, making the very vessels themselves seem alive with celestial power.

Eliza counted the days in her head. Five. It had been five agonizing days since she had delivered the charity baskets in the Barrens. Five days since copies of a book she had helped to steal had been disseminated among the Riftborn families who lived there. Five days since she had watched Praesidio soldiers deliver bottles of Riftmead to every single household in the district, cloaking their actions in the guise of benevolence. She shuddered just thinking about it.

Society in Post-Rift London was divided into two unbridgeable groups. On one side, the Dignus, free of the curse of magic. On the other, the Riftborn, whose magic marked them as weak, sinful, and inferior. The Illustratum, at once the religious and governmental authority of the land, ruled over both groups, preserving the power of the Dignus and subjugating the Riftborn into lives of servitude. And how had this come to be? All her life, Eliza had believed it to be the will of the Creator, but that belief slipped further and further away by the day.

The knowledge that Riftmead was not a mere symbolic casting away of their Riftmagic but an actual poisoning of their bodies was a knowledge that Eliza had carried with her for several weeks now, and the burden only grew heavier with every passing day. And the new policies of the Illustratum were only making it worse. It was all Eliza could do not to smash every bottle of Riftmead she saw upon the shelves in her father's office, not to knock every glass of it out of the hands of her friends who served with her as one of the household staff at Larkspur Manor, where Elder Hallewell ruled over them all with an iron fist. And now, as she stood right within the beating heart of the Illustratum, partaking in Sunday services, reality hit her with the force of a speeding locomotive.

Her life was a lie. Her life had always been a lie.

The golden chalice was being passed along the row before her now. She watched helplessly as the goblet was handed along and pressed to one set of lips after another. She watched as her own father, who stood just a few feet in front of her, lifted his prayerful eyes to the sky before drinking deeply. She knew what he was experiencing in those silent moments after the Riftmead entered his body: a sense of freedom, the sensation that his Riftmagic was releasing its hold on him. In reality, it was he who was losing his hold on his Riftmagic—the gift was being somehow dulled and weakened by whatever was inside the cup. Watching it happen was almost unbearable.

The voice of the High Elder droned on, but Eliza could not focus on what he was saying. The words, once so familiar and comforting to her, had no meaning, like so much buzzing in her ears, like irksome flies she wished she could bat away. An unexpected wave of grief crashed over her, for the loss of the comfort and reassurance she had once found standing in this pew. Where once she had felt safely anchored to her faith she now felt dangerously adrift.

So battered was she by this new storm, so busy trying to keep her head above the water, that she was startled by the appearance of the chalice at her elbow. She froze as it glinted in the periphery of her vision, and she was seized by a sudden and violent impulse to knock it from Peppa Milton's hands. Several seconds passed as she tried to master herself, and it was only when Peppa, wide-eyed, gave her a

8

nudge with her elbow that Eliza forced herself to reach out and take the cup. Her hands shook. She couldn't bear to look at it, couldn't stand to see the golden liquid sloshing around inside it. Her blood thundering in her ears, she closed her eyes, lifted the chalice to her mouth, and tilted it upward, so that the Riftmead sloshed against her tightly closed lips. Lowering the cup again, she made an exaggerated swallowing movement, and then turned, handing it to Mary Carter, who accepted it with her face full of reverence and her eyes full of tears. Eliza dropped her eyes to her own hands, now clasped tightly in front of her, knuckles white from the effort to stop their shaking. She was holding her breath, waiting for something to happen.

She had refused to drink the Riftmead, and she had disguised her refusal by pretending to drink. Surely something would happen? She half-wondered if the heavens above her would open up and strike her dead where she stood. Surely an Elder would stand up, pointing an accusatory finger at her, announcing her duplicity to the entire Sacrarium before having her dragged straight out to the gallows.

But the chalice continued its lilting progress along the row of servants, and the mumbled prayers around her continued unabated. No lightning bolts. No claps of thunder. No deep, authoritative voice of the Creator boomed through the rafters, no chasm opened beneath her to swallow her up for the heretical act she had just committed. And at last, the chalices were carried back up to the altaria and stowed away beneath it, and the service continued as though nothing at all had happened.

The lack of instant retribution did nothing to calm her nerves.

The truth was that she'd been waiting for divine punishment for days now, and her fears were only mounting. Eliza had not dared to correspond with Eli Turner again, not since the books had been distributed. It felt too risky, reaching out to him so soon. She wondered if Colin was able to pass along her message, that she wanted to join his next efforts, whatever they might be. She wondered if Eli would even welcome her help. Perhaps they were all happy to be rid of her now that she had played her part. She was, after all, a manor servant, and as such, it would be much harder for them to trust her. The social divide between the Riftborn manor servants and the Riftborn that populated the poverty-ridden lanes of the Barrens was nearly as great as the divide between the Riftborn and the Dignus themselves. But of course, Eliza thought with a new and pungent bitterness, this was all by design.

If they mistrusted each other, there was little chance of them banding together. Divide and conquer, that was the Illustratum's key to maintaining their power.

She felt as though she'd been walking through her life with a blindfold on, not only accepting the darkness, but grateful for it. Eli, Sully, and the others had given her a peek at the world on the other side of the blindfold, and now she could never be satisfied to stumble around again, feeling her way through the world, trusting to faith to guide her when she had perfectly good vision of her own.

This did not mean, of course, that a part of her didn't still long for the peace and quiet and blissful ignorance of the blindfold, though she despised herself for admitting it. In many ways, her life had been easier before she'd known. The Path had stretched out before her with nary a twist nor a turn—it never occurred to her that a life ought not to look like that, every decision easy because your choice had already been made for you. And now her Path had vanished in the misty indecision before her, and she felt she could only see a few steps in front of her, the destination no longer clear. The anxiety was almost enough to make her run up the aisle and ask for the chalice back.

There was a great shifting of bodies around her; lost in her thoughts, the end of the service had taken Eliza by surprise. She shook her head to clear it, and composed her face before anyone around her could remark upon her distraction. She waited as the rows emptied one by one, as the Dignus made their way up the aisles to rejoin their awaiting servants. As Jessamine swept alongside her, Eliza caught her eye and was unsurprised to see the same distraction in her mistress's expression.

After all, Jessamine's clear Path had likewise disappeared from beneath her feet, and she had yet to regain her footing.

They joined the solemn queue shuffling toward the entrance hall, where the sounds of their feet and the rumblings and mutterings of quiet voices were amplified in the vast, cavernous space. Eliza could not help but glance at the place on the floor where, a few short weeks ago, a Riftborn man had been shot and killed during services. The smears of his blood had long since been scrubbed away, but the echoing sounds of his demise remained, ringing in Eliza's head as she tried to avert her eyes.

She had wondered, as they had gotten into the carriage that morning, if there would be another disturbance at services. After all, the books that she had helped to disseminate would have been read by now, their vile and violent truths about the Illustratum laid bare in the Elders' own words. Surely the Barrens would be abuzz with it by now? Surely the rebellious undercurrent of the past few weeks would only grow stronger, the demonstrations bigger and harder to quash?

Unless the Illustratum's plan to distribute Riftmead to the masses had worked, she told herself bitterly. Unless the Barrens was too deeply in the clutches of Riftmead to muster a care for the fact that the Dignus were abandoning and even murdering their own Riftborn children. The thought that they might continue to get away with it made Eliza's blood boil in her veins even as she cowered away from the stony glares of the Elder statues watching them from above like gargoyles.

They rode back to Larkspur Manor in silence. Elder Hallewell did not join them, having remained behind with the other Elders for yet another legislative session, though they knew he would be home for dinner, for he had demanded that Jessamine be there to join him. It was a pointless demand; Jessamine was always there for dinner on Sundays before she left for her charity circle. She had eaten far too many meals there staring down the length of an empty table to the place where her father ought to have sat.

"Miss Jessamine, would you like me to accompany you upstairs, miss?" Eliza asked as the carriage crunched to a halt in the gravel drive.

"Thank you, but no, Eliza," Jessamine replied with a sigh. "I think I'd like to be alone for a little while. My father will want to discuss the service when he returns, and so I think I may spend some time going over today's readings from the Book of the Rift. I do not want to disappoint him if I am unable to converse upon the subject."

"Very well, miss. Ring if you need me. I'll just be tending to some mending," Eliza said, bobbing a curtsy. She stepped back and allowed her mistress to enter the house first, watching her drift all the way up the grand staircase and vanish into the upper reaches of the house before starting down through the warren of narrow hallways and dark staircases that led to the servants' quarters below.

The hour or two after Sunday services was the only time one could find silence downstairs. It was expected that the staff would return to their quarters for quiet reflection and prayer. Now, Eliza suspected, it was also to allow the initial haze of the Riftmead to clear from their heads before they returned to their work. The quiet had always felt wrong to her—unnatural, in a place of such continuous hustle and bustle. Now, it just felt heavy, weighted with dark and unspoken things. She hurried to her room, desperate to escape it.

Bridie was there, as Eliza knew she would be. She snatched her prayer book up from the bed in a hasty attempt to appear to be studying it, but when she saw who was standing in the doorway, she cast it aside again with a sigh of relief and scooted across the bed to make room for Eliza.

"Thank goodness it's you. Your father has been making the rounds, checking up on us all to ensure we're reflecting properly. He caught one of the footmen napping. I could hear the shouting all the way from the men's quarters," Bridie said with a smothered grin. Eliza dropped onto the bed beside her and began unlacing her boots.

"Is that so?" Eliza said automatically.

"Oh, yes. It was ever so loud. I'm not sure why we have to spend so much time reflecting on the service after we've just had to sit through it, but I'm not complaining about the break," she said, stretching her limbs like a cat.

"Shh, don't say things like that out loud," Eliza scolded. "Do you want him in here next? These walls have ears, you know."

Bridie rolled her eyes, but dropped her voice to a whisper. "How is Miss Jessamine?"

"She is bearing up well, considering," Eliza said stiffly. Personally, she thought Miss Jessamine was falling apart, but she was not about to reveal as much to Bridie who, despite her clear empathy for their mistress, was likely to take whatever details she could wring from Eliza and scatter them like seeds to the wind. She simply couldn't help herself.

"I don't know how. I think I should die of a broken heart if it was me," Bridie said, and a dreamy look came into her eyes, as though no girl could ask for a more romantic fate than to die of unbearable heartbreak.

"I hope you would have more sense than that," Eliza replied. "If a heart can break, then it can mend. Surely some of the greatest love is found in the wake of heartbreak."

"Well, I'm not likely to find out either way, am I?" Bridie

grumbled. "Where am I supposed to meet someone capable of breaking my heart, anyway?"

"Do you want your heart broken?"

Bridie scoffed. "Perhaps not, but I'd like the chance to find something worth breaking it for."

"Where does anyone meet anyone? It's all by chance, Bridie. We just have to keep our eyes open to the possibility."

"I suppose it's a *possibility* that a handsome chimney sweep might fall into the grate while I'm sweeping up the ashes, but I shan't hold my breath," Bridie said.

Eliza chuckled, feeling just a bit of her tension melt away as Bridie prattled on. It was almost possible to forget the heavier things weighing on her when they were together like this, curled on the bed and whispering like schoolgirls.

"Do you ever feel like you're missing the life you're meant to live?" Bridie whispered, her voice suddenly tinged with melancholy. "Like, the world up there is spinning away and down here it's just... still?"

Eliza gave a wry laugh. "Still? This place? Perhaps for an hour or two on a Sunday afternoon; but otherwise, I can safely say our lives are anything but still."

"I don't mean work, Eliza," Bridie said, impatience thick in her voice. "I mean the other things... the things that make life worth living."

Eliza frowned up at the ceiling. "If this is your way of reflecting on the Path, I think you might be going about it the wrong way."

"Oh, for Creator's sake, Eliza, you know what I mean! I'm grateful for my position here, you know that. I'd still be in that blasted workhouse if it weren't for this opportunity. But does that mean I must resign myself to having no other dreams at all? Is it so wrong to dream of a life beyond kneeling in filthy grates, up to my elbows in soot?"

Eliza turned and looked into Bridie's earnest face and smiled. "No, it's not wrong. I just worry about you, Bridie. I worry that what you have will never be enough."

Bridie's mouth twisted, and she turned her gaze back to the ceiling. "Sometimes I worry about that, too."

Eliza turned her head to adjust her pillow and caught sight of the picture on her bedside table: her mother. Eliza stared into Emmaline Braxton's serene countenance and wondered, as she had wondered every day since she was a small child, what had caused the devoted wife, mother, and servant to run off and disappear without a trace. Had she, like Bridie, been consumed with the thought that life was passing by without her? Had she abandoned her family and the only life she'd ever known to chase after something beyond the walls of Larkspur Manor? Eliza had wasted many years wishing ardently for her mother to come back. Now, she simply wished that, wherever her mother was, she had found what she was looking for, though that wish came at the aching cost of knowing that she had not been reason enough for her mother to stay.

Eliza felt herself sinking very close to something like despair, and so she tore her gaze from her mother's portrait, cleared her throat, and said very seriously, "I heard from a very reliable source that Peter Bennett offered to walk you home from town two days ago. Perhaps *he* might be willing to break your heart, if you asked him."

Bridie broke into a snorting laugh and immediately had to clamp her hand over her mouth to stifle it. "Who told you that? No, don't answer, I know jolly well who it was. Ooh, when I get my hands on Millie…"

"Why don't you let him walk you home? What's the worst thing that could happen?" Eliza said.

"I suppose that he might get it in his head to ask me again!" Bridie said, continuing to giggle. "Eliza, you can't be serious! What possible hope of romance could I have with Peter Bennett?"

"He's a nice enough lad," Eliza said.

"Nice he may be, but he's a dreadful bore," Bridie countered. "Have you ever tried to carry on a conversation with him? One may as well try pulling teeth from his head as words from his mouth. And he's so tall! I'd crick my neck just trying to look him in the eye!"

"Well, now you're just being silly," Eliza said.

"Silly, am I? The next time you see Peter Bennett, you try carrying on a conversation with him. If you can get him to string together more than five words at a time on any mildly interesting subject, I'll walk home with him every Sunday for a month."

Eliza sat up. "Hmm. I think I fancy a chat with him right now."

Bridie's face fell. "Eliza, don't tease me."

"Every Sunday for a month, you say?"

"Eliza!"

14

"I'll be right back. I just remembered something I needed to ask him."

"Eliza! Stop! We're supposed to be reflecting!" Bridie hissed. She reached out to grab Eliza's arm, but Eliza was too quick for her. She had already hopped out of the bed and slipped her feet back into her boots.

"Would you consider stable mucking 'mildly interesting'?" Eliza asked seriously.

"Eliza, don't you dare!"

But Eliza had already flashed a mischievous grin and slipped out the door. She could not lay around and reflect, not today—avoiding her troubled thoughts by teasing Bridie was a much more tempting prospect.

She did not really intend to track down Peter Bennett—she merely wanted Bridie to think she was. Instead, she slipped out of the door by the kitchen and into the glow of the midday sun. It was a truly glorious spring day—her anxiety about services had blinded her to the clear skies and balmy temperature. She took a deep breath, inhaling the sweet, heady scent of early roses that wafted on the warm breeze from the garden. She gazed out over the grounds to the fringe of trees and the rolling hills beyond. A pair of starlings swooped and darted overhead, their twittering like the playful banter of lovers in pursuit of one another. *Yes,* Eliza thought, *this was the kind of reflection she needed.*

But the untroubled moment was not to last.

"Psst! Eliza!"

Eliza jumped in surprise and whirled around to spot James Whippet waving his arms frantically at her from the threshold of the stables. After ensuring that no one was about, Eliza strolled in the direction of the stables, taking her time, lest anyone spot her from the windows. Not wanting to attract any attention, she stooped to pluck a pale yellow bloom from the patch of wild primrose that grew near the stable door before slipping quietly inside.

"For me? I'm flattered," James said, nodding his head toward the flower and winking roguishly.

Eliza rolled her eyes. "I was attempting to appear casual—a trick you might want to try, rather than waving your arms like a windmill in a hurricane," she said rather tartly. "Now, what is it, and be quick

15

about it. You know it isn't safe for us to be seen conversing together too frequently."

James' grin widened. "We could close the door if you like. No one would see us then."

"What do you want, James?" Eliza sighed. He was perhaps the last person at Larkspur Manor Eliza would have chosen to trust and confide in, but she had little say in the matter. If she hoped to continue as part of the Resistance, she would have to put up with him.

"I've got a letter for you," James said, pulling the slightly crumpled missive from his pocket and holding it out for her.

"When did it come?" Eliza asked, all aggravation forgotten as she lunged forward to snatch it from him.

"Last night. Colin brought it."

"And you've only just brought it to me now?" she snapped even as she broke the seal to read it.

"Don't blame me! It's not my fault you were gone all morning at services. I did my best to track you down, you know, but I couldn't draw attention to m'self. After all, what business should I have with you?"

But Eliza wasn't even listening to his excuses. Her eyes flew over the words on the page before her—words in a familiar hand. She looked up to see him scowling at her.

"Well? What's it say?"

She folded it back up and tucked it into her pocket. "I'm not at liberty to tell you. But thank you for seeing that it was delivered to me safely," she replied.

She turned her back on James Whippet's crestfallen expression and hurried out of the stable and back toward the house, barely able to conceal a grim smile. It looked like the Resistance might just want a lady's maid in their ranks after all.

Night could not come quickly enough.

(Letter from Eli to Eliza)

Eliza—

I hope this letter finds you well. Colin gave me your message. If you still desire to help the cause, meet us Sunday night at half twelve at the Bell and Flagon. There is much to be discussed and no time to lose. We will be grateful to have you in the fold.

Burn this letter as soon as you have read it. Tell no one.

—Eli

.

TWO

T HE LETTER LAY on a gleaming silver tray, upon what felt like an ocean of pristine white table linen that separated Jessamine from her father. It drew her eye like a dead thing, and she had to force herself to look away from it, dropping her eyes to her dinner plate and forcing the food down forkful by agonizing forkful.

Her father did not mention the letter. He was content, it seemed, to allow it to sit, unremarked upon, through course after course. Jessamine dug her fingernails into her palms in an effort to ignore the missive and focus instead on the sound of her father's voice as he lectured at length on the content of that morning's service at the Illustratum.

Jessamine tried to be grateful that she was, at last, sitting down to a meal with her father after weeks of his being conspicuous only by his absence. She tried to feel the pride she used to feel, the sense of importance when he would take the time to talk to her. As a child, she would sit poker-straight, hands squeezed together in her lap with the concerted effort to both absorb and understand every word. Perhaps, she thought, if she proved herself a worthy vessel of his knowledge, he would give her more of the attention she so craved. Now, it was all she could do not to leap up from the table and shout at him to say something—*anything*—about Reginald Morgan and the letter now lying between them.

It had arrived that morning, but as it was not addressed to her, she dared not open it, though the envelope's return address made it perfectly clear that she was the subject of the letter within. She could think of nothing more maddening than the fact that decisions regarding her future were being made and casually passed back and forth under her very nose in sealed envelopes that she was not even permitted to open.

Of course, she had had no shortage of mail arrive for her, either. In the several weeks following her disastrous Presentation ball, it seemed every acquaintance with whom she'd ever exchanged a casual word or two had taken it upon themselves to personally express their shock and horror *on her behalf* as to the troubling events that had ended her Presentation in confusion and flames. And among these letters were those from closer "friends" who also could not miss the opportunity to express their further surprise at the fact that it was Reginald Morgan, not Teddy Potter, who had claimed Jessamine's first dance, and then congratulating her on the match. After the first few of these letters, Jessamine refused to open any more, demanding instead that Eliza open and read them, and only to pass the letter along to her if it required answering.

"If it's nothing but gloating beneath a delicate veil of pity, throw it straight in the fire and let Bridie sweep it out with the ashes in the morning. I'll have none of it," she had declared.

Bridie had subsequently done a great deal of sweeping.

There was, however, a growing stack of letters that Eliza would not burn and refused to open: those addressed to Jessamine from Teddy Potter. These were piled upon the silver tray at Jessamine's bedside, and she would stare intently at them as she lay in bed at night, as though hoping they would stand up and start reading themselves, or else fling themselves onto the smoldering piles of correspondence in her hearth, for it seemed she lacked the will to either read or burn them. Every time she reached out her hand for one, she thought about the last time she watched Teddy Potter sign his name, in a meaningless space upon her dance card, breaking her heart with a single swipe of a pen, and this memory was enough to shore up her determination never to read another word he wrote.

"Jessamine?"

Jessamine looked up with a start from her plate, as disoriented as if she had just been shaken awake from a dream.

"I'm... I'm sorry, Father?"

Josiah was frowning at her, his fork suspended in the air halfway to his mouth. "I asked you whether you'd had a chance to read the High Elder's declaration on the Feast of the Chosen? It was in the Weekly Word."

"Oh," Jessamine wracked her brain for some detail she could dredge up to prove she'd read it. In truth, she had given up halfway through and abandoned the Illustratum's weekly printed newsletter on the seat of the carriage. "I... I was pleased to see that a fasting will be observed on the eve of the Feast this year."

To Jessamine's relief, her father seemed mollified. He nodded curtly and went on. "Yes, I quite agree. The Elders voted upon it, and it was passed *nearly* unanimously." He barely refrained from rolling his eyes, and Jessamine knew why. There were several Elders on the Council who would sooner vote to lose a limb than lose a night of indulgence in fine food and wine. Her father went on, "It will set a good example, for the Riftborn to see the Dignus abstaining in this way."

"I suppose setting an example holds particular importance now," Jessamine said, dropping the words carefully one by one, afraid to cross some invisible line her father had drawn in the conversation, "what with the unrest."

Though he did look sharply at her upon the depositing of this last and most controversial of words between them, he did not reprimand her. After all, it could hardly be supposed she did not know about the unrest in the Barrens now that it had quite literally exploded before her very eyes. "Well, quite," he agreed grudgingly. "Though I have argued in the past few days that if we made a better show of setting such examples, we might not be here in the first place."

Jessamine nodded and looked down at her pudding. It was her favorite: a lovely sponge cake, layered with cream and strawberry jam and dusted in a snowy layer of powdered sugar. Mrs. Keats' sponges were, as a rule, light as air, but as Jessamine forced down a bite, it felt like sand in her mouth. She persisted, though, because Mrs. Keats had been sending up all of her favorite foods over the past couple of weeks, as a wordless attempt to cheer her up, and she didn't want the poor woman's efforts to go unappreciated, despite the fact that she had never felt less like eating in her life. And so she forced down several more bites before setting her fork down upon the plate and turning to the footman who stood silently by the serving board, awaiting the moment he could clear the plates.

"Higgins, please be sure to send my compliments down to Mrs. Keats on this triumph of a sponge. She really is too good to me."

Higgins started at being addressed by the lady of the house, but

21

cleared his throat and replied promptly, "Of course, miss. I will be sure to pass on the message directly."

"Thank you, Higgins," Jessamine replied.

There was the sound of another fork upon a plate and a deep sigh. Jessamine turned back to see her father reaching across the table for the letter on the tray. Her stomach twisted itself instantly into a knot, making her heartily regret forcing down the sponge, which now seemed in danger of making its way back up.

"I have just had a letter from the High Elder. He has requested that we dine with him and his family on Thursday next."

Jessamine dared not open her mouth in reply, for fear she could not control herself. Whomever might be included in "family," there was only one member Jessamine could call to mind: Reginald Morgan, the man it now seemed a foregone conclusion that she would marry. The very thought sent a sensation of icy fingers creeping up the bones of her spine, and she could barely repress a violent shudder.

"I... I realize we have not had much time to discuss the matter," Josiah continued, frowning down at the letter, it seemed to Jessamine, so that he would not have to look at her. "But I trust I do not need to impress upon you how important it is to accept Reginald's attentions with pleasure."

Jessamine bit down on her tongue until she tasted blood, startling herself. It was her turn to avoid her father's eye.

"The Morgans are the most powerful family in the Illustratum. You cannot hope to be more prosperously or influentially placed for your future. I understand that there were certain... expectations regarding your Presentation, but I trust you have had, by now, the proper time to consider the matter rationally and sensibly."

It was not a question—it wasn't even an assumption. It was an instruction, and Jessamine took it as such. There would be no apology, no words of comfort, no acknowledgment of her broken heart beyond a demand that it be patched and hidden before it could embarrass him further. Where a moment before her stomach had been writhing, it now seemed to have gone completely, leaving a gaping, aching hole behind.

Seemingly oblivious to all of this, her father plowed relentlessly onward. "You have always had to shoulder more of the responsibilities around the manor, in a way that many of your peers have not due to your mother's... *condition*." He said the word with

22

a delicacy that bordered on disgust—as though he was disappointed to have married a woman who was so susceptible to the inherent weaknesses of femininity. "You have always proved yourself equal to the tasks of playing hostess and mistress of the manor, a point of distinct pride for the Hallewell name. I would hate for that aptitude to fail us both at this most important of junctures. Do you take my meaning, Jessamine?"

"Yes, Father," she murmured. What else could she say when he glared at her in that manner? She had always known her marriage would have to be one of political expedience, but she had also managed—somehow—to convince herself that hers would be a match of houses and of hearts. She would be one of the lucky ones, she had deluded herself, to just happen to fall madly in love with her future husband. Why should she be so shocked that she—like nearly every young woman in her circle—should be auctioned off to the highest bidder, regardless of any emotional attachment on either of their parts?

Suddenly, as though giving voice to the anguish Jessamine was not permitted to express, a guttural wail echoed faintly down from the far reaches of the house. Jessamine froze, her eyes on her father, whose face had become a blank mask—utterly unreadable.

The occasional ghost of a wail was one of the only hints that Jessamine's mother, Lillian Hallewell, still resided in the house. She had been confined to her quarters for years, under the watchful eye of her nursemaid, Mrs. Spratt. Her cry of pain, though, was not for Jessamine's sake, but her own; she had never recovered from the loss of her only son—indeed, had lost herself so deeply in her sorrow that she did not even know who Jessamine was anymore. Her father, Jessamine knew, saw it as weakness. Jessamine had, until recently, even thought of it as selfishness. After all, her mother may have lost one child, but she still had another who needed her. Now, though, in the weeks since her own world had been torn asunder, Jessamine had begun to wonder if she was not being too harsh on her mother. She now knew what it felt like to want to close herself off from the world, to ignore letters and social calls and gatherings and even the presence of the people around her. Indeed, she had become almost jealous of the tiny, separate reality her mother had constructed to protect herself. The moment this feeling sparked within her, though, Jessamine snuffed it violently out.

No. There was nothing to be envied in Lillian Hallewell's

condition, and everything to be pitied. Her solitude was constructed entirely of pain, and there was no escape from it. Jessamine was determined not to allow herself to forget it again.

The wail died away, leaving the heaviest of silences in its wake. Jessamine both longed and feared to break it, but fortunately, her father placed his napkin on the table and rose from his seat.

"Do excuse me. It appears I have something to see to," he said rather stiffly, and left the dining room.

Jessamine sat quietly while Higgins swept around the room, scooping up plates and glasses and cutlery and piling them neatly on a tray to be returned to the kitchen. And as she sat there, bedecked in her sparkling jewels and finely trimmed satin gown, she felt so small, so insignificant, that she wondered why he didn't just sweep her up with the crumbs and toss her away, too.

THREE

J OSIAH CLIMBED THE STAIRS in an ill humor. He prided himself on being a man who had his daily life in impeccable order. He had molded and shaped every aspect of his existence—from his household staff to his professional career into a model of perfection. He even used his position as an Elder to shape the world around him, building brick by legislative brick, the post-Rift London in which he now lived. He could look down upon it from his office windows, surveying the city stretching out before him, and know that he had made it so.

And so the fact that within his own house, in the closest most intimate relationship of his life, he had lost nearly all control, was intolerable.

Lillian Hallewell had been the loveliest young woman of his acquaintance. She had been a suitable match, her father being a powerful Elder in his own right, but Josiah had fallen helplessly in love with her, and probably would have fallen to his knees to propose to her even if she'd been the daughter of a chimney sweep. Not that he would have admitted as much, even to himself. His choice had been logical. Practical. Politically strategic. Just like every other decision he made, he intended his choice of a wife to advance his prospects. And at first, it had seemed that this plan like so many of his others, would flourish. Lillian bore him a healthy son almost immediately, and he watched his dreams and ambitions expand as the child grew. Jessamine followed her brother, bright-eyed and beautiful. Josiah seemed poised to achieve every ambition he had ever set for himself.

And then the magic appeared. That insidious curse wrapped its tendrils around his son, his pride and joy—corrupting him as it corrupted everything it touched, poisoning all of Josiah's well-laid plans.

It could not be borne. Something had to be done. And Josiah was not a man who shied away from what needed to be done. He knew his decision would make his future and his family's prospects stronger. What he did not predict was that it would destroy his wife.

Feminine weakness. How he detested it.

At first, when the boy was gone and they had gone through the public motions of mourning him, he thought the grief would pass. She knew what the boy had been—what he would become. They were young and healthy—they would simply have another child, and another, until they produced another boy who could carry on the family legacy. Surely these children would fill the hole left behind. It was logical.

But the hole would not be filled. It expanded until it swallowed his wife whole. He watched her slip away from him to a place where he could not follow. And so he let go of her, of the dreams he had for their life together, of the visions of how she would assist him and lift him up. Instead, he put his energy into forgetting about her—an effort that was wasted entirely when Mrs. Spratt lost control of her charge, like now.

He knocked sharply upon the door, and it flew open before he had even lowered his hand. Mrs. Spratt had anticipated his visit. She had probably stood at that door, fear eating at her, listening for his footsteps, listening to them draw nearer with mounting panic.

The thought satisfied him.

"Elder Hallewell," Mrs. Spratt mumbled, dropping into a curtsy, not daring to raise her eyes to him.

"Mrs. Spratt."

Josiah pushed past her into the room, which was dim and musty, the curtains having been drawn. His wife sat upon the floor in the corner, her knees pulled up under her chin, her face buried in her arms. Her body shook with quiet sobs, her long curtains of dark hair obscuring her features. If she had heard her husband's voice, she showed no sign of it. Josiah looked down at her and felt the familiar disgust welling up from his belly. He detested the weakness of tears.

"Mrs. Spratt, how long have you been tending to my wife?" Josiah asked, keeping his voice dispassionate.

Mrs. Spratt swallowed hard and cleared her throat nervously before she dared to answer. "Near on to seventeen years, sir, unless I am mistaken."

"You are not mistaken. Seventeen years. So why is it, after so many years of being employed in the same job are you still so incompetent at it?"

What little color there was in Mrs. Spratt's face drained away. Her hands began to shake, and she pressed them together to still them. Josiah did not miss the gesture, and it pleased him to see evidence of the fear he inspired.

"Mrs. Spratt, your role here in this household is clear. You are to keep my wife calm and subdued. You are to prevent outbursts such as the one you have just allowed. You do understand that, do you not?"

"I... I do, sir," Mrs. Spratt replied breathlessly.

"Then I am at a loss to understand why the screams emanating from this room have just interrupted our peaceful dinner downstairs. Today, it was only my daughter and I present. But at any time, we could have visitors here. We entertain. We attend to business. We cannot live under the constant threat that someone will discover the truth of my wife's condition. We count on you to avoid such a situation. Am I wrong to place this trust in you?"

"N-no, sir," Mrs. Spratt breathed, the panic clear in her tone now. "Please, sir, I... I am doing my very best."

"Perhaps your best is not good enough anymore?" suggested Josiah, cocking his head to one side and examining the effect of his words on the woman. "Perhaps your Riftmagic is not up to the task—or perhaps you are not properly faithful in the application of your gift? Perhaps you do not wish, in your heart, to serve your Creator and the Illustratum in the ways we ask of you?"

"No!" The word burst from Mrs. Spratt's lips like an explosion, and she slapped a hand over her mouth in horror at the outburst. When she removed it, her voice was trembling with fear. "Please, Elder Hallewell, forgive me. Please, sir, I did not mean to raise my voice. I am devoted to my position, and I do my utmost to discharge it to your satisfaction."

"And yet, I am not satisfied," Josiah said coldly. "What ought I to do, Mrs. Spratt? We have another Influencer in this household—and a powerful one at that. Would she perhaps be a more reliable caretaker for my wife?"

Mrs. Spratt shook her head. "No, sir! No, I... I can do it, sir. Please, do not dismiss me."

"You better had, Mrs. Spratt. Because you know what will happen if I have to dismiss you. Need I remind you? Shall I perhaps send a letter to the Praesidio regarding the placement of—"

"No! No, please, sir, I beg of you! I shall—I shall do better. Please, give me another chance!" Tears streamed down Mrs. Spratt's face now, and she was struggling to keep her feet. She clutched at the back of a chair beside her to help keep herself upright.

Josiah stayed silent for a few moments, allowing some time for the woman's fear to crest and peak, before replying, "You are fortunate that I'm in a humor to be merciful today. I shall keep you in my employ, but you should know that you are on very thin ice, Mrs. Spratt. Very thin, indeed. I'm sure I need not remind you that a single missive to the palace can ruin everything your—"

"No!" Mrs. Spratt was barely upright now, leaning heavily against the chair so that it tipped precariously. "No, I beg of you, do not write to the palace! Let her be, please! I will not fail you, sir, I swear it!"

"See that you do not," Josiah said. "There is every possibility that we will be hosting a wedding here at Larkspur Manor very soon, and I cannot allow my wife's condition to cast a pall over the event. She has come too close to destroying this family as it is. I will not allow Jessamine's wedding day to fall prey to her weakness and selfishness as well."

Mrs. Spratt's face twisted suddenly, as though she was about to shout, but the moment passed. She swallowed back whatever she had been about to say and composed her face once more. "Yes, of course, Elder Hallewell."

Josiah gave the woman one last, hard look, and then turned away from her. The moment he had released her from his gaze, Mrs. Spratt sank into the chair and dropped her face into her shaking hands. But Josiah had nothing more to say to her. He turned to his wife, who had not moved from her crouched posture in the corner of the room, though she had gone deathly still. He crossed the room until he towered over her, and then bent down so that his lips were mere inches from her ear. He had not been this close to her in years, and his heart sped up at the familiar heady scent of her perfume. He whispered to her, so quietly that Mrs. Spratt could not possibly hear, even if she hadn't dissolved into tears.

"Jessamine is to be married to the High Elder's son. I am poised to take the highest seat. Everything is in place. Our family is upon the precipice of everything we ever dreamed and schemed for, Lillian. You tried to destroy it all once before. I will not allow it again, do you understand me? You will never again prevent me from doing what I must to preserve the Hallewell legacy, I promise you that."

His wife might have been carved of marble for all the response she gave, but he was sure she had heard him—even understood him. Satisfied that both mistress and servant were once again under his control, he straightened, strode from the room, and slammed the door behind him.

Testimony of Charles Thacker, Physician, to the Elder Council.
Recorded 12 February 1817

"I have concluded my research, undertaken at your behest, into the various effects of herbs and tinctures upon the Riftborn, with special emphasis on the strength and control over the use of Riftmagic. I am happy to report that I have found a combination of elements that, when taken carefully in small doses, can dull the effects of Riftmagic while creating few ill effects in the rest of the body. I have included the exact preparation and measurements for the resulting paste in my notes. It is my recommendation that the paste is best administered diluted, perhaps in wine or mead, so that the taste is masked from those who must take it, for the compound is somewhat bitter, and unpleasant to the palate.

It is my duty, however, to warn the Elder Council that, like any toxic elements, too much over a long period of time can cause damage to the rest of the body. In the subjects I have tested, I have recorded a number of troubling symptoms, from confusion and dizziness, to loss of speech and physical abilities. There was also a case of what I can only describe as hysteria, where the subject fell victim to intense paranoia and even hallucinations. Great care must be taken in the preparation and administration of this paste if it is to succeed in the broader population as a control measure, for overuse will surely result in an outbreak of great illness and even death…"

FOUR

T HE BELL AND FLAGON was full when Eliza arrived, but the raucous energy had quieted and congealed into a human stew of mumbled song and drowsy stumbling. No one so much as looked up from the sticky bottoms of their glasses when she slipped through the door, which suited her fine—the street clothes she had donned for the occasion were itchy and ill-fitting, and she felt like a child playing dress up in a costume. It was with a great sigh of relief that she reached the bar and caught Zeke's attention.

"Well now, look what the cat dragged in!" he muttered at the sight of her. "And to what do we owe the pleasure, Miss Braxton?"

"I'm here for the meeting. I had a letter from Eli inviting me here."

"Is that so? And here I'd thought you'd have run for the hills by now. My mistake, clearly. Go on back, then. You fancy a drink?"

"No thank you," Eliza said quickly. The last thing she wanted to do was dull her senses in a place like this. "Where do I...?"

"Through there, and be smart about it," Zeke muttered, hitching his thumb toward the door behind the bar, "before one of these sods sobers up enough to notice you."

Eliza scurried around the bar counter and hesitated in front of the door, debating whether to knock. She decided it would draw too much attention, and slipped through it silently, closing it behind her.

The room was quite large with a fireplace at one end, but it had been crammed with shelves and stacked with crates and barrels so that it felt cramped. A long, battered wooden table had been jammed into the middle of the room with ten mismatched chairs around it, and at this table, six people were gathered, all gawking in surprise at Eliza's sudden appearance.

33

"Um...hello," she said to announce her presence, but her mouth had gone dry and her voice was barely more than a hoarse whisper.

Sully rose from her chair. "Eliza! We weren't sure if you'd... that is, Eli warned us you were coming."

"Warned you? That doesn't sound very promising," Eliza said with a wan smile.

"That's not what I meant," Sully said quickly. "I just meant, we've been expecting you. Any trouble getting here?"

"None at all," Eliza said, shrugging out of her cloak and laying it over the back of an unoccupied chair. "I was very cautious."

Zeke slumped in from the bar, wiping his hands on a scrap of rag tied to his apron. He collapsed into a chair with a sigh. "Mick's minding the bar, so I've got an hour. Chuck us the tobacco pouch, will ya?"

Sully reached down and slid the pouch across the table to Zeke, who caught it deftly and started filling his pipe. "Well we're all here now, so we may as well get started."

"Where's Eli?" Eliza said, glancing around. "I thought he would be here."

"Out on a job for the Resistance. Don't worry, he can look after himself sure enough," Sully added, scrutinizing Eliza's face.

"Oh. Yes, I'm... I'm sure he can," Eliza stammered. The truth was that she was less worried about what would happen to Eli and more worried about what would happen to her in this room without him here. She'd come to trust him... well, perhaps not implicitly, but certainly more than anyone else in the room. She'd counted on him being here, an ally of sorts...

"You sure you don't fancy a drink, manor girl?" Zeke asked. She stiffened a little at being addressed that way, but his smile seemed genuine, if a bit teasing.

"Oh, no. No, thank you very much. I'm not thirsty," she replied.

A red-faced man chuckled from beside the fire, brandishing his tankard. "Nor am I, love, but that's by the by, innit?"

"I reckon you're a tidy two pints past 'by the by,' Michael," Zeke declared. "You might as well stick your head in the ale barrel and be done with it."

"Ah, sod off," Michael mumbled into his tankard, draining the contents.

"Well, I, for one, am less interested in whether she's thirsty and more interested in how the hell she knew where to find us."

Eliza knew who had spoken before she'd registered his presence. Jasper was sitting with his feet on the table and a sour expression on his face. His eyes were narrowed in suspicion, for all the world as though he thought she was hiding a Praesidio guard under her cloak.

"I sent a message to Eli, letting him know I... I still wanted to help," Eliza replied, and she was frustrated to hear the tremor in her voice, betraying how intimidated she felt. "He sent me a letter back telling me when the next meeting was."

"Oh, well, why don't we just hang a sign on the door so any stranger off the street can join up?" Jasper cried, throwing his hands into the air.

"She's not a stranger off the street, ya pillock, she's one of us, now, whether you fancy the idea or not," Sully snapped, pulling a chair violently out from the table and then glaring pointedly at Eliza, who realized a moment later that this was an invitation to sit down. She hurriedly did so.

"I'm, um... I'm sorry to interrupt..."

Jasper snorted. The woman sitting beside him cuffed him none too gently over the head.

"It's no bother," Sully said, waving a hand dismissively. "We were just getting started anyhow, weren't we, lads?"

"Aye, that we were," a lanky, wheezy man agreed, scratching at his stubbled chin. "So this is the manor lass, is she now?"

"That's right," Sully replied, and began pointing around the room. "This here is Fergus," she pointed to the wheezy man who had just spoken, "and that's Michael. You're already acquainted with his boy, Colin," she gestured to the red-faced man by the fire. "Jasper you know, of course, and Zeke. And this here is Cora." She pointed to the woman who had hit Jasper around the head. "And that's all that's managed to turn up tonight."

"I'm very pleased to meet you all," Eliza mumbled. Everyone was staring avidly at her, as though she was some sort of fairground oddity. She could feel her face burning.

"I'll be honest, I wasn't sure you'd be back, after the business with the book deliveries," Sully said, dropping back into her chair. She was dressed in trousers again, brown tweed ones, with a wide leather belt. "Thought we'd seen the last of you. What changed your mind?"

Eliza swallowed. "I... well, I had meant for the books to be the end of my work with you, but then, when I was delivering them, I saw the Praesidio come through with their wagons full of Riftmead."

Everyone around the table exchanged dark looks. Apparently, she had struck a chord.

"I thought that might have damaged our efforts," Eliza said tentatively. "Based on what I know about Riftmead, and the timing of when it was distributed... do you think the Illustratum somehow knew?"

"Knew? You mean about our plot with the books?" Sully asked.
"Yes."

Sully shook her head. "No, or they'd have seized the baskets, wouldn't they? There's not a chance they'd have allowed the books to stay out there circulating through the Barrens, Riftmead or no Riftmead."

Eliza blew out a relieved sigh. "I'm glad to hear you say that. I had wondered."

"Yeah, well, don't get too excited," Zeke said, blowing a smoke ring into the air. "It may have been a coincidence, but the damage to our efforts was real. They subdued the masses with Riftmead just as we were trying to rile them up to action."

Eliza's relief curdled in the pit of her stomach. "So it was all for nothing?"

Jasper snorted and nodded his head.

"I wouldn't say that, no," Sully said through tightly clenched teeth, throwing a nasty look at Jasper, who glared insolently back. "We still got the truth out there. But we'd hoped to light a fire with that truth, and instead, the Illustratum has gone and poured water all over it instead. The Riftborn know, but they won't act on that knowledge, not while they're all lulled into a stupor on Riftmead.

The room had gone quiet. Everyone was staring at her. Her palms began to sweat. Oh, why hadn't she just stayed home? Because she had to know everything. She had to understand the world in which she was living and choose her place in it. She couldn't be kept in the dark any longer. She took a deep breath. "I need to understand more about Riftmead. Or rather, I need to understand what happens if someone stops drinking it."

Sully's eyebrows disappeared into her dark curls. "Is that so?"
"Yes."

"And is that because you're thinking about cutting yourself off?" Jasper asked, a condescending smirk on his face.

"I have cut myself off. I haven't had a drop of it since I found the letter."

"Come off it," Michael snorted, his expression incredulous. "You're a manor servant. Surely they force it down your throat three times a day at least."

"Certainly not," Eliza replied, stiffening. "We have it once a week at services and three times a week at dinner. I've managed to avoid swallowing any of it for the last two weeks."

"Aren't you worried about what will happen if someone notices you aren't drinking it?" Fergus asked.

"I'm more worried about what will happen to me if I *keep* drinking it!" Eliza said.

"Aye, and so you should be, love," Sully muttered darkly.

Eliza turned to Sully, the panic rising like bile in her throat. "But why? I understand they are using it to weaken us, but how? How does it work?"

"Why, it's the Creator's own nectar, sent down to cleanse us of our weakness," Jasper said, his eyes widening in mock innocence. "Or haven't you been listening in services every Sunday like a good girl?"

Eliza glared at him. "I admit that I've swallowed an awful lot for a very long time, and I'm not just talking about Riftmead, but I'm not swallowing that nonsense anymore." She turned to Sully, who was looking at her with renewed interest. "Now will someone please answer my question? How does the Riftmead work? Why does it have such an effect on us and our gifts?"

"I think Cora is the best one to explain it," Sully replied. "She's the witch, after all."

Eliza started in alarm, but the woman named Cora merely chuckled. "Don't frighten the child, Sully."

Sully waggled her eyebrows and grinned, snatching Zeke's pipe from his hand and giving it a puff before handing it back to him. Zeke barely looked up from his maps.

"Are… are you really a witch?" Eliza asked in little more than a whisper. Her blood felt like ice water running through her veins.

Cora cocked her head to one side, looking amused. "Why? Do I look like one?"

Eliza hesitated. Every tale she'd ever heard of witches spoke of

37

dirty old crones and familiars and evil curses. As she gazed at Cora, whose mouth was turned up in a good-natured expression, she could not reconcile this woman with such images. Still, there was something a little... *wild* about her. Her hair, whether it resisted being tamed or whether Cora simply never bothered to try, sprung rebelliously out from her scalp in tight red curls, which were only unsuccessful in obscuring her face by virtue of the braided rag band she had tied around her head. Her face had a permanently sunbaked look to it, and even her freckles had freckles. Her dress was a colorful collection of fabric scraps that had been stitched together, and there was earth beneath her fingernails. She smelled faintly of herbs and something mossy, almost like she'd climbed out of the hollow of a tree to attend the meeting. Perhaps she was, indeed, everything a witch *ought* to be.

Eliza's silent assessment only seemed to entertain Cora more. She threw back her head and gave a hearty, gravelly laugh that made Eliza jump and then grin sheepishly.

"I've been called 'witch' too many times in my life to count, and I've always thought the word explained much more about the person saying it than it ever said about me," Cora offered when Eliza still didn't answer. "I'm an herbalist, love, which means 'witch' to some as don't bother to learn about things they don't understand. My mother before me and her mother before her used the bounty of nature around them to blend remedies and tonics and teas and the like."

"It's thanks to Cora's witchy brews that I can move my blasted joints," Zeke piped up distractedly, flexing his fingers. "Ain't no doctor that can give you a salve like she makes."

"Sometimes in the race to make new remedies, the virtues of the old ones, the ones right under our noses, get left behind and forgotten," Cora said, nodding. "The doctors can't make no money selling you a remedy you can grow in your own back garden, now can they?"

"And let's not forget, it's as much a condemnation of the healer as it is the remedy," Sully added. "A woman and a Riftborn one at that, daring to presume that she can heal people? The nerve!"

"Aye, there is that," Cora agreed wryly.

"But medicine is one of the Exceptions," Eliza said quickly. "Riftborn aren't allowed to work in medicine. Won't you get caught?"

Cora shrugged. "They ain't burned me yet, so I reckon I'll keep

38

on. Besides, what hospital have you seen what treats Riftborn with the same respect as the Dignus?"

Eliza pressed her lips together. She'd heard stories of Riftborn who'd been turned away when they were ill, but in those cases, their magic was always cited as the cause of their illness. Riftmagic could turn in on a person, the Illustratum said, and poison them from the inside out if they did not stay the Path and work to tame their gifts. It was called Riftsickness, and it came in many forms. And as the Riftborn could not be cured of their own magic, they were deemed beyond the help of medicine and shipped off to filthy crowded Riftwards to wither and die.

"Are... are you talking about Riftsickness?" she asked.

Cora snorted. "Riftsickness, indeed. Nothing but an excuse to turn away the Riftborn and deny them the care they need."

"I'm afraid I don't understand," Eliza admitted.

"She means Riftsickness is a load of bollucks, just like the rest of the Book of the Rift," Michael said, much too loudly. Fergus shushed him, and he fell to muttering into his tankard again.

"Now, what you need to understand about our magic is, it's part of who we are, and I'm not talking spiritually," Cora said. "Just a natural part of our bodies—our make-up, like our blood and our bones. It's not some thing apart, as it's made out to seem. Some folks have blue eyes, some have brown. Some folks are tall, others can barely see fit to grow their way out of short pants. It's just a part of who we are and how we work."

Eliza did not reply. She'd never heard anyone talk about Riftmagic in this way, divorced from the concept of souls and Creators and inherent goodness.

"Now, how Riftmagic came to be, I cannot fathom," Cora went on, "but there had to be a first person what had blue eyes, a first person to grow to six foot tall. I reckon Riftmagic appeared in just the same way—humankind just sort of grew into it."

"And that's not just some unfounded whim of Cora's. There are fascinating writings on the subject," Sully jumped in, her eyes alight with the fervor only books could ignite in her. "There's a scientist, Charles Darwin, whose theories on the evolution of creatures offer real insight into how Riftmagic could have simply appeared in the population as an adaptation to—" she trailed off, registering the blank stares all around her. "Right, sorry, carry on," she muttered, snatching

Zeke's pipe from his hand and taking a long drag on it. Zeke relinquished it to her with a resigned sort of sigh.

"Anyway," Cora continued, "It's not Riftmagic what causes Riftsickness—it's the Riftmead what does it! Too much o' the stuff, and our bodies and minds start to break down."

"Are you suggesting that Riftsickness is... is a lie?!" Eliza gasped.

"I ain't suggestin' it, I'm bloody well tellin' you!" Cora said. "There ain't a bout of Riftsickness in all our history that hasn't been caused by too much Riftmead, you mark my words, lass."

Eliza sat blinking and spluttering, trying to absorb this information. She supposed she shouldn't have been surprised, after everything she'd learned in recent weeks, and yet the news hit her like a slap to the face. All those people in the Riftwards, thinking their magic and their own weakness was killing them when it was really the Illustratum all along...

"I just... just can't believe it," she whispered.

"Can't you, love?" Cora asked softly. Eliza met her eye and realized she already did believe it. Soon there would be nothing at all that she could not believe of the Illustratum and their methods.

"But why?" she whispered. "Why are they doing this to us?"

"You already know the answer to that question: because they're a pack of bloody cowards," Sully said from beneath her halo of pipe smoke. "They're terrified our magic will grow and strengthen. They fear we will become so powerful that they will be the ones at our mercy, the ones who are subjugated."

"Now, that's a lovely thought, isn't it?" Jasper sighed dreamily, staring off into the middle distance.

"No, it bloody well isn't, or we'd be no better than them, would we?" Sully snapped.

Jasper appeared ready to make a spirited retort, but at that moment, the door that led to the bar opened and Eli walked in, out of breath and clutching at a stitch in his side.

"All clear. The delivery came off without a hitch," Eli panted, crossing the room and dropping into a chair. His eyes found Eliza at once, and he gave her a searching look, like he was assessing her for damage. "Are you all right? I'm sorry I wasn't here when you arrived, but the damn wagon was late."

"I... I'm fine, thank you," Eliza mumbled, flustered as she realized that she was the reason he was out of breath; he'd been hurrying back for her.

Eli darted a glance at Jasper before helping himself to the pitcher of ale and pouring himself a brimming tankard full. "So? What have I missed? Solved all the problems of post-Rift London in my absence, have you?"

"We were just getting into a discussion about Riftmead. Eliza wanted to understand how it works," Zeke said helpfully, before turning to Sully and bellowing, "And for the love of God, woman, can a man get his pipe back so he can smoke in peace?"

Sully threw her head back and roared with laughter before tossing the pipe back into Zeke's waiting hands. He thrust it back between his teeth, still muttering grumpily.

"We were discussing the effect of Riftmead on Riftmagic. Or, I should say, Cora was explainin' it. Go on, Cora," Sully said, still chuckling.

Cora nodded and cleared her throat. "I was just going to say that our Riftmagic has to be cared for, like any other part of our bodies. It needs exercise to get more powerful. And it can be weakened by outside influences, such as Riftmead."

"How so?" Eliza asked, turning her attention back to the woman. Here, at last, they were approaching the answer to her question.

"Well, take a look at Fergus, for example," Cora said, gesturing over to Fergus, who was dozing and wheezing, his chair tipped precariously back on two legs. "He spends his life down in those ruddy, dusty mines, and listen to him breathing. His lungs is weakened by the dust and the poor air down there. If he stopped working in the shafts, I reckon they'd start to improve. But the longer he carries on with it, the worse it will get."

"So, are you saying that Riftmead is like the air in the mines?" Eliza asked.

"That's right. Whatever they've put in it, it weakens Riftmagic the same way that blasted mine has weakened Fergus' lungs. It dulls the potency of the magic, see? Take Colin, for example. You've seen his Riftmagic at work, haven't you?"

Eliza nodded, and her face broke into an incredulous smile. "I've never seen anything like it," she said. "The way he can manipulate the light and the dark. It's... it's the first time I ever thought a Riftborn's gift was truly magical."

Cora returned her smile, encouragingly. "That's right. He's got complete control over it. And do you know why that is? Because that boy has never had a drop of Riftmead in his short life."

Eliza shuddered. She still carried the terror in her heart from the morning's services, the fear that somehow, someone would realize that she had not drunk from the chalice, nor swallowed even a sip of the Riftmead that had made more regular appearances at the staff dinners below stairs.

"What you need to understand," Jasper said suddenly, as though he was growing impatient with all the explanations and metaphors, "is that the Riftmead is a means of control. The Dignus fear our Riftmagic. They fear what we will do with it if we have full mastery of it. And so they have created Riftmead as one of the many means to ensure we never do."

"How long have you known this... about Riftmead?" Eliza asked.

"A little more than ten years," Eli replied. "It was after Sully started making contact with Davies inside the Praeteritum."

"There's very little contact with the prisoners held in there," Zeke chimed in, "and so we never had a clear picture of what really went on. What you've got to understand is, very few Riftborn are ever released from the Praeteritum, regardless of the length of their sentence. And those what are... well, they ain't got no fight left in 'em."

"Fight?" Eliza asked.

"Empty, some might call 'em. Defeated." Zeke gave a shudder. "And every one of 'em is terribly addicted to Riftmead, and fraught with Riftsickness."

"What Davies was able to tell us was that Riftmead is used as a sort of tool in the Praeteritum," Sully explained. "It was administered daily, and in larger doses. Davies told us that since he'd been inside, he'd not only grown physically weaker, but his Riftmagic had dulled so significantly that he could barely work it. It took him a gargantuan effort to produce a single spark, and he was one of the most powerful Catalysts I'd ever met before he got locked up. He suspected—but could not prove at the time—that the Riftmead was the cause of it."

"So, how did he discover that it was?" Eliza asked.

"Did a little experiment of his own," Zeke replied. "Stopped drinking it. It took him ages to do, because whatever they put in it has a powerful effect on the body—makes a person crave it, see, and when they're thrusting it at you night and day, it makes it difficult to stop drinking it. But eventually he managed it, and the results were remarkable. His strength came back, and so did his Riftmagic, more powerful than ever it had been."

"Once he got word to us what had happened, we all stopped drinking it, everyone in the Resistance—or at least, those of us who were able to. Some people are more... drawn to it than others," Eli said, and here he threw a glance into the corner at Michael Webb, who was staring into the fire, a tankard dangling from his hand, forgotten.

"And have all of your... your gifts strengthened as a result?" Eliza asked, fascinated now.

All around her heads nodded. Jasper winked roguishly, and levitated the glass in front of him, twirling it in mid-air several times before setting it down again. Eliza's eyes widened. She'd never seen his Manipulator gift in action.

"And all those people in the Riftwards—if they simply stopped drinking Riftmead, they'd get well?" Eliza pressed.

Cora nodded. "Most of them, I reckon, yeah. Mind you, some of their bodies or minds might have permanent damage by now, but..."

"And you've known this for ten years?! So, why haven't you told everyone about Riftmead? Why aren't you telling everyone to stop drinking it?" Eliza asked, staring around the table. "Surely people deserve to know what's happening to them?"

Jasper raised an eyebrow. "Have you told the other servants at Larkspur Manor?"

Eliza flushed a deep scarlet. "No, I... I can't do that. It's not safe and anyway, why would anyone believe me?"

Sully gave Jasper a sour look before jumping in. "That's just it. Telling a man something and getting him to believe it are two very different things," Sully replied. "It's the same reason we needed to put out the truth about the Lamplighters Confederacy in the Illustratum's own words. To a lot of the Riftborn, we're a pack of upstart troublemakers. They don't trust us, not enough to overcome their fear of the Illustratum's retribution should they dare to step out of line. We have no chance unless we can expose it in a public way."

"But how?"

"That's why we were working so hard to break Davies out," Jasper said. "We hoped he could help us in the effort since he had knowledge of how the Riftmead was being used inside the Praeteritum walls. But of course, that all went to hell." His expression darkened, and he looked away into the leaping flames of the fire, pressing his lips together as though trying to prevent himself from saying any more on the subject.

"And now?" Eliza asked into the heavy silence that followed Jasper's words.

Cora sighed. "And now we're back where we started."

"Not exactly," Sully said. "Many in the Barrens now know the truth about the Lamplighters Confederacy—they know what the Dignus do to Riftborn children, and that knowledge will continue to spread, even if Riftmead is dulling the response. And thanks to Eliza, we know about the correspondence between Elder Hallewell and Elder Potter. We know the Illustratum have voted to increase the use of Riftmead in the Barrens and we know they've been experimenting with dosing."

"Yes, but we can't prove any of it, so what does it matter?" Jasper grumbled and then gestured at Eliza. "I mean, maybe if she'd had the sense to grab the letter off of the desk—"

"Call that sense, do you?" Eli said, firing up at once. "And you think Elder Hallewell wouldn't have noticed a letter disappearing out of his private study when he was still in the middle of writing it?"

"I think that was the proof we needed, and she let it get away!" Jasper snapped back.

"You know what your problem is, Jasper?" Sully began, her voice rising like a tide.

"No, but I reckon you'll enlighten me," Jasper muttered into his tankard before draining the dregs.

"You don't consider consequences. It's like we've set up a chessboard and you think the way across it is to blow the whole damn thing up with dynamite," Sully went on.

Jasper snorted but did not reply. Sully seemed to take his silence for confirmation of her accusation. She continued, "What's the point of changing this world for the better if none of us can escape the gallows long enough to enjoy the fruits of our labor?"

Jasper glared at Eliza, and it was as though she could read his thoughts right there on his face. He didn't care a jot whether *she* lived to see the fruits of their hard work. As far as he was concerned, she was practically the enemy, a Riftborn so cozied up to the Dignus that she must surely be loyal to them. She shuddered and looked away from him, half-ashamed that she'd even dared to come tonight.

"Eliza didn't take the letter, and it's a bloody good thing she didn't, or we'd have no eyes and ears inside the walls of Larkspur Manor," Sully said. "But she read it, and she's told us about it, and now we've got information we didn't have before. So, let's decide what we're going to do with it, because it's clear we have to do something before they successfully drug us all into a stupor we can't climb out of."

Cora spoke up then, for Jasper looked as though he was gearing up for another argument. "I've made it my work since joining the Resistance to discover what's in the Riftmead, and though I've been able to rule out some basic garden variety herbs and plants, I still don't know what ingredient is reacting with our Riftmagic. I thought at first it might be oleander or nightshade in small amounts, but a bit of experimentation ruled them out."

"What if you can find out what's in the Riftmead? What then?" Eliza asked.

"Then I'd seek what every poison needs: a reliable antidote," Cora said.

"If we could counteract the effects of Riftmead, the Illustratum would lose one of their most potent weapons over us," Eli said. "It would turn the tide against them."

"So, how do we do it, then?" Eliza asked, leaning eagerly across the table. "What's the plan?"

No one replied. The other Resistance members looked around at each other, and in their silence, the answer to her question was clear: they had no plan. Not yet.

"We're still working on that," Sully grumbled finally. "But in the meantime, we're trying to lessen the impact of the Riftmead crackdown."

"How?" Eliza asked.

"Well, by smuggling in alternatives, for a start," Zeke said. "My bar is one of the only places in the city where a Riftborn can buy himself a drink that won't poison him, but we've begun to change that."

"That's where I was tonight," Eli said. "Overseeing the shipment of bootlegged mead and ale into the city. We're slowly convincing other Riftborn-owned pubs to serve it."

"The Illustratum controls all production of alcohol in the country," Sully explained, for Eliza's confusion was plain on her face. "A stiff drink at the end of the day is one of the only pleasures allowed to a Riftborn man under our current laws, so the Illustratum has made damn sure that drink will keep him under their thumb."

"Serving alcohol that the Illustratum hasn't tampered with is punishable by death," Zeke added, drawing a finger across his own throat for emphasis, "in case you were wondering why we've had a bit of trouble convincing the other pub owners to risk it."

"Yes, but the problem remains that if we can't convince the Riftborn that the Illustratum is poisoning them, we'll never break the hold that Riftmead has over us all," Jasper said, crossing his arms over his chest and glaring around the table, daring them all to contradict him.

No one did.

"So now you need incontrovertible proof that the Riftmead is poison," Eliza concluded, "and also a means of distributing that proof to the masses."

"Neither of which we've gotten sorted yet," Zeke replied.

"So, we sit around here with our thumbs up our arses, arguing and waiting to see which of us will have to carry Michael home," Jasper said, jerking a thumb over his shoulder at Michael, who was now snoring softly, his tankard having dropped to the floor with a soft clunk.

"Some of us are doing a bit more than that," Cora snapped at him. "But yes, that's our next big goal."

"All right then, how can I help?" Eliza asked. "I'm positioned at Larkspur Manor, so there surely must be something I can do that no one else can."

Sully rubbed her chin thoughtfully. "I reckon the moment will come when that is true. Until we figure out what that something is, though, you'll have two jobs. First, keep your eyes and ears peeled, especially around the Hallewells. Any tidbit of information you pick up, relay it back to us. You never know what might be helpful."

Eliza nodded. She had expected this. "And second?"

"Second, keep well clear of the Riftmead for as long as you can and work on strengthening your gift," Sully said. "An Influencer with your power, you may come in very handy, especially if you've got full control of your abilities."

Eliza stiffened. "I daresay I manage my abilities very well."

"That may be so, but you've never tested their boundaries outside of the effects of Riftmead, have you?" Sully countered.

Eliza hesitated and then shook her head. Fear blossomed in the pit of her stomach. Elder Hallewell had already forced her to abuse her magic, pushing her far beyond what she had ever attempted before, and the result had not only made her violently ill, but she had forced her mistress to be complicit in the very public breaking of her own heart. The thought of pushing again into uncharted magical territory terrified her.

"There you have it, then. Start practicing, and I daresay you'll soon have fashioned a weapon to rival Riftmead," Sully said with a smirk. Several of the others laughed. Zeke gave a whoop of encouragement, for which Sully shushed him impatiently. "That's enough all of you, settle down! Now, Eli, let's get an update on that shipment."

But Eliza was no longer listening. The meeting continued all around her, but she was staring down at her own hands and wondering if she could really be as dangerous as they all wanted to believe.

FIVE

T HE MEETING FINALLY broke up around one-thirty in the morning. Eli tried to focus on the discussion, but his eyes and his brain kept wandering to Eliza. It was almost surreal to see her there, sitting at first among the other Resistance members as though she had wandered in by accident and didn't know how to leave without appearing rude. She had gained confidence, though, as the meeting had gone on, posing questions and even making a few suggestions. By the end, even Jasper had stopped rolling his eyes at her and taken to sulking in the corner instead.

Like many of the others, Eli hadn't been at all sure that he would see or hear from her again after the clandestine book deliveries in the Barrens. The plan had been a dangerous one, and there had been every chance that she would be caught. Once she had emerged safely on the other side, Eli was not at all sure that she would want to endanger herself in such a manner again, and he did not blame her. But then Colin delivered her message, and Eli realized that she might just be one of them.

He could not help but feel smug about this. After all, it had been almost entirely on his gut feeling that she'd gotten involved in the Resistance at all. It was gratifying to know that he could trust his instincts, at least.

He caught her as she refastened her cloak for the journey back to Larkspur Manor.

"You came back."

She frowned. "I told you I would."

Eli smiled an easy smile. "Sure, but people say things all the time. It doesn't mean they'll follow through on them."

49

"Flawed though I may be in many respects, Mr. Turner, I hope I can at least call myself a woman of my word."

Eli raised an eyebrow. "So it's Mr. Turner again, is it?"

"Eli," she corrected herself with the hint of a smile.

"That's more like it." He hesitated, then said what he wanted to say. "I'm glad you came."

A delicate pink flush crept into her cheeks as she replied. "I'm not sure if glad is the word, but I don't regret coming. I can't stand by anymore. I just wish there was more I could do. I feel a bit helpless, actually."

"You'll get used to that feeling, I'm sorry to say," Eli said. "Frustration is part and parcel with life in the Resistance. Just ask Jasper."

He cocked his head over his shoulder at his adopted brother, who was still in his chair, picking moodily at his teeth with his fingernail.

"I think I'd rather not," Eliza said, eyeing Jasper's unfriendly countenance. She finished with her fastenings and sighed. "Well, I'd best get back to Larkspur Manor before anyone misses me. Thank you for... well, just thank you. I'll try not to let you down."

And before Eli could reply, she pulled her hood up over her golden hair and hurried out the door.

Only Jasper and Sully remained in the back room. Eli could hear Zeke rousing his remaining patrons from their stupor and herding them toward the exit.

"Well?"

Eli turned to see Sully staring expectantly at him, hands on hips, foot tapping impatiently.

"Well, what?"

"Did you get it?" she asked. "The book!" she cried exasperatedly when he continued to stare blankly at her.

"Oh!" he cried, at last, clapping a hand to his forehead. "Apologies, Sully. Yeah, I got it." And he returned to his chair to retrieve the package from his overcoat pocket. Sully snatched it from him like a greedy child claiming a sweet.

"Finally!" she muttered, tugging at the string and carefully removing the brown paper wrappings. A single book fell into her hands.

"Is it the one you wanted?" Eli asked, staring down at it.

"I don't know yet," Sully muttered. Her fingers worked around the

50

edges of the cover until they found purchase and began peeling back the false cover that had been pasted over it. Many of the books that were smuggled across the border to her were disguised in some way, in case the shipment went astray.

"It won't fool anyone who actually opens the damn thing, of course," Sully had once told him. "But then again, those who burn books are rarely concerned with the reality of what's between the covers, are they?"

At last, when she had carefully stripped away the disguise, she let out a satisfied sigh. "It's a collection of work by an American writer, Edgar Allan Poe. It's supposed to be fascinating stuff, can't believe I've finally gotten my hands on a copy." The cover she had peeled away was stamped with the title: *A Woman's Place in the Creator's Kingdom*. Sully dropped the curling paper to the floor and kicked it into the grate with a grunt of disgust. It caught almost immediately in the glowing bed of embers, curling and blackening into oblivion. With a groan, she flopped back into her chair, flipped open the first page, and dropped her face into her hand. The silence lengthened.

Zeke slumped back into the room, throwing a rag over his shoulder and muttering darkly. He snapped his fingers at Jasper. "Oi. I need some help collecting the glasses out there. Get a shift on, will ya?"

Jasper groaned. "Why me?"

"Because of the people left in this room, you're the only one who hasn't paid for their liquor. And since I'm unlikely ever to see that money, I'll settle for a bit of manual labor instead."

Jasper grumbled, but heaved himself out of his chair and shuffled toward the bar. Zeke looked down at Sully and then back at Eli in exasperation.

"You've gone and given her a new book."

"Huh? Oh, yeah, I have. Just came in with the mead shipment."

"Ain't you got no sense, boy? I'll never get her out of here now, not when she's started reading!" Zeke cried. He balled up his filthy bar rag and chucked it at Eli's head for emphasis.

"Sorry, Zeke," Eli mumbled, shamefaced.

"Don't apologize, just deal with it! I need some sleep, lad!" And he stomped back out into the pub.

Eli nodded and approached Sully again, who had heard not a single word of their conversation.

"Um... Sully?"

"Hmm?"

"Not that I want to interrupt your reading—after all, I would very much like to keep living—but are you planning on going home tonight?" Eli asked.

Sully's face popped up and she glanced around, surprised, it seemed, to find that she and Eli were the only remaining people in the room.

"Oh, right. Blast," she muttered, closing the book reluctantly and tucking it into the breast pocket of her jacket. "While I've got you a moment, I want to talk to you about Eliza."

Eli stiffened. "What about her?"

"I think she's going to need some guidance getting a proper handle on her Riftmagic."

Eli gave a little laugh. "I think she's got a pretty damn good handle on it already, Sully. That day in the carriage—"

Sully swatted his words away impatiently. "I know she's powerful, Eli, that's not what I mean."

Eli frowned. "Well then, what do you mean?"

"She's raw, Eli. She's only ever used her gift under the influence of Riftmead, and she's bound to be startled by what she's able to do without it. She will need to learn to temper her approach, adjust her technique, and test the boundaries of what she can do in a safe and controlled way. She can't achieve any of that with her mistress or anywhere in Larkspur Manor, for that matter. If they realized she was growing more powerful, that could mean trouble for her."

"Yeah, I see your point. So what does this have to do with me?"

"I want you to train her."

"I... what?" Eli blinked.

"You heard me," Sully snapped.

"But I'm not an Influencer! I don't know how to—"

"Stuff and nonsense. You don't need to be an Influencer to help her. You just need to show her how to exercise self-control, how to let her gift surge, and how to pull it back. Nothing you can't handle."

"I... I suppose," Eli said. "I've never taught anyone else how to do it, though."

"No time like the present to try. She needs a steady hand. I'm up to my eyeballs in new stock to translate, and Jasper would bully her to tears like as not. It's got to be you. Besides, she trusts you."

"You think so?"

"Well, a damn sight more than she trusts the rest of us, I reckon. So, get word to her and set something up. In fact, I'd go after her now—try to catch her before she makes it back to her horse. It would be irresponsible to lead her to the truth and then abandon her to the consequences. Besides, the better understanding you have of what she can do, the better we can use her in the Resistance, yeah?"

"Uh, yeah. No, that... that makes perfect sense," Eli admitted.

Sully squinted at him. "Then why do you sound so confused? Can you do it or can't you?"

"Of course I can!" Eli said, a little too loudly. He cleared his throat and tried again. "I'll, uh... I'll go catch up with her and we'll get started as soon as she's able to get away."

"That's a good lad, I'll leave you to it. The sooner the better, mind," Sully replied, standing up and stretching. "Then we'd better get home. The patrols may not be as frequent, but they'll delight in harassing us if we meet one on the way back to the Commons."

"Sully."

"Hmm?"

"You don't think it's a mistake, do you? Inviting Eliza to join the Resistance?"

Sully looked up at him. He expected a sarcastic remark—something along the lines of only having himself to blame if it was, seeing as he was the one who brought her in. And so, he was surprised when she gave him the piercing look that she only gave when she was deep in consideration.

"No, I don't," she said at last. "For all their high-falutin' manners and fancy uniforms, manor servants see a side of the Dignus we never see. In some ways their lot is more difficult than ours—and I'm not talking about the daily struggle for food and money and the like that plagues the Barrens. Their whole lives are like a performance with a constant and critical audience, and they dare not trip up even once. They can never rest—never let their guard down. But once their eyes have been opened, like Eliza's have, they could be one of the most powerful weapons the Resistance could ask for. And opening one pair of eyes could well be the key to opening the rest of them. When I'm wrong, I'll damn well say it, and I was wrong to doubt her. She's an asset I'm glad to have, and you were right to listen to your instincts. I don't know exactly what part she's going to play, but I believe she'll find her place in the end, and that's down to you."

It was so rare for Sully to express praise of any kind that Eli could only splutter in response. He was still trying to wrap his tongue around an answer when Jasper slouched back in from the bar area, looking grumpy.

"Can we clear out already, before Zeke makes me sweep and mop the bloody place as well?" he snapped.

"Aye, let's get going," Eli agreed. "That book is fair burning a hole in Sully's pocket. She'd best head home before her trousers catch fire, and I still need to catch up with Eliza."

As Eli turned for the door, he heard the swish and then felt the whack and a dull pain as Sully cuffed him sharply over the top of his head with the aforementioned book. Now, *that* was more like the Sully he knew. He grinned as he followed her out the door and into the night.

Report from the Captain of the Praesidio Guard, presented to the Elder Council, 24 April 1887

It is with great pride and relief that I report a significant decrease in the unrest that has, until recently, caused a great disturbance in the Barrens. Reports from all corners of the district are encouraging. I have compiled the most significant of the reported developments to illustrate the Guard's success in calming the masses within Riftborn districts of London.

- Praesidio patrols were increased tenfold in frequency when the troubles began several weeks ago, resulting in more than 30 arrests and three executions. In the past three days, there have been no arrests, and we have been able to reduce the number of patrols by half.

- The High Street market has been under heavy guard for the past two weeks, and we are glad to report that there have been no further instances of rioting. Two shopfronts damaged in the previous riots were boarded up, and the damage to the parish office there has been repaired and the office has resumed normal operations.

- The Barrens constables report fewer than ten curfew infractions in the past week. Fines were collected in all cases, and no arrests were made.

- The most marked improvement in the Barrens, however, has come about since the Guard has begun distributing Riftmead. In the days immediately following the first rounds, not only have arrests all but ceased, but there has been scarcely a confrontation. My men have reported more respectful interactions as well as a significant rise in compliance to orders when given.

- The investigation into the events at Larkspur Manor continue, though no arrests have been made. We request that the Elder Council offer a bounty for information leading to the discovery of the culprits, so that we may entice a now placated populace to come forward with any clues they may have to aid us in our search.

SIX

"ELIZA, THERE YOU ARE."

Eliza turned to see her father walking down the hallway toward her where she sat in the little closet off the laundry room, working her way slowly through a pile of mending. His countenance, as he approached her, was untroubled, but Eliza noticed the tiny throbbing of a vein in his left temple, a small but telltale sign that he was under some kind of strain. Her pulse quickened even as she stifled a yawn. Her attendance at the previous night's meeting at the Bell and Flagon meant she had gotten very little sleep, and she'd been delayed even further when Eli Turner had caught up with her and offered his help honing her Riftmagic. She'd been surprised, but grateful at the prospect of his assistance. By the time they'd settled on a day and time for their first practice session, and she'd made it back to Larkspur Manor, she could hardly see straight for exhaustion. She'd practically sleepwalked through Jessamine's morning routine, and had almost nodded off over her mending just moments before her father's appearance. If she was going to maintain this charade—lady's maid by day, rebel by night, she was going to have to figure out when she could steal some moments to sleep. She immediately tried to look alert.

"Father? What is it?"

"I've been looking for you. Elder Hallewell would like to see you in his study," Braxton replied, coming to a stop in front of her.

All sense of exhaustion evaporated. The numbness of terror spread through her until it seemed she was nothing more than a pair of wide eyes attached to a thumping heart.

"Why?" she squeaked.

Braxton frowned. "He did not divulge that information to me, but I must say, it hardly matters. He has summoned you and you must go. Be quick about it, too, for it took me nearly ten minutes to find you."

"He... he must have said something," Eliza breathed.

"He said he wanted to speak with you, which should be reason enough for you to take to your heels and be prompt about it," her father replied, eyebrows raised. Eliza dared not question him further, though the panicked questions were gathering in her mouth like marbles, threatening to choke her.

She set down her mending and tucked her hands into her pockets to hide the trembling. She hesitated only a moment before deciding to take the main staircase that would bring her up through the entrance hall. It would give a better impression, she thought, trying to think rationally through her mounting fear, knocking upon the door from the public spaces of the house rather than appearing through the back wall like a specter.

As she climbed, her thoughts raced each other around the inside of her head, colliding and exploding. What had Elder Hallewell discovered? That she had snuck out the previous night? Or the book, perhaps? Had he realized it had been missing, or else discovered one of the copies in the Barrens and realized they had come from his study? Did he perhaps even know about the baskets? Or had someone in the Resistance perhaps been caught? Would there be any point at all in trying to deny her involvement? Ought she to claim ignorance, or just admit what she'd done? Or—her heart thumped even harder—did he somehow know she hadn't drunk the Riftmead like the rest of the staff? She couldn't imagine how he could have known such a thing, having been at the very front of the church with his head bowed in prayer at the time, and yet suddenly it seemed entirely possible. Of course he knew. What would he do? Force her to drink it in front of him? Pour it down her protesting throat, which was now beginning to close up, like she had forgotten entirely how to breathe.

Lost as she was in a fog of speculation, Eliza allowed her feet to carry her where she was headed without conscious thought, and so it was with a start of surprise that she suddenly found herself standing outside the door to Elder Hallewell's study. She said a frantic prayer, and then immediately regretted it—why would the Creator answer such a prayer?

She knocked on the door.

"Enter."

She made a last desperate effort to compose her face, then pushed the door open.

"You wanted to see me, sir?"

Elder Hallewell looked up from the work upon his desk and smiled. "Ah, yes, Eliza, please come here." Eliza hastened to obey him, feeling more flummoxed than ever. Surely he wouldn't be smiling if she was in trouble?

"I wanted to speak with you about an invitation Jessamine and I have received."

"An invitation, sir?"

"Yes. We will be dining with the High Elder and his family on Thursday."

Eliza blinked, wondering how in the world this could concern her. "That's... that's nice, sir."

Elder Hallewell frowned down at his hands. "It is more than nice. It is an important night for our family. I'm sure you understand enough about the events of the Presentation to understand that Jessamine and Reginald Morgan are now intended for each other?"

Eliza tried to keep her face smooth, even as she felt a sharp pang in her heart for her mistress. Yes, she knew this was likely, but she couldn't deny that a part of her had been hoping it was all a misunderstanding, or that it wouldn't work out for some reason. Aloud, however, she said, "Yes, sir."

"I greatly appreciated your assistance on the night of the Presentation. Without it—the night could have ended disastrously—that is, disastrously in more ways than one," Elder Hallewell corrected himself with a grimace.

Eliza swallowed hard against the memory, which rose like bile in her throat. "I... I only did what you asked of me, sir, as was my duty," she managed to choke out, curtsying and dropping her gaze, hoping he would not see how the words tore at her.

"I am... uneasy in my mind about Jessamine. I do not sense she has come around to the idea of her match to Reginald," Elder Hallewell went on, evidently oblivious to Eliza's distress.

Eliza shifted nervously. It was becoming increasingly clear that this conversation had nothing to do at all with her transgressions being found out. She cleared her throat. "Did she say as much, sir?"

Elder Hallewell raised his troubled gaze from the fire to Eliza's face. She felt her cheeks flush. "Not in so many words, no."

"Did you... begging your pardon sir, but did you talk to her about it?" Eliza asked tentatively.

Elder Hallewell frowned. "I expressed my expectations in the matter."

Eliza's hands twisted in her apron pocket. "But did you ask her how she felt, sir?"

His face twisted in confusion, as though the idea had never occurred to him and that he found it to be quite a foreign one, indeed. "I must say, I'm not sure how that's relevant. It's not as though she has any choice in the matter."

It took every ounce of Eliza's self-control to keep her real thoughts from bursting from her lips in a torrent of indignation on her mistress's behalf. She took a slow, measured breath, trying to cobble together a reply that would not earn her a reputation for impudence—that was the last thing she needed at the moment. "Sometimes... sometimes, for women, just talking through such things can be very helpful in moving past them."

Elder Hallewell did not look angry, but he did appear somewhat overwhelmed as he ran his hand through his hair. "I can see that I'm out of my depth here with Jessamine. This is the sort of thing her mother ought to handle."

But her mother can't, can she? Which is why you need to step forward and do it! Eliza wanted to shout. Instead, she nodded agreeably. "Yes, of course, sir."

He cleared his throat, attempting to steer the conversation back onto a road he was able to navigate. "Well, as you can see, I need your help."

Eliza blinked. "My help, sir?"

"Yes," Elder Hallewell went on, his tone slowly returning to its usual surety and authority, "which brings me round again to the invitation I mentioned. We are attending a dinner at High Elder Morgan's house. There are, of course, lady's maids in abundance to tend to their guests, but I would like for you to accompany Jessamine there. I fear that she may still be unpredictable in her behavior regarding Reginald. She clearly needs help dealing with these... these *feelings*, as you say, and your gift will be valuable in that effort, should her feelings overwhelm her while we are guests at the palace. I want you on hand to ensure that she does not disgrace us with another outburst like the one she had on the night of her Presentation."

Eliza felt the horror rise inside of her, filling her up. She wanted to run from the room, to run and run and run and never stop running.

The night of the Presentation had been perhaps the worst night of her life—she and Jessamine had that much in common. That night, Eliza had been called down to this very study to find Jessamine in hysterics over the discovery of her match with Reginald, and Eliza had been commanded to use her Riftmagic to subdue the poor girl. By the time she had finished calming her down, Jessamine was nothing more than a zombie, stripped of her free will and dazedly following whatever instructions were given to her. Eliza had always felt shame about her Riftmagic, but had comforted herself in the knowledge that she was using it for good—to help and guide her mistress, to offer comfort and encouragement and confidence when Jessamine could not find it in herself. But in that moment, as she watched Jessamine disappear into the ballroom, Eliza had wanted to tear her Riftmagic from her very fingertips, to cast it from her and cleanse herself of its terrible power.

And now it was happening again. She knew it must—knew she could not escape it, now that Elder Hallewell understood just how powerful she could be—but she had hoped for more time. Eliza looked up to see Elder Hallewell staring at her, and she felt her flush deepen.

"Come here, child," he said, gesturing her toward him.

Eliza forced herself forward, first one step, then another, until she stood before this man who held so much power over her. And for the first time in her life, she felt something else mixed with her fear and her anxiety—something sharp and unfamiliar that sent a shiver down her spine.

"I understand your hesitation," he said, in a softer voice than he usually employed with servants.

Eliza's breath caught in her throat. "You do?" she whispered.

"Of course. You have been taught all of your life that your Riftmagic is to be tamed. You have been taught not to embrace it. And now I am asking you to exercise its full power. That must feel like something of a contradiction."

Eliza nodded blankly.

"I want you to know that what you do at my behest is the will of the Creator. It is He whom we serve by joining Jessamine and

61

Reginald together. It is His will that our families be joined and our positions within His hierarchy be ensured. What I ask you to do is in service of this most devout of pursuits. Do you understand?"

Eliza bit her lip to stop the tears that threatened to spring into her eyes. If she allowed even a single tear, she would surely fall apart.

"Of course, you want Jessamine to be happy," Elder Hallewell went on. "But you must see that the path to true happiness is to serve the Creator. Trivial school girl notions of love and romance are easy to mistake for deeper callings. And guiding her along the Path to that calling is how you can serve in your own way, to stay your own Path to salvation, Eliza."

For the briefest of moments, Eliza imagined refusing Elder Hallewell's request. She could do it. She could open her mouth and say that single word.

No.

A simple enough word to say, and she might truly have said it, had an onslaught of images not descended upon her at that moment, of what would happen after the no. Eliza would have to leave to avoid terrible punishment if she was not turned out on the spot. She would be an outcast, with nowhere to go, no livelihood. Her father would surely disown her. No one on the household staff would dare speak a word to her for fear of being thought disobedient or worse. And what would become of Miss Jessamine without her? Who would care for her? Who would comfort her?

Who would manipulate and control her? Eliza asked herself bitterly. She pushed this question aside. The answer was simple enough. If she didn't do it, Josiah would find someone who would, and she would lose her chance to pass information to the Resistance from inside Larkspur Manor.

"Yes sir," she replied. Her voice betrayed none of the turmoil she felt churning in her breast, for which she was grateful.

"Very good. I knew I could count on you, Eliza. You are your father's daughter, and you shall be rewarded for your commitment to your duty and your faith," Josiah declared. Then he replaced his spectacles on his nose and gave a wave of his hand. "You may go."

"Thank you, sir," Eliza muttered, and left the room as swiftly as she could without breaking into a run. She eased the door shut behind her, and suddenly it was as though her legs had turned to water. They spilled out from beneath her and she sank to the floor, her breath coming in sharp, painful gasps. She quickly slapped her hand over her mouth so that Elder Hallewell would not hear.

She almost wished she'd been caught red-handed in the book distribution scheme—in some ways that would have been better than what had transpired in the study. It was as she had feared since the night of the Presentation—Elder Hallewell had at last discovered just how useful Eliza could be, and now her magic was being weaponized. Would Jessamine ever be allowed to make a single decision on her own again, or would Eliza spend the rest of her life as some kind of puppeteer, reluctantly pulling her mistress' strings every step of the way?

The sudden clicking of polished shoes upon the floorboards forced her to her feet. She had barely managed to wipe the tears from her cheeks and compose her expression before Bridie appeared around the corner, a coal scuttle in her hand and a snatch of a hum on her lips. She stopped suddenly when she saw Eliza.

"Eliza? What are you doing? You look ill, are you all right?"

"I'm quite well, thank you, Bridie," Eliza said, attempting a smile. "I'm just dreadfully tired. I didn't sleep well last night."

"I should say not!" Bridie replied. "When I woke up around two o'clock, you weren't even in bed! I nearly went to look for you, but I was too comfortable. Having a cup of warm milk, were you?"

Eliza tried to mask her panic with a laugh. "Yes. Had a dreadful nightmare and just couldn't settle again. I hope I didn't wake you with my restlessness."

"Not at all. You know me, Eliza. I sleep like the dead," Bridie replied. It was true enough, and Eliza was grateful for it. She'd never have been able to slip out to Eli Turner's clandestine nocturnal gatherings if she'd shared a bed with anyone other than Bridie, who could have cheerfully slept through the apocalypse. Still, she'd have to come up with better excuses than nightmares in case Bridie made a habit of waking at two in the morning. Of course, she could always invent something of a romantic nature—Bridie would fall all over herself to keep the secret if Eliza told her she was meeting some beau for a romantic tryst. For the briefest of moments, her imagination produced an image of her and Eli riding off together on the back of a horse, but she pushed it away, color rising in her cheeks.

"May as well give this to you," Bridie went on, oblivious to the scandalous turn Eliza's thoughts had just taken. "It just came for Miss

Jessamine. Your father asked me to deliver it to her room, but that's only because you'd already come upstairs. I reckon she'd rather have it from you."

Eliza reached out and took the letter. She gazed down upon the return address and sighed. Teddy Potter. Again. How many times would the poor man write before he finally accepted that Jessamine would not reply?

"Do you think it's a love letter?" Bridie asked in a whisper.

"Perhaps, but it's a lost cause," Eliza murmured, slipping the letter into her apron. "I've just been to see Elder Hallewell, and he's asked me to accompany him and Miss Jessamine on a visit to the palace."

Bridie nearly dropped her coal scuttle in excitement. "The palace! Oh, Eliza! I've only ever heard stories of how grand it is! And you're going *with* them? Oh, I could fairly die of jealousy!"

"I don't know what there is to be jealous about," Eliza replied. "It's not as though they shall be entertaining me. I shall be lucky to see any part of the place except for the servants' quarters and perhaps Miss Jessamine's rooms."

"Yes, but still... just to go inside... I'd give almost anything to be in your shoes, Eliza!"

Eliza pressed her lips together in what she hoped was an approximation of a smile. Between her budding role as a member of the Resistance, Elder Hallewell's new expectations of her Riftmagic, and the weight of all the secrets she now carried, her shoes had never been a more uncomfortable—or potentially dangerous—place to be.

SEVEN

"**N**EVER THOUGHT I'D LIVE to see the day," Jasper sighed.

Eli did not move from his place by the window where he was keeping watch over the darkened street outside the house, expecting a cloaked figure to appear at any moment. "What are you on about, Jasper?"

Despite Eliza's meeting being with Eli and Eli only, Jasper had been sprawling about on the chaise lounge in the front parlor for the last quarter of an hour, solely for the purpose, or so it seemed to Eli, of taunting him.

"I just can't believe I have to watch my own brother, mooning around like a fool after some stuck-up manor girl."

Eli pressed his lips together and flared his nostrils. "I'm not mooning. I'm waiting for her to arrive, and then I'm going to open the door before someone sees her. I realize you don't have much experience with it, but we call this 'common courtesy,' not 'mooning.' If you weren't such a miserable bastard, you'd be able to spot the difference."

Jasper clicked his tongue. "My, my, my, touchy, aren't we? Have we perhaps struck a nerve?"

"Jasper, I've lived with you for seventeen years. Do you really think I've got a nerve left you haven't gotten on?"

Jasper chuckled. At least someone was enjoying himself. Eli, on the other hand, was wound tighter than a bowstring. Ever since he'd agreed to help Eliza with her Riftmagic, he'd been on edge, and he couldn't quite put his finger on why. Perhaps it was simply his guilt over Davies; the last time the Resistance had put him in charge of something, the whole plan had blown up in his face. He didn't think he could bear it if Eliza met a similar fate, all because she'd been unfortunate enough to cross his path.

"Don't you have somewhere you're supposed to be?" Eli asked over his shoulder.

Jasper looked at the clock on the mantel and groaned. "Blast it all. Is it that late already?" He rolled off the chaise and stretched his arms over his head, yawning. "Well, I'll be sorry to miss what I'm sure would have been a very entertaining evening. Maybe Eliza can practice some of her mind tricks on me when next we meet."

But Eli did not answer; a dark figure was sweeping up the pavement toward the house, glancing repeatedly over its shoulder as it came. Eli twitched the curtains shut and ran for the front door. Jasper, for all his taunting and teasing, dropped his light-hearted manner and joined his brother behind the door, hands tensed, listening hard for the sound of footfalls upon the steps.

A few moments later, a soft knock sounded upon the door in a familiar pattern: three, two, three again. Eli pulled the door open, and Eliza slipped wordlessly through it.

"Any trouble?" Eli asked as he shut and locked the door behind her.

"No. I haven't seen a soul in two blocks," Eliza replied breathlessly.

"Well, you wouldn't see them if they were any good at hiding, would you?" Jasper muttered. He had shifted to the window and was watching the street for signs of pursuers.

Eliza glared at him. "I'm quite confident I wasn't followed."

Jasper moved away from the window. "Oh, well, if you're confident, then I won't bother checking. Surely manor servants are experts at avoiding late-night Praesidio patrols."

"Speaking of late, shouldn't you be going?" Eli asked Jasper pointedly.

Jasper rolled his eyes and then turned back to Eliza, sweeping into an exaggerated bow. "Until next time, m'lady's maid," he sneered, then loped from the room. Eliza watched him with narrowed eyes until he vanished down the hallway.

"You know, I don't think Jasper likes me very much," she said rather dryly.

Eli threw back his head and laughed so loudly that Eliza stiffened

66

beside him. He smothered the laugh and tried to arrange his face so that he didn't look as amused as he felt.

"Forgive me," he said, clearing his throat. "I wasn't laughing at you, truly. It's just... well, Jasper doesn't really like anyone, if truth be told. What I mean to say is, Jasper is... well, he's quite angry, actually."

Eliza's eyebrows pulled together. "Angry? About what? I haven't done anything to him. I barely know him."

"I didn't say he was angry at you," Eli pointed out.

"Well, who is he angry at, then?"

Eli gestured broadly. "Everything. The world. His lot in life."

Eliza stared at him for a moment and then replied, "I'm afraid I don't follow."

Eli sighed. "Jasper's like me. He's from a Dignus family—quite a wealthy one, from what Sully has let slip. If he'd simply been born without his Riftmagic, like the rest of his family, he'd have grown up like a pampered little prince."

"And how is that my fault?" Eliza asked, an edge of exasperation still audible in her tone.

"It's not, of course," Eli said. "It's not anyone's fault, really. It's just what happened. Well, actually, I think a good case could be made for blaming the family that abandoned him."

"But he doesn't know who they are," Eliza said.

"That's right. So, he can hardly punish them. The sorry alternative is punishing himself—and everyone around him—every chance he gets."

"That can't have been very pleasant, growing up with him," Eliza said, dropping her gaze just as Eli met it.

He shrugged. "It wasn't so bad, not really. For a long time we were two peas in a pod, him and me. Had to stick together, didn't we, under Sully's roof."

Eli couldn't be sure, but he thought Eliza might have smiled for just a moment. "Sully isn't very... motherly, is she?"

Eli frowned. "Whatever gave you that impression?"

Eliza froze for a moment, as though afraid she had insulted him, but Eli couldn't carry off the joke a moment longer. He burst into laughter again, but this time Eliza joined in, allowing herself a quiet giggle before stifling it behind her gloved hand. Eli's laugh caught in his throat as he watched her face transformed by the laughter—it was as though a veil had been lifted for the first time, that ever-present veil of careful decorum and duty. She was—for a moment—transfigured.

And then it was gone.

Eliza looked nervously around the room. "You don't suppose he'll be back while I'm still here, will he?"

Eli shook his head, trying to jar loose the glimpse of the radiant girl that was now distracting him from paying proper attention to the serious-faced girl now staring at him. "Who, Jasper? No. He's heading out on a job for Sully. We don't expect him back until tomorrow night."

"What kind of job?" Eliza asked, curiosity coloring her tone.

Eli shook his head. "Ah, I could tell you, but then I'd have to kill you."

Eli watched as Eliza's face drained of color, and quickly added, "That was a joke! Blimey, I can see I'm going to have to speak literally for a while."

"I... I knew you were joking," Eliza muttered shakily, raising her chin sharply, as though daring him to contradict her. He dared not, he decided.

"Right," he said. "Well, to answer your question, it's a delivery. See, Sully's got contacts over the borders, and they bring her books."

Eliza's eyes widened. "You risk discovery at the borders just for books?"

Eli smiled. "Surely you, of all people, no longer doubt the power of a book in the right hands?"

Eli watched as the girl's face flushed with embarrassment.

"No, I... of course not. It's just..."

But Eli was already waving off her stammers. "I know, I know. Believe me, Zeke thinks she's out of her bloody mind as well. But those deliveries keep us connected to the outside world. Without them, we have no touchstone... no counterpoint to the Illustratum's narrative."

"What kinds of books are they?" Eliza asked.

"All kinds. Literature. Poetry. Science. Political Discourse. Everything she can get her hands on from as many countries as possible. The Illustratum has cut us off from the rest of the world. Those books help to connect us again, to understand what's happening outside our borders."

"And that's important?" Eliza asked.

68

"Crucial. We don't exist in a bubble, as much as the Illustratum would like us to believe that we do. Riftmagic has appeared in other countries as well, but they haven't all reacted the way we have here. In other countries, Riftmagic is accepted. It's being studied, certainly, but it doesn't brand a person for life as some sort of leper."

"That's not what the Illustratum has told us."

"Add it to the very long list of things the Illustratum hasn't told us."

Eliza did not reply. Eli let the silence lengthen, giving her time to absorb this information. At last, he cleared his throat and, trying to strike a lighter tone, said, "Well, shall we get started, then?"

Eliza's eyes snapped up, full of an animal terror. "What, now?"

"Well, it is after midnight, so I thought we might as well crack on," Eli said with a slight smirk.

"Before we start there's something I think I should tell you," Eliza said.

"Eliza, I already know how powerful you are, there's no need to—"

"No, it's not about my Riftmagic. It's about... well, I'm going to the palace."

Eli blinked. "Now?"

"No, not now. On Thursday afternoon. I've been asked to accompany Miss Jessamine and Elder Hallewell on a visit to the palace. We're to stay the night and all."

Eli's eyes went wide. "Bloody hell," he murmured.

"I know. It's all been arranged since the last time I saw you. I thought Sully would want to know."

"Yes, I... I will be sure to tell her," Eli said.

"Do you think... is there anything I ought to... to *do* while I'm there?" Eliza asked.

Eli frowned. "Like what?"

"I don't know!" she snapped defensively. "You're the Resistance leader, not me!"

"I'm sorry, I was just caught off guard," Eli replied. "What I meant to say was, our plans haven't evolved to the point of trying to breach the palace. So, I think the best course of action while you're there is to keep your head down and your eyes and ears open. If you happen to hear anything of interest, be sure to relay it back to us at the next meeting.

69

Eliza looked slightly crestfallen, as though this was a less exciting prospect than she was expecting. "All right, then."

"Unless of course, you see an opportunity to overthrow the entirety of the Illustratum and re-establish a fairer, more representative form of government that values the contributions and humanity of our Riftborn brethren, in which case, do that," Eli added seriously.

Eliza narrowed her eyes at him. He answered with his most charming smile.

"Now that that's sorted, shall we move on to your Riftmagic? That is why we're here, after all."

Eliza shook her head as though to clear it. "Yes. Yes, of course. Where do we start?"

"With a little information," Eli said, gesturing to the chaise and dropping into the chair at the desk. He pulled out a file folder, flipped it open, and picked up a pen.

"What is that?" Eliza asked, pointing to the folder.

"It's a file."

"About me?"

"Yes. We keep one on everyone whose magic we've tested. It helps us to understand the effects of Riftmead more clearly if we have the evidence compiled."

"What's... what's in it?" Eliza asked nervously.

"Right now? Just your name, age, and occupation," Eli said with another smile. "Do you object?"

Eliza hesitated. "I... well, I'm not sure..."

Eli leaned forward. "Eliza, we would never let this information fall into anyone's hands. It's quite safe with us. But what we learn from your magic could help us understand other people's gifts as well."

Eliza's expression cleared. "Yes. Yes, of course. Please, do continue."

Eli gestured again to the chaise across from him, and Eliza settled herself onto it. Her face looked composed, but Eli noticed her hands were very tightly knotted together in her lap.

"First, can you tell me, how often did you drink Riftmead before you discovered what it did?"

Eliza furrowed her brow. "Well, once a week at services, and then usually once more, at Sunday dinner in the staff chambers."

"Twice in one day?"

"Yes."

"And not again until the following week?" Eli asked.

"Yes," Eliza replied, then bit her lip. "At least, I don't think so. Not knowingly, at any rate. But recently, with the new edicts from the Illustratum, the Riftmead has been served to us more often. Over the last few weeks, it has been three times a week at dinner, though I knew better by then not to consume it."

Eli recorded the information. "And did you notice any weakness in your magic that occurred with the drinking of the Riftmead?"

Eliza squirmed. "I'm not really sure. Well…"

"Go on," Eli encouraged her.

"There was always this feeling I experienced during the services, immediately after I drank the Riftmead. It was a sort of… untethering."

"Untethering? Could you explain?"

She shifted again. The subject clearly made her uncomfortable. Her color was rising, flooding the porcelain planes of her face. "I always imagined it as though… as though my Riftmagic and I were bound together. And then, when I drank the Riftmead, in that moment, it felt as though those bonds were broken—like I was free from it, in some way. It was… euphoric."

Eli nodded and recorded the information, trying to keep his face deliberately smooth, free from judgment.

"Do you think that feeling was caused by the Riftmead itself, or do you suppose it arose from your mind?" he asked.

Eliza made a sound—something between a sigh and a groan. "You make it sound as though I must be mad."

"No, not at all," Eli replied calmly. "I do not cast aspersions on your sanity, Eliza, not at all. I am merely trying to understand if the sensation you describe was a mental or a physical one."

Eliza opened her mouth, and then pressed her lips shut again. She seemed to be thinking. At last, she responded with "Both."

Eli nodded. "Very well. And can you recall an instance when you had to use your Riftmagic shortly after consuming Riftmead? Within a few hours, for instance?"

"Of course."

"And? Did you notice any waning of your abilities?"

Again, she paused to consider. "There is one time I recall, when I was riding home with Miss Jessamine in the carriage after the services. She got it in her head that she wanted to stop in at Lionel

71

Park, to inquire after the health of one of her friends. She had come down with a cold, you see, and had not been well enough to attend services that day. I knew that her father would never approve—not only would he wish her to look after her own health, but he would surely consider it a social call, which he expressly forbids on Sundays. I tried to—to use my gift to persuade her out of it, but I couldn't seem to exert the kind of influence I usually do. She shrugged off my protestations and ordered the driver to divert the coach. She was roundly told-off when she arrived home, and I was reprimanded rather strongly as well for allowing it to occur. I remember something Elder Hallewell said to me... something that made little sense at the time, but now..." She trailed off.

"Go on," Eli said eagerly. "What was it?"

"When he had finished with the shouting, Miss Jessamine fled the room in tears, but I could not follow her because I had not yet been dismissed. He looked over at me and his face softened a bit, which surprised me. Then he said, 'You're not to blame, child. You weren't up to the task, so soon after services.' Then he sent me off. I was so relieved to escape punishment, I didn't stop to think what in the world he meant. I don't think I've ever stopped to think about it again, until now. I feel so stupid."

She looked at Eli, and the horror on his face was clear. He felt guilty—almost voyeuristic—watching her world crumble, brick by brick. It felt wrong, like being a spectator to someone's private grief. He closed the file and put down the pen.

"That's enough of that for now," he said briskly, pretending he hadn't noticed her pain, and looking pointedly away from her, so as to give her a private moment to compose herself. "Let's see what you can do, shall we?"

If he'd been hoping to calm her, he failed. She looked more frazzled than ever when he chanced another glance at her. "Eliza, you don't have to do this, you know. I'm not going to force you."

"I know, I know. It's not your fault, Mr. Turner. I mean... Eli. It's just... very recently, I had a terrible experience using my Riftmagic and I don't wish to relive it."

Eli leaned in. "Look, if this was about the day I first met you, you needn't feel guilty. I startled you and you acted instinctively to protect yourself..."

Eliza looked almost affronted. "I'm not talking about your accosting me in the carriage!"

Eli frowned. "Accosting is a strong word."

"Well, that's not the incident I am referring to. It... was something that happened with Miss Jessamine the night of the Presentation."

The word "Presentation" jarred loose a memory from Eli's brain, of the night that Eliza had appeared upon his front steps with the stolen book. He had felt certain that there was more to her sudden conversion than she was letting on, and he told her so. She replied with words that had left him rabid with curiosity, words he had nearly forgotten in all that had happened since.

"The night of the attack at Larkspur Manor, I was asked to use my Riftmagic in a way I have never been asked to use it before—in a way that made me question everything I've devoted my life to."

"Can you... do you want to tell me about it? You can trust me, you know," Eli said quietly.

"I know," Eliza replied. "That's why I'm here."

Eli held his breath, waiting to see if that new and tenuous trust would be enough. At last, Eliza sighed and slumped her shoulders. She looked ashamed.

"I'm afraid if I tell you, you'll think less of me. That is, less than you already do."

Eli was taken aback at that. "What in the world would make you think I don't think highly of you?"

Eliza gave a short, bitter laugh. "I've seen the way you all look at me when I show up to meetings—like I'm this naïve little thing that's getting under everyone's feet and needs to have everything explained to her. I know I don't actually belong here."

"That's not true!" Eli replied. "Well, okay, maybe Jasper, but everyone else—"

"Everyone else barely tolerates me," Eliza cut in.

"Look, if some members of the Resistance seem a bit... well, hostile, it's not anything personal. You must understand, they've all been brought up to mistrust manor servants, just as you've always been taught that you were better than the Riftborn skulking around in the Barrens."

Eliza opened her mouth as though she wanted to contradict what he had said, but closed it again almost at once. Her cheeks flushed.

"We've all got to learn to trust each other now," Eli went on.

"We're all on the same side. The only ones who will benefit from our continued division are the Illustratum itself, which is precisely why they created those divisions in the first place. So, maybe you could start by telling me about the night of the Presentation."

It took several seconds for Eliza to work up the courage, and when she finally lifted her head to speak, her eyes were shining with tears, but her voice was steady.

"It had been understood that Miss Jessamine was intended for the son of Elder Potter."

"Intended?"

She frowned at him, evidently wondering if he was pulling her leg. "That they would marry."

"Oh, I see. Right. Do go on."

"But then at the Presentation, she was promised instead to another young man, the son of the High Elder."

Eli sat up very straight. "Are you telling me the Hallewells and the Morgans are creating a political alliance?"

Eliza frowned. "I... well, I suppose you could look at it that way."

Eli stood up. "But this is really important! Is that why the Hallewells have been invited to the palace?"

"I believe so, yes. I believe Elder Hallewell is hoping to settle things with a proper engagement."

"This is exactly the kind of information we should be..." his voice trailed away at the look of consternation on Eliza's face. "Right. We'll deal with that bit of news later. Please, continue. I promise I won't interrupt you again."

"Miss Jessamine was—understandably—upset about the arrangement. No one had told her, you see, and so she was utterly gobsmacked when it became clear what was happening. She became hysterical and... and Elder Hallewell summoned me."

There was a tremor in her voice now. Eli held his breath.

"He... he forced me to subdue her with my magic. Then, after that, I... I was made to compel her to walk back out into the ballroom and smile and dance with a man she despises."

"And she did it? Even after you no longer had physical contact with her?" Eli's voice was barely more than an incredulous whisper.

"Yes."

Eli did his best to stay composed, but he could barely restrain himself from whooping for joy. The possibilities of such a gift, the power it could wield in their fight... and yet...

He came down from his cloud with a thump, staring into the devastated face of the girl before him, the girl looking down at her own hands as though they had betrayed her to her core. He would have to be very careful how he proceeded if he wanted her to truly explore what her magic could do.

"There's something else, too," Eliza said, her voice thick with suppressed tears. "Once I had done as Elder Hallewell had bid me, I fainted dead away. And when I finally woke up, I was unwell."

Eli frowned. "Unwell? In what way?"

"I was feverish and dizzy. I vomited. I didn't feel well again until I woke up the next morning."

"Hmmm..." Eli went back to the file, opened it, and was about to touch pen to paper when he hesitated. He looked up and caught Eliza's eye. "Is it all right with you that I'm writing this down?"

Eliza shrugged, but her face was tense. "I suppose so. If you think it might help someone else—Cora perhaps, with her work for the Resistance?"

Eli tried to smile reassuringly. "Yes, I'm quite sure she'll be glad to have this kind of information."

Eliza nodded, seemingly mollified. Eli ventured forward, choosing his words carefully.

"You have not consumed Riftmead now for several weeks, is that correct?" he asked, as casually as he dared.

"Yes." She sounded almost ashamed. This might be harder than he thought.

"And have you noticed any change in your gift? Anything unusual?"

"Well, no, because..." Eliza broke off, dropping her eyes again, but not before Eli had noticed they had filled with tears again.

"Because why?" he asked, his voice as gentle as he could manage.

"Miss Jessamine is very... cautious around me, at present. I think she fears my gift, and what I might compel her to do next."

There was grief in her voice now—Eli recognized it at once, the ache of it. She longed for her role as protector and pacifier. It was the measure by which she had always defined herself. Eli tried to imagine, for a moment, what it would feel like for his magic to turn on him, to betray him in some way. He couldn't wrap his mind around it. His magic had always been a source of comfort and pride for him, which, he supposed, was a result of Sully and his upbringing far from the family who wanted to stamp him out before he could understand what a gift magic truly was.

"All right then," Eli said, his tone betraying none of the depth to which he'd just delved to better understand her. "This will be a trial run—best way to do it, in my opinion." He tried to sound robust and cheerful so that Eliza might rouse herself out of her emotional torpor. "Let's see what you've got, lady's maid."

He picked up his chair and arranged it so that they were sitting face to face, only a few feet between them. He was close enough that he could have reached out and laid his hand upon her arm, but it was not his touch that was his main concern: it was hers.

"We're going to keep this very simple. You shall remove your gloves, lay your hand upon me, and compel me to do something. We will see if I am, indeed, compelled to do it. Should be good fun, eh?"

He smiled encouragingly, but Eliza looked merely skeptical.

"Are you sure?" she asked.

"Of course," Eli replied, with a confident grin. "What, you think I'm scared of a little slip of a thing like you? Do your worst, Braxton!"

Eliza looked taken aback at first by the use of her surname, but rallied almost at once, a shadow of a smile ghosting its way across her face.

"You're asking for it, Turner," she replied, arching a single eyebrow.

Eli smiled again in encouragement, but all trace of humor left Eliza's features as she plucked the glove from her hand and stared down upon the exposed skin as though it was a dangerous weapon. And it would be, Eli thought to himself, by the time they were done, though he had no intention of expressing such a thought to Eliza.

The air between them suddenly seemed charged with crackling energy. Eli fought to keep his hands steady upon his knees and his face composed, when all the while he was practically vibrating with anticipation. What would she compel him to do? What would it feel like? Would he have the will to resist? These thoughts chased each other through his brain until he felt quite dizzy, and yet nowhere in his thoughts was there room for fear. All was anticipation and fascination.

Eliza's eyes met his, and asked silently for permission. He recognized it as such and nodded his head. She sat perfectly still for

76

a moment, apparently coming to a decision. Then, she slowly reached out a hand and laid it upon Eli's.

He had not had the chance, the last time she'd used her gift upon him, to appreciate the sensation of it. He had been so distracted, so paranoid about the Praesidio finding him, that he hadn't realized what she had done until after it was over. Now, poised for the experience, he felt the initial thrum of energy hit his system. It was a curious sensation, a kind of instant slicing through of the strings that tethered him to his own will. And even as he felt his control slip away, he welcomed it. It was lovely not to have to think, or feel, or decide...

And then, quite suddenly, he knew that his life's ambition was in this moment and, indeed, had always been, to leap onto Sully's desk and dance. He'd never been so eager in all his life to do anything as he was to stand upon that table and dance a jig. And then, before he could decide to do it, he had leaped upon the tabletop, his feet flying nimbly beneath him. He marveled at his own grace, the way his feet executed the steps with confidence and unadulterated joy.

He was elated.

He was delighted.

He was...

Confused.

The wonderful weightless sensation drained from him, and his feet became like lumps of lead at the ends of his legs. He stumbled and fell, cursing, to his knees upon the desktop. As he blinked around dazedly, a sound began to fill his ears. He shook his head to clear it, but the sound only got louder. He stared around for the source of it.

It was Eliza. She was laughing.

Eli felt the heat rise to his face, but he was laughing, too, as he clambered down from the desk and fell into his seat again. Eliza had both her hands pressed over her mouth to stifle the laughter. When he had composed himself enough to speak, Eli asked, "How long was I up there dancing before I came to my senses?"

"Not very long at all," Eliza replied between giggles. "Perhaps ten seconds? But each one of them was highly amusing."

"Very well, if I'm going to put you through this, I suppose it's only fair that you have a bit of fun at my expense."

"I'd tell you I'm sorry, but that would be a lie," Eliza chuckled.

Eli shook his head once more, still grinning, and pulled the file toward him so he could record the details of the incident before they slipped away. He was already finding that his perception of the experience was very vague and spotty.

"Did you remove your Influence from me, or did it wear off on its own?" Eli asked, after jotting down his thoughts.

"It wore off on its own. If I'd maintained physical contact with you, I might have compelled you to stop. But what you felt was your own will taking back over. My Influence doesn't last very long after I lose contact with someone—usually."

"Usually?"

"Well, as I said, the incident with Miss Jessamine was an exception to many rules."

"Not to harp on a difficult subject, but did Miss Hallewell mention if she could remember anything about being under your Influence?"

"We… we didn't discuss it at length," Eliza replied, all trace of humor gone now. "I was too ashamed. But she did mention it being a bit like finding herself in a dream."

Eli nodded thoughtfully. "Yes. Yes, I'd say that's an apt description." He added it to his notes and then closed the file again. "Right, then. Well, shall we try it again?"

"Eli, before we go any further, could I just… can I show you something?"

Eli leaned back in his chair. "Of course you can."

Eliza pressed her fingers together, looking down at them with an almost wistful expression. "Can I show you how I've always believed my gift is meant to work?"

Eli nodded, his curiosity piqued.

Eliza shifted toward him and Eli mirrored her, so that they were both leaning out into the empty space between them. Eliza held out her hands—an invitation. Eli placed his hands in hers.

"I need you to tell me about something that troubles you. It can be something you fear or something that burdens you," Eliza said softly.

Playing for time, Eli gave an uncomfortable laugh. "I'm fairly good at keeping those kinds of things to myself, if I'm honest."

Eliza narrowed her eyes at him. "Eli, you were the one lecturing me about trust when this exercise began, remember?"

Eli grinned sheepishly. "Good point. Okay, let's see… something that burdens me…"

He felt the grin fade from his face as he began poking around at things inside his head that he usually tried to ignore, averting his

78

eyes from them, as he might anything he stumbled across that was unpleasant to look at. He knew, though, that he had made this girl incredibly vulnerable, and if he did not show some vulnerability in return, he might never gain her trust completely. He sighed. It wasn't hard to choose what to tell her, once he allowed himself to consider it.

"I worry about what's to come, and I'm afraid I'm going to be responsible for the deaths of my friends," he said. It surprised him, hearing the words fall out of his mouth so baldly. Now that he thought of it, he wasn't sure he'd ever expressed this fear out loud.

Eliza's eyes went wider than usual, and Eli guessed she had not been expecting such a bold admission either. But she cleared her throat and, as she did so, gently squeezed his hands. "Tell me more. Why do you think you would be responsible?"

Eli shrugged. He tried to give a casual laugh, but he couldn't quite manage it. "I suppose it's because it's all happening now, isn't it? It feels like we've reached a kind of tipping point, and the only way forward is..." he trailed off, not wanting to frighten her, but she was not to be deterred.

"Dangerous," she said, completing the sentence for him.

"Yes."

"But how is any of that your fault? If your friends are committed to this cause, and they have all chosen to move forward together, they are making their own choices."

"I..." A sense of calm was flooding through Eli even as he tried to form his argument. It was his fault... he just suddenly couldn't remember why...

"Surely you can see none of this will be your fault..."

"But John Davies... I was the one who... who..." he tried to remember what it was he had done, why he had been so sure Davies' death was his fault, but his reasoning was slipping away from him, like sand through his fingers, grain by grain.

"John Davies made his choices, too. You are a good leader, Eli. You are doing the best you can. You are not to blame for what happens." Eliza's voice was like a lullaby, and Eli felt the pain and guilt that had been lodged in his chest melting away, draining down and out and away from him, so that he felt as though he could take a proper deep breath for the first time in months. She was right, of course. There was nothing to feel guilty about, nothing to fear...

Eli looked up and was almost startled to see Eliza sitting there, smiling at him serenely, as though she knew exactly what he was thinking.

"That's remarkable," he whispered.

"Thank you," Eliza replied, a dull pink flush of pleasure creeping into her cheeks. She was still holding his hands, but neither of them made any move to let go of each other.

"How long will it last, the... serenity?" Eli asked.

Eliza shrugged. "It depends. The physical effects will start to fade as soon as I break contact with you, but the mental effects usually linger for a while. Miss Jessamine is usually more contented for many hours before she begins to worry again."

Eli shook his head. "I hope it won't embarrass you if I said I'm very reluctant for you to let go of my hands."

The pink in Eliza's cheeks deepened, but she did not pull away from him. "This is how I imagine my gift can do the most good—soothing people who are in pain or mental anguish. I've always been so proud of what I can do—how I can serve. It felt like the silver lining to having been cursed with Riftmagic in the first place." Her smile faded. "I am afraid of what this gift will become if I am made to wield it for the wrong reasons."

This gave Eli pause. He wondered for a moment if she would think his cause—the Resistance's cause—would be the wrong reason. Helping her to hone her magic had seemed a simple enough prospect when he had agreed to undertake it, but now a seed of worry buried itself deep inside him; what if she grew to resent him the way she resented Elder Hallewell? He cast the worry away. He would never ask her to do anything like what the Illustratum asked of her. He could never do such a thing.

"You must start by telling yourself that your Riftmagic is not a curse at all—that is what the Illustratum wants us to believe. As long as we are ashamed, we can never rise."

"You make it sound so easy, to simply stop believing something."

Eli hesitated. He could barely remember a day when he'd felt anything but awe and pride in his Riftmagic. Sully had drilled it into him from his earliest days in her care. It was one of the reasons he'd never understood manor servants or many of the other Riftborn eking out their meager livings in the Barrens, unable to imagine aspiring to something else, heads bent, eyes downcast, spirits trodden in the dust beneath their boots. The thing that was broken inside them had always been full and alive in his own heart.

"Don't think of it as stopping believing in something," Eli said at last. "Think of it as beginning to believe in something new."

"That... sounds a little easier," Eliza admitted.

They looked down at their joined hands once more and Eli reluctantly pulled his away. They felt very empty as he returned to the table. "I should write down my experience before I forget the details," he said, smiling.

"Yes of course," Eliza said, folding her own hands together and returning a small smile of her own.

"And then, if you're up for it, perhaps you can find another way to make a fool of me?" Eli suggested.

Eliza laughed. "Very well, Eli. If you insist."

EIGHT

T HE MORNING OF THE PALACE VISIT dawned bright and clear, but Bridie could see no reason to be cheerful. Once again, she was going to miss out on all the fun. Though she tried not to dwell on it, she could not help but think that the opportunity was being wasted on Eliza, who could not seem to summon even an ounce of enthusiasm. She was already awake when Bridie rose to begin tending the fires, and by the time she'd finished, Eliza had settled herself to nothing except muttering over her packing lists and biting anxiously at her fingernails. It wasn't until she swept into the kitchen for Miss Jessamine's breakfast tray that she spotted the charity baskets all lined up upon the counter and spoke to Bridie for the first time.

"Oh, no! The baskets! In all the chaos of packing, I'd completely forgotten! Will you be able to manage, Bridie?"

But it was Mrs. Keats who answered as she bustled by balancing five freshly baked loaves of bread on a tray. "She most certainly can! What, do you think her arms will have stopped working? She's perfectly capable of delivering a few baskets on her own, or one of the scullery maids can tag along. Now get that tray upstairs before Miss Jessamine's bell starts ringing right off the rope!"

"Yes, Mrs. Keats," Eliza replied, snatching up the little porcelain sugar bowl and filling it. "*Will* you be able to manage?" she added in a whisper to Bridie.

Bridie pouted. "Of course I can manage, but that doesn't mean I want to! Oh, Eliza, can't you get out of it?"

Eliza laughed. "Get out of it? Are you mad? I haven't got a choice here, Bridie! We're going to the High Elder's palace, for goodness sake! Do you honestly think I can just say no?"

"Well… well, no, I suppose you can't," Bridie groaned, "but… oh, Eliza, with you gone I'll be forced to bring Millie along and you know how she natters on. I won't be able to hear myself think!"

"I know how she vexes you, Bridie, and I'm sorry I can't be there."

Bridie shrugged. "I suppose I'll have to get used to it now, won't I?"

"What do you mean?" Eliza asked, frowning.

"Well, you aren't going to be at Larkspur Manor for much longer, are you? Not with Miss Jessamine getting engaged to Mr. Morgan. After the wedding you'll be packing up and moving with her to the palace, won't you?"

Eliza's face fell. "I… hadn't even thought about that, not yet. After all, she's… she's not engaged yet."

Bridie laughed bitterly. "Oh, come off it, Eliza. You know as well as I do that the engagement is just a formality now. Once he claimed her dances at the Presentation, that was as good as a march down the aisle to the Dignus."

Eliza bit her lip but did not argue. Bridie took advantage of the pause and went on, allowing a month's worth of bitter thoughts to spill from her mouth.

"You'll be off, dressing her for the most lavish parties and balls, night after night, and I'll be stuck here, rotting away in this basement and lighting fires in the dark and the cold for the rest of my life."

"Bridie, don't… you mustn't say it like that!" Eliza cried, and it was clear from her expression that her feelings had been pricked. "You make it sound like I'm abandoning you on purpose!"

"I never said it was on purpose," Bridie mumbled rather sullenly, crossing her arms over her chest.

Eliza reached out and tugged Bridie's hands out from under her arms, grasping them tightly and squeezing them until Bridie, rolling her eyes, deigned to look up into her face. "I'm not abandoning you. You will always be my friend, even if we're working in separate houses."

"Can't you take me with you?" Bridie whispered, dropping her eyes as they filled with tears. She knew the question was childish, knew what the answer must be, but couldn't help asking it all the same. "They must have fires that need lighting at the palace."

"I'm sure they do," Eliza said, her voice full of pity which only

84

made Bridie feel worse. "Bridie, I'd put you right in my trunk if I could, you know that. But I'm only a few miles up the road. I'm sure I'll still get to see you all the time."

Bridie just sniffed. She didn't trust herself to open her mouth and say what she really thought: that she'd be lonely and miserable without Eliza, that Eliza would forget all about her in all the excitement of palace life, that soon they'd be passing in the street like strangers.

"Please don't be angry with me," Eliza said, breaking into Bridie's tangle of thoughts. "Please, Bridie, I can't stand it if I thought you were angry."

Bridie ground her teeth together and then sighed. "I'm not angry at you, Eliza. I just... don't want you to go."

"I don't want to go either," Eliza admitted. "Nor does Miss Jessamine, come to that."

Something in Eliza's tone jerked Bridie up out of her morass of self-pity for just a moment. "Is she all right, Miss Jessamine?"

Eliza shook her head. "I'm not sure. She's... withdrawn. And I don't blame her one bit. Her life as she'd known it has fallen apart."

Bridie bit her tongue. She tried to imagine being miserable over the fact that she was going to live in a palace and marry a tall, rich, handsome man and wear jewels and silk gowns every day, but she couldn't quite manage it.

Eliza leaned across the table and planted a quick kiss on Bridie's cheek. "I am sorry, Bridie, about this morning. I'll make it up to you."

Bridie looked up into Eliza's face, raising one inquisitive eyebrow. "Is that so? And how do you propose to do that?"

Eliza pursed her lips and tapped on her chin. "Would some smuggled sweets from my stay at the palace put me back in your good graces?"

Try as she might to suppress it, a hint of a smile tugged at the corners of Bridie's mouth. "It would be a start," she said.

"That's my girl," Eliza said, smiling broadly now herself. "Well, I'd best get packing."

And she flounced out the door, leaving Bridie alone with the polishing.

§

The Barrens were bustling that morning, in direct contradiction to their name. The sun was out, not just poking its rosy head meekly from the clouds, but shining brightly and unabashedly down from a clear blue sky. Bridie could feel the warm welcome of it on her cheeks, head tilted back, eyes closed as she savored it, though she quickly regretted the decision to wear her wool cape over her uniform. She'd only been walking for a few minutes when she felt the sweat starting to drip down between her shoulder blades.

"The patrols have quieted things down, haven't they?" Millie observed, peeking down each narrow alleyway they passed as though expecting to see a full-scale riot breaking out therein. "It's not at all the way you and Eliza described it."

Bridie fancied there was something accusatory in Millie's tone, like she had anticipated an adventure and was now disappointed in the distinct lack of excitement. "What did you expect? They wouldn't have let us come if the place was still in an uproar, you know that."

Millie gave a non-committal sort of shrug, but continued to peer around corners with an unhealthy amount of anticipation.

The manor maids were gathered in the High Street as usual; Bridie spotted them at once, like a flock of oversized birds. She hastened her footsteps to join them, eager for better conversation than Millie's prattling.

"Bridie! There you are! I wondered if—but where's Eliza?" Nell Porter, lady's maid from Elder Smythe's estate, greeted them first, looking all around as though Bridie might very well be hiding Eliza under her cloak.

"Morning, Nell," Bridie replied, smiling determinedly. "Eliza couldn't be spared this morning. She's needed for preparations for the mistress' departure to the palace this afternoon."

The flock of twittering birds became instantly as still as stone. Every eye turned to stare at Bridie, who felt her cheeks flush with pleasure. She did so dearly love to be the bearer of information that none of the others had heard yet, and she so rarely got to do so. When Eliza was present, the eyes of the other girls usually passed right over her. After all, nearly all of the other girls were lady's maids, which meant they carried with them a mark of status within the homes they served that Bridie could never hope to achieve.

"The palace? Indeed?" Katherine Maguire exclaimed, eyes bright with curiosity. "But there's no ball this week, is there?"

"Of course there isn't, you ninny, or we'd all be as busy as Eliza, wouldn't we?" Nell replied with a roll of her eyes. "Honestly, haven't you a lick of sense?"

Katherine blushed, and Bridie spoke up, "It's not a ball. Elder Hallewell and Miss Jessamine have been invited to dine and stay the night as well."

Many looks were exchanged from beneath frilly bonnets. Bridie stood up a little straighter, the better to bear all the attention.

"Is it true, then, what my mistress said?" Charlotte Cooper asked, stepping closer to Bridie so that the many baskets on their arms crunched against each other. "That your mistress is going to marry the young Master Morgan?"

"Mine certainly seems to think so," Eleanor Upton chimed in, her freckled face pink and dewy with the heat of the day. "Miss Rebecca has been quite distraught about it, in fact. She was so sure that..." Eleanor's voice broke off and her blush deepened. It seemed she didn't think it proper to expound on her mistress' thoughts on the matter. Nell, however, harbored no such discreet tendencies within her narrow frame.

"Well, we all thought she was going to marry the young Master Potter, there's no denying that," she said. "But it sounds like Miss Jessamine had her sights set on even greener pastures. Well, she certainly strung poor Master Potter along, didn't she?"

Several of the girls gasped, covering their mouths in shock at Nell's boldness. Nell scrunched her face up into a smug little knot of an expression, evidently quite pleased with herself. Bridie, however, felt as though her own Riftmagic had suddenly lit a fire right in her belly.

"Miss Jessamine did no such thing, and you'll keep such indelicate remarks to yourself, Nell Porter!" Bridie snapped, surprised at the intensity with which the defense sprang to her tongue. It was all well and good for Bridie to feel less than sympathetic towards her mistress, but she would not tolerate it from gossiping maids in the street. In the absence of Eliza, she found herself feeling quite protective. Nell snapped her mouth shut, looking angry. *Her* mistress would never marry, everyone knew that. Bridie supposed this was why she was always pouncing upon matrimonial gossip from other households like a hungry tabby on a mouse.

"There's no cause to take that tone with me, Bridie Sloane!" Nell retorted, though her cheeks were still flushed with embarrassment. "What business is it of yours how we speak of our mistresses? You're naught but a workhouse orphan in a house maid's uniform."

Several of the other maids turned their faces away, as though the insult was beneath them. But others lifted their faces excitedly, scenting blood.

"Crawling about in fireplaces, covered in soot," Nell went on, sneering. "You've hardly spoken two words to Miss Jessamine in all your life, I don't doubt, unless it was while you were scrubbing out her chamber pot."

It was Bridie's turn now to feel the heat flooding her cheeks. The truth was she'd had more than a passing conversation with Miss Jessamine—in fact, she'd traded places with her just a few short weeks ago, spending the whole morning lying in Miss Jessamine's bed, wearing her nightgown, all so that Miss Jessamine could sneak into the Barrens herself, and in Bridie's own uniform, no less. But Bridie could not say any of this out loud, of course, not without getting Miss Jessamine into terrible trouble and stirring up a scandal that could get her fired.

"I may be just a workhouse orphan, but at least my mistress can trust me not to engage in frivolous gossip at her expense, which is more than any of your mistresses can say for you," Bridie shot back, riled beyond the ability to keep her temper. On sudden inspiration, she slipped her hand into her pocket and pulled out a *venia*. She held it out to Nell who, looking puzzled, opened her palm to receive it.

"A *venia*? What do I want with this?" she snapped.

"Because after so much time today spent insulting the family of an Elder, I reckon you'll need a blessing today far more than any of the guttersnipes running around the Barrens. My treat."

Nell gasped but seemed too insulted to verbalize a response. Bridie, recognizing her victory, squared her shoulders and tried to imitate the tone Eliza took any time their conversations strayed too far from the Path. "Well, these baskets aren't getting any lighter, and we've much to do back at Larkspur Manor to prepare for Miss Jessamine and Elder Hallewell's departure to the palace," she announced to the group at large. This wasn't exactly a lie—after all, there were many preparations to be made, even if she was not the one in charge of making them. She tossed her head. "Millie and I should be on our way. Creator be with you and your good works today."

She turned on her heel even as the rest of the girls mumbled their replies. Nell's face was still slack with shock, her hand still held out in front of her, the *venia* glinting in the morning sun. As soon as they had turned the corner, and the rest of the maids were out of sight, Millie sucked in a scandalized breath.

"Bridie! I've never heard you speak to the other girls like that!" She sounded both awed and impressed. "What's gotten into you?"

"I don't know," Bridie replied, striding along briskly. And she wasn't just trying to avoid a conversation with Millie—she really didn't know how to interpret the tangled, stormy mess of emotions chasing each other through her mind. "But whatever's gotten into me, it's too late to escape it now." She'd never dared speak up like that in the company of the other maids—she was always just so happy to be included. Now she'd be shunned by the whole lot of them. She knew she ought to be upset about this self-inflicted social exile, but she found she couldn't summon the appropriate feelings of remorse.

They trudged through the narrow, dirty lanes, dropping baskets on doorsteps, exchanging hardly a word with each other—Bridie began to wonder if Millie was afraid she might shout at her as well. If Bridie had been less distracted, she might have noticed the way Riftborn were peering out of windows warily at them, and the way they peered suspiciously into the baskets as they lifted them from their doorsteps.

But she did not. She noticed nothing, lost in her own confused thoughts, until they reached the corner of Butler Street, one of the narrowest, most run-down lanes in all of Whitechapel. As they approached the first building on the corner, with its sagging walls and shuddered windows, the door flew open.

"What do you mean by it, coming here again?" A wild-eyed woman stood in the doorway, her hair like a matted mane around her face, which was glassy-eyed and slick with sweat. She looked feverish. Bridie was so taken aback by her sudden appearance that it took her several seconds to realize it was Bridget Mahoney, a washerwoman with whom Bridie had engaged in friendly conversation many times.

"Good… good morning Bridget," she said slowly, attempting a friendly smile. "It's lovely to see—"

"Sssshhhhh!" the woman hissed, flapping her arms madly like she was attempting to take flight. "Someone might hear you!"

"Hear me say good morning?" Bridie asked with a nervous laugh. "Well, I certainly don't mind that."

The words had barely parted company with her tongue when Bridget's hand suddenly shot out and grabbed a fold of her cloak. Millie let out a shriek and dropped her baskets, taking off back toward Commercial Street. Too shocked to resist, Bridie allowed herself to be dragged, baskets and all, into the dingy front room of Bridget's house.

The place was a shambles, even for the Barrens. Dirty plates and tankards littered the table, and piles of filthy linens spilling out of baskets shoved into the corners. A baby was crying fitfully from a sagging bed in the corner, being rocked by a small child with sooty cheeks and a vacant expression. All of the curtains were drawn so that the only dim light came from the embers of the fire still glowing in the bottom of the grate.

"You've got to take it back!" Bridget whispered, still dragging Bridie by her cloak.

"Take… take what back?" Bridie asked, trying to keep her voice calm even as her heart beat against her ribs like a wild animal trapped in a cage.

"They'll know. They'll know I have it. They'll find out," Bridget gasped.

"Bridget, what are you talking about?" Bridie asked, but Bridget had released her and was now digging through one of the linen baskets, dumping the contents onto the dirty floor and digging through the pile. If she'd had her wits about her, Bridie would have run back out the door the moment Bridget had released her, but instead, she stood rooted to the spot, watching in horrified fascination as the woman continued to tear the room apart.

"I know you said to burn it, but I can't be doin' with burnin' it," Bridget said, jumping to her feet and stumbling forward so that Bridie had to thrust out her arms to steady the woman. Bridget looked up into Bridie's face, eyes wild with fear and something else—perhaps drink? Sure enough, Bridget gave a wracking cough and Bridie could smell the Riftmead on her breath.

90

"Bridget, I don't know what you're on about. I haven't asked you to burn anything!" Bridie said, but Bridget shook her head.

"You did, girl. I read it for meself. 'Burn after reading,' that's what it said. But I can't, y' see? I can't be burnin' it!" She gripped Bridie by the shoulders, her jagged, filthy fingernails digging right through the fabric and finding purchase on Bridie's skin, making her gasp aloud with pain. "The smoke, y' see, it goes right up, doesn't it? It goes right up into the sky, right up to the Creator Himself and he'll know! He'll know what I've read! It's blasphemy, Bridie, and He'll strike me down where I stand!"

Bridie pried at Bridget's hands, her shock giving way to true fright. She had never seen Bridget like this, so clearly divorced from reality. What had happened to her? Was she sick? Intoxicated? She decided the safest thing to do would be to just go along with the woman's ravings, in the hopes that she would be mollified and let Bridie go.

"Yes, you... you're quite right. You mustn't burn it," Bridie said, nodding along vigorously.

"It can't stay here. He'll know, Bridie. He'll know what I've done. You never should have brought it here!" Bridget went on, her eyes bulging.

"I'm... I'm sorry, Bridget. I, er... it was a mistake."

Bridget nodded, then gave a hysterical sob and released her hold on Bridie, diving again for the linens on the floor. In the corner, the baby's cries had turned to screams, and the elder child was now humming monotonously in a half-hearted attempt to calm it.

"Here!" Bridget staggered to her feet again and crashed sideways into her table, knocking a ceramic cup to the floor, where it shattered. Bridie reached out to help her upright, and as she did so, Bridget thrust a square parcel against her chest. It had been hastily rewrapped in brown paper, and through the tears in the edges, Bridie could make out the corner of a book. "You take it. Take it away, and don't bring it 'round here again!"

"All right, Bridget, don't fret, now. I'll take it," Bridie said soothingly, tucking the package into her cloak. "You don't worry about a thing now, you hear? Do you want your basket? I've got some lovely preserves and fresh veg this week for you. And scones as well."

The child on the bed sat up a little straighter, hungrily eyeing the baskets resting against Bridie's hip. Bridget, however, backed away from the baskets with a look of terror on her face. "I can't be doin' with those baskets. You keep them outta here."

Bridie tried to smile. "There's nothing in the baskets you oughtn't to have, Bridget. Come on now, love. For the children, eh?" And she opened one of the baskets and placed the items inside it on the table. Bridget flinched away from each one as though it would explode. A jar of jam. Half a dozen currant scones. New potatoes and a head of lettuce. Half a loaf of bread. "See? Just some food, all right?"

Bridget still wouldn't approach the table, though. She was shaking from head to foot. Bridie turned to the child, who had abandoned the baby to squall on the bed while he helped himself to a scone. "How long has she been like this?" Bridie asked under her breath.

The boy shrugged, his mouth too full of scone to answer. He pocketed a second and returned to the bed. Bridie felt a tug on her sleeve and turned to see that Bridget had gotten a hold of her cloak again and was pulling her back toward the door. "Take it away, Bridie. Take it away. They'll be watching now. We can't let them know. They can't ever know."

"Of course, Bridget," Bridie said, hoisting what she dearly hoped was a convincing smile onto her face. "I'm... I'm taking it right now. You'll never see it again. Your secret is safe with me."

"It's not my secret! It's yours! You brought it here and you'll take it back again!" Bridget shouted, eyes popping madly. The baby's cries turned to shrieks from its nest of filthy blankets on the bed.

"Yes, that's what I meant to say. My secret. Well, goodbye, then," Bridie gasped, slipping through the open door and stumbling out into the street where she collided with the body of a Praesidio guard.

"Begging your pardon, sir," Bridie mumbled as the man set her on her feet.

"Bridie, thank goodness! Are you all right?"

Bridie looked up to see Millie standing beside the officer, looking wild-eyed and terrified.

"I didn't know what else to do, so I went for help!" Millie went on, gesturing to the Praesidio guard. Then she pointed a shaking finger at Bridget's closed door. "That's the place, there, sir, that's where the woman drug her into!"

"This maid here says you were attacked," the guard said in a clipped voice.

Bridie could not have imagined being more frightened than she had been in Bridget's house, but panic leaped in her heart now as the guard took a decisive step toward Bridget's door.

"No, sir! It was a... a misunderstanding," Bridie gasped, grasping the man's arm and then immediately releasing it again as he glared down at her clutching fingers.

"A misunderstanding?"

"Yes, sir. She's just... a bit panicked, sir. It's her baby, see. Her baby is ill, and when she saw me coming, she thought I might... might be able to help."

In a stroke of providence, the baby inside the house chose that moment to unleash a particularly ear-splitting cry. The guard frowned.

"But she laid hands on you?"

"I... I wouldn't say laid hands, sir. She just... just brought me inside, is all. I know her, you see. I've spoken to her many times when we've made our rounds with the baskets."

The guard turned and looked back at Millie, whose face had gone white. "But Bridie..."

"I said I'm fine!" Bridie insisted, staring meaningfully at Millie, willing her silently to shut her mouth. Millie seemed to get the hint, for she cleared her throat.

"I... I must have misunderstood," she said in a hoarse voice.

"There, now. That's right. Just a misunderstanding," Bridie said, nodding encouragingly at Millie before turning to look at the guard again, who was still staring at Bridget's door as though weighing whether or not he ought still to barge through it and arrest the woman. "Officer, I offer my sincerest apologies to you for wasting your time. We know how... how important your job is, sir, and we won't keep you a moment longer." On sudden inspiration, Bridie reached into one of the baskets and pulled out a scone. "A scone for your troubles, sir? Baked in the Larkspur Manor kitchens, by the finest cook in the country, no less."

The officer looked down at the scone, and the stony planes of his face seemed to soften. "Are those currants?"

"They are indeed, sir," Bridie said, daring a small, encouraging smile. "We must thank you somehow, for your diligence. Won't you take it?"

The guard wavered for a moment, then his hand shot out and snatched the scone from Bridie's outstretched fingers. He gave a grunting nod of thanks and then turned to Millie. "See to it that you take more care in the future not to raise false alarms. I could just as easily arrest you for wasting an officer's time on hysterical nonsense."

"It will never happen again, sir. We promise you that," Bridie said, sinking into a curtsy. The man grunted again, shoved the scone into his mouth, and stalked away, trailing scone crumbs behind him.

Neither Bridie nor Millie spoke until the guard had reached the end of the narrow lane and disappeared around the corner in the direction of the High Street. Bridie shoved her hand into her cloak pocket and closed it around the book, heaving a sigh of relief that she had not been ordered to turn out her pockets. But before she could speculate further on what the book might actually be, Millie rounded on Bridie, looking furious.

"What are you on about, Bridie? That woman attacked you! I saw it! I thought you'd be dead before I could get back with help!" Millie hissed. Though the guard was gone, several bystanders had stopped to gawk at the confrontation and were still lingering around in hopes something more dramatic might happen.

"If you thought I might be killed, it's a wonder you left at all," Bridie said, a bite of sarcasm managing to work its way into her voice despite the fact that she was still shaking from fear.

Millie looked affronted. "I suppose you think I should have tried to arrest that woman myself?"

"I think you should have left well enough alone. What were you thinking, bringing a Praesidio guard down here? What if they had arrested Bridget? What would have happened to her children, left alone in there?"

Millie flushed, but her expression remained defiant. "What is the point of having the guards if they can't protect people? It's her own fault if she gets herself arrested! She can't do things like that to a manor servant and expect she won't get into trouble!"

"Never mind all that. We can't go making a scene in the Barrens. We might be manor servants, but we are still Riftborn, and we need to keep our heads down. That guard could have arrested you just for bothering him, did you ever think of that?"

Millie bit her lip. "Bothering someone isn't a crime."

"Millie, being Riftborn is half a crime already. Let's not tempt fate. Now, come on. We've got to hurry up and finish delivering these or Martin will get cross, and I don't much fancy walking back to Larkspur Manor, do you?"

Millie did not indeed fancy it, and so they hurried through the rest of their route in near silence. As for Bridie, she felt she hardly knew where she was or what she was doing. She could not tear her brain away from the tattered package against her chest. It whispered to her as she walked the cobbles, both a temptation and a warning.

NINE

T HE PALACE ROSE BEFORE THEM, imposing and austere. Jessamine had been here before, as a mere child of twelve for her Dedication. She felt even more nervous now than she had been then, and she still remembered the way her knees had knocked together beneath her petticoats. Then, it had been the mere façade of the building that had set her heart to racing. Now, she knew, it was what waited behind it that left her breathless with fear. Eyes still focused out the window, Jessamine reached out until she found Eliza's hand and squeezed it. Eliza, taking the cue, shifted her glove so that her palm could rest skin to skin against Jessamine's. Jessamine felt a wave of calm rush over her, loosening the hold her fear had on her, easing her breathing. She turned to Eliza to give her a quick, grateful smile, already dreading the moment Eliza would have to let go. Elder Hallewell's eyes flickered to their clasped hands and then away again.

The carriage pulled up the long drive and curved around to stop in front of the doors, where it was greeted by a column of stony-faced servants who curtsied and bowed in unison as Jessamine reluctantly released Eliza's hand and stepped out. Before Jessamine could so much as arrange her face into a smile, they descended wordlessly upon her conveyance, unstrapping luggage and seeing to the horses. Their efficiency was at once impressive and slightly disconcerting. No one looked her in the face—every set of eyes was carefully cast downward, either upon their tasks or upon their own feet. Even Eliza, who lived her life belowstairs amidst the constant buzz and hum of servants, seemed taken aback.

As the staff swarmed the carriage, Jessamine's father swept forward. His hat and cane were plucked from his hands even as he held them out. He paid no notice to the servants at all, his eyes trained upon the doors themselves, which were slowly creaking open. Brother Flannigan, the High Elder's assistant, stood on the other side of them, chest puffed out so that he looked like a songbird, his arms raised in welcome.

"Elder Hallewell. Miss Hallewell." His tone was unctuous, and he rolled the 'l's around in his mouth unnecessarily, as though he was savoring them. "We welcome you warmly to the palace and are honored by your presence today. The High Elder is expecting you. Please do follow me this way. The staff will show your servants to their entrance."

Jessamine threw a glance back at Eliza, who had dropped into a curtsy at the arrival of Brother Flannigan. She did not want to be separated from her so soon. She felt like a small child being parted from a favorite toy; Eliza was her security blanket, and she felt lost and rather afraid without her. As though she could hear her mistress' frantic thoughts, Eliza straightened out of her curtsy and gave Jessamine a reassuring smile. "I'll see you up in your room, miss," she murmured as she passed. Jessamine repressed the urge to call after her, but it was a near thing. She clenched her hands to stop them from shaking, took a deep, steadying breath, and followed her father up the stone steps and into the breathtaking splendor of the High Elder's palace.

Brother Flannigan was still talking, expounding upon the details of the entrance hall and the virtues of a new painting of the Morgans which had just been hung beside the grand staircase, but Jessamine could not focus on his words, nor any of the splendor now surrounding her. She was too busy devoting every ounce of her concentration to staying calm. She tried to hold on to the feeling she got when Eliza used her gift—that weightless, almost dreamy quality, as her fears and doubts faded away, but it slipped like grains of sand from between her fingers.

"The mistress of the house is ready to greet you," Brother Flannigan was saying, as he made a sweeping gesture to follow him through a door on the righthand side of the staircase. Jessamine forced her feet to shuffle forward behind her father, wishing she could disappear behind him like a small child behind her mother's petticoats.

A young woman hovered near the fireplace, her hands fidgeting restlessly with the pearls on her long gloves. As they entered the room, she clasped her hands in front of her and her face broke into a radiant smile.

"Welcome!" she said, her voice and demeanor as girlish as her face. "It is such a pleasure to see you again, Elder Hallewell! And Miss Jessamine! What a delight." She swept over to them, extending first one hand to Elder Hallewell, which he kissed, and then both hands to Jessamine, who, flustered, reached out to take them. Jessamine was quite sure that she saw her father throw her a look of warning out of the corner of her eye, but she paid him no mind. The young woman looked Jessamine up and down, approval written all over her face. "Reginald was right. You are simply lovely."

Jessamine found herself utterly unable to respond. She had attended the marriage of the High Elder to his second wife five years ago when she was still but a child. At the time, she had heard a few rumors that the bride was young—barely a woman at all, but of course had not seen even a glimpse of the woman, draped as she was in a pearl-encrusted veil that hid her features. And even if she had been young, what could anyone have said about it? The High Elder had consulted with the Rift to find his new wife. If the decree from on high had led the High Elder to this particular woman, what could anyone have to say against the union? But this woman... no, this *girl,* was barely older than Jessamine, it seemed. These thoughts chased each other through Jessamine's head rapidly as she struggled to control her face and her voice so that she could greet her hostess. Her father, apparently noticing the delay, cleared his throat and stepped in.

"Jessamine, this is the High Elder's wife, Mrs. Amelia Morgan," her father said. He turned back to their hostess. "Mrs. Morgan, it is a pleasure as always. We thank you for your hospitality."

Amelia Morgan waved the gratitude away with a sparkling laugh. "Not at all, Elder Hallewell. The pleasure is all mine. I thought we might enjoy some tea out in the garden. The weather is always a gamble in May, but the Creator has blessed us with an afternoon of sunshine to brighten our meeting. He shines His approval down upon us."

"Indeed, He does," Elder Hallewell replied, by which time Jessamine had pulled herself together and found her own, most bewitching smile.

"Thank you very much, Mrs. Morgan. I've heard the roses in your gardens at this time of year are a sight to behold. I look forward to feasting my eyes upon them."

"Then I shall have to give you a personal tour of the flowerbeds after our tea," Amelia replied, the picture of graciousness. "Reginald and the High Elder Morgan will be joining us shortly. My husband did not expect to still be engaged in business when you arrived, but it could not be helped. Such is his responsibility, of course. I pray you will not hold it against him, for he is most anxious to see you both."

"Not at all," Elder Hallewell was saying, launching into a treatise about duty and commitment while Jessamine spiraled into her own silent thoughts. Mrs. Morgan had not said why Reginald was not there to meet them as they had expected. Was he caught up in the same business as the High Elder, or had something else delayed him? Regardless of the reason, Jessamine felt unabashedly relieved that she did not yet have to face him for the first time since her Presentation.

She could not remember all of the events of the night, which troubled her. She remembered the ceremony—the giddy anticipation of it all, the excitement and heady feeling of accomplishment that carried her down to her guests like a wind filling her sails. She remembered the moment of crashing devastation when she realized what had happened—that her future with Teddy had been negotiated away in a political backroom somewhere, and that she was now to be promised to a man she barely knew, though what she knew of him was despicable. After that, the night was a hazy blur, a pleasant whirling confusion that soured like milk and ended in an explosion that awoke her to both the dangers outside and the clawing grief within. Even when she found the courage to dig through the memories, she could not remember what she had said to Reginald, nor he to her, as they'd danced together amidst a circle of onlookers, and she could hardly ask him. What would he think of her, unable to recall the simplest details of their interaction?

She only remembered spinning... spinning in a cloying, hazy dream from which consciousness would steal all memory.

"Jessamine? Shall we proceed to the garden?"

Jessamine pulled herself heavily out of the quicksand of her thoughts. Mrs. Morgan was looking curiously at her, her hand extended in a gesture toward the open glass doors that led outside.

"Yes, of course," she replied, and swept after her hostess.

100

§

Eliza followed the footpath around the side of the palace, following in the wake of a string of silent servants, including several footmen who were carrying the luggage between them. There was no chattering of the sort that tended to break out between servants when out of sight of the family, no whispers or relaxing of postures. Everyone conducted themselves like they were under inspection by the High Elder himself. Eyes remained downcast, hands remained clasped in front of aprons. She tried to catch someone's eye, to exchange a friendly smile or a nod of the head, but everyone ignored her as thoroughly as if she was a ghost floating along invisibly beside them. Her stomach gave a nervous twist.

The footpath branched off into many different directions, the various servants scuttling off down them like ants. The footmen disappeared through a door with the trunks. She wondered for a moment if she ought to follow them—surely they would be headed for the Hallewells' sleeping quarters? But before she could open her mouth to ask someone, or make a decision on her own, someone cleared their throat sharply and she turned around.

A sour-faced maid stood in the shadow of an overhang, a door set back into the wall behind her, half-concealed by a creeping curtain of ivy. She beckoned to Eliza when Eliza looked up, looking impatient. Eliza backtracked a few paces and crunched down the path to meet her.

"How do you do?" Eliza murmured, inclining her head.

The woman pursed her lips disapprovingly. "You are Miss Jessamine's lady's maid?"

"I am," Eliza replied, wondering how this fact could be in doubt. Surely her uniform made her position clear? It was the same uniform the woman herself wore, after all.

The woman looked her over again. "You're awfully young."

Eliza was not sure how to respond to this, so she gave a small, tight smile instead.

"I'm Martha, Mrs. Morgan's lady's maid. I'm to show you to Miss Jessamine's quarters and see that you have everything you need to tend to her. Follow me please, and quickly. You're late."

Eliza bit her tongue. They had left the manor at the intended time and met no difficulties along the way. It seemed Martha just wanted something to complain about.

Eliza hurried along behind Martha into a long white paneled hallway lined with door after door, all with gold filigree handles. Between the doors, huge oil paintings hung on the walls like windows, but instead of depicting pleasant bucolic scenery, each seemed to be an illustration of a scene from the Book of the Rift, some of them quite gruesome. She tried not to stare at them, but the bleakness of many of them drew her eye like violence, and she was profoundly relieved when they reached the end of the hall and began to ascend a narrow staircase, where the walls were mercifully bare.

Much like Larkspur Manor, the servants' paths through the house were hidden away from the palatial rooms, like animal burrows running behind the walls. Eliza knew that she would likely not even catch a glimpse of the places that made the palace so famous—the grand ballroom, the extensive libraries, and room after room full of priceless antiques and sumptuous furnishings—at least until they reached whatever hallway Miss Jessamine was staying on.

After climbing several stories, Martha opened a door on the landing and they emerged into one of the many guest wings in the palace. Here the carpets were thick and richly woven, the walls tapestried and set with niches in which stood priceless vases and statues. Chandeliers scattered shards of rainbow light and cherubs pouted down at her from delicate frescoes painted upon the ceilings.

Much of her life, she had dreamed of setting foot inside the palace, even if only in the servants' spaces; but now that she was here, she felt none of the thrill she had anticipated, none of the pride and happiness that her commitment to the Path and her duty to her mistress had resulted in this rarest of opportunities. No, instead of soaking in the details of this most inner sanctum of Illustratum power, she found her mind wandering to the squalid conditions of the Barrens and Miss Jessamine's anxious, trembling hands in the carriage, reaching out for a small scrap of comfort.

Whatever this place was, it was not magic. It was the absence of it.

Martha stopped suddenly in front of a door at the end of the hallway, tucked into the corner. "Here are the chambers that have been set aside for Miss Hallewell's use during her stay with us. Everything you require has been prepared for you, but should you find yourself lacking something you need, you can ring the bell and someone will attend to you. Your meals will be brought here for you, and there is a small chamber off the sitting room where you may sleep. There will be no reason to stray from these chambers until the Hallewells are ready to return home to Larkspur Manor."

Eliza dropped into a neat curtsy. "Yes, of course." She understood. She was not to be seen or heard from during their visit. She was to stay, for all intents and purposes, completely invisible. The collective demeanor of the other servants was starting to make more sense. It was simply the way things were done here.

Martha gave a curt nod, her mouth twisted into a skeptical little knot, and then turned the handle and pushed the door inward. The room beyond was decorated in soft creams and golds, from the silken hangings sweeping down from the impossibly tall windows to the richly embroidered bedding on the enormous four-poster bed. Carved mahogany furniture was grouped around the fire that crackled merrily in the marble fireplace. Beyond, through another open door, Eliza could see a claw-footed bathtub, and stacks of fluffy white towels beside a gold filigree vanity and mirror. The room was lit with another chandelier, dripping with crystals that dangled like unshed teardrops over their heads. The ceiling was painted, like in the hallway outside, with a celestial tableau of angels and clouds and flowers so beautiful they might have been plucked from the gardens outside and tossed upward to brush their petals against the heavens. In the corner, Miss Jessamine's luggage had already been stacked neatly between a tall gilt-framed mirror and a folding screen painted with trailing sprays of white roses. And as she had expected, Eliza felt none of the awe, none of the excitement she would once have felt—only a strange hollowness that the splendor of the palace could not fill.

Eliza turned to thank Martha, only to find that the woman had already left, closing the door behind her without so much as taking her leave. Eliza sighed, realizing how tense her body had become in the stiff, starched presence of the palace servants. She felt her shoulders relax and her hands unclench themselves. Left on her own, she felt she could perform her usual duties without feeling the pressure to meet some kind of unspoken standard being forced upon her. She opened the trunk and tended to the garments within, hanging and smoothing them, seeing to creases and wilted bows. She opened the hat boxes and jewelry cases, removing each piece carefully and laying everything out upon the dressing table, fluffing feathers and polishing already gleaming gemstones. She arranged the hairpins and combs and a brush upon the vanity. Then, supposing she may as well prepare everything while she had the time, she laid out everything in preparation for bedtime as well, knowing it could easily be many hours before Miss Jessamine was prepared to return to her room and retire for the evening. Finally, when she could find nothing else to do to distract herself, she sat down in a chair by the window and looked out over the gardens decked out in all their springtime finery.

Inexplicably, she thought of Bridie—about how her friend would be flitting around like a butterfly, exclaiming over each and every beautiful detail of the rooms and admonishing Eliza for her lack of enthusiasm. She would be running her hands over the linens and imagining dashing suitors standing under the windows, determined to woo her. From the time she arrived, Bridie would have enjoyed every solitary moment of glimpsing the inner workings of the palace. And here was Eliza, moping by the window and half-wishing she was back at home. Bridie had been so envious. Eliza almost wished she had allowed her friend to come in her place. She would have talked of nothing else for years.

A strange sound issued from the hallway—a muffled shriek followed by thumping. Eliza stood up from her chair, her heart racing. She crossed the room to the door, all thought of Martha's warnings to stay in the chambers gone. She pressed her ear to the door and listened hard.

Someone out in the hallway was running, their feet slapping against the carpets, their breath coming in hard gasps. And there was another sound—the frantic jiggling of door handles. Before she could make sense of what she was hearing, before she could decide whether she ought to open the door, the handle turned beneath her fingers and she sprang back as the door flung inward and a girl fell through it. Eliza was too stunned to scream, and before she could properly gather the breath, the girl had scrambled to her feet and stumbled right into her, clutching at Eliza's apron and hissing, "I've got to hide. Please. You've got to hide me."

Eliza looked down at the girl, her eyes swimming in bright, animal panic. In less than a second, she took in the rumpled maid's uniform, the mussed hair, the red mark angry and swelling across her tear-soaked cheekbone. And then, before she'd realized she'd made a decision, she was dragging the girl across the room and into the adjoining bathroom.

"Get into the tub. Lie down," Eliza ordered, her breath hoarse with fear. The girl did as she was bid without hesitation. Eliza snatched the pile of fresh towels and laid them on top of the girl, obscuring her from view. She hesitated only a moment to be sure the girl was well covered before she dashed out into the main bedroom again. She did not have time to reach the door, to close it again, when a second figure stumbled through it.

He was tall and rakishly handsome, with tousled blonde hair and an angular, square-jawed face that was set in an expression of delighted amusement. He looked around the room twice before his eyes fell on Eliza. Eliza knew him at once.

"Where did you go, you saucy little... oh. You're not who I'm looking for," Reginald Morgan said, straightening up out of his playful posture and looking, for one absurd moment, like a child who'd lost his favorite toy.

"Begging your pardon, sir," Eliza mumbled, folding into a deep curtsy and dropping her gaze to the floor, but not before she took in the bright, watery eyes, the reddened face, the sharp tang of whiskey.

"Are you alone in here?" Reginald asked.

"Yes, sir," Eliza said promptly.

"Did you happen to see someone—a maid—come by this way? Bloody hell, but she was fast when she decided to—" He blinked and looked at Eliza again as though seeing her for the first time. "Wait a moment. You don't work here, do you?"

"No, sir."

"No. I'd remember you, I'm sure of it," he said, his face breaking into a lazy grin. Fear curdled in Eliza's stomach, but the grin quickly slid off Reginald's features as another realization bloomed in his mind.

"This is Jessamine's room. You're her lady's maid."

It wasn't a question, but Eliza answered anyway. "Yes, sir."

"Blast it all. What time did she arrive?"

"Only just, sir. Perhaps half an hour ago now."

Reginald Morgan hardly seemed to be listening to her answer, though he had asked the question. He was crossing the room now, his eyes alight with curiosity. Eliza's heart hammered against her ribs.

105

She forced herself not to let her eyes flick toward the bathtub, where the maid still crouched under the pile of towels.

Reginald strolled through the room, examining all of Jessamine's things, running his fingers over her gowns and picking up her hairbrush, turning it over in his hands. He plucked her bottle of perfume from the table, pulled out the stopper, and sniffed it. Then he slunk over toward the bed, where Eliza had, only minutes before, laid Miss Jessamine's nightdress upon the crisp satin coverlet. He ran his fingers over it, smirking. Eliza felt angry heat explode behind her eyeballs and she bit down hard on her tongue before she could shout at him to get his filthy hands off her mistress' possessions. He surely saw them as his, she realized, watching him. There was a possessiveness in every gesture, every leer.

"Well, it looks like I'd better go observe the niceties, oughtn't I?" he sighed. "Saints alive, the *ceremony* of it all."

He looked up at Eliza, his eyes raking her figure in a way that made her blood run cold. He stepped toward her and opened his mouth to speak. Every muscle in her body tensed, ready to run, to claw at him, to…

A laugh echoed up from the garden below, a feminine, ringing sound. It seemed to alert Reginald, once again, to his guests. He turned with a reluctant sigh and walked to the door, pausing only to survey his appearance in a mirror hanging on the wall. He straightened his cuffs, fastened a button at his collar, and ran a hand through his hair until it fell across his forehead to his satisfaction. Then, without so much as a backward glance, he loped from the room, leaving the door gaping as he had found it.

Eliza did not allow herself to relax—not yet. She followed his path to the door and peeked around the threshold just in time to watch him vanish around the corner at the far end of the hall. Her breath escaped her in a pressurized *whoosh*, and she hastened to close the door, taking care this time to turn the golden key that sat in the lock. Then she hurried for the bathroom.

"It's all right. You can come out. He's gone," Eliza said, unable to coax her voice above a breathless whisper. The mound of towels shifted and parted, and the maid emerged, her entire frame shaking. Eliza took hold of the girl's upper arm and helped her swing her leg over the bathtub's edge. Once she was sure the girl was steady on her feet, Eliza turned and refolded all of the towels, placing them once

106

again upon the chair beside the tub. She kept her eyes averted from the girl, allowing her a few moments to compose herself before turning to look at her properly.

She was no older than Eliza. Her skin was pale but clear, with a smattering of pretty freckles across her nose. Her large blue eyes were red-rimmed and her full lips were quivering as she hastened to tuck the stray tendrils of her auburn hair back into her bun, but her fingers were shaking so badly she was only making more of a mess of herself.

"Here. Let me do that."

The girl shook her head, opened her mouth to protest, but Eliza had already stepped forward and begun to tug and pin. The girl dropped her hands to her sides in surrender and worked to slow her breathing instead.

"There you are. Neat as a pin," Eliza said, ignoring the impulse to remove her gloves and compel the girl's anxiety to ebb away.

"Th-thank you," the girl replied.

"What's your name?"

"C-Corinne."

"Are you all right, Corinne?"

"I am, thank you." Corinne was gathering herself now, straightening and angling herself into the erect posture modeled by every other servant Eliza had seen thus far since arriving at the palace. Already, the emotion was fading from the girl's expression, already a veil of unshakable calm was settling over her, cloaking the terror of just moments ago. When it was clear she had gathered herself, she turned an almost accusatory glare on Eliza.

"You're the lady's maid to Miss Hallewell," she said, a bite in her voice. It was not a question.

"Yes," Eliza replied, off balance at the sudden, hostile shift in tone.

"You mustn't tell her what... please, you must say nothing." The words were harsh, and yet there was a pleading note. "It is not the young master's fault, of course. Our inward wantonness and sinfulness manifests in many ways."

Eliza froze. What was she hearing?

"I must look inward. I must understand what faults have led me to this moment and pray for the strength to correct them, by the Creator's hand." Corinne's eyes were closed, and she nearly whispered these words, a mantra to herself. Then her eyes snapped open and she was glaring at Eliza again. "Please, I beg of you, say nothing of this to your mistress. I cannot lose my post. I've only just started. My family…" Corinne's voice cut off with a choking sound. Her face somehow managed to look both fearful and defiant at the same time.

Eliza wanted to shake the girl. To tell her none of it was her fault. To promise her that no job was worth the pain and humiliation of what she had just experienced. But she saw the almost fanatical gleam in the girl's eye, the fever-bright glow of conviction, and she knew that her words could not penetrate it, not here, not in these few stolen moments when the fear and the shame was so fresh and painful. So instead, she nodded and said, "Not a word to anyone, Corinne. I give you my word."

Perhaps it was the sound of her own name, but the girl's defenses seemed to drop. Her shoulders sagged with relief and she nodded her thanks. She looked down at her uniform and gave it a few more adjustments. She looked up at Eliza and asked the silent question. Eliza answered it with a nod.

You look fine. No one will know.

Corinne lifted her chin and found whatever it was that women have inside them that allows them to walk back out into the world with a steady gaze. She left without another word, closing the door behind her. Eliza sank down upon the rug right where she stood, fighting back a sob and the urge to be sick. She looked around the room and found herself wondering how she had seen any beauty in it moments before.

All she could see now were lies. Lies painted gold.

108

TEN

J OSIAH WATCHED HIS DAUGHTER CAREFULLY. He tried to be discreet about it, of course, but he found himself dissecting her every expression, analyzing her every gesture with a knot of unpleasant expectation in his throat, as though he was simply waiting for the inevitable moment that she would fall apart and he would be forced to step in to control the damage.

She had given not the slightest indication that his worries were anything other than a nasty combination of guilt and unfounded fear. She had held herself with poise and calm expectation during the whole of the journey from Larkspur Manor, and every moment since their arrival—save, perhaps, a moment's stunned silence when she first laid eyes upon Mrs. Morgan—had been a masterclass in social grace. Still, her histrionics at the Presentation had shocked and alarmed him, and ever since he had felt as though he'd spent every moment in her company holding his breath, waiting for the next outburst to shock him and ruin all of his carefully constructed plans.

It was the way he had felt about his wife before he had relegated her to the upper reaches of the house. He only hoped he could get Jessamine securely ensconced in the palace before any such similar emotional instability could jeopardize his future.

Her future, he corrected himself. Despite what she may believe, he did want what was best for her. And what was best for her was entirely dependent on securing the match with Reginald. The High Elder had given his word, and Reginald had agreed, but Josiah would not rest easy until the union was complete.

Josiah drew himself out of his whirling thoughts to find that Jessamine was speaking eloquently on the topic of charitable outreach, explaining in great detail to a fascinated Mrs. Morgan all about the projects that she and the other daughters of the Elder families had been so busy with at their charity circle meetings.

"We coordinate with the kitchen staff at each manor as well. We plan each week's baskets around what the cooks have on hand and what they need to use up and, of course, what they have in abundance to spare," she was saying.

"What a wonderful use of resources," Mrs. Morgan exclaimed. "And of course, the outreach must be met with much joy and gratitude in the Barrens."

Jessamine took a long sip of tea before she answered. "Our lady's maids are responsible for the distribution of the baskets, naturally, as it would be unseemly for the daughters of Elders to frequent such neighborhoods. But I am sure the families they visit look forward to the baskets as answers to prayers."

"As indeed they are! Blessings, to be sure," Mrs. Morgan said. Josiah allowed himself a few moments pause in scrutinizing his daughter's face to note Mrs. Morgan's mannerisms with something akin to fascination.

Truly, when John Morgan had announced he would take a second wife, the other Elders were wary of his choice. The woman was barely a woman at all, hardly old enough to carry the mantle of High Elder's wife. The position required such gravitas, such unerring piety. But John was not to be dissuaded—he had communed with the Rift, and his righteous Path forward was clear. There could be no argument, and now Josiah was pleased to see that he was wrong to harbor doubts. Mrs. Morgan was almost eerily poised and handled her guests with an ease that suggested she had been entertaining for decades rather than a measly handful of years. Certainly, she had no trouble improvising while her husband was unexpectedly detained. What the devil was keeping him, Josiah wondered to himself. After all, it had been John who had arranged for the visit, and now he wasn't even present for it. Josiah felt uneasy that there might be Illustratum business that could be both important enough to keep them waiting and yet mysterious enough that he himself was not privy to it.

He wondered if the delay was due not to John, but to Reginald. Josiah knew the boy needed to be taken in hand, but to miss the first courting outing with his intended bride? He may be more work than Josiah was anticipating, even just to get him down the aisle.

The thought had barely passed through his mind when the butler appeared in the doorway. "Mr. Reginald Morgan," he announced in a voice like a crisp starched shirt.

"Terribly sorry I'm late," Reginald said, though there was no sign of contriteness in the casual way he loped out onto the terrace. "Unavoidable delay, couldn't be helped. I hope you haven't been waiting long?" He said this all very quickly, without seeming to expect a reply from anyone. Josiah hid his aggravation as he stood to accept the boy's handshake.

"Not at all," he said, surprised to see that he had to look up slightly to meet the boy's eye and realizing, as he looked him over, that the word "boy" no longer applied. Reginald was a man now by every measure of the word, it seemed, unless one took into account his habitual flouting of responsibility. Well, Josiah thought, he would soon have that well in hand. John had always been too indulgent with him. Reginald would find no such indulgence with his father-in-law.

"Miss Jessamine. Looking just as lovely as ever. You are a sight for sore eyes," Reginald said, sweeping himself into quite a graceful bow. Jessamine extended her hand and Reginald took it, planting a chaste kiss lightly upon her knuckles.

"Thank you, Mr. Morgan. And please do not apologize. We have been enjoying the beautiful grounds and Mrs. Morgan's company in your absence," Jessamine replied, a careful smile on her face.

"Glad to hear it! Old mumsie really is the most smashing hostess, isn't she?" Reginald said, beaming mischievously at Mrs. Morgan, whose face reddened at once.

She dropped her gaze to her own hands and said, in tones of clear reproval, "Now, Reginald. I've asked you not to call me that."

Reginald slapped his palm against his forehead in an exaggerated manner. "That's right! It must have slipped my mind again. My apologies. Goodness, so much to apologize for, and I've only just arrived. That doesn't bode well for the rest of the day, does it now?"

He laughed boisterously, and everyone else gave the obligatory half-hearted chuckle.

Mrs. Morgan seemed to have lost the thread of what she had been talking about. For the first time since they had arrived at the palace, she looked flustered. Her hands were actually shaking in her lap. Josiah had barely time to note the fact when Mrs. Morgan suddenly rose to her feet. "Miss Jessamine, I think the weather might be turning.

I would never forgive myself if I broke my promise to take you on a tour of the rose garden. That is, if you are still keen to see it?"

Mrs. Morgan looked at Jessamine and a strange something seemed to pass between them. Josiah could not quite put his finger on it—a kind of understanding. He opened his mouth to protest, for Reginald had only just arrived—surely Jessamine should remain in his company, seeing as their intended union was the focus of their visit. But Reginald waved them off with an exaggerated gesture.

"Yes, yes, by all means, visit the flowers, so Elder Hallewell and I can avail ourselves of something stronger than this dratted tea. Haven't you offered him a drink by now?" He tossed this last question to Mrs. Morgan, who had risen from her seat and taken Jessamine's arm.

"Don't be silly, Reginald, it's not even noon," Mrs. Morgan said, her tone one of gentle disapproval, though she smiled good-naturedly. "But I daresay you gentlemen can do as you please. Reginald, your father should be joining us shortly as well, when his business is concluded."

Reginald pressed his lips together and nodded curtly, all amusement vanishing momentarily from his features. Then he waved the women off, turning to Josiah with a long-suffering sigh.

"Now, then, Elder Hallewell. I think we might be able to find something to amuse us in the library."

Josiah inclined his head and gestured. "I daresay we might. Lead on, then." And most uneasily, he followed the young man back inside the palace, leaving Jessamine to stroll the gardens with their hostess.

§

Jessamine allowed herself to be steered around the many flowerbeds, periodically exclaiming over the fine specimens of everything from cannas and dahlias to more types of roses than she'd have believed existed. All the while, though she exuded keen interest in the plant life, she took the opportunity to study her hostess. It was unlikely that she'd get another chance to be alone with her. She was desperate to learn what she could of Reginald, but she was still unsure what, if anything useful, she might be able to coax from the woman. The moment Reginald had arrived in the gardens was the very first hint that there might be a crack in her veneer. Jessamine wondered if

112

she probed at it just right, that she mightn't get a glimpse behind it. It was a slim chance, but one she felt she must exploit, for the sake of her own future happiness.

"...and I spent a good deal of time with the gardener, you see, to redesign this area here so that I could include a few of the exotic plants that were gifted to us to celebrate our wedding," Mrs. Morgan was saying, bestowing a fond smile on the beds overflowing with vibrant color.

"Truly magnificent," Jessamine said. "Do you find you have very much time to oversee the gardens? Your social calendar must be truly overwhelming."

Mrs. Morgan laughed. "I make the time. These gardens are one of the only places I can..." she stopped, faltering over a word.

"Make your mark?" Jessamine suggested.

Mrs. Morgan's smile slipped into place again. "Yes, precisely. A woman likes to make a home her own, you know, but when your home is the palace, well..." she laughed again, and the joke was clear. One did not attempt to improve upon or change a palace.

"But with all the other responsibilities—don't you find it overwhelming?" Jessamine asked.

Mrs. Morgan shrugged. "I like to stay busy. And besides, lately our social obligations have not been nearly as onerous, since..." Her eyes went wide and she pressed her lips tightly together, as though she had misspoken. Jessamine wondered what that was about, but decided not to press it. Mrs. Morgan's social calendar was not what she truly wanted to know about. It was merely a way to steer the conversation away from flowers. She stared down at the confetti of blossoms, wondering how to proceed when suddenly Mrs. Morgan's hand was on her arm. Jessamine looked up in surprise.

"Jessamine, I must confess something to you."

Jessamine raised her eyebrows. "A confession? How very mysterious."

Mrs. Morgan smiled, though it was a mere shadow of her usual expression. "I had an ulterior motive for asking you to take a walk with me."

"I confess myself intrigued," Jessamine said, and though her tone was lighthearted, her heart was thumping unevenly. "Please, do go on."

"Let's keep walking," Mrs. Morgan said, slipping her arm through

Jessamine's once more and continuing down the path. It seemed that keeping still made her more anxious.

"Very well."

"I hope you'll understand that I mean you no ill will in what I have to say," Mrs. Morgan began. "And before I venture to say any of it, I must tell you that it is not my place, and that, if you ever speak of it to anyone else, I shall deny this conversation ever happened."

Jessamine took a moment to ensure she was in control of her voice before she replied, "Understood. I have no intention of betraying your confidences, Mrs. Morgan, should I be so lucky as to be invited into them."

Mrs. Morgan gave Jessamine a searching look, as though trying to detect a false note in her promise. Finding none, she took a deep breath and went on. "I want to... put you on your guard. Regarding Reginald."

When she did not elaborate, Jessamine replied. "In what regard, Mrs. Morgan?"

"In as much as... please do not interpret this as a criticism. It is not my place to—" She seemed to be panicking now, and Jessamine, tensed to understand what the woman meant, did not want to afford her the opportunity of backing out.

"Mrs. Morgan, I promise you, I have no wish to interpret your words in any way other than how you offer them to me. Please, speak freely, and without fear of misunderstanding."

This seemed to settle Mrs. Morgan's mind. She took another fortifying breath and said, "Thank you. Your frankness puts my mind at ease. The expectations regarding marriage and... well, the expectations are different between men and women."

Jessamine let the pause spiral before she said, "Yes, that is true enough."

"Reginald has always been a bit... well, wild. As a young man, out in the world. Well, he has plenty of worldly experience," Mrs. Morgan said. Her face was scarlet, and Jessamine could see that this was almost excruciating for her to talk about. She understood, therefore, the meaning of her words "worldly experience."

"I think, Mrs. Morgan, that you will find that Reginald's reputation precedes him, in this regard," Jessamine said gently.

Mrs. Morgan's face contorted, as though she couldn't decide whether she was pleased or horrified by this news. "I see. Well, I am not convinced that this… this *reputation* will cease to be well earned once he has married."

Jessamine froze. "Oh."

Mrs. Morgan looked up and met Jessamine squarely eye-to-eye for the first time since she had embarked upon this highly uncomfortable topic. "You will need to be vigilant, Jessamine," she said, her voice quite serious now. "Not just around other society women, but your staff as well. Reginald is accustomed to having his way. He will see what he wants and he will take it." Her voice cracked and she dropped her eyes to the hands twisting wildly in her lap.

Jessamine could barely breathe. Something about the expression on the woman's face… the tone of her voice…

"Mrs. Morgan, did he… did you…?" But she could not bring herself to finish the question any more than she could bear to force Mrs. Morgan to answer it. She let it die on her tongue and clamped her mouth closed, pressing her lips into a thin line.

"I wanted you to know. I think a wife ought to know before… well, I would have wanted someone to tell me if I were in your position."

Jessamine nodded once, swiftly. It was all she could manage. She was afraid if she opened her mouth, she would be ill. Mrs. Morgan did not seem to expect any further reply though. She smiled tightly, reached out to squeeze Jessamine's hand, and gestured. "Come along, now. I haven't yet shown you the lilies, and they're my personal favorite."

And Jessamine allowed herself to be pulled along, looking down upon blossom after blossom but seeing nothing.

ELEVEN

T HE PACKAGE LAY UPON THE BED in the dark, but Bridie still had not opened it. Each time she looked at it, she thought of the animal panic in Bridget's glassy eyes, and her fingers twitched to simply light the thing on fire and be done with it, whatever it was.

She could, after all. With just a touch of her fingers. Poof. Flames. But she didn't.

The quiet pressed in on her, heavy and curious, like every particle of air in the room was leaning over her shoulder, waiting to see what she would do. She might not have another chance, she told herself. Eliza would be home soon. Eliza, who was at the palace. Eliza, who would soon be riding about in palace carriages, subject of the jealous whispers of the other maids while Bridie swept the grates and emptied the chamber pots beneath all of their notice.

She looked down at the package again, the corner of a book peeking through the wrinkled brown wrapping. What was it, and why did Bridget think Bridie had been responsible for it? One possible answer to that question was that Bridget was simply mad. Yes, it would be quite easy to attribute the entire exchange to a break from reality — a bout of fever from Riftsickness, perhaps. But Bridie knew Bridget — had spoken to her many times. Bridget wasn't mad — she was boisterous and loud, and a bit outspoken, but her feet had always seemed to be planted firmly on the ground. But now something had frightened her beyond reason, and that something was lying on the bed in front of her. A reckless curiosity seized her, and Bridie tore the paper from the package with trembling fingers.

A book fell out onto the threadbare quilt, small and square and completely unremarkable. Bridie picked it up and turned it over in her hands. It had no title, no markings on the outside. She opened the front cover and read the title: *A Historical Account of the Downfall of the Lamplighters Confederacy* by Elder Hiram Sloane. The room seemed to press in harder. The very motes of dust sang, *read it*.

And Bridie did.

§

Many hours later, Bridie was still looking down at the book, though her unfocused eyes had long since turned it into a pale, amorphous blur in her hands. Her mind was spinning. Riftborn children, born to Dignus families—even wealthy and important Dignus families—left abandoned on the doorsteps of workhouses or even killed, all to avoid the scandal of having Riftmagic infect the family tree.

Somewhere deep in the back of that spinning brain, were the questions she knew she ought to be asking. Where had this book come from? How had Bridget gotten her hands on it? Had it really come to her, as she had suggested, in a previous charity basket, or had that been simply more lunatic raving?

But she could not bring herself to care at that moment what the answers to any of those questions might be. A larger question loomed over her, threatening to consume her:

Had she been one of those children?

Plenty of Riftborn families had to abandon their children to the workhouses. Poverty ran rampant in the Barrens, and a surplus of children amidst a dearth of money and food meant that many families were left with little choice but to lessen their burdens. It was grim, but Bridie, who had always assumed she had been a casualty of such desperation, could at least understand it. She could conjure pity for a family caught in an impossible situation, on the verge of starvation or victims of illness that left them unable to care for their children. She could envision love as the motivation for her abandonment. And she had always done so, to protect her own heart.

But this? This was altogether different. This was monstrous.

She could conceive of no unselfish motives in such rejection. She could conjure only revulsion. Embarrassment. Hatred. The specters of these feelings slid through her veins, chilling her from the inside, hollowing her out, emptying her.

She looked down at her hands and, for the first time since Liesel had brought her to Larkspur Manor, she wanted to cast out the magic that hummed in her fingertips, to scratch and scrape it away until she was left raw and bleeding and powerless.

She thought of the maids in the square, glaring down their noses at her for daring to walk among them when she was nothing but a workhouse drudge. But what if she wasn't? What if she, had she not been abandoned, ought to be looking down on them? What if they, by rights, ought to be calling her "mistress" and fastening her buttons and arranging her curls?

She knew she was a pretty girl. She had always been too vain for her own good—how many times had Eliza and Liesel chastised her for it? She had straight white teeth, a clear, rosy complexion, and lavishly lashed blue eyes. She still remembered the way she'd cried when the matron had cut off her gorgeous auburn hair during an outbreak of lice when she was nine years old. She'd begged to be allowed to simply tuck her curls up under her cap, but the woman had scoffed at her.

"Believe me, child, I'm doing you a favor," she'd muttered darkly. "You're too pretty for the likes of this place, and I'm not the only one who's noticed." And sure enough, Bridie soon found herself shrinking away from the leers of the workhouse Master as she sat at her spinning wheel with the other children, spinning yarn for mops. It seemed likely that Liesel had gotten her out of that place just in time.

Now she found herself thinking of the Dignus girls she'd seen arriving at Larkspur Manor for balls and dinner parties. She had skulked in the shrubbery near the kitchen door, stealing glimpses of their finery through the leaves as they alighted from carriages like birds of paradise touching down from flight. She had fervently wished to be one of them, to twirl about just once in such a fine dress, or to know the weight of a bejeweled necklace nestled in the hollow of her throat. Now she wondered, as she flipped back through their faces in her mind, like a gallery of portraits, if one of those gowns or tiaras or fluttering fans might, by rights, be hers. Had any of their faces resembled hers? Had she glanced, perhaps, upon a nose or a pair of eyes or a crown of red curls too similar to be explained away by chance? Had she cousins or perhaps even siblings among the laughing, drinking, dancing throngs?

119

And they looked down on her. They pitied and laughed at her. They made jokes at her expense, and she had never questioned their right to do so, pitying and laughing at herself as she knelt in filthy grates and dumped out chamber pots and polished and scrubbed until her hands were blistered and raw. She looked down at those hands now, hands full of magic and shame and blisters and ash, that would forever mark her as an outcast. Had those hands cost her the knowledge of who she really was?

There was only one person she could talk to who might know.

§

"Bridie? Creator preserve us, what are you doin' hovering over my bed like a ghoul in the middle of the night? What do you mean by it?" Liesel gasped. Her face was scrunched up with sleep, the bedclothes pulled up to her chin. Between the frilly white cap pulled down over her hair and the fierce expression on her face, she looked much more the wolf of fairytales than the grandmother he was impersonating.

"Well?" she cried, for Bridie had still said nothing. Bridie cleared her throat, trying to find a way to hold on to the courage that was rapidly draining out of her.

"I'm sorry to wake you, Liesel, but I have to ask you something," Bridie whispered.

"And you couldn't have waited until morning?" Liesel demanded.

"No."

Liesel gave a long, exasperated sigh and pulled herself into a sitting position with much groaning of joints and mumbling of curses. When she had arranged herself comfortably, she gestured to Bridie to put the candle down on the bedside table. Bridie complied and then settled herself on the edge of the bed.

"Let's have it, then. Out with it. What is it that couldn't wait for daylight?" Liesel sighed, crossing her arms over her chest and stifling a yawn.

Bridie hesitated. Now that Liesel was sitting in front of her, it was hard to pry the words from her tongue. She licked her lips. "Liesel, why did you choose me?"

Liesel's eyebrows pulled sharply together. "Choose you for what? What are you on about?"

"At the workhouse. They sent you to find a maid. There were

120

hundreds of kids there, plenty of them better behaved than I was and most of them not half so scrawny. So why did you choose me?"

"Scrawny don't mean you can't work," Liesel hedged.

"Just answer the question," Bridie said.

Bridie couldn't be sure, because it was so dark, but it didn't feel like Liesel was quite meeting her eye. "Well, now, I can't say," Liesel said. "You seemed eager enough. And you had sharp eyes—like you were a quick learner, if someone would just bother to teach you something."

"And that's it?" Bridie asked.

"What else ought I to have been looking for?" Liesel asked, sounding exasperated.

Bridie shrugged. "I don't know."

"Are you regretting that I chose you? Should we ship you back?" Liesel asked with a huff.

"No, no, it's not that," Bridie replied. She was making a mess of this. She tried again. "Liesel, when you chose me, did the workhouse matron... did she tell you anything about me?"

"She didn't warn me you were liable to scare me to death in the middle of the night, if that's what you mean," Liesel grumbled.

"No, that's not what I mean," Bridie replied, frustration creeping into her own voice now. "I mean about my... about where I came from."

Bridie was looking at her own fingers now, and so she could not be sure what caused Liesel to hesitate before she replied. "She said you were a foundling."

"A foundling?"

"Yes. Like most of the children there, you'd been abandoned to their care."

"But didn't they tell you anything else? Anything about my family, or... or anything?"

"No."

"Why not?"

"Because I didn't ask, I suppose."

"But didn't you wonder?" Bridie asked, a tremor in her voice that she could not quite suppress.

"No, I didn't wonder," Liesel said, her voice sharp and snappish, and yet her eyes were soft. "Because every child in that sordid place has a sad story, Bridie, and there's no good to come from dwelling on them."

"I'm not dwelling," Bridie replied, angry to hear that her voice sounded like that of the petulant child she had not been for many years now.

"Why are you asking me this now, in the middle of the night?" Liesel asked. Something in her voice made Bridie look up, but a study of the lined old face she knew so well betrayed nothing. She wondered if her own face could be such a mystery, or if the reason for her sudden appearance was as clearly written there as the words on the book back in her room.

"I just... had a dream. About the workhouse," she blurted out finally.

Liesel's eyes narrowed. "What kind of dream?"

Bridie shook her head. "Just... just a dream about being back in the workhouse. I guess it just left me wondering."

Liesel sighed, running a weary hand over her face and stifling a yawn. "Well, for the love of the Creator, Bridie, can't you wonder about it at a reasonable hour? I've already told you, I don't know nothing about your life before you arrived there. They don't provide such information. Your age, your health, and your temperament, that was all I needed to know for my purposes."

"You asked about temperament and still took me home?" Bridie asked with a sad half-smile.

Liesel's mouth crooked into an answering smile. "Well, we all make mistakes, don't we? Off with you, now. Get some sleep, child, and set your mind at rest. No one ever found their way in life by looking backward."

Bridie sighed and nodded, recognizing defeat. She kissed Liesel on the cheek, despite the woman's protests about "sentimental nonsense," and slipped back out into the hallway.

"I suppose I'll just have to find out for myself," she whispered to her own shadow, which crept along in her wake, unable to voice a protest.

TWELVE

J OSIAH WAS UNEASY. Though he tried to hide it behind an easy smile and a casual conversation over drinks, he could not entirely dispel the feeling that Reginald had changed his mind about Jessamine. Reginald did not say as much, but there were certain clues that Josiah had begun to pick up on. Reginald refused to bring the conversation around to their engagement, though Josiah made several attempts to steer it in that direction. He had barely so much as glanced at Jessamine when they were all together in the garden, and seemed far too eager to see the back of her when the women strolled off into the flowerbeds together. Jessamine, too, looked far too relieved to be stepping out of Reginald's company, though she was all politeness and smiling grace when speaking to him. Josiah began to wonder, as he nursed the dregs of his second whiskey, if the matter was as settled as he had allowed himself to assume. Perhaps, he thought, there was more work to be done—work he was not sure he should try to undertake without the High Elder. The problem was, however, that their host had not yet arrived.

Josiah was just beginning to wonder if the High Elder was going to join them at all when the doors to the library opened and John Morgan walked through them—though, as Josiah watched him, he realized that "walked" was quite the wrong word to use. Even in the several days since he had seen the High Elder, it was clear that his health had deteriorated considerably. His feet shuffled laboriously across the floor, each step seeming to cost him rather a great effort, so that by the time he had settled himself into a chair by the fireplace, he was out of breath and his hands were shaking upon his knees. A footman followed anxiously behind him, his hands hovering around his master as though anticipating he may have to catch him at any moment. He seemed quite relieved when the High Elder finally sat down, and hurried off to see to the refreshments.

"Josiah, delighted you could join us. My sincerest apologies for my inexcusable delay. I had much work to catch up on that could not be put off."

"Of course, High Elder. Please do not speak of it. Your son and your lovely wife have kept us well entertained in your absence," Josiah said, pasting a smile onto his face to cover his concern. He was no fool. He knew that work had had nothing at all to do with the High Elder's tardiness. Indeed, he would have been surprised if there were not a doctor's carriage pulling away from the palace at that very moment. Reginald, too, seemed to be trying not to look too closely at his father, throwing him a quick frown and then concentrating instead on draining the remainder of the whiskey from his glass before pouring himself another. Josiah wondered how much of the seriousness of his condition the High Elder had shared with his son.

"Speaking of my lovely wife, where are the ladies at present? I expected to find you all together," Morgan said, in a tone that suggested he would tolerate no questions.

"They are taking a turn about the garden," Josiah replied. "Jessamine was most enamored of your roses and Mrs. Morgan offered a guided tour."

"And there is only so much talk of vegetation that a sane man can take," Reginald added, rolling his eyes. "How can anyone be that interested in flowerbeds?"

"Ah, well, flowerbeds are one of the few areas over which a woman can claim dominion, and so they do, with perhaps more enthusiasm than is warranted, but we must allow them their little projects," Morgan said, with an airy wave of his hand. "It is one of the many lessons marriage will teach you, my son."

Reginald snorted and turned his gaze toward the windows, making it quite clear that he had no interest in lessons of the sort.

"Have you been pleased with the reports out of the Barrens, your Grace?" Josiah asked.

"Yes, indeed, I've just been reading them," Morgan said. "Your proposal to use Riftmead as a balm of sorts to quell the unrest was a brilliant one, Josiah. The patrols have reported a great decrease in violence and resistance since we have implemented the weekly rounds."

"Thank you, your Grace. I am pleased to hear it," Josiah said, as though he had not read every word of those reports several times over before they were sent to the High Elder's office. He would have been a fool not to ensure they cast his solutions in as positive a light as possible. Luckily, the news out of the Barrens had required no finessing— his plans had unfolded even more smoothly and effectively than he could have hoped. He had had to work rather hard to keep the smug look off his face as the reports were read aloud in the last legislative meeting of the Elders. Even the most vocal of his detractors could not deny his success. One rung higher on his climb, one more triumph to tip the scales in his favor when the time came to select the new High Elder. Josiah tore his mind from the notion and forced himself to focus on the man before him, who was still very much alive and whom he still needed to throw his weight behind his nomination.

"We shall have to be careful, of course," Josiah said. "There will be those among the Elders who get carried away by our success and will wish to expand the policy still further."

"Why not expand it further?" Reginald asked, still staring out the window. "Haven't you just said how well it's been working?"

"There is a delicate balance that must be struck," Josiah said patiently. "There is a very real risk of abusing the benefits of Riftmead. Too much of it can cause illness and addiction. We want the Barrens docile, yes, but they still have important functions to serve, and we cannot risk poisoning our own workforces."

Reginald shrugged his shoulders, as though to suggest poisoning the masses might still be an amusing prospect.

"The reports out of the asylums and workhouses make it clear that we must tread carefully with the dosing," Josiah went on. "The doctors there have provided us with much research that is guiding our policy at present. Thus far, it has worked much better than we had hoped. It will be important to keep that research at the forefront of our discussions."

"Oh, yes," Morgan agreed. "There is many a hot-headed Elder on the benches who would just as soon shower the Barrens in Riftmead than do the work necessary to maintain the balance between obedience and usefulness."

"We shall rein them in, sir," Josiah said confidently.

"I have no doubt," Morgan said. "So, gentlemen, what have I missed? Have you already discussed the matter of Miss Hallewell?"

"Certainly not, father," Reginald said, his tone hardening. "Creator knows I'd never have the audacity to discuss the matter of my own future without you present to make all the decisions."

"You sound like a petulant child," Morgan said.

"Perhaps I am a petulant child," Reginald countered. "If I embraced the moniker, would you stop trying to herd me like a sheep up the aisle, snapping at my heels like a hound?"

Morgan closed his eyes as though praying for patience. "Reginald, you left childhood behind long ago, desperately though you try to cling to it. Marriage is not an inconvenience, it is a moral and social obligation."

"Ah, yes, and we all know what a smashing record I have with obligations," Reginald said dryly.

"Yes, well, try as you may to ignore it, the responsibility to carry on our family name and lineage now rests squarely on your shoulders," Morgan said, a bit wearily, as though he had given this very speech more times than he cared to remember.

"Peter's shoulders were more suited to the burden," Reginald muttered.

"Undoubtedly," Morgan replied tartly. "But as those shoulders are now rotting away in the family plot, that leaves yours. Now pull yourself together before Josiah starts to believe your attitude is a reflection on his own admirable daughter rather than your inability to commit to anything like a man."

Josiah cleared his throat. "You needn't worry about that, your Grace. I remember what it was to be young, with the world at my fingertips. It was intolerable to think of settling down, and I must admit I did so grudgingly."

Reginald raised a skeptical eyebrow. "Somehow I find that hard to believe, Elder Hallewell, you shirking responsibility."

Josiah shrugged and smirked. "What can I say? The world was full of possibilities and I felt no drive to limit them. But I must say, I soon found the benefits of marriage to far outweigh the tedium that often defines it."

Reginald had the good grace to look intrigued. "Is that so?"

"Oh, yes, indeed," Josiah said. "You must realize that a dutiful wife assumes many burdens that would otherwise fall to a man. A good and faithful wife will lighten your load, not weigh you down."

But the curiosity had already slipped from Reginald's features, leaving an amused skepticism behind. "You'll forgive me, Elder Hallewell, but you are hardly a neutral party in this discussion. As Jessamine's father, you have every reason in the world to make marriage sound as palatable as possible. Your words are encouraging, but they do not ring true in the ears of a young man who tends to hear within his circles rather different anecdotes about matrimony."

Morgan laughed humorlessly. "And what circles are those, pray tell? The gambling dens? The pubs? The brothels? What good do you expect to hear about marriage in places like that?"

Josiah nodded in agreement. "The men you meet in those places cannot even control their own excesses, let alone control a wife. You are a clever enough man never to make that mistake, I am sure."

"I will be frank with you, Elder Hallewell," Reginald said, sighing deeply and setting down his glass. "I agreed to my father's suggestion of a betrothal with Jessamine because it seemed sensible at the time."

Morgan let out another bitter bark of laughter that dissolved almost at once into a hacking cough, and his reply came out choked. "You agreed because I threatened to cut you off without a penny. If you're going to be frank, Reginald, for Creator's sake, be frank!"

Reginald's mouth twisted and he glared at his father for a moment before nodding curtly. "Very well. I was strong-armed into it, is that what you want me to say? But regardless of how I came to agree, the fact remains that I'm not interested in tying myself to a girl who will not submit herself to me, but who seeks to assert her own sort of control over my life. I do not care to set my watch to a woman's expectations."

"Only a fool who marries for love would fall prey to such things," Josiah said bluntly. "I do not think you are a fool."

Reginald blinked. "Don't you? He certainly does. Makes sure to inform me as much at least twice a day."

Morgan opened his mouth but Josiah held up a hand to silence him, a thing he would never ordinarily have done, but he could see that Morgan's input would only further alienate the boy. Too much had gone sour between them, and it was threatening to poison the entire arrangement before it could be finalized. Josiah could not allow that to happen. There was too much at stake. Morgan swallowed his words and seemed to choke on them again, coughing violently into his handkerchief and his complexion turning swiftly from papery white to scarlet.

"Pardon me," he managed to say, before rising laboriously from his chair and walking out of the room. His footman met him at the door, beginning some sort of ministrations with a damp cloth and offering Morgan a tincture of some kind from a small glass bottle. Josiah seized the opportunity of being out of Morgan's hearing and turned back to Reginald.

"Perhaps you think I am interested only in what this arrangement can bring to me, personally," Josiah said flatly. The bluntness of the pronouncement brought Reginald up short. He tore his eyes from his father, still in the throes of a coughing fit, and gawked at Josiah instead. Sure of the boy's undivided attention now, Josiah went on, "I would not blame you for coming to such a conclusion. There are many people who will see it that way, especially those in the benches at the Illustratum who would like nothing better than to see me unseated. But I assure you, I thought about much more than my own aspirations when your father and I first discussed the merits of this arrangement. I thought of you, of the kind of man you are. I thought about your reputation for excess, which I believe to be much less a flaw than a lack of direction. You have the drive to go after what you desire and seize it. That is not a bad thing. That is determination. That is hunger. When channeled in the right way, that is a recipe for success. I see potential in you, Reginald. A great deal of it."

Josiah congratulated himself silently as he watched the effects of his words on Reginald. The boy looked frankly stunned to be told he was anything other than a failure and a disappointment. Josiah took advantage of the silence and plowed on.

"I also thought of Jessamine. I thought of how she would be uniquely suited to you. You may think I am indifferent to my daughter's feelings, given the whole mess with Teddy Potter, but you couldn't be more wrong. I thought very carefully about her temperament and the role for which she has been groomed all her life. Teddy Potter is a fine young man, but he can rub along comfortably with nearly anyone. He will not find it difficult to build a pleasant life with any one of a dozen amiable young women from Elder families. He's like his father—easily contented and never too keen to reach beyond what he knows for certain he can attain. You are not so easily contented. You are restless. I think you want more out of your life, and the right woman can help you to attain it."

Reginald looked deep in thought now as Josiah's words sank through his armor. Josiah stood up, closed the distance between them, and clapped a hand firmly on Reginald's shoulder.

"Jessamine is sensible and practical. She has never been one to fall prey to sentimentality—my wife has never been well enough to fill our daughter's head with the romantic drivel so many mothers poison their daughters with. Jessamine understands better than most girls of her age and rank how the world works." He ignored the nagging voice in the back of his mind, the one that told him he wanted this to be true more than he believed it to be true—the one that reminded him that he had likely broken his daughter's heart when he had promised her to this man. He pushed it away, as he did any thought that did not serve to further his cause. He squeezed Reginald's shoulder, and the boy met his eye.

"With her by your side, you could achieve great things," Josiah whispered. "You can forge your own path, Reginald. Don't worry about the man others want you to be. Think about the man you want to be."

Reginald smiled his bitter smile, but the effect was ruined by the genuine emotion that had crept into his eyes as he listened to Josiah's speech. "I don't know what man I want to be," he murmured.

"I do. I can see him in you, despite your best attempts to ignore him," Josiah said. "Your father may not see him, but I do."

"I hate him," Reginald whispered. "When I see how he's failing, all I can feel is relief. What kind of son thinks like that?"

"A son who is ready to spread his wings and become his own man," Josiah said bracingly. "The expectations of a father can weigh heavily on a young man, and that is all the more true for you, as you have no ordinary father. This marriage may just seem like another means by which he means to control your life, but I beg of you not to look at it that way. See this arrangement for what it is: a gift. Let Jessamine lift the burdens of society from your shoulders so you can be free to make your mark. Do it not for your father, and not for me. Do it for yourself."

Josiah watched as his words landed, scrutinizing the young man before him. Whether it was Josiah's own powers of persuasion or the healthy measure of whiskey Reginald had already consumed, something in his demeanor softened, the resistance melting until, when he met Josiah's eyes again, Josiah could see the decision that had crystallized there. His heart sang with triumph before Reginald could even open his mouth.

"Thank you, Elder Hallewell. You're quite right, sir. I mustn't destroy this arrangement simply to spite my father, however tempting that prospect may be. I have my own future to think about, and though marriage was not my priority, it has become something of a necessity, given my financial situation. And a wife needn't be a burden if she is handled properly."

Ought these words to have troubled Josiah Hallewell? Perhaps so, but he would not allow them to dull the shine of this further victory. Reginald was still young. It would be possible to curb the bad habits he had not yet outgrown, he was sure of it. A firm hand and some carefully applied persuasion had proven effective. Perhaps Morgan had simply neglected the boy, having found everything he desired in an heir in his firstborn son. And if he remained as stubbornly unprincipled a lout as he appeared at present? Well, that would be Jessamine's problem to sort out. The boy will have served his purpose.

Morgan chose that moment to shuffle back into the room and rejoin them by the fireplace. His lips had a slightly bluish tinge to them, and his eyes were bloodshot. His hands shook upon the top of his cane as he lowered himself into his seat, from which place he seemed unlikely to rise again for quite some time.

"Reginald, I think we need to have a serious talk about—" Morgan began in a quavering voice, but Reginald cut him off.

"There's no need for that, father. Elder Hallewell and I have spoken. I do not intend to dishonor our agreement. We shall settle everything this evening."

Morgan's mouth dropped open and he quickly snapped it closed again. He turned his gaze on Josiah and smiled for the first time since he had appeared to greet them.

"Well, well, well," he chuckled. "It seems I underestimated you, Josiah."

"Not at all, sir. Your son is a reasonable young man. We've merely struck up an understanding," Josiah said, inclining his head toward Reginald, who returned a grudging smile.

Morgan clapped his gnarled hands together. "Then it seems we have a wedding to plan! Reginald, ring the bell for Graves, would

130

you? And have him call the ladies in from the garden! We shall be a merry party for dinner tonight!"

An excerpt from *Duties of the Dignus Wife* written by Elder Emerson Cuthbert, published 1824

"…It would be easy, therefore, to believe that a wife's greatest duties lie in the rearing of her husband's children and management of her husband's household. These duties are, of course, vital to the success of the marriage and family, but I beg of you not to see it in that light. A much greater duty exists, one that every faithful Dignus wife must acknowledge as her most sacred task—the one upon which she must pray each and every day, the one upon which all her other tasks and duties rest. This duty, the foundation upon which all others must build, is the unwavering support of her husband in his faith.

A good Dignus wife will care not only for her husband's physical well-being, but his spiritual well-being also. Dignus men must walk out in the world, facing temptations and tests of faith that women cannot even conceive of. His wife, therefore, must serve as a constant reminder of the importance of centering the Creator in all things. She must be the light when the world becomes dark, guiding her husband back to faith in all things. If she does this, she shall find the rest of her duties a joy rather than a burden, for she has kept her husband upon the Path, and therefore she is assured the Creator's favor in all her family's endeavors…"

THIRTEEN

J ESSAMINE'S OWN EMERALD GREEN EYES stared back at her from the mirror in her palace quarters. Every detail of her appearance, from her raven hair piled high on her head to the satin slippers adorning her feet, had been meticulously seen to with such care that she felt as though she was attending her Presentation all over again. In some ways, she thought to herself, it was a continuation of the same performance—the culmination of what she had begun when she stepped out onto the floor of the ballroom on Reginald Morgan's arm. The thought made her eyes suddenly sparkle.

"You look positively lovely, Miss Jessamine," Eliza said quietly, fussing unnecessarily with an already perfectly positioned bloom in Jessamine's hair. "A vision, miss."

"A vision of what?" Jessamine asked. "Fear? Obedience?"

Eliza pressed her lips together in a guilty expression, and Jessamine regretted her candid words at once. "I'm sorry Eliza. I do not wish to devalue your work. You've seen to each detail with such care. Thank you."

"Don't thank me, miss. And don't apologize. I understand."

Jessamine almost laughed dismissively, but stifled the sound. She realized that Eliza probably did understand, better than Jessamine had ever considered before. After all, wasn't Eliza's entire life a performance, a constant dance to prove her competency and obedience, and skill? The expectations placed upon them might have been different, but the people for whom they were expected to display perfection were the very same.

She rose from her seat at the vanity and took as deep a breath as her corset would allow. Not even Eliza's magical ministrations could calm her tonight, even if Jessamine had allowed them. If she was going to face this night, she wanted to do it with her mind clear and her eyes wide open.

The dinner laid before her that evening was the most sumptuous of banquets, but while the rest of the party were deeply engrossed in the food before them, Jessamine could not take her eyes off of Mrs. Morgan. Try as she might to focus on the conversation that was bouncing back and forth across the vast dining table, she found herself studying the woman's face, scrutinizing her facial expressions and gestures. She was so lovely, so flawlessly styled, and yet there was something incredibly fragile about her—a porcelain doll come to life. Her moment of vulnerability in the garden, when she gave Jessamine her warning, had peeled back her carefully constructed veneer, and now that Jessamine had seen behind it, she could sense what was beneath it. As she watched Mrs. Morgan entertain her guests, Jessamine began to notice the effort behind her smile, the spark of something in her eyes that was harder to define, and yet Jessamine thought it might be fear—fear of saying the wrong thing, fear of not performing up to the standards that were expected of her. It was almost heartbreaking to watch, this constant underlying terror of a misstep. Was this what every moment of her life was like, a tightrope performance that hinged on absolute perfection?

Was this what Jessamine's life would be like as Reginald's wife? A constant pantomime of contentedness while her emotions roiled and raged beneath? How long could a person possibly keep that up? How long would it be before Mrs. Morgan cracked and crumbled under the pressure? And how long could Jessamine herself last, when it was her turn to assume the performance? She suddenly felt terribly, deeply tired.

When she managed to tear her eyes from Mrs. Morgan, she found herself scrutinizing the men at the table. They were too wrapped up in their conversation to notice the unladylike way in which she stared pointedly at them, and she found, to her surprise, that she could peel their layers away much in the same way she had peeled them away from Mrs. Morgan. Reginald was just barely keeping his resentment at bay with the steady refilling of his wine glass, his conversation becoming louder and less coherent as the evening wore on. Her father was coating every word he uttered in a thick layer of deference and flattery, weighing the High Elder's response each

136

time he spoke, adjusting his tone and topic to fit Morgan's every whim. Mrs. Morgan interjected primly at the appropriate moments, but otherwise let the men guide the discourse. No one seemed to expect much from Jessamine, which suited her well, for she was finding her scrutiny of the speakers far more interesting than the conversation itself. That is until the topic turned at last to the reason for their visit.

Jessamine looked up from the remains of her blancmange to find everyone staring at her.

"Jessamine? Did you hear Mr. Morgan?" Her father's eyes were boring into hers.

Jessamine cleared her throat and attempted a smile. "I'm terribly sorry. I was so intent upon this delicious dessert, I did not realize I had been addressed. Mrs. Morgan, you must send my compliments to your cook."

Mrs. Morgan nodded agreeably, and Jessamine turned her attention reluctantly to Reginald. "My apologies, Mr. Morgan. What did you say?"

Reginald drained the remainder of the wine in his glass and set it down, rather harder than was necessary, upon the tabletop. "I asked if you would care to take a turn about the garden with me."

Jessamine felt her heart seem to leap into her throat. Wild panic coursed through her limbs, and she fought back a mad desire to flee from the table. Instead, she clenched her fists in her lap as hard as she could, willing her body to calm and obey her before rising to her feet. Her voice did not tremble when she replied, "I'd be delighted, Mr. Morgan."

Jessamine felt every pair of eyes upon her as she crossed the room to Reginald's side. The High Elder's expression was bleary but satisfied. Her father's bordered on smug. Mrs. Morgan, however, was biting her lip, and when Jessamine caught her eye, she dropped her gaze to her plate, her cheeks flushing.

No one was going to rescue her. There would be no more delaying this moment. It had come, and she had to face it. She expected Reginald to offer his arm, but when he saw that she had risen to join him, he simply charged toward the doors, leaving her to hurry along behind him. Rather than allowing herself to smart over the indignity of it, she took the opportunity to smooth her dress, ensure her hair was still in place, and pinch some color into her pallid cheeks. She wished desperately that Eliza was with her, that she could use her Influencer magic to calm and soothe her, and then chided herself for her childishness. She had already decided she would face this on her own, and blast it all, she would.

Reginald did not walk all the way out into the gardens, as Jessamine expected him to. As she stepped through the glass-paned doors to the balcony that led to the gardens, she found him standing in a bright patch of moonlight, staring up into the face of the full moon that had cast the gardens in a ghostly brightness. She cleared her throat, so that she would not startle him, and then stepped forward until she stood just beside him.

"The moonlight is beautiful," she said at last, for it seemed that someone ought to say something, and resorting to inane comments about the weather was all she could manage.

"Moonlight is deceiving," Reginald replied. "It turns the world into a pale imitation of itself—nothing is quite as it should be."

"Perhaps so. Nevertheless, I've always enjoyed it," Jessamine said quietly.

Reginald turned to her. His face was florid from the wine, and he squinted at her with glazed and watery eyes, as though trying to get her to come into focus. "I suppose you know why we're all here," he said flatly.

Jessamine hesitated. She knew it wasn't proper to make assumptions about his intentions, but then again, he was the one who was choosing to broach the subject in such a straightforward manner. She decided to follow his lead, at least for the moment, and be truthful.

"Yes, I suppose I do," she replied, lifting her eyes to the moon again.

"Look, you should know I had no bloody intention of getting married." The words stumbled over each other on the way out of his mouth, coming out garbled. "And as much as I can't stand the fellow, it wasn't my idea to break off your arrangement with Potter. I don't know if that makes any difference at all to you, but I wanted you to know anyway."

The mention of Teddy stung, but Jessamine swallowed back the pain. "Thank you for telling me."

"You're not going to cry, are you?" Reginald asked suddenly, leaning closer and nearly stumbling into her as he squinted into her face.

"No, I certainly am not," Jessamine said indignantly. Apparently, the pain had flashed as clearly across her face as it had sliced through her heart, and she cursed herself for it. The very last thing she wanted was to make herself vulnerable in front of this man.

Reginald mumbled something about handkerchiefs and then stared back at the moon again. Silence hung heavily over them. Jessamine longed for the evening to be over.

"My father is dying, you know."

Jessamine's head snapped up. "I beg your pardon?"

"Surely you knew."

"I... I did not. I... I thought perhaps he was unwell when I saw him this evening, but I had no idea that..." her words trailed away as the horror sunk in. The High Elder, the Creator's interpreter on Earth, was dying. It felt wrong, impossible. And then...

"That's why this has happened. That's why they've arranged *this*," Reginald said, gesturing between the two of them, a mocking smirk upon his face.

"I beg your pardon?" Jessamine barely managed to whisper.

"It's an arrangement, you see. A political one."

Jessamine felt her mouth open and close stupidly. "I... I'm sorry?"

"Well, all marriages between Elder families are political arrangements, aren't they?" Reginald said. "We're all just pawns in their quest for power and alliances."

Jessamine had never heard a man speak so baldly about such matters. It had never occurred to her that the sons might harbor similar feelings to the daughters. She had always assumed that the sons of Elders were masters of their own destiny, just as their fathers were. Fleetingly, she wondered if she had been too harsh on Teddy, refusing to so much as open his letters after her disastrous Presentation.

"Well, I'm no better," Reginald said, bitterness saturating every syllable. "I always said I wasn't going to let my father control my life, and here I am, submitting to his will like all the rest of them. At least my brother had the good sense to die young."

Jessamine could not reply; she was too shocked. Each time Reginald opened his mouth felt like another slap to the face.

"Well, your Father will get what he wants, I suppose," Reginald said with a sigh and a poorly suppressed belch. "A daughter married off in wealth and influence, and the highest seat in the land. A fair exchange for your future happiness, eh?"

Jessamine felt as though her brain was working in slow motion, her thoughts struggling to keep up with Reginald's words. "Do you mean... is my father..."

"My God, they really don't tell their daughters anything, do they?" Reginald said with a mocking laugh. "Yes, your dear Papa is first in the line of succession—or at least, my father will make him so when our union is ensured. Once upon a time, my father might have thought to pass it right along the family line, but now..." He pointed to himself and shrugged. "So, he'll settle for a trusty lieutenant whom he can rope into reining me in after he's gone. Your father ought to do the job admirably. He convinced me to go through with it, at least. I'm still not quite sure how he managed it. Maybe he slipped something into my drink." He grinned lazily, as though this was a very witty joke.

"So, my father drugged you into agreeing to marry me, is that what you're implying?" Jessamine snapped, her anger roused at her father's betrayal. "I suggest you do not make a habit of proposing to young women, Reginald. You've no talent for it at all."

"My father is dying. I'm doing this for him. Damned if I know why—I've never felt the need to appease him much before, as anyone can tell you. In fact, I seem to have expended most of my energy in this life doing exactly the opposite of what he would have wished me to do."

Jessamine stared at Reginald in mild shock. First, the lout implied her father was drugging him, and now she had been reduced to a prop with which he could assuage his guilt. It was like watching a man propose with a gun to his head. Her stomach twisted. She felt ill.

He looked down at her and laughed at the expression on her face. "You needn't look so horrified. I'm a man of my word, on the rare occasion that I choose to give it."

Jessamine cleared her throat. "I'm sorry, but am I meant to understand this as a proposal?"

Reginald laughed, a bitter, twisted thing. "I suppose so."

"Well, I'm not sure what you've heard about proposals, Reginald, but your technique leaves a lot to be desired. I'm not sure if you thought the moonlight was going to do all of the work for you, but there's just a bit more to romance than that."

Reginald snorted loudly. "Romance? Is that what you're after?"

"I'd settle for a modicum of respect," she shot back.

"I don't think there's going to be much in the way of romance or respect in this arrangement, do you? I mean, bloody hell, they've all but danced us down the aisle on puppet strings."

Jessamine felt resentment flare up inside her. "And am I so insignificant in this process that I do not even warrant the question to be asked of me? Am I not allowed even to answer for myself?"

Reginald shrugged. "What does it matter? It's not as though you are going to refuse me."

Jessamine actually bit down on her own tongue to hold back the vicious diatribe she longed to spit at him. She wanted to tell him she would refuse him, right there in the garden, and leave him alone to marinate in his own alcohol-soaked bitterness. She wanted to tell him she'd rather marry any man in England than waste a single moment of her life with him. But she couldn't. She loathed the fact that he was right. She would not refuse him. She had no choice.

He watched, clearly amused, while her struggle played across her face. "So it's settled, then?"

"No, it certainly is not!" Jessamine ground out through her clenched teeth. "I know we've little choice in the matter, but I will not be cast aside in this manner. The question must be asked and answered. You will do me this courtesy at least, if no other."

"Why?" Reginald asked, exasperated.

"Because every young woman of my acquaintance will be pressing me for details the next time they see me, and I should not like to have to lie to them. You took me on a stroll in a moonlit garden at the palace. You got down on one knee amidst the roses and promised to love me forever. You presented me with a ring, which I accepted."

"I've already told you, I detest moonlight. And I'm allergic to roses."

"I will settle," Jessamine growled, "for the kneeling and the ring."

Reginald merely looked amused for a moment, and then, expelling a dramatic, long-suffering sigh, he got unsteadily to one knee. Jessamine gasped—she had not expected him to comply with her request. Then he reached into his pocket and pulled out a small gold filigree box. He flipped open the catch and held it out to her.

Jessamine did not reach for it. She simply stared. The ring nestled in the cushion of silk was stunning, set with an enormous rose-cut diamond in an elaborate golden setting with a halo of tiny diamonds set all around it. It glittered unnaturally in the moonlight.

"If it doesn't suit you, there are dozens of others to choose from.

My father's child bride selected it. I don't know the first thing about jewelry, but it seemed an appropriate enough choice."

"It's beautiful," Jessamine whispered. Even as she imagined flinging it back in Reginald's smug face, she had to admire it.

"It will do," Reginald conceded. "So. I've knelt. I've presented you with a ring. The bloody moon is out. What have I missed? Oh yes." He cleared his throat obnoxiously and said, in a ridiculously formal tone, "Miss Jessamine Hallewell, will you marry me?"

Jessamine could not bring herself to answer out loud. With a feeling like she was stepping off a cliff, she closed her eyes and nodded her head.

Reginald plucked the ring from the box, snatched up Jessamine's hand, and slid it onto her finger. She stared down at it, with the unshakable impression that she was staring down at a stranger's hand rather than her own. That ring could not belong to her any more than she could ever belong to Reginald Morgan. She was convinced the sight of it upon her finger would surprise her every day for the rest of her life—a thought that made her feel positively faint.

She was so intent on steadying her breathing and avoiding the impulse to swoon that it was a moment before she realized Reginald had not let go of her hand. She tried to pull it away, but his grip did not loosen. She met his eye and felt her blood run cold. He had gotten unsteadily to his feet and was now staring down at her with a kind of hunger that left her frozen with fear. His thumb stroked against the bare skin of her wrist.

"Maybe this won't be as terrible as I feared," Reginald said, his voice low and husky now. "You really are a delectable little thing, aren't you?"

Jessamine tensed. His grip on her wrist tightened. As she watched, he lifted it to his lips and planted a kiss upon it. Then he pressed his nose to her skin and inhaled her scent.

"Reginald…" she began breathlessly, but he did not allow her to finish. He yanked her forward, crushed her against him, and kissed her. She could not even scream. His hot, sour breath was in her mouth. His hands were groping everywhere. His voice was a growl of animal desire.

"No… you mustn't… NO!"

Somehow, she gathered the strength to shove against him. It mightn't have made the slightest difference if he'd been sober, but he was already off balance from the wine, and he stumbled backward and fell, landing flat on his back in a border of tulips. He swore incoherently as she backed away from him. His face was thunderous for a moment, then broke into a vicious smile.

"That's not a word I will tolerate once we are married, my darling," he said, a sneer in his voice. "Others might find your spirited nature endearing, but I promise you, I shall tire of it very swiftly."

Jessamine continued to back away from him, trying to wipe the smell of him from her lips. While he struggled clumsily to his feet, she smoothed her hair and tugged at her dress, ensuring there was no evidence of his advances. A sudden voice from the balcony echoed down into the grounds, and she went as still as stone.

"Jessamine? Reginald? We have champagne! Do join us so that we may celebrate together!" Mrs. Morgan's voice drifted down, like a snatch of music in the wind.

"We're just coming!" Jessamine called back, relieved to hear that her voice was quite steady. Then she turned back to Reginald. "Pull yourself together. You look a mess, and I won't have them thinking I allowed you to take liberties with me."

And before she had to endure whatever hideous reply he dredged up from his wine-soaked stupor, she turned and marched into the house, the ring heavy and glittering upon her shaking hand.

FOURTEEN

E LIZA COULD BARELY SIT STILL. Every time she tried to settle herself down she had sprung to her feet again, pacing the room, reorganizing the dressing table, smoothing the dresses, peering out through the windows. She was brimming with a nervous energy she could not contain, and it animated her like a dark magic spell so that she hardly felt in control of herself. Her mind was racing. What ought she to do? Should she tell Miss Jessamine what she had witnessed? It would be nothing short of pure insanity to betray the confidence of the man who would shortly become her master, and yet it felt like an impossibility to keep such information from her mistress. The palms of Eliza's hands were sore from the number of times she had dug her fingernails into them, leaving painful pink crescents in her flesh. She felt almost dizzy with anxiety. The hours crawled by at an impossibly slow pace—Eliza thought she would go mad with the anticipation.

At last, the door opened and Miss Jessamine entered her room, having been led there by the housekeeper, a stern-faced woman with a pocket watch in her hand and a spark of almost manic servitude in her eye.

"We have striven to ensure that everything is to your liking, Miss Hallewell, but if you require anything at all, please do not hesitate to ring, and we shall see to your request at once," the housekeeper said, her shoulders hunched into a constant near-bow.

Jessamine barely gave the room a cursory glance before saying, "Everything looks wonderful, thank you. I have no doubt I shall be very comfortable."

The housekeeper bowed lower, shot Eliza a sharp, almost warning look, as though to say, "You'd best be up to our standards!" and backed out of the room, easing the door soundlessly closed as she went.

The moment the woman was out of sight, Jessamine sighed deeply and sat heavily on the bed before allowing herself to fall backward onto the pillows with a groan.

"Miss Jessamine? Are you quite well?" Eliza asked anxiously, hurrying over to hover near the bed.

Jessamine sighed again. "All I want to do is get out of this dress as quickly as possible and forget this whole night ever happened."

Eliza bit her lip. "Did... did something happen, miss?"

"Oh, yes. I think it's safe to say that something has, indeed, happened," Jessamine replied glumly, and stuck her left hand up in the air, wiggling her fingers. The light caught the diamond now resting there so that a glittering like sparks from a fire dazzled Eliza's eyes. She gasped and threw her hand up over her mouth.

"You're... you're engaged, miss!" Eliza cried, her voice muffled behind her hand.

"Don't remind me," Jessamine said, letting her hand drop again.

"I... I didn't... congratulations, miss!" Eliza gasped, trying to muster some excitement to overcome her shock, with the effect that her words came out more like a question than a declaration.

Jessamine must have heard the inflection, for she let out a single humorless chuckle before replying. "It's all right, Eliza. You needn't pretend for me. We'll have to do plenty of pretending when the engagement parties and wedding preparations start. For tonight, in this room, just the two of us, let's not pretend."

Eliza let her hand drop. "I'm sorry, miss. How... I admit I am at a loss for what to say."

"That's just fine, Eliza. I am at a loss for what to feel. We shall suit each other well tonight, I think," Jessamine said with a sigh. She lowered her hand, holding the ring in front of her eyes. "It's terribly sad, Eliza, having dreamed for such a long time to see a ring on this finger, only to find I can hardly bear the sight of it. And it's such a pretty ring, too."

Eliza ventured closer to the bed until she was able to perch herself on the very corner. "It really is, miss. It looks just lovely on you."

"I know it does," Jessamine said. "I suppose that's part of why I can barely stand to look at it. It ought to be everything I want. All

146

of this," she gestured broadly to the opulence that surrounded them, "should be exactly what I want. And yet, it's all I can do not to burst into tears."

"Do... would you like me to help, miss?" Eliza asked. She held up her own hand, encased in its white glove.

Jessamine considered for a moment and then smiled sadly, shaking her head. "Thank you, Eliza, but not this time. I'm not sure why, but I think I need to sit with this—all of it—and let it do its worst. I don't think it shall do me any good to put it off."

"Very well, miss. Shall we get you changed, then? The ring can do its worst, but surely we needn't continue the torture of the corset?"

Jessamine managed a laugh. "Oh, yes indeed. An excellent idea."

But when they had gotten her extricated from her confection of a gown, with all its undergarments, Jessamine decided that what she really needed was a bath. Eliza ran the hot water, and when the tub was filled, Jessamine sank down into it. After a few moments, she slipped the ring from her finger and held it out to Eliza. "If I have to think about it relentlessly, I shouldn't have to look at it, too. Please put it in the box."

Eliza carried the ring, perhaps the most valuable thing she'd ever been allowed to handle, and placed it gingerly in its silk-lined box, where it twinkled up at her as though it knew its own terrible power. She closed the box upon it, deciding that she, too, no longer wanted to look at it.

Carefully, Eliza removed her gloves and rolled up her sleeves. Then, she wrapped a soft cotton cloth over her bare fingers, so that there would be no danger of using her Influence. Then she sat beside the tub, wringing warm water over Miss Jessamine's shoulders and neck. Miss Jessamine lay quite still, her eyes closed, but a deep crease between her eyebrows betrayed that she was not as relaxed as she seemed. Looking down at her mistress's expression, a battle raged in Eliza's mind. What ought she to tell Miss Jessamine, if anything? The tub in which she now soaked had served as a hiding place for a frightened maid hiding from her future husband's advances! Surely this was something she ought to know?

"Miss Jessamine, I—"

A tentative knock sounded upon the door. It was such a gentle sound that Eliza thought she might have imagined it at first, but then it sounded again, just a trifle louder. Eliza excused herself and crossed the bedroom to open the door.

A maid stood on the other side of it, white-faced and wide-eyed. For one heart-stopping moment, Eliza thought it might be the same maid she had hidden from Master Reginald, but a closer look revealed this girl was taller, her face narrower, her complexion fairer. Eliza felt her shoulders relax and she tried to smile.

"Can I help you?"

"Are you Eliza Braxton?"

Eliza was taken aback, but nodded all the same. "At your service. And you are?"

"My name is Bette. I wondered whether you know a woman named Eleanor Spratt?"

Eliza's smile faltered. Barely anyone outside of Larkspur Manor knew that Mrs. Spratt worked there. Elder Hallewell had made sure of it, for he had wanted to draw as little attention to his wife's condition as possible. However, she decided she could answer the question without betraying anything about Mrs. Hallewell.

"I do. Why do you ask?"

The girl let out a sigh of relief. "I must beg a favor of you. Would you see to it that she gets this letter?" And without waiting for an answer, she thrust the letter hastily into Eliza's hands.

"Excuse me?" Eliza looked down at the slightly crumpled letter in surprise.

"Please," the girl added, her voice breaking slightly. Eliza peered at her more closely and saw that her eyes were bright with unshed tears and that she was twisting her apron in her hands. "I have no other way to deliver it to her, and I thought... I heard... that you would be here with Miss Jessamine, so I took the chance to sneak up here to see you."

Eliza was bewildered but could think of no good reason to refuse the girl's request. Nevertheless, she asked, "Why didn't you just send it by post?"

Bette bit her lip. "I did not think it was safe."

"Not safe? The post?" Eliza asked with an incredulous laugh.

Bette shook her head solemnly. "I could not run the risk that it would not make it into her hands. Can you help me ensure she receives it? Please. I would not ask if it was not important."

Eliza hesitated only a moment, gazing into the girl's earnest face, before making her decision. "Yes, of course."

Bette's entire body sagged with relief. The tight line of her mouth relaxed into a grateful smile. "I am indebted to you, Eliza Braxton. If I can ever do anything for you, you need only say the word."

Eliza tried to smile. "I require no favors of you, Bette. However, I would be grateful if you could ask someone to bring up a tea tray for my mistress."

"Of course." She bobbed a quick curtsy and turned on her heel at once, scurrying down the hall and out of sight.

Eliza looked down at the letter in her hands, curiosity burning within her. Of course, she would never read another person's private correspondence, but that did not mean she was not desperate to know what was within it. Suppressing the almost overwhelming urge to tear it open, Eliza tucked it into her apron pocket and composed herself on the surface, even as the questions roiled under her smooth demeanor.

She'd barely been at the palace half a day, and already she'd had two very strange encounters with servants here, the first of which had been disturbing and the second merely mysterious. She thought back to earlier that day when their arrival had been greeted by a veritable army of staff, every face smooth and blank, every movement practiced and choreographed. She would have thought the servants here were a single, impenetrable unit—a united front that could not be shaken. It gave her a strange hollow feeling, knowing how much discontent and secrecy roiled beneath the surface of the perfect façade. But then, she thought to herself, hadn't she learned in the past few weeks that that was the way of things in post-Rift London? The order imposed did not kill what seethed beneath it, after all. It only fed the fury.

"Who was that, Eliza?" Jessamine asked when Eliza returned to her stool by the soaking tub.

"Oh, just one of the servants, checking in to see that we had everything we require for the night. I took the liberty of asking her to send up some tea."

"That's perfect, Eliza, thank you. A cup of tea and some sleep, I think."

"Yes, indeed, miss."

The silence settled over them, heavy with all of the things neither of them would say. Eliza did not think she could bear it.

"Miss."

149

"Hmm?"

"You don't have to marry him."

Jessamine's eyes fluttered open, but she did not look at Eliza. She kept her eyes fixed carefully on the ceiling. "I very much wish that was true, Eliza."

"But if your father knew what kind of man he is—"

Jessamine made a choked sound, half-laughter, half-sob. "But he does know. Everyone does. Master Reginald's reputation precedes him in all of the Dignus circles, I am sorry to say."

Eliza's eyes went wide. "You... you know that he's... well..."

"A gambler? A heavy drinker? A famous philanderer? There's not a member of the Elder circles that doesn't know it. Why do you suppose I've been regarded with such pity over the past few weeks? The other girls can't breathe for telling me how sorry they are, and how they're sure it's not as bad as they've heard. But it is. His reputation has been well and truly earned, and he has made no efforts to disguise it."

Eliza felt the words she was going to speak shrivel and die on her tongue. "And your father promises you to him regardless?"

"He does."

Eliza grappled for something to say. She had been so horrified that she might have to be the one to tell Miss Jessamine what Master Reginald was truly like, but somehow this was worse.

"But why?"

"Because of this," Jessamine said, gesturing around again. "Don't you see, Eliza? It's not about me. It never was. My father seeks power. He seeks the High Elder's seat. And my marriage is how he will secure it."

"The High Elder's seat? But I don't understand."

"Don't you? Oh, I suppose you might not, having stayed locked away up here all night. When was the last time you saw the High Elder?"

Eliza thought for a moment. "I suppose... at services several weeks ago?"

Jessamine nodded. "And haven't you wondered why he has not been leading the services?"

"I just assumed he was away on state business, or something of that nature," Eliza said, shrugging. After all, the High Elder did not always appear at services. There had been plenty of instances

150

throughout her life when she could recall the other Elders running the services.

"Not this time, I'm afraid," Jessamine said. "The High Elder joined us for dinner this evening. By all appearances, he is extremely unwell. He and Mrs. Morgan have not admitted such, but Reginald told me all about it."

"He's sick?" Eliza asked, her voice barely more than a whisper.

"Quite. In fact, he's dying. And he wishes to settle his affairs, both political and familial. My father is the answer to the first. And I am the reluctant answer to the second. That's why all of this has come about. It had nothing to do with Teddy at all."

"Miss Jessamine, I hardly know what to say. I'm so sorry," Eliza whispered.

"I am sorry, too, most of all because I know I won't stop it. I could run away, I suppose. I could pack a bag and hire a coach and leave the country. I could start a new life somewhere. But I won't, Eliza. I'm selfish and coddled and scared. I don't want to give up my position. I don't want to leave all my friends and everything I know. I don't want to invent a new reality for myself. The very thought of it makes me want to crawl into a hole and never come out. I'd rather make do with the world I know, even if I hate it, because bearing it is a less frightening prospect than navigating the unknown."

Miss Jessamine said all of this quite calmly, quite matter-of-factly. She was not looking, as women so often did, for someone to contradict her, or to tell her that everything she said about herself was untrue. She was not looking for advice, or to be talked into anything. She was simply stating the facts. She knew she would be unhappy, knew her marriage was destined for misery, and she was going to go through with it anyway. Eliza did not even attempt to talk her out of it. What would be the point? Escaping was a fantasy, and they both knew it.

A mere few months ago, Eliza would have used her skills to convince her mistress that her marriage was the right choice, that her husband would love her, that all would be well. She would have gone on and on about the Path, and how Miss Jessamine would be rewarded for doing her duty to the Creator and the Illustratum by submitting to her match without question. She would have expounded on the expectations of daughters, wives, and mothers. She would, in short, have done Elder Hallewell's bidding, without even being asked to do so. Now, she would do no such thing. She would not sweeten this bitter twist of fate. She would not dress it up in the trappings of deception. She would simply listen. If Miss Jessamine was going to have to face down this marriage, she would do it with a clear head, entirely of her own accord. Eliza owed her that, at the very least.

And so she simply sat, pouring water over her mistress' shoulders until it had run cool and goosebumps began to form on her bare arms. Then she helped her to stand, wrapped her in a large, white, fluffy towel, and walked her to the changing screen, where she helped her into her snowy white nightgown. Next, she led her to the dressing table, where they sat in silence while Eliza brushed, pinned, and tied up her hair under her cap. She helped her up into the massive bed, removing the warming pan down by her feet and lowering the lamp on the table. Finally, she went to the window, meaning to draw the curtains, but, catching a glimpse of the remarkable array of stars on display on this unusually cloudless night, she threw them wide instead.

And they stared at the stars in silence, each girl contemplating her existence beneath them, and wondering if, in some other place, where the stars looked quite different, her life might be something—*anything*—else.

An excerpt from *The Illustratum Code on Riftborn in Society* as voted upon by the Elder Council and signed into law on 7 September 1803

"...A Riftborn shall toil in the name of the Creator in any of a number of capacities, but there shall be fields of employment, known henceforth as "The Exceptions" from which the Riftborn shall be excluded, for the safety of all, Riftborn and Dignus alike. These fields have been chosen carefully to help maintain the proper societal structure and to ensure that Riftmagic, and its accompanying moral degradation, shall not infect the integrity of said fields. The Exceptions shall include, but shall not be limited to, the fields of law, medicine, education, and all levels of governance. Further restrictions shall be made within other fields as pertains to management and ownership as the Council sees fit.

Furthermore, a system of workhouses shall be established to ensure that all Riftborn are put to use. Idleness in the Riftborn population shall surely lead to moral degradation and improper use of Riftmagic. It must remain a top priority that all Riftborn citizens are employed at all times, and those who are not shall be conscripted to the workhouses until such time as gainful employment can be found to help them stay the Path. These workhouses shall function under the purview of the Illustratum and be maintained by a system of management filled by upper levels of the Dignus. Each workhouse shall..."

FIFTEEN

C LERKENWELL WORKHOUSE LOOMED like a reaper over Farringdon Road, its windows staring down like empty eyes, its shadow threatening to swallow whole the little figure standing before its entrance.

Bridie had sworn when she walked out of this place that she would never enter it again. She knew she had a job waiting for her, but if that job did not work out, she decided, she would rather starve in the gutters than throw herself once again on the violent mercies of the workhouses. Now, as she stared up at the dirty brick walls, all of it came back to her; the overwhelming stench, the crowded wards that were never quiet, even in the dead of night, the way every muscle in her body ached after hours sitting at a spinning wheel, squinting at her work in the half-light, the pervasive illness and death hanging over the place like an unshakable fog.

And now here she was, doing the one thing she had sworn she would never do again: walk through those doors of her own free will. A violent shudder shook her from cap to boot, and she cursed under her breath.

"This place ain't got no power over you anymore, Bridie Sloane. It doesn't own you anymore. Just get what you came for and get out," she whispered. She imagined the words came from another person, a braver person, whispering in her ear to bolster her up. It sounded like the kind of thing Eliza might tell her. Then she remembered that there were many things Eliza did not tell her anymore, and she shook the image of her friend from her mind. It was clear this was something she would have to do on her own. There would be no borrowing of courage from anyone else.

The great soot-blackened brick face of the building rose in four stories on either side of her, seeming to grow larger with each step she took toward the front doors—or perhaps she was growing smaller, shrinking inch by inch into the scrawny girl she had been within those walls. By the time she reached the front door and lifted her hand to knock upon it, she was almost surprised to see it wasn't a child's tiny fist banging against the wood.

After a few moments of muffled shouting, the door opened. A middle-aged woman stood there, looking harassed at the very act of having to answer Bridie's insistent knocks. She glared down at her, as though expecting Bridie to apologize for having disturbed her. When Bridie did not, she sighed and grumbled. "Well? Can I help you?"

"Yes," Bridie said, clearing her throat. "I wish to see the matron, please."

"What for?" the woman asked, narrowing her eyes suspiciously as she took in Bridie's uniform and tidy appearance. "We ain't got no more room in the women's ward."

"I am not concerned with finding accommodations," Bridie said. "I simply wish to speak to the matron."

The woman seemed to be trying to find something in this request to take issue with. Bridie waited silently. After a few moments, it became clear that she could think of no reasonable excuse to deny the request. "Very well. She's quite busy, you know. You may have to wait."

"I understand," Bridie replied, smiling patiently. "I do not mind waiting."

The woman stepped back to allow Bridie entrance and pulled the door shut behind her. The smell of human misery was cloying, even in the entryway. Though the morning outside was bright and cloudless, the light that filtered down through the grimy windows was dull, and it took Bridie's eyes a few moments to adjust as she followed the woman down the hallway. Narrow stairwells rose on either side, leading to the women's wards on the left-hand side, and the men's wards on the right, but they did not ascend them. The matron's office was down the main hallway on the right, a hallway which, if you followed it to its end, opened up into the stone courtyard where they hung out the washing. Bridie kept her eyes fixed firmly on the back of the woman's bonnet, afraid even to glance into the spaces where the memories reared up like phantoms, though she could not help but watch as a line

156

of somber, scrawny children in brown shapeless dresses passed them, several of the older children bouncing wailing babies on their hips. She eased her face into a gentle smile as one of the little girls turned to stare at her, but the child did not return it, gaping wordlessly instead, as if she thought Bridie might be a phantom herself. Bridie tore her eyes from the child to find the woman had turned and was glaring at her.

"Matron's office," she announced sourly, before raising a fist and knocking on the door. "Someone to see you, Mrs. Langford."

"Show them in," came a gravelly voice Bridie remembered well.

The woman stepped aside reluctantly and Bridie walked past her, murmuring her thanks as she turned the handle and pushed the door open.

Hattie Langford was one of those unfortunate individuals who had appeared to be in middle age from the time she was still a fairly young woman, and so to Bridie, she seemed hardly changed at all. Her colorless hair was parted severely in the center and pulled tightly back from her face in a bun. Her eyes were pouchy and sunken, and her mouth grim. She wore the very same uniform Bridie remembered—a high-necked brown dress and a starched white apron embroidered with the emblem of the Illustratum-run institutions: a sun shining between two cupped hands. The only difference was a pair of wire-rim glasses now perched precariously on the end of her long, beak-like nose, over which she was now squinting curiously at Bridie.

"May I help you?" Mrs. Langford asked, setting down the paper in her hand and folding her hands on her desk. "I'm sorry, I wasn't expecting..." Her eyes fell on the Larkspur Manor insignia on Bridie's cloak, and widened. She scrutinized Bridie's face again and whispered, "Saints alive! Bridie Sloane?"

Bridie did her best to muster a polite smile. "Yes, indeed, Mrs. Langford. It's been a long time. How have you been keeping?"

"As well as can be expected," Mrs. Langford replied dryly. There was something odd in her stare, a sort of wariness, as though she wasn't seeing a flesh-and-blood housemaid in front of her, but the ghost of one. "And what brings you back here, Bridie? I confess I never expected to see you again once you took your post at Larkspur Manor."

"I confess I did not expect to return," Bridie admitted. She could feel the color in her cheeks. Standing in this office brought back a horde of unpleasant memories of whippings and harsh lectures. A wave of terror used to break over the children when one of them would be called to this office or, more frightening still, to the master's office. Even now, knowing she was no longer subject to their authority, Bridie could still feel the cold sweat beading up on her palms.

"What can I do for you, Bridie? Is Larkspur Manor in need of another housemaid? I've got a number of young ladies who could be quite suitable," Mrs. Langford said, pulling open a drawer and extracting a pile of papers.

"No, Mrs. Langford, I haven't come on Larkspur Manor business. I've come on a personal matter," Bridie said. She waited for Mrs. Langford to ask her to sit down, but the invitation never came, so she pulled out the rickety wooden chair across from the matron and settled herself in it.

"A personal matter, you say?" Mrs. Langford repeated, shoving the papers back into the drawer.

"Yes," Bridie said, her voice escaping in something of a squeak. She was suddenly feeling quite nervous. Her decision to come to the workhouse had been made in the dead of night while she was emotionally drained and sleep-deprived. She hadn't thought through anything beyond arriving at the doors and demanding answers. She had given not a thought to how she would procure those answers, or what she would do with them if she did in fact manage to get any. She opened her mouth and closed it again, suddenly struck with the fear that this entire trip was terribly foolish. Mrs. Langford was staring at her with a penetrating gaze that Bridie remembered— the kind of gaze that stripped you bare.

"I was hoping you might be able to give a bit of information about... about my family." The words tumbled over each other as they sped out of her mouth, sounding jumbled.

Mrs. Langford's eyebrows disappeared into the frizzy tendrils of hair that framed her face. "Your family?"

"Yes," Bridie said, her voice more sure now. "I have been wondering about them—who they are and if they might still be alive?"

Did Bridie imagine it, or was there a flicker of panic in the woman's eyes? But before she could be sure of what she had seen, Mrs. Langford's face settled into an unpleasant smirk. "Bridie, you know that most of the children here are dumped on our doorstep without an explanation."

"Yes, but I also know that not *all* of them are," Bridie pressed. "I thought there was a chance I might be one of them."

"I'm going to tell you the same thing I told you when you were a child: there's no point in looking back. Keep your eyes on the future and how you can be useful in serving your Creator," Mrs. Langford said, in a schoolmarm tone which, in her opinion, quite settled the matter.

But Bridie would not be deterred. She felt the anger rising in her, the feeling that she was being shoved aside and dismissed, just as she did with the lady's maids the previous morning in the Barrens. Why did everyone insist on treating her as though she did not matter?

"I am useful to my Creator every day in my work for the Hallewell family," Bridie said, trying to unclench her jaw so that she would not sound disrespectful. "I assure you, I am grateful for my position and happy in my duties. Wanting to know more about where I came from takes nothing away from my commitment to stay the Path."

"Well, I'm sorry, child, but there's nothing I can tell you."

"Don't you remember anything about when I was brought in?" Bridie asked with an air of clutching at straws. "Do you remember if I was simply left abandoned on the steps? Or was I brought in by someone? Surely you must—"

"I cannot be expected to remember the circumstances of every foundling cast off in this place," Mrs. Langford said, almost angrily.

Undeterred, Bridie pointed to the papers on the desk that Mrs. Langford had been shuffling through when she had entered. "But you have files on all the wards here, don't you? Couldn't you look up mine? Even if you don't remember, the details must surely be recorded somewhere."

Mrs. Langford's face twisted, as though she had swallowed something sour. "We don't keep the files on old wards. I haven't the room to store them, and anyway, what would be the point? Once you are out of our care, what does it matter?"

"It matters a great deal!" Bridie cried, her voice rising now despite her best efforts to keep herself calm. "Those files might be all any of us ever know about our own lives! What have you done with them? Are they sent elsewhere, or—"

"We burn them," Mrs. Langford replied, finality ringing in every syllable. "And as I know you are intimately acquainted with burning things, I imagine I need not explain any further why your requests will

159

find no further satisfaction here." She crossed her arms and settled her face into a triumphant smirk, as though daring Bridie to challenge her.

A fury such as she had never known rose up in Bridie's chest, as though her very magic was igniting her innards. She could feel the sparks tingling in her fingertips, and she might have done something extraordinarily foolish were it not for the scream.

A wailing, piercing shriek echoed through the hallways, making Bridie jump. Mrs. Langford gave almost no indication she had heard the sound, other than closing her eyes for a moment with a little sigh. Then she continued to stare expectantly at Bridie.

Bridie squirmed uncomfortably. The shrieking continued—someone was in great distress. "I... I can wait here if that's something you need to see to," Bridie said.

Mrs. Langford snorted with amusement. "If I went running every time someone shouted in this place, I'd never sit down again!"

Bridie tried to regather herself, tried to ask her question, but the sounds from the hallway seemed to be boring their way into her skull, scrambling her thoughts.

Rather than fading away, the screaming was only growing louder. Soon it was accompanied by the scurrying sounds of footsteps and pounding of fists against doors and windowpanes. A man's vehement cursing joined the din, along with the voices of several women.

"I can't get ahold of her properly, not when she's soaking wet. It's a miracle she didn't drown poor Agnes."

"We've got to corner her. Blast it all, I told Langford we should chain her up, inspections be damned."

At the sound of her own name, it seemed that Mrs. Langford decided she could ignore the situation no longer. With a sigh that was half a groan, she heaved herself out of her chair and said, "Excuse me, won't you?" Then she opened her office door and closed it again, leaving Bridie alone.

At first, Bridie considered simply walking around to the far side of the desk and having a good rifle through the files, despite Mrs. Langford's insistence that the files on former wards such as herself had all been burned. After all, the woman had acted very oddly. Perhaps she had been lying about the files being destroyed, just to stop Bridie from asking further questions. But she brushed this notion aside impatiently. Even if she was right, and the matron was lying, Bridie would never find what she was looking for before Mrs. Langford returned, and she'd surely be booted from the premises or perhaps even arrested if she was caught digging around in the matron's private files. She wondered if any of the other staff now shouting on the other side of the door mightn't remember her? Surely some of them had been there for decades—maybe one of them might know something about Bridie's past if she asked them? It could be anything—something she'd said to them when she was little, a question she asked about the family she had been too young to remember? She'd come all this way—it was certainly worth a try, however unlikely the chances of success.

Steeling herself, Bridie rose from her seat and pushed open the office door, peering out into the corridor beyond.

The scene was utter chaos. A woman clad in nothing but a thin muslin nightshirt was cowering in the corner. She was dripping wet, her blonde hair stuck all over her face and streaming water down her back. The nightshirt, too, was drenched, clinging to every angle of her frail and skeletal frame, so that she might as well not be wearing anything at all. Water pooled around her filthy bare feet as she struggled to stay upright. In her hands, she clutched a long, lethal-looking shard of broken glass, which she was swinging wildly at anyone who tried to approach her. Bridie knew instantly she must have come from the medical ward, where lunatics were sometimes unceremoniously dumped when there was no room for them in the equally crowded and squalid asylums.

Mrs. Langford had joined the efforts of the other staff members to subdue the woman. She had ordered for the ends of the hall to be blocked off. There were now men standing at the bottom of the staircases on either side of the corridor, their postures coiled and prepared to spring should the woman come running at them. Another man stood at the far end of the hallway, his back to the door which Bridie knew led to the crumbling stone courtyard beyond. He was holding what looked like a bedsheet to his forearm. Both the sheet and his shirt were stained with blood, and he was hissing curses through his clenched teeth.

As Bridie watched, mouth agape, the dripping wet woman let out a guttural moan and began to feel along the brick wall behind her, fingers scrabbling madly over the bricks like pale, frantic spiders, searching for—what? Another weapon? A means of escape? Whatever it was she was seeking, it continued to elude her as she

161

swiped at the air with the glass shard, the men moving in around her now, slowly closing the space between them. Any moment now, they would be within reach of the woman's weapon. Surely more blood was about to be spilled; Bridie could hardly bear to look.

And that's when it happened. One of the men shifted on the balls of his feet to his right and at the same moment, the wailing woman jerked her chin upward to keep him in view, so that her tangle of sopping hair flew back over her shoulder, and Bridie got her first clear look at the woman's face. She recognized her at once, a face she had only ever seen smiling gently at her in the darkness from a tarnished silver frame.

"Mrs. Braxton!" The words sprang free from Bridie's mouth as she sprang out of the office and into the hallway. Everything seemed to stop as all of the staff and Mrs. Langford turned to gawk at her. The cowering woman, too, turned and stared right at Bridie with enormous, hollow grey eyes, and Bridie was even more sure than she had been a moment before. This woman was Eliza's mother.

"Mrs. Braxton, what are you doing here?" Bridie cried, all fear gone, breaking into a run toward her, but the burly man nearest to her flung out an arm, catching her in the chest and knocking the breath from her. She gasped, but fought against his restraining grasp as she continued to call out. "They all think you've run off! Or that you're dead! What are you doing here?"

Emmaline Braxton was now gaping at Bridie as though she was a ghost. Her eyes filled up with tears and the hand holding the shard of mirror dropped limply to her side. Then she lifted her other shaking hand and pressed it to her chest and moaned softly.

"Would you get back, you daft girl? She'll hurt you! She ain't right!" grunted the man who was restraining Bridie, but Bridie continued to struggle against his grip.

"No! What is she doing here? Mrs. Braxton—"

"This woman's name isn't Mrs. Braxton," Mrs. Langford said suddenly, her voice ringing like a bell against the stone walls of the hallway. "Now get back in that office and shut the door before you get yourself injured. This is no place for you."

But Bridie did not go back to the office. Gone were the days when she cowered and curtsied at every order barked at her by Mrs. Langford. There was no doubt in her mind whom she was looking at, and she would not be ignored any longer. She shoved again at the

162

man who was now using all of his considerable strength to restrain her, trying to break away, to close the space between herself and the woman whom she was more certain with every passing second was exactly who she believed her to be.

"I know that's Emmaline Braxton! I know it is, I recognize her! Her daughter Eliza is my—"

Emmaline Braxton—if that was indeed who she was—let out a keening wail at the mention of her daughter's name. She began to reach her hands out toward Bridie, beckoning her closer even as she swung her shard of glass at the attendants closing in on her.

"Bridie, you stop that now! This woman isn't who you think she is and you're upsetting her further!" Mrs. Langford shouted, her voice tinged with something akin to panic.

"Mrs. Langford, please, you must listen to me! I know it's her! I know it's Emmaline Braxton! Her family thinks she's dead or lost! They have no idea she's here! Please, just let me—"

"Enough of this!" Mrs. Langford shrieked. "Mullins, for Creator's sake, subdue her and get her back upstairs!"

The man named Mullins nodded to his companion, and the two of them charged at Mrs. Braxton, whose attention was divided trying to communicate with Bridie. Mullins dodged a vicious swipe of the jagged glass and managed to close a hand around Mrs. Braxton's wrist, bending it backward with a grunt of effort. Mrs. Braxton gave a cry of pain and the glass clattered to the floor and skittered away across the stones. Then the two men pinned her to the ground and yanked her arms behind her back, securing them with a length of rope before hauling her roughly to her feet. All the while, the man kept a tight grip on Bridie as she struggled and watched helplessly.

"Take her upstairs and sedate her," Mrs. Langford ordered, and the two attendants, still panting with the effort of subduing their prisoner, began to drag Emmaline Braxton toward the stairs that led to the women's wards. Bridie watched the woman go, her eyes full of tears. She tried to think of something to call after her—some words of comfort, but she could think of none. Her mind was still reeling. How could Eliza's mother be here, in the same city, all these years later? What had happened to her?

"Bridie I must insist that you come back to my office. You look pale. I'll get someone to fetch us a pot of tea," Mrs. Langford said briskly, and Bridie, too distracted and upset to argue, allowed the

163

burly attendant to steer her back toward Mrs. Langford's office and deposit her in the very same chair she'd left only a few minutes before. Mrs. Langford entered as well, after a few moments whispered conversation with the attendant who disappeared back out into the hallway.

Bridie realized in the sudden and pressing quiet of the office that she was panting as though she had run a mile. She closed her eyes and tried to slow her breath.

"There now," Mrs. Langford said, in what she clearly thought was a motherly tone. "That's right. Just calm yourself down now. I think you've had quite a fright. A few years of working in a fancy home and you've lost your nerve, child."

"I haven't lost my... my nerve," Bridie gasped, "and I'm not frightened."

Mrs. Langford gave a humorless bark of laughter. "Not frightened indeed. You're white as a sheet."

"I'm upset, not scared!" Bridie snapped, feeling her breath and her anger return in equal measure. "Mrs. Langford, that woman—"

"Is very unwell," Mrs. Langford cut in. "Has been since she arrived. She ought to be in Bedlam, but they haven't the room, what with the latest outbreak of Riftsickness."

"Yes, I can see she's not well, but I recognize her!" Bridie insisted. "I'm sure of it! I share sleeping quarters with her daughter, she's got a picture of her right beside the—"

But Mrs. Langford had already raised an impatient hand in protest. "The woman you thought you recognized is named Jane McCreary. She has no family, let alone a daughter with whom you happen to share a blanket."

"Well, then, she's using a false name," Bridie said stubbornly.

"Why on Creator's good earth would she do something like that?" Mrs. Langford asked, her eyebrows drawing together in a forbidding way.

"I don't know!" Bridie cried, abandoning all attempts at calming herself. "Perhaps someone ought to ask her! All I do know is that when I said her daughter's name, she recognized it. She was trying to speak to me!"

"That lunatic can't even recognize that my staff members aren't trying to murder her!" Mrs. Langford shot back. She seemed to be swelling with anger, her cheeks reddening, her chest expanding.

164

Bridie opened her mouth to argue further when a tall, sallow-faced woman appeared in the doorway, a tea tray balanced on her hip.

"Ah, yes, thank you, Sarah," Mrs. Langford said, forcing a smile. "You can just set that down here on my desk. Our guest is a little out of sorts."

Bridie did not argue the point, but sat glaring at Mrs. Langford while Sarah poured two cups of tea, set them down steaming before them, and slipped back through the door without so much as a word.

"There now. Nothing like a nice cup of tea to put us back in the right frame of mind," Mrs. Langford said.

"I don't want any tea," Bridie said.

"I won't discuss another word of this nonsense until you've gathered yourself and had some tea. I'll not have you behaving as though I never taught you any manners in your time here."

Bridie could not have said whether it was the familiar, soothing scent of the tea or a lingering impulse to obey the woman who had once whipped her for being insolent, but she picked up the cup of tea and sipped it. It was slightly bitter, but there was no sugar on the tray. She took another sip.

Mrs. Langford's shoulders relaxed. "There now, that's a good girl. Everything looks a bit clearer after a nice cup of tea."

Bridie did not reply, but kept drinking. Everything was already crystal clear, as far as she was concerned, but she did not think it would do any good to belabor the point. For whatever reason, Mrs. Langford refused to see reason, but it did not matter; Bridie did not need her to see reason. All she needed to do was politely finish her tea and excuse herself so that she could get home as quickly as possible and tell Eliza where her mother was. Mr. Braxton could certainly sort out the rest—there was no one who could hold a candle to William Braxton when it came to efficiency. He'd probably have his wife released before bedtime tonight. Bridie drained the rest of her tea and threw one last longing look at the files still sitting atop the desk. She had not gotten what she'd come for, but all of that would keep for another day.

"Would you like another cup?" Mrs. Langford asked.

"No, thank you. I really should be going. I've taken up enough of your time this morning," Bridie said, and rose to her feet.

She knew immediately that something was wrong. The entire room spun as she got to her feet and she swayed on the spot, clutching the back of the chair to prevent herself from falling what suddenly felt like a very great distance to the floor.

"I... I feel strange," she said, and the words stuck to her tongue like porridge. She looked over at Mrs. Langford, who said nothing, but simply stared at her expectantly. Horror dawning inside her, Bridie looked down at her empty teacup, and then at the teacup resting untouched at Mrs. Langford's elbow. The matron had not taken so much as a single sip.

"The tea... what have you done to me?" Bridie whispered.

"Sit down, child," Mrs. Langford said. She sounded weary. "No one wants you to fall and hurt yourself."

Bridie shook her head, in which every tiny sound was now warping and ringing like a chorus of bells. "How... why would you..." She stumbled back from the desk, a single thought clarifying itself amidst the fog now clouding her brain: she must get out of there. Now.

Bridie made a break for the door, the floor seeming to slip and slide beneath her with every step, like the deck of a storm-tossed ship.

"Bridie, stop. You'll only make this harder on yourself, child."

"I'm... not a ...child," Bridie slurred. "And I'm... I'm going..."

She heard Mrs. Langford rise from her chair behind her, but she did not turn to investigate. Her panic was building—she had been drugged, she knew it. She had to get to the street, she had to get help. Her fingers felt numb and clumsy as she struggled to turn the doorknob. Finally, in desperation, she flung her shoulder against the door and stumbled out into the hallway.

She started running, with no clear notion of where she was going, only that she needed to get away, to find a way out. She struggled to remember which way she had come to get to the office. She skidded to a halt at the sight of a door ahead and nearly cried with relief.

Voices were calling after her and feet were stomping behind her, all of it warping into a cacophony inside her skull, making her wince with pain. Sheer animal panic urged her feet forward, even as they seemed to turn to great lumps of stone at the ends of her ankles so that she had to drag them across the floor. Something caught at the back of her cloak, and she swung out wildly with her fist, making contact with someone's head, for whoever it was grunted with pain and released their grip and the cloak swung heavily against her legs again. Bridie ran past a line of little girls in their shapeless brown smocks, a dozen sets of wide terrified eyes set into gaunt little faces staring at her as she passed, reflecting her fear back to her like mirrors. One child shook her head sadly at her, as though to say, *Just let them catch you. What's the use of running?*

I have to try. I have to tell Eliza, Bridie told the child… or perhaps she only thought it. Her face felt numb, her tongue like a rock. She wasn't sure that words would be able to find their way out of her mouth, even if she'd had the breath to shout them.

Though she ran with every ounce of strength within her, the door didn't seem to be coming any closer. The walls felt like they were closing in around her. A voice screeched "Don't let her get out!" and her panic peaked. She stumbled sideways into the wall, catching her cloak on the rough stone. With a tug, she freed herself from it, abandoning it on the floor behind her in her last desperate attempt to get to the door. At last, she reached it and, with a cry of relief, shoved her shoulder against it and burst out, not into the bustling street, but into the stone-walled courtyard.

She had gone the wrong way. Damn it all, she had gone the wrong bloody way. How could she have been so stupid?

Her legs were turning to sand beneath her, slipping grain by grain out of the soles of her shoes. She glanced around the courtyard and spotted a pile of rotting wooden crates leaning up against the wall. Even as she looked at them, her vision darkened. She was running out of time—whatever they'd put in the tea was trying to pull her down into unconsciousness. She shook her head to clear it. If she could just get on top of those crates, maybe she could scale the wall. It was the only chance she had. She dragged herself forward focusing every fiber of her being on reaching the crates, batting away the darkness, fighting to maintain control of her limbs, but she was like a puppet whose strings were being snipped one by one.

"Help! Please, someone help me!" she screeched, but the words came out slurred, unrecognizable. She tried to jump onto the crates but she had lost control of her legs, and she crashed headlong into them instead, reducing them to a splintered, rotting heap. A pair of huge, calloused hands seized her by the back of her dress and dragged her backward across the mossy, muddy ground. The attendant tried to set her on her feet, but she could no longer support her own weight. Cursing, he scooped her up into his arms. Bridie looked up into the red, foul-breathed face swimming above her, tried to beg him to let her go, to help her…

"Please…"

The man did not so much as glance at her. Bridie's vision went nearly black. The last thing she heard before unconsciousness swallowed her was the flustered voice of Mrs. Langford which echoed through her head like an explosion.

"Get her upstairs and secure her. We must alert the Elders."

SIXTEEN

E LIZA DID NOT EXPECT TO SLEEP; her pity for Jessamine
felt as though it was eating a hole straight through her abdomen.
It was clear Jessamine did not trust sleep to take her anywhere
pleasant—after an hour's tossing and turning, she seemed to decide
she could not settle into her bed, and curled herself into the chaise
lounge by the windows, watching the moon and the stars and the
coming dawn perform their celestial dance across the sky. Eliza sat
with her, Jessamine's head on her shoulder, running her gloved fingers
through her mistress' hair, watching it spring up into curls as it dried.
She remembered seeing the first hints of orange tinting the clouds
gathered at the horizon and then, quite suddenly, she was startled
awake. She blinked around, disoriented, every muscle stiff and bent at
wrong angles. Miss Jessamine still lay upon her shoulder, snoring very
softly, her thick eyelashes resting upon her cheeks. Bright sunlight
was streaming through the window and birds could be heard calling
and answering each other in the gardens beyond. She glanced at the
clock and realized they were dangerously close to being late for
breakfast.

Eliza tried to extricate herself out from under her mistress, but
her legs were cramped and her arm completely numbed of all
sensation—she had no choice but to wake Jessamine with a gentle
prod.

"Miss Jessamine? It's time to wake up. We've got to get you ready
to have breakfast with the Morgans."

Jessamine groaned. "I'm not hungry," she said blearily.

Eliza laughed. "Unfortunately, hunger has very little to do with it.
You will still be expected downstairs."

Jessamine rubbed her eyes and looked first at Eliza, and then around the room. Eliza watched the confusion in her face drain away, to be replaced by realization and then, unmistakably, dread. "Oh. Yes, of course. I'd forgotten."

Jessamine dressed in a daze, barely speaking more than a few words to Eliza as she readied her for breakfast with the Morgans.

"Miss?"

"Hmm?" Jessamine had risen from her seat at the dressing table and was making her way to the door when Eliza called out to her.

"You... I suppose you ought to wear the ring, don't you think?" Eliza asked tentatively.

Jessamine blinked and then pressed her lips together. "Yes. I suppose I ought." She swept across the room in a rustle of peach satin, and plucked the ring from the box, barely looking at it as she slid it onto her slender finger. "Please see that my blue afternoon dress is laid out, along with my peacock feather hat. I was informed last night at dinner that blue is young Master Morgan's favorite color."

"Yes, miss. Of course."

The day passed in much the same way as the previous one, with Eliza pacing the floors waiting for her mistress' return prior to each meal, when she would listen to Jessamine's exasperated rants about Reginald while Eliza pinned, buttoned, and tied her into her next gown. There were no more sudden appearances by frightened housemaids, although this might have been due to the fact that Master Reginald had a devil of a hangover and had not joined the rest of the party until well after lunch. By the time Eliza was readying her mistress for bed again, she thought she had never been so anxious to leave a place as she was to depart the palace.

Eliza was up with the sun on Thursday morning, stowing her mistress' belongings in their various trunks and cases, and readying them for the footmen, who arrived to carry them all down to the carriage just as Miss Jessamine went down for breakfast. When Eliza closed the door on the sumptuous palace bedroom in which they had spent the last two nights, it was with a sigh of relief.

She wanted to go home. She thought of Bridie and how she would be wild with anticipation to hear all the details of their visit to the palace; what a disappointment it would be to her that Eliza would be in no mood to gush about the splendor of the place. Eliza felt sure she would never be able to think back on her time at the palace without

170

a shudder of horror. Luckily, Eliza had had the presence of mind to grab a handful of chocolates and boiled sweets from the bowl in Miss Jessamine's sitting room and stow them in a handkerchief; she'd never hear the end of it if she hadn't at least returned with the promised pocketful of palace sweets.

Eliza was already settled in the carriage out on the drive when Jessamine and Elder Hallewell appeared. Walking side by side, Eliza thought she could see something of Elder Hallewell in his daughter's demeanor and bearing; both of them carried themselves with remarkable poise and purpose. They strolled down the gravel drive together, both tall and slim, their faces unreadable masks of composure. Whatever might be brewing inside of them, passersby would never catch even a glimpse of it marring their features. Jessamine had made the mistake of letting that façade slip in front of her father once, and the result had been so catastrophic that Elder Hallewell had forced Eliza to step in and compel his daughter's calm and compliance. Eliza was sure that Jessamine would never allow herself to be so unguarded and vulnerable in front of her father again, which meant, of course, that Elder Hallewell would be insulated from ever knowing how much his matchmaking scheme had wounded his only child. Eliza knew that Jessamine was protecting herself, but she could not help but wish that Elder Hallewell might feel just a fraction of the keen sting that he himself had inflicted when he broke his daughter's heart.

But Jessamine would show none of her hesitancy, none of the fear and resentment and horror clawing about within her as they bumped and jostled their way back to Larkspur Manor. Instead, she nodded and smiled along as her father launched into a long-winded monologue about the upcoming nuptials—when they ought to be held and to whom they ought to entrust the details of the grand affair, from the floral arrangements to the dressmaker and the guest list. Jessamine quietly deferred to him in every aspect, despite having dreamed about her wedding day endlessly since she was old enough to wear long skirts, and Eliza knew why: having been reduced to a pawn in the schemes of powerful men, it seemed Jessamine planned to live into the part thoroughly. Let them dress her and place flowers in her hands and march her down the aisle to the dulcet sounds of her own undoing; what did any of it matter anymore?

Eliza felt a wave of gratitude wash over her as they passed through the gates at Larkspur Manor; she did not think she could bear to sit silently by for another second. Every word out of Elder Hallewell's mouth felt like a slap to her mistress' face, and Eliza had bitten her tongue until she tasted blood in her attempts not to say something. She knew her interference would do much more harm than good. Eliza practically raced for the servants' entrance to the kitchens—it would be loud and hectic down there, but at least she could let her guard down and speak freely. She had much to tell Bridie, though none of it would meet with Bridie's fairy tale expectations.

If she hadn't been so distracted with the events of the previous day, Eliza might have noticed that the usually bustling downstairs was more subdued than usual, and that faces of the other servants were grimmer, more solemn. As she walked by the entrance to the kitchen, Eliza waved to Penny, who looked up from her tray of scones with a start.

"Eliza! We weren't expecting you until a bit later!"

"Yes, we set out straight after breakfast. I think the High Elder had Illustratum business to tend to this afternoon."

"Have you seen your father yet?"

"No, not yet. Just going to lay my things down, and I'll pop into his office. I'm sure he wants to know all about the palace visit." *And I'm sure he's not the only one,* Eliza added silently to herself as she started back down the hallway again toward her bedroom.

"Eliza, wait! Your father wanted to see you as soon as you—"

But Eliza was already halfway down the hallway. Her father could be patient long enough for her to put her suitcase down, surely. Penny came hurrying down the hallway after her, but Eliza had already reached her bedroom door and thrown it wide.

"What in heaven's name...?" she gasped.

She stared in open-mouthed shock at the disarray that lay before her. The bed had been stripped to the bare mattress, the drawers emptied and left gaping or lying upon the floor. The bedside table had been cleared of all Bridie's personal belongings: her collection of buttons, her starched white handkerchiefs, her book full of pictures of gowns, clipped from discarded newspaper advertisements and pasted together—all gone. Only Eliza's possessions remained, strewn about like so much rubbish.

Penny appeared behind her in the doorway, huffing and puffing.

"I'm sorry, Eliza, I tried to tell you, but you ran past me so fast. Bridie's gone."

"Gone? What do you mean, gone? Gone where?" Eliza demanded, turning on Penny, who jumped back at the look on Eliza's face.

"Sick. She come down with Riftsickness, real sudden like. She seemed well enough when I saw her Thursday morning, but she was real quiet at dinner on Thursday night. Hardly ate a bite she did, and excused herself early to go to bed. It was the same on Friday morning, pale as you please, and said she didn't want no breakfast. She left before the rest of us had sat down properly to eat, and that was the last any of us saw her. They say she took ill while she was out."

"Out? Out where?" Eliza asked.

Penny shrugged helplessly. "I'm afraid I don't know. Just out in town, running an errand. They came for her things and ordered that the bed be stripped and the linens washed and aired, in case it were catching."

"Who came for her things?" Eliza demanded.

"I'm 'fraid I don't know, Eliza. I'm sorry," Penny whispered, her eyes filling with tears. "It were your father that let them into the—"

But Eliza had already dropped her bags in the doorway and taken off down the hall to her father's office, her cloak streaming behind her like a banner. She knocked hastily but did not wait for her father to reply, pushing the door open at once. Her father looked up from his ledger in mild surprise, which quickly gave way to pleasure at the sight of his daughter.

"Eliza, I wasn't expecting you until—but whatever's the matter, my dear?" His face fell as he took in Eliza's disheveled appearance and starkly white face.

"Bridie!" Eliza gasped, clutching a stitch in her side. "Where is Bridie?"

William Braxton's face fell, and he set down his pencil with a sigh. "Ah, yes. I had hoped to speak to you before you found out from someone else."

"Penny says she took ill?"

"It appears so, yes," he said with a solemn nod.

"Well, where is she? I want to see her!" Eliza demanded.

"I'm afraid that's not possible," he said, frowning. "Riftsickness is a serious matter. We can't risk it spreading, to you or to anyone else."

Eliza clenched her fists so hard that she could feel her fingernails digging into the soft skin of her palms, even through the gloves she nearly always wore. She wanted to scream. She knew what caused Riftsickness. She knew it wasn't catching. And most certainly of all, she knew that Bridie, whatever may be wrong with her, did not have it.

"Where have they taken her?" Eliza asked again, trying to keep her voice calm, though she could hear the anger trembling in it.

"Eliza, I know you are upset about your chum, but I've already told you—"

"Where?" The word rang out, startling her father into wide-eyed silence. Eliza knew she had crossed a line, but could not bring herself to care.

"I do not know where," her father said slowly.

"And you just... just let them take her things?" Eliza gasped.

"Let them?" Braxton's eyebrows pulled together into a deep "v" of disapproval. "You speak as though I had some kind of choice in the matter. It was on the Illustratum's orders that her things were taken and that she was given over to the care of some institution or other that has the means to accommodate her. I was not consulted and had no desire to interfere with their orders. It is my duty to keep you all safe and the household running smoothly, and that means taking the proper precautions to protect you."

"But you didn't even ask where she was being taken?" Eliza asked.

"Does it matter?"

"Of course it matters!" Eliza cried. "This was Bridie, father, not some poor nameless stranger off the street! She's worked here for years, she is my best friend! Don't you care?"

"I will not allow this to descend into hysteria," Braxton snapped. "Eliza, I must insist you control yourself. Of course, I care what happens to Bridie. She's a good girl, and a good worker, if somewhat consumed at times with silly frivolities. But you needn't worry, my dear. The Illustratum will see to it that she is well cared for."

Eliza took a long, unsteady breath. It was clear she would get no further help from her father if she did not give at least the appearance of decorum. Unclenching her fists with difficulty, she clasped her hands primly in front of her and tried to arrange her face into a mask of calm, though her heart continued to pound against her ribcage like a desperate prisoner. "Please, Father. I want to know what's become

174

of my friend. Couldn't you inquire as to where she might have been taken? You manage the household of one of the most powerful Elders in the country. Surely they would not begrudge you information on your own staff, even if only to determine if you need to find someone to replace her?"

Braxton pursed his lips and seemed to consider the matter. "I will ask for word on her condition, but no more. I do not want you running off to try to visit her, wherever she might be. You have far too much responsibility now with Miss Jessamine's impending nuptials to be running around Riftwards in unsavory parts of town. Let it be, my dear. The Illustratum will see to it that the girl is taken care of. I have no doubt she will be well and back to lighting the fires in no time at all, as long as she can see her way clear to recommitting to the Path."

"Thank you, father," Eliza said. The words barely escaped through her clenched teeth. With a greater effort than ever it had cost her before, she curtsied to her father and then took off down the hallway, slowly at first, and then broke into a run when she had rounded the corner. She had absolutely no intention of letting anything be.

She questioned Mrs. Keats and every kitchen maid she could find, but no one knew what the mysterious errand was that Bridie had slipped out to run on the morning she vanished. Frustrated, she returned to her room and, ignoring the bags she was meant to unpack and the laundry she was meant to begin washing, she set about searching the room. She wasn't even sure what it was she was looking for—some kind of clue, perhaps, to where Bridie had gone the previous day? There was also the chance that Bridie knew she was not coming back, and if that were the case, Eliza thought desperately, she was sure that Bridie would have left her some kind of note.

Eliza dug pointlessly through the empty drawers and felt around inside the wardrobe. She ran her hands along the underside of the curtains that separated the washbasin from the rest of the room. She felt inside the pockets and creases of the starched and folded aprons in the wash basket in the corner. She got down on her hands and knees and ran her hand along the baseboard behind the bed, but all she found was a dirty handkerchief and her own framed portrait of her mother, which she usually kept on her bedside table. The Praesidio had clearly knocked it from the tabletop in their haste to complete their search; a jagged crack now ran the length of the glass that encased her mother's photograph. Defeated, clutching the broken portrait in her hands, Eliza sank down onto the bare mattress, ready to succumb to tears. It was then that she felt it: a strange lump beneath the ticking. Heart pounding, she reached underneath the mattress itself and felt a tear in the fabric. She crammed her hand inside the tear and felt around with desperate fingers until her grip closed around something flat and hard. She tugged and wiggled it back and forth until finally, it popped free of the mattress.

It was a book. A single glimpse beneath the front cover told her exactly *which* book. The room seemed to be closing in, the walls collapsing, the air being squeezed out until Eliza felt sure she would suffocate with the panic.

They were meant to be burned. Every copy was meant to be burned. Why did this book still exist and how in the world had it fallen into Bridie's hands? Had she read it? Had she perhaps told someone about it?

A gasp for air that was half a sob escaped Eliza's lips before she clamped them shut again against the violent urge to be sick. There was no way this could be a coincidence, that Bridie somehow managed to get her hands on this book, and then suddenly disappeared. Whatever had happened to Bridie, Eliza was absolutely, terrifyingly sure of two things.

The first: Bridie was not lying in a Riftward somewhere with a case of Riftsickness.

The second: wherever Bridie was and whatever had befallen her, it was entirely Eliza's fault.

"Eliza."

Eliza jumped at the sound of the voice, though it was no more than an anxious whisper. Liesel stood in the doorway, wringing her hands. Eliza quickly dropped the book she was holding onto the mattress and slid a pillow on top of it.

"Liesel! I'm sorry, I didn't see you there," Eliza said, trying to compose herself enough to smile. Liesel was not smiling, however. Her face was pale and drawn, and there were dark, half-moon shadows nestled under her eyes. "Are you all right?"

"Of course I'm not all right," Liesel replied, and though her tone was sharp, Eliza recognized the grief behind it. "I suppose they've told you, have they? About Bridie?"

"Yes. I... I can't believe it," Eliza said, which was true enough.

"I'm not sure I can believe it either," Liesel said, and something in her tone gave Eliza pause. She narrowed her eyes at Liesel, who did not flinch away from her gaze, but met it steadily.

"Liesel, is there something you want to tell me?" Eliza whispered.

Liesel glanced into the hallway behind her and then eased the door shut. She moved toward the bed as though she might sit on it, but then seemed to reconsider, staying on her feet and beginning to pace instead. "I'm afraid something's happened to Bridie."

"My father said she came down with Riftsickness, and..."

But Liesel was shaking her head. "That child weren't Riftsick, and we all know it. She was fit as a fiddle when she walked out the door. It don't come on that fast. And besides, she put her Riftmagic to use every day in service to the Hallewells. How could she have come down with it? How could that make even the slightest sense?"

"What do you think happened then?" Eliza asked.

Liesel bit her lip. "This is my fault. All my fault."

Eliza reached out and snatched at Liesel's hand as she passed the end of the bed. "Liesel, calm down and tell me what's happened."

Liesel took a deep shuddering breath. "She came to me the other night. Said she couldn't sleep, thinking about her parents."

Eliza started. This was not at all what she'd expected Liesel to say. "Her parents?"

"That's right. Wanted to know if I knew anything about them, seeing as I was the one who brought her home from the workhouse," Liesel said.

"And... and do you? Know anything about them?"

Liesel bit her lip, her eyes filling with tears. "I do, although I didn't breathe a word of it to Bridie."

"What is it, Liesel? You can trust me. What do you know about her parents?"

"It's not somethin' I know so much as it's something I guessed," Liesel said, sinking onto the bed beside Eliza. "When I was sent to find a new maid, I knew what I had in mind: a Catalyst who could tend the fires, someone well-behaved and quick to learn. When I sat down with the matron and explained what I needed, her eyes lit up at once. 'I've got just the girl for you,' she told me, and left the office. While I was waiting for her to come back, I heard arguing out in the hallway—it's the way that place was built, see, voices carry. You could hear someone whisper from the other end of the corridor clear as day. I weren't eavesdropping!" Liesel's voice rose, as though Eliza were accusing her of something.

"I understand, Liesel. You didn't mean to overhear. Please, do go on," Eliza said with a placating pat on Liesel's shoulder.

"The matron and the master, they were arguing. Seems the master wasn't too happy with who the matron had chosen to send to Larkspur Manor. Complainin' he was, that she was one of their better workers. 'Don't make me laugh, John. We all know why you want the girl to stay, and I'll be damned if I'm going to let you make a fool of yourself over a Riftborn girl. I've seen the way you look at her. It's disgusting, and I won't stand for it, you hear me?' And the man sneers at her, 'Look at you, green with envy over a workhouse drudge.' And the woman responds, 'She ain't just some orphan from the gutter and you know it. I suppose that's part of the appeal, is it? You make me sick.' And then she marched off to fetch Bridie."

Eliza's pulse had quickened. "What do you think she meant?" she whispered.

"Not every workhouse orphan's story starts in the Barrens," Liesel mumbled. "Do you understand my meaning?"

Eliza nodded. A few short weeks ago, Liesel's statement would have baffled her. But she was wiser now. Liesel was referring to those Riftborn children unfortunate enough to be born into Dignus families who would rather abandon them than admit they had produced them.

"I resolved to put it out of my mind. I never said a word to Bridie about what I heard the matron say. Wasn't my place to fill the girl's head with fantasies about where she might have come from. It wouldn't change where she *was*, see?" There was an edge of remorse in Liesel's voice, a plea for understanding. "What's best for the girl is to learn her new place and be grateful for it."

"It's okay, Liesel. You did what you thought was best," Eliza said.

"It was best, when she was a wee thing. But then two nights ago, when she came to me in the dark... she had worked herself up into such a state. I can't think what might have set her off, but she was desperate to know something about her family. And I... I just couldn't tell her, Eliza. She was so unsettled, and anyway, all I'd be able to give her to go on were secondhand scraps, overheard nearly seven years ago now. What good would it do her?"

Eliza didn't answer. Her mind was on the book now hidden beneath the pillow. Bridie must have read it; it was the only way to explain why she would suddenly have such a keen interest in finding out where she came from.

"Do you know where she went, Liesel? My father said she took ill while she was out running an errand, but I've asked the entire staff, and no one sent her on an errand, as far as I can tell."

Liesel shook her head. "I didn't see her again. She was done with the fires before I was even awake, and she had left before breakfast. But..." She hesitated, biting her lip.

"But what?" Eliza urged her. "Liesel, please. This is important. If you think you know where she might have gone, you have to tell me."

Liesel squirmed. "Well, now, it's just a guess, mind, but... Martin said he dropped her on Roseberry Avenue but that she turned south toward Farringdon Street. I think she might have gone to the Clerkenwell Workhouse."

Eliza turned this possibility over in her mind. Yes, Bridie might have thought to go to the workhouse. After all, if she was looking for answers about her family, where better to find it than at the very place she had grown up?

But what would happen, Eliza suddenly wondered, if she had asked the wrong questions? What if the matron got suspicious? Or what if, Creator forbid, Bridie had somehow let slip that she was there because of something she'd read in that book? Perhaps the people who had come to "collect her things" were really searching for some sign of the book? If they had, it seemed they had overlooked it, but that didn't mean that Bridie wasn't now in very serious trouble. If Eliza had been panicked before, it was nothing to how she felt now.

"Eliza? Are you all right?" Liesel's anxious voice pierced Eliza's thoughts. She struggled to bring her face and voice under control before she replied.

"I'm fine, Liesel," she said.

"Did you hear what I said?"

"Yes, yes. The workhouse in Clerkenwell. I think you may be right, Liesel. It sounds like just the sort of thing Bridie might do. You know what she's like when she gets something in her head."

"What should we do?" Liesel asked. "I've half a mind to go down there and bang the door down myself, and I would have done already if I weren't worried about making things worse."

"No. No, don't do that," Eliza said swiftly. "You're right, it won't do any good. I've... I've got a friend who might be able to help. I'm going to write to him now."

"A friend?" Liesel's eyes were full of questions which, she seemed to decide a moment later, were better left unasked. "Well, you tell this friend of yours to hurry up. You've never seen the inside of one of those places, I reckon, and I hope you never have to. We need our girl home, you hear me?"

Eliza did indeed hear her—heard the strained maternal note in Liesel's voice, the way her words were both a request and a promise. Liesel would not rest until she found Bridie, and so neither must Eliza.

"I hear you. Have faith, Liesel," Eliza said grimly; and for the first time, when she said the word 'faith' she realized she was not thinking of holy books or prayers or even the Creator himself.

She was learning to put her faith in the people she trusted and, she realized, in herself.

It was terrifying and beautiful blasphemy, and she held tight to it.

(Letter from Eliza to Eli)

Dear Eli,

I know I will see you again later this week to continue my tutelage, but this cannot wait until then. I need your help. My friend Bridie has vanished. She is one of the maids at Larkspur Manor, and also my best friend in the world. My father says she was taken ill suddenly with Riftsickness while I was away at the palace, but I don't believe a word of it. Bridie has been as healthy as a horse every day since I've known her, and I refuse to believe that she could have stepped out to run an errand in perfect health, only to be taken so ill in the city that she had to be carted off to a Riftward at once. It doesn't make sense—and of course, I understand enough about Riftsickness now to know that isn't at all how it works.

There's more. The Praesidio came and ransacked our room as well. They said it was to gather her possessions for her, but if that were so, why would they have torn the place apart as though they were looking for something? If that was indeed their true intention, I believe they were unsuccessful in their search, for I hold in my hands the only thing I believe could have caused such a violent invasion of our sleeping quarters. It is a copy of the book—you know the one of which I speak, the only book that might have meaning for the both of us. I do not have any idea how Bridie could have gotten her hands on it, but I believe the information within it drove her to seek out the truth about her parentage—Bridie was abandoned at Clerkenwell Workhouse, you see, when she was just two years old. You understand perhaps better than anyone what the information in that book might have meant to her.

I fear Bridie may be in terrible danger, Eli. I am terrified of what may have befallen her if she asked the wrong question of the wrong person. The book is safe, but my friend is in grave danger, I can feel it deep in my bones. Please. You have to help me find out what happened to her.

Awaiting your reply,

Eliza

SEVENTEEN

J OSIAH SET DOWN HIS PEN and read through the first page of his speech. He'd never even gone home after his visit to the palace, but had continued on straight to the Illustratum to get started on it. He'd reworked the opening lines half a dozen times, but had yet to strike just the right tone. He was confident he would know it when he'd achieved it; it had to be authoritative and yet humble. He knew much of his uphill battle toward the position of High Elder could be conquered if he could just win over a few more of his brethren early on in the process; and while many would be dead set against his nomination to the seat, there were many who could be persuaded into his corner with a few veiled promises.

A knock upon the door interrupted his ruminations, and he swore under his breath.

"Come in," he called, though he'd have much preferred to send whomever it was packing.

He was surprised when the door swung open to see a woman standing there—he had expected Brother Goodwin or another of the Elders. It took him a moment to recognize Mrs. Langford, the sour-faced woman who ran the Clerkenwell Workhouse for the Illustratum.

"Mrs. Langford. To what do I owe the pleasure?"

"Pardon the intrusion Elder Hallewell. I would never presume to trouble you here, sir, but a... well, a delicate matter has come up, and I thought I ought to come to see you directly, seeing as we couldn't reach you at home."

"Certainly," Josiah said with a sigh. "And what is this delicate matter you wish to discuss? Do sit, please." He gestured to the seat in front of his desk, for the woman was still hovering like a ghost halfway across the room. She nodded gratefully, then marched across the room and perched herself upon the very edge of the seat, like a bird who would spook and take flight at any moment.

"Well, you see, sir, it's Bridie Sloane," the woman said.

Josiah frowned. "Who?"

"Your... your housemaid, sir? Bridie Sloane?"

"Ah, yes, Bridie," Josiah said, nodding along. Did the woman really expect him to know the names of all the Riftborn scurrying around the bowels of his estate? He had a bloody country to run. "What about her?"

"Well sir, she showed up at the workhouse yesterday morning, wanting to see me," the woman began. She had taken up the corner of her apron in her hands and was twisting it anxiously. "I thought she might have been sent by Mr. Braxton to seek out additional help in the kitchens or some such business, but it weren't nothing of the sort. She wanted to know if I had any information about... about her parents, sir. All worked up she was, sir, wondering if I had any information about them."

Josiah blinked, wondering what on earth this could have to do with him. Was he to concern himself with the sentimental notions taken up by his kitchen staff? Unless, of course... he sat up a little straighter.

"I assume you sent her packing?" Josiah said sternly. "We've made it clear, I am sure, how dangerous it could be for records to be kept concerning—"

"Yes, of course, sir," Mrs. Langford said hastily. "I assure you, she got no information from me on that score. No, I came to you because of an incident that she witnessed while she was in my office."

"And what incident was this?"

Mrs. Langford swallowed hard and cleared her throat. "Well, sir, it's... there was a situation. One of our inmates from the lunatic ward gave our attendants the slip when they were taking her down for a washing. She got all the way down to the main entrance hall and attacked several of my staff violently before we were able to subdue her."

Josiah sighed. "I'm struggling to see why this requires my involvement, unless you're here to beg for more funding, which I must remind you, good lady, we have a strict process for. You're not doing yourself any favors by wasting my time with—"

"Please, sir, this isn't about money, though Creator knows we are barely scraping by and overcrowded to the rafters. No, sir, it's about the patient, sir. Bridie Sloane recognized her."

"And?"

"It's Emmeline Braxton, sir."

Josiah's impatience drained out of him, as dawning horror began to fill him up. "That's impossible. She can't have recognized the woman. She's never met her."

"Yes, I know that, sir, but she recognized her just the same. She says she shares sleeping quarters with the Braxton girl. Apparently, there's a photograph?"

Josiah ran a hand over his face. "Where is the Sloane girl now?"

"At the workhouse, sir, being detained. She... we had to drug her, sir, to stop her from running off," Mrs. Langford admitted.

"You drugged her?!" Josiah stood up. "Why didn't you just tell her she was mistaken in the woman's identity and send her on her way?"

"I tried that, sir, but the girl was quite insistent. She would not be deterred. I knew we couldn't risk her returning home and telling the Braxton girl, or then we'd have both of them banging down our door."

"No. No, of course, you are quite right," Josiah said, starting to pace back and forth behind his desk. "But when was this?"

"Yesterday morning, sir."

"But surely my staff must already be in an uproar looking for her!"

"We thought of that, sir," Mrs. Langford said. "We tried to get in touch with you there but were informed you were at the palace. And so, we... that is to say, my husband and I—made the decision to send the Praesidio to the house, sir. We cited a case of Riftsickness, and asked them to collect her things."

Josiah nodded. "That was very quick thinking, Mrs. Langford. Damn it all, I would have known about it at once, but I haven't been home yet. I had the carriage drop my daughter at Larkspur Manor and then bring me right along to the office. Did my staff give them any trouble?"

"Of course not, sir. Your butler let them right in and pointed out the girl's room to them. They explained she was being taken to a Riftward, and then they were gone. I gave 'em strict instructions not to mention me or the workhouse. Your butler seemed to accept the story without question."

"Yes, yes, of course, Braxton would give you no trouble," Josiah muttered. "But surely the other servants will want to know what's become of her. Blast it all, I need a moment to *think*."

Mrs. Langford pressed her lips together and looked down at the wrinkled twist of apron in her lap.

Josiah pressed his palms together under his chin. He could not risk exposure, not now, not with so much at stake. He was days away from achieving his life's ambition, and he could not jeopardize it because some nosy little chit of a housemaid started asking too many questions. No, there had to be a way to contain this before it went any further. The Langford woman, incompetent though she had been to allow this to happen in the first place, had at least been clever enough to control the damage. But there was more work to be done.

"Keep the girl locked up where she is for now," Josiah said at last. "I must confer with some of the other Elders. I will send word with further instructions."

Mrs. Langford closed her eyes and exhaled, apparently relieved that she was not going to be further chastised. "And what am I to say if anyone comes looking for Bridie Sloane, sir? She might have told someone where she was going."

"Feign ignorance," Josiah said at once. "You've not seen the girl since she left your care. Stick to it, and make sure all your staff does the same."

"Yes, sir," Mrs. Langford said, taking to her feet and dropping into a respectful curtsy. "Thank you, sir. I will keep the girl hidden and await your instructions."

"Very good. Now leave me, please, so that I can attend to this matter. And tell Brother Goodwin in the outer office that I wish to see Elder Potter at his earliest convenience," Josiah said, flicking his hand dismissively toward the door, through which the woman immediately scuttled, closing it behind her.

Josiah went to his window and threw it wide. A warm breeze swept around him, carrying with it the stagnant smell of the Thames nearby. Below him, the residents of the Bankside scurried to and fro, as small as insects and no more significant from where he stood. He had not thought about Emmeline Braxton—*really* thought about her—for perhaps ten years now. Over time, he had reduced her in his mind to a faceless figure in the background, a cog in the machine that had raised him to the very precipice of his heart's deepest desires.

Once an existential threat to his very position, now the woman was nothing to him—neutralized and locked away.

He should have had her killed—of course, he knew that now. But he had been so eager to avoid the scandal, so sure he could sweep it all under the rug, and her along with it. He had fancied himself merciful, though he had seen the inner workings of those workhouses with his own eyes, and he knew a sentence there was a far cry from mercy. But he had convinced himself that killing the woman would be wasteful when the Illustratum could use her—a young and healthy woman with exceptional Riftmagic abilities—she could serve a much higher purpose in the experimental wards.

A lot of bloody good those wards would do, though, if they couldn't even contain the woman. Nearly escaping? Attacking staff? He would need to impose harsher restrictions if the woman was to be allowed to stay there. Or, indeed, anywhere.

And now this housemaid, Bridie Sloane... this would have to be handled very carefully.

A sharp knock on the door drew a gasp from his lungs, and Josiah turned to see Francis Potter standing in his doorway, a pipe clenched in his teeth.

"You're not going to jump, are you? I don't much fancy having to fish you out of the bloody river."

"Come in, Francis, and close the door behind you," Josiah said, ignoring the jest.

Francis did so and crossed the room to sit on the corner of Josiah's desk, puffing away thoughtfully. "Well? Let's hear the worst of it."

"The worst of what?"

Francis chuckled. "Goodwin looked in danger of reducing himself to a puddle of perspiration, the poor chap. I knew something had to be wrong. You haven't called me to your office like this in weeks."

Josiah looked his friend in the eye. "I know. I'm sorry, Francis."

Francis waved the apology away. "I don't need your apologies, Josiah. Creator knows I'd have done the same thing if it had been my daughter. Hell, I probably would have married off my son to the Morgan lad if I'd been asked to."

Josiah attempted a smile. "No, you wouldn't have. That's always been the difference between us, hasn't it?"

Francis puffed thoughtfully on his pipe for a moment. "Morgan's always been a smart man. He might have inherited the post of High

Elder from his father, but he'd have earned it regardless, we all know that. And when he took the two of us on as his Councilors, there was little doubt as to why. He took me on because he trusted me. He took you on because he couldn't trust you."

Josiah bristled. "I beg your—"

"Come on now, man. Hear me out, you owe me that."

Josiah ground his teeth together and held his tongue.

"I've never wanted the High Elder's position. You know it, I know it, and Morgan knows it. Therein lies my value to him; I'm not a threat, so he knows he can trust me. You, on the other hand, have always had your sights set on the top seat. You're ambitious to your core, Josiah, and that makes you a man to be wary of. Morgan was smart enough to see it. He saw your potential, assessed you as a threat, and decided to keep you close. In doing so, he has turned you from a potential enemy to a devoted ally, and therefore protected himself."

Josiah wanted to argue but found he could not. "I want to earn the seat, Francis, not steal it," he finally said.

"And so you have," Francis agreed. "I said you were a threat, Josiah, but not an underhanded one. You have always been clear and forthright in your ambition. It's the reason I can be friends with you. It's also the reason so many of the others detest you with a passion hot as hell."

Francis allowed himself a good chuckle. Josiah, again, struggled to disagree.

"And do you think I've finally become underhanded, promising Jessamine to the Morgan boy? Have I finally crossed that line?"

Again, Francis took a moment to consider it. "I'll wager you flirted with it. But the fact is, Morgan would have put your name forward anyway. He knows you're the right man for the job when the time comes. But he played your loyalty against your ambition and he won. You've won, too. It's only the children who've lost."

"And you? Have you lost?" Josiah asked quietly.

Francis spread his hands out in front of him, like a king surveying his domain. "Of course not! You came to me, didn't you? We agreed it was the prudent thing to do. I pity Teddy, but the boy will buck up and find some other pretty young thing to marry. His prospects are bright, and I know you'll take care of him once you've taken your seat. You've promised me as much, haven't you?"

"Yes, I certainly have, and I'll stand by that promise, Francis."

"I know you will, or I wouldn't be sitting here," Francis said, sounding uncharacteristically serious for a moment. "So, since I am sitting here, what's happened? Let's have it, man, come on."

Josiah sighed, walking back to his chair and sinking into it. Then, without preamble, he told Francis what Mrs. Langford had come to report.

Francis let out a low whistle. All trace of levity was gone from his round face. "I'd have thought the woman was dead long ago, the state of that place."

Josiah nodded. "What should I do now, Francis? I can't let this get out. The scandal it would cause…"

"The housemaid is still there, you say?" Francis asked.

"Yes. They've locked her up in one of the wards, and they are awaiting my instructions."

Francis bit the end of his pipe, his brow furrowed. "Well, there's no question of letting her go. She's seen too much, and there's no guarantee she'll keep it a secret, regardless of what you threaten her with."

"What do you suggest, then? I don't know what good it would be to keep her locked up in Clerkenwell. The place is clearly overrun as it is."

"And poorly run, it seems. We may need to address that, too, but one mess at a time," Francis said. "No, I think the safest course of action is to transfer her to one of the higher security institutions. An asylum, perhaps?"

Josiah had to repress a shudder just thinking of the madhouses, which he had only toured once, in his first days as an Elder. It was as grim a place to sentence a person as could be found. And yet, what choice did he have? It was regrettable, of course, but the girl could not be allowed to reveal what she knew.

"And you think that's all that's… necessary?" Josiah asked, dancing around the question because he knew that Francis would understand the implication.

"I think that's all that's prudent," Francis replied with a grim nod. "Any further and you've got yet another scandal to cover up. Riftsickness and a stint in an asylum will damage her credibility beyond repair. Even if she ever does manage to get out or tell someone what she knows—"

"She won't," Josiah muttered darkly.

"—no one will believe her. It will be the Illustratum's word against the lunatic ravings of a Riftsick madwoman," Francis finished with a shrug.

"Yes. Yes, you're right," Josiah agreed, feeling the tight knot of anxiety in his chest start to loosen for the first time since the matron had appeared in his doorway. "And for good measure, I think I ought to have the Braxton woman transferred there as well."

Francis grunted his approval of this added precaution. "Indeed. You'll need to get the matron to help cover the tracks, of course. Sweetening her pay, perhaps, in return for her assistance? Or agreeing to revisit their budgetary requests. No point in leaving a bad taste in the woman's mouth, if she's meant to keep your secrets."

"Thank you, Francis," Josiah sighed, leaning back in his chair.

"What for?" Francis asked, his pipe now clenched between his teeth again as he hoisted his bulk up off the desk. "I didn't tell you anything you didn't already know."

"I appreciate your counsel, as ever," Josiah said. "One last question."

"What's that?"

"Do you think I ought to tell Morgan?"

Francis considered this for a moment, then shook his head. "Morgan's got one foot in the grave as it is. What he doesn't know won't hurt him now. Be thorough, Josiah. Seal up all the cracks. We've come too far to falter now."

Josiah nodded. They had, indeed.

Tom o' Bedlam (an excerpt from the anonymous poem, dated to approximately 1620)

From the hag and hungry goblin
That into rags would rend ye,
The spirit that stands by the naked man
In the Book of Moons defend ye,
That of your five sound senses,
You never be forsaken,
Nor wander from yourselves with Tom
Abroad to beg your bacon,
While I do sing, Any food, any feeding,
Feeding, drink, or clothing;
Come dame or maid, be not afraid,
Poor Tom will injure nothing.
Of thirty bare years have I
Twice twenty been enragèd,
And of forty been three times fifteen
In durance soundly cagèd
On the lordly lofts of Bedlam
With stubble soft and dainty,
Brave bracelets strong, sweet whips ding dong
And now I sing, Any food, any feeding,
Feeding, drink, or clothing;
Come dame or maid, be not afraid,
Poor Tom will injure nothing.
With a thought I took for Maudlin
And a cruse of cockle pottage,
With a thing thus tall, sky bless you all,
I befell into this dotage.

I slept not since the Conquest,
Till then I never wakèd,
Till the roguish boy of love where I lay
Me found and stripped me nakèd.
And now I sing, Any food, any feeding,
Feeding, drink, or clothing;
Come dame or maid, be not afraid,
Poor Tom will injure nothing…

EIGHTEEN

I T WAS THE PAIN IN HER HEAD that first woke Bridie. The pounding made it feel as though her whole head was pulsating, and for a few moments she just lay there with her eyes still closed, trying to think through the pain.

She was lying down.

She was very, very cold.

The inside of her mouth felt like it was full of sand.

She tried to open her eyes, but her vision was blurry and the room swam, making her stomach heave. She quickly shut her eyes again.

Think, Bridie, think.

She tried to reach back into her memory, to remember where she was or how she had gotten there, but the images were like a tangled ball of yarn, impossible to extricate from each other and hopelessly knotted together. Slowly, she tugged at the ends, willing them into focus.

Mrs. Langford's office…

Emmeline Braxton, cowering in the corner…

The tea…

The attempted escape, the dead end in the courtyard…

She groaned and shifted herself. Every muscle felt like it had been torched, like her own Riftmagic had been set off inside her, burning as it went. She was afraid to try to open her eyes again, afraid to see that every inch of her had been scorched beyond recognition.

The room swam into view: a dank and filthy cell, bare stone walls, sunlight filtering weakly through a high, barred window. Beneath her was a ragged mattress made from burlap sacking and stuffed with straw. She dared a glance at her own body— she was whole and unscathed, aside from a few scrapes and bruises she had acquired during her attempted escape over the courtyard wall. She was no longer wearing her Larkspur Manor uniform, but a shapeless white garment that hung down past her knees, revealing bare legs and feet.

She was also not alone.

Three other women occupied three other corners of the room, each of them wearing the same white uniform, each of them crouching or lying upon their own filthy mattress. Not one of them was paying Bridie the slightest bit of attention as she took in her surroundings. Two of them appeared to be sleeping. The third had her face pressed up against the stone of the wall, crooning a song to her own bloody fingertips as she scratched at the rough stone.

Bridie's gaze took all of this in before her sluggish mind was able to catch up. When it finally did, she felt something new burning through her with the pain: terror.

She pushed herself into a sitting position with difficulty; every inch of her was stiff and sore. How long had she been lying here? She could feel the hunger pulling at her beneath the nausea, felt the thirst in her parched throat. She tried to speak but no sound came out. She cleared her throat and tried fruitlessly to moisten her lips with her tongue before she tried again. She addressed the only person she could: the singing woman in the corner.

"Excuse me?"

Her voice sounded strangely loud in the little room. The woman flinched, as though bothered by the sound, but otherwise did not respond.

"Please, can you tell me where we are?" Bridie tried again. "What is this place?"

The woman shook her head, like she was trying to displace a buzzing insect, and sang on.

Bridie gave up and looked around her more carefully now, searching for any clue that might help her understand what had happened.

She tested her legs and found they could bear her weight, though they shook madly. Clutching at the wall for support, she shuffled her way along the floor until she was standing beneath the solitary window. It was set so high in the wall that she had to dig her bare toes into the grooves of the stones to gain a foothold so that she could hoist herself up to see. It took several attempts before she managed to catch a glimpse. The grime that coated the glass obscured almost everything, and she had to squint to make out anything at all. In the distance, the hallowed halls of the Illustratum loomed over the Thames, but the perspective was wrong; it was on the wrong side... so she wasn't still in the workhouse at Clerkenwell. She was somewhere on the South bank of the river, then. Her still-shaky limbs gave out and she collapsed back onto the floor, panting from the effort. Still, none of the other women in the room had acknowledged her presence.

She turned her attention now to the only door to the room. She knew instinctively that it would be locked, but it would have been foolish not to at least try it. She walked unsteadily across to the far side of the room and tugged fruitlessly at the door handle. There was a small opening in the top of the door, too high for her to see out of, and the door itself offered no footholds to hoist herself up so that she could see out into the corridor beyond. On the other side of the door, however, a cacophony of human misery was echoing through the halls—a constant hum of moaning and muttering and crying, punctuated by discordant shrieks and curses and maniacal laughter.

What was this place? And dear Creator, how was she going to get out of it? A mistake had been made. A terrible, terrible mistake.

Bridie turned her back on the door and slid down it until she was sitting on the floor. She fought back against the panic that threatened to overtake her. She would achieve nothing by losing her head, she told herself, and drew several long, deep breaths. This was a mistake. The room stank of urine and sweat and all manner of unspeakable filth. She retched violently, but her stomach was empty. She tried to breathe through her mouth instead. She closed her eyes.

Think, Bridie. Think.

She turned her attention back to the women sharing the room with her and examined them more closely. The one nearest her, the woman who was singing, could not have been much older than she was, perhaps twenty-five, though it was difficult to pinpoint her age because of how gaunt and ill she looked. Her hair was dark and had been shorn nearly to the scalp, sticking out in messy patches, as though a child had taken the scissors to her head. Her knees and elbows were scabbed and sore-looking, and her fingernails were bloodied from her obsessive picking at the walls. Her song had continued unabated since Bridie had regained consciousness.

A second woman lay curled up in a nest of straw, breathing slowly and evenly. A large purple birthmark obscured what little of her face could be seen; the rest was hidden beneath a matted curtain of grey hair. As Bridie watched her, she stirred feebly, gave a soft moan, and rolled over to face the wall. As she did so, there was a clattering sound, and Bridie realized with a gasp of horror that there was a shackle around one of the woman's ankles; she was chained to the wall. The third woman was curled into a tight ball in the furthest corner, her arms wrapped around her knees. She, too, had been shackled—Bridie could see the heavy chains snaking away across the floor. At first glance, Bridie had thought she was asleep, but now that her vision had cleared, she could see the woman's eyes, like deep wells, staring out from behind her long, tangled blonde hair.

Very blonde, nearly white... and the eyes... were they grey?

"Mrs. Braxton?" Bridie whispered, her voice coming out choked with fear.

The woman picked her pointed chin up off her knees and turned her gaze on Bridie. The white-blonde hair fell away from her face and Bridie could see now that it was indeed Emmeline Braxton. Her eyes—the exact color as Eliza's—were set like deep and brooding globes into the deathly pale planes of her face, and they blinked at her, as though trying to make sense of the words Bridie had just spoken.

Bridie pulled herself forward onto her hands and knees and began to crawl toward Mrs. Braxton, who did not flinch away but watched her progress with those wide, wary eyes. Bridie crouched on her heels, just beyond the woman's reach, just in case she lashed out as she had at the workhouse.

"Mrs. Braxton? Emmeline?" Bridie murmured softly.

It was dim in the cell, but Bridie thought she saw something like recognition spark in the woman's eyes. Encouraged, she continued in the same gentle tone.

"Emmeline, my name is Bridie Sloane. You don't know me, but I'm friends with your daughter, Eliza."

There was no doubt about it; those grey eyes lit like torches with recognition. Emmeline's lips trembled as she silently mouthed the word: *Eliza*.

"Yes, that's right!" Bridie said, her voice cracking with emotion as she tried to offer the woman a smile. "Yes, Eliza! We work together at Larkspur Manor."

Emmeline flinched at the sound of her former place of

employment, and her eyes suddenly shone with tears. She began to shake her head violently.

"No, Emmeline, no! It's okay! Eliza is okay! She's... she's safe!"

Emmeline's head stopped its whipping back and forth. *Safe?* she asked silently.

"Yes. Eliza is safe. But I'm... I'm afraid we may not be. Do you know... can you tell me where we are?"

Emmeline unwound one painfully thin arm from around her knees and lifted it slowly, pointing over at the singing woman, whom Bridie had all but forgotten in the moments since she'd realized it was Emmeline crouched in the corner.

Bridie followed with her eyes, but only saw more of what she had already witnessed from the woman—singing and scraping away at the walls with raw, bloody fingertips.

"What do you—" Bridie began to ask, but Emmeline interrupted her, making sound for the first time. It was little more than a hoarse hum, a snatch of the tune that the other woman had been singing since Bridie had first come to. Cautiously, Bridie shifted closer to the young woman, whose voice rose and fell softly on the lilting tune of the song. Bridie leaned in, listening.

"From the hag and hungry goblin
That into rags would rend ye,
The spirit that stands by the naked man
In the Book of Moons defend ye,
That of your five sound senses,
You never be forsaken,
Nor wander from yourselves with Tom
Abroad to beg your bacon..."

Bridie gasped and threw a hand over her mouth to keep herself from crying out. She knew the song—everyone knew the song, the words to which had been taken from a poem so old that no one knew who had written it. Despite the best efforts of the Illustratum to stamp out everything that had come before the Awakening, little snatches still existed, whispering through the Barrens, hummed to babies dandled on knees, whistled by drunkards as they weaved and tottered through the streets.

"Of thirty bare years have I
Twice twenty been enragèd,
And of forty been three times fifteen

197

In durance soundly cagèd
On the lordly lofts of Bedlam
With stubble soft and dainty,
Brave bracelets strong, sweet whips ding dong
With wholesome hunger plenty,
    And now I sing, Any food, any feeding,
Feeding, drink, or clothing;
Come dame or maid, be not afraid,
Poor Tom will injure nothing."

Tom o' Bedlam, the tune was called. And though Bridie had heard it a hundred times in her life, never had the words caused sheer dread to shoot down her spine like a bolt of lightning.

She knew where she was, and the realization struck a fear into her heart the likes of which she had never known. She turned back to Emmeline, whose solemn eyes stared back, and in them, Bridie could see her own terror reflected back to her.

Bedlam.

Bethlem Hospital was its proper name, but no one ever used it. The most notorious of madhouses, stuffed to the gills with the most dangerous lunatics the city could spawn, where the wealthy could come and gawk at the patients like delighted spectators at a carnival sideshow. A tidal wave of fear broke over her, and Bridie jumped to her feet, stumbling across the room to the door once again. Tears welled up in her eyes as she began to pound on the door with her fists.

"Someone, please! Help me! I'm not supposed to be here! I'm not mad! This is a mistake! This is a terrible mistake, please! Somebody! Anybody!"

The only answer, apart from the echoes of her cries, was a wheezy, cackling laugh from somewhere on the other side of the door, followed by the words, "Save your breath, duck. We've all said the same thing. Ain't no one listenin'."

And behind her, the madwoman sang on.

NINETEEN

I T HAD BEEN THREE DAYS since she'd sent her letter to Eli.
Three endless days that dragged by in a haze of restless sleep
broken apart by nightmares so intense they left her screaming into
her pillow. Shadowy figures in Illustratum robes loomed silently over
her as she begged on her knees to know what had become of Bridie,
even as Bridie cried out for help from behind heavy doors that would
not open. Or else she ran, her skirts filthy and torn and waterlogged,
through endless fog-laden forests, calling out for Bridie, whose
terrified pleas she could hear but never find. Wolves howled in the
trees, and figures seemed to form and dissolve in the shadows,
dogging her steps and whispering promises of her demise.

If Jessamine had noticed that her lady's maid had been driven to
distraction by her worry, she did not mention it. On one hand, Eliza
was relieved—she did not want to draw any more attention to Bridie's
plight than she needed to, and the last thing she wanted was to try
to invent excuses for her low spirits. On the other hand, she was
desperately worried about Miss Jessamine, who seemed lost in her
own troubles.

This was not to say that Jessamine lay in bed all day—on the
contrary, she was up each morning before Eliza came in with her
tea, and she had committed herself to a relentless schedule of charity
groups and social outings. But though she rose from her bed, readied
herself without complaint, and went briskly through the motions of her
days, there was something in her eyes—a sort of defeat that was even
worse to watch than if she'd locked herself in her room, screaming
and throwing things at the walls. It was as if all the fight had gone out
of her—a flame had been snuffed, and Eliza was not convinced that

enough of a spark remained within her mistress to rekindle her spirit again. Between this and her concerns about Bridie, Eliza worried she, too, would sink irretrievably beneath the weight of her own despair.

Eliza clung to the hope each day that she would hear from Eli, and kept herself as busy as possible to avoid any chance of sitting around driving herself mad with worry inventing wilder and wilder scenarios of what might have happened to Bridie—what might, even at that very moment, *still* be happening to her. As a result, she not only caught up on every bit of mending, pressing, and polishing she had to do, but she also began offering her services in the kitchen and around the rest of the house, taking on any task anyone would allow her to perform until she fell into her bed each night almost too tired to remove her boots. Perhaps, she thought wryly, as she drifted off to sleep, she would have a better chance of catching up with Bridie in her dreams if she kept the boots on.

It was on the fourth afternoon after they arrived home from the palace that Eliza decided to occupy her racing mind by starching all of her aprons again. The aprons were not in need of starching, but Eliza certainly seemed to be. She went to her wardrobe and pulled down every apron she had. As she carried them across the room to lay them out on her bed, however, something white fell from one of them and fluttered to the ground. Perplexed, Eliza bent to retrieve the item and realized, with a gasp of realization, that it was the letter she was meant to deliver to Mrs. Spratt.

She cursed herself for her own distraction. What if the content of the letter were of a time-sensitive nature? Why, that maid, whoever she was, might even now be pacing about, as desperate for a response to her missive as Eliza was to hear back from Eli. Slipping the letter into the pocket of her apron, she abandoned her starching and hurried as quickly as her feet would carry her all the way into the upper reaches of the house, where Mrs. Spratt tended her charge.

As she climbed the many flights of stairs, Eliza realized that she could not remember seeing Mrs. Spratt at all downstairs since she arrived home from the palace. This was unusual; while it was true that Mrs. Spratt spent the vast majority of her time up in Mrs. Hallewell's chambers, she did nip down to have a break and a cup of tea with Mrs. Keats most evenings, when Mrs. Hallewell had been put to bed for the night. Many times, Eliza had slipped out of bed and into the kitchen for a biscuit and a cup of milk, and seen the two women, huddled together with their hands wrapped around their teacups, whispering seriously together. Somehow, even when she was very young, she knew not to disturb them—their weary expressions did not invite interruptions.

Eliza rounded the last landing to Mrs. Hallewell's chambers and knocked softly upon the door; she did not expect that Mrs. Hallewell would be sleeping this early in the day, but it would not do to disturb her if she was. The door eased open just a crack, and Eliza was startled to see Mrs. Spratt's wide and bloodshot eyes taking her in as though she might be an apparition before pulling the door wide.

"Eliza! What are you doing here?" Mrs. Spratt asked, her gaze darting all around the hallway beyond. Eliza could not blame her. The last time she had visited Mrs. Hallewell's chambers, it had been on Jessamine's insistence, and the results of that brief reunion between mother and daughter had been disastrous.

"It's all right, Mrs. Spratt, it's just me this time." She peered over Mrs. Spratt's shoulder and saw that Mrs. Hallewell was in her usual place in the rocking chair by the window. She had not so much as stirred when Mrs. Spratt opened the door. "May I come in?"

Mrs. Spratt shook her head violently. "I can't let no one in, I'm afraid. I'm under very strict orders to keep her calm and quiet, Eliza, and I can't afford to allow anything that might upset her, and that includes visitors."

Eliza looked anxiously back down the hallway to ensure it was empty before she extracted the letter from her pocket. "I have something for you."

She held it out. Mrs. Spratt looked down at it warily. "What is it?"

"It's a letter. One of the maids at the palace asked me to—"

But Mrs. Spratt's eyes had gone wide and her hand shot out, snatching the letter from Eliza's fingers and pulling her roughly into the room, closing the door behind her.

"Have you told anyone about this?" Mrs. Spratt hissed, shaking the letter in Eliza's face.

"N-no," Eliza replied, startled by the sudden change that had come over Mrs. Spratt. "I told no one. I'm sorry, I ought to have given it to you several days ago, but I've been so... so..."

Mrs. Spratt was not listening. She had scurried over to her wingback chair in the corner and tore the letter eagerly open. Her eyes were now racing back and forth over the words written there. After a few silent moments, she pressed the letter to her heart, closed her eyes, and heaved a great sigh. "Thank the Creator she's all right," she whispered. Tears squeezed their way out from under her eyelids and rolled down her face.

"Mrs. Spratt, are... is everything okay?"

"Did you see her? You must have seen her! What did she look like? How was she?" Mrs. Spratt was on her feet again and had stumbled forward to Eliza, clutching at her arm. Eliza tried to back away, but Mrs. Spratt followed, her questions burning in her tear-filled eyes.

"I don't understand what you mean, Mrs. Spratt. Who are you—"

"My daughter! My only child, Bette. She works at the palace as a maid. I haven't seen her in... Please, did she... does she look well? Did she seem anxious or... or troubled at all?"

Eliza struggled to bite back a thousand questions and tried to provide answers first. "She... she looks well. Quite pretty. Taller than me by several inches, fair skin and hair. She seemed nervous, but only until I agreed to deliver her letter to you."

Mrs. Spratt closed her eyes and let all these little nuggets of information wash over her as though Eliza had dropped them directly from heaven, the letter still pressed against her heart.

"Mrs. Spratt, I... I didn't know you had a daughter," Eliza said quietly.

Mrs. Spratt's eyes fluttered open, and she seemed to be trying to pull herself back together. She brushed the tears impatiently from her cheeks and cleared her throat. "Not many people do. I haven't seen her in many, many years."

"But why?" Eliza whispered. "Have you had a... a falling out, or...?"

Mrs. Spratt shook her head. "No, no, nothing like that. I want to see her, more than you could possibly imagine. I think of her every day, dream of her every night."

"But she's... she's only a few miles away. Surely on a day off you could..."

Mrs. Spratt laughed harshly. "A day off? When have I ever had a day off? I've barely left this house in more than fifteen years."

Eliza could not understand it. Several of the servants had been married and had families over the years. A few of them lived in small cottages on the grounds, and there was even a tutor who came and taught the little ones how to read their Illustratum-issued books and how to do arithmetic. She could remember Mrs. Keats' boys when they were younger, learning to help out in the stables. One of them still worked there, mucking out stalls and tending the horses.

"Surely you could ask for one?" Eliza suggested timidly. "My father isn't entirely unreasonable, you know."

"My position is not like that of the other servants. Your father does not determine whether or not I get a day off. Only Elder Hallewell can grant such a privilege." She said it in a dry husk of a voice, a voice with no hope.

"But why don't you ask him to—"

"NO!" The word burst from Mrs. Spratt's lips and she clapped a hand over her mouth in horror. Then she was out of her chair and halfway across the room to Mrs. Hallewell, hovering anxiously over her, waiting for a response to the shouting, but there was none: if Mrs. Hallewell had heard her caretaker's cry, she showed no sign of it. Mrs. Spratt sagged with relief and returned to her chair. When she looked at Eliza again, her face looked impossibly old.

"I am bound to stay here with Mrs. Hallewell. I do not have a choice."

"Everyone has a choice," Eliza said quietly. "Why don't you just resign?"

Mrs. Spratt laughed again. "I can't."

"But why not?"

"Because they will kill my daughter!"

For the second time in a minute, Mrs. Spratt had her hand clapped over her own mouth in horror. She reached her other hand out into the space between them, as though she could pluck the words right out of the air and take them back.

Eliza fought to compose herself, and when she broke the silence she was relieved to hear that her voice was quite steady. "Mrs. Spratt, who are you talking about? Who is threatening to kill Bette?"

It was the mention of her daughter's name that shattered whatever remaining composure Mrs. Spratt had. She wilted back into her chair, slumped and sobbing. Eliza hurried forward and knelt at her side, reaching out for one of her hands and grasping it tightly; she took it as a good sign that Mrs. Spratt did not push her away.

"The Illustratum. Well, really I suppose it's Elder Hallewell, but he brings the full power of the Illustratum to bear," she mumbled through the onslaught of tears.

Eliza fished a handkerchief from her pocket and handed it to Mrs. Spratt, who dabbed at her glistening cheeks. "Why would he do such a thing?"

Mrs. Spratt looked Eliza straight in the eyes. Indecision clouded her gaze, and Eliza knew she was not at all sure that she could trust Eliza. Eliza could not blame her. She herself had always been such a model of piety and obedience. Her father had seen to that.

"I just don't think you'd understand, dear," Mrs. Spratt hedged.

"Maybe I would. Maybe I would understand much better than you think. Maybe I've learned enough recently to understand that the world we live in—the Dignus and the Riftborn—is much darker and more complicated than the Book of the Rift would ever dare to tell us."

Mrs. Spratt's eyes widened, and Eliza tried, with all her might, to meet that gaze levelly, to express wordlessly what she could not say outright. And then, she felt a strange energy flowing through her, and she looked down with a gasp at Mrs. Spratt's hand clasped in hers. She had been too distracted, too focused on their conversation to realize that their hands were pressed against each other, no gloves between them, for Mrs. Spratt never wore them, and Eliza had neglected to put hers back on in her haste to deliver the forgotten letter. Two Influencers, their magic melding and flowing freely between them—Eliza thrilled at the raw power she could feel in her fingertips.

The women's eyes met again, and at that moment, a rush of feelings, of understanding, of empathy and epiphany ran through them, binding them so tightly that Eliza was not sure she would ever have the strength to pull her hand away. She could feel Mrs. Spratt mining her for truth, willing her to explain herself, to earn the woman's trust. And Eliza was likewise pressing for information, for comprehension, for any way she might be able to help ease the terrible suffering smoldering in Mrs. Spratt's eyes. And then, it was as though their gifts met, entwined, and exploded. If they had been visible, Eliza would have expected to see sparks. Her head whirled, filled for a moment with flashes of insight and stabs of pain that were not her own. Frightened, she pulled her hand away just as Mrs. Spratt released it.

"I... I wasn't trying to... I didn't... what happened?" Eliza whispered.

"We saw into each other, as only Influencers can do," Mrs. Spratt said.

Eliza rubbed at her hand, which was still tingling. "And...w-what did you see?"

"I saw that I can trust you, Eliza."

"H-how do you know?"

"Because we have known the same pain at the same hands," Mrs. Spratt whispered.

She did not elaborate, and Eliza did not want her to. Before she could try to gather her thoughts into a reply to such a remarkable pronouncement, Mrs. Spratt heaved a sigh and spoke.

"You may be too young to remember, I don't know, but there was a time when I worked as one of Mrs. Hallewell's maids. She was very kind to me. When I met my husband, I was afraid to tell her, but she knew me well. She figured out that I was in love and she encouraged me to seek happiness. She insisted I accept his proposal, said that tending to her should not preclude me from living my own life as well. She was over the moon when I found out I was with child. She came to visit me while I was recovering from the birth, and rocked Bette for me while I slept. She doted on Bette as though she were one of her own beloved children. But then..."

Mrs. Spratt swallowed back tears, and her eyes darted to Mrs. Hallewell, still oblivious to their conversation over in the corner. Nevertheless, she lowered her voice to the softest of whispers as she went on, "But then young Master William was kidnapped."

Eliza did not need Mrs. Spratt to remind her of what that time at Larkspur Manor had been like—they were the most cutting of her early memories—the fear and sorrow that had permeated the house, the long, silent days that grew darker and darker when the boy wasn't found.

"Mrs. Hallewell went mad with grief. She was locked in her rooms, screaming, and throwing things, and crying herself to sleep. And then, three days after Master William vanished, Elder Hallewell came to me. He told me that I must give up my family and my other duties around the manor and dedicate myself to Mrs. Hallewell's care, night and day. I begged him to choose someone else—how could I be a mother to my child if I could never leave my mistress' side? And so he took her."

"He... he what?" Eliza whispered.

"He sent her away, just a wee thing, to live in an Illustratum-run orphanage. He told me that the only way I'd ever see her again was if I agreed to his demands. What did I have to live for, if not for Bette? My husband had died the previous spring—it was a fever what took him. Bette was all I had left. And so I agreed. What choice did I have, really?"

She looked at Eliza again, and there was a plea in her eyes, as though Eliza could somehow offer her the forgiveness she could not give herself.

"You had no choice, Mrs. Spratt. None at all."

Mrs. Spratt nodded gratefully, though the pain in her eyes did not fade. "His instructions were—and have always been—to keep his wife calm and quiet. It was not easy at first—as I said, she was beyond reason, beyond sanity. It took every ounce of my gift to keep her subdued in the early years. It's easier now—I think some of the fight has gone out of her—out of us both, if truth be told."

She looked over at her mistress, and there was genuine affection in her gaze. She did not blame Mrs. Hallewell for her lot, that much was clear.

"I've done everything that has been asked of me, and I have survived on scraps—scraps of news about my daughter, tossed to me through a half-closed door perhaps once a year. I have begged, nearly every time I've seen Elder Hallewell, to allow me to see Bette, and every time his answer is the same: perhaps soon. I'd been starting to wonder if everything he told me was a fabrication, that she might be dead or missing or Creator knows what else, but now..." She held up the letter, and a smile fought its way onto her face. "She's written me. She knows how much trouble she'd be in if anyone found out, but she's done it!"

Eliza forced a smile, too. "I'm so glad. I'm only sorry I didn't give it to you three days ago when I arrived home."

Mrs. Spratt waved her hand dismissively. "Don't you give that another thought, child. There is no greater gift you could have given me than this letter." She held it up with a watery chuckle. "She's getting married. That's what she wanted to tell me. She's getting married in a fortnight's time and she wants me to be there. Oh, if only I could!" She dissolved into tears once again.

"You must," Eliza told her firmly. "We must find a way to get you there."

Mrs. Spratt wiped viciously at the tear-tracks on her prematurely lined face. "No. No, I can't. I just need to accept it. It is enough that she wrote to me, that she knows I would want to be there. It is enough that I have this, written in her own hand, that I know that she's safe and happy."

"No, it's not enough!" Eliza said, forgetting that she had to keep her voice down. She threw an anxious look at Mrs. Hallewell, who was still lost in her own world. "You yourself just said that you have been forced to survive on scraps, but I would venture to say you've had to survive on even less than that. The idea that you have to miss watching your only child get married is absurd. I will not allow it."

Mrs. Spratt smiled wearily. "Eliza, I appreciate your passion, but it's impossible. There's no chance that Elder Hallewell will agree."

"If we do not try, there is no chance at all," Eliza said. "Let me talk to him. Let me see if I can persuade him. Forgive me, but he has expressed great satisfaction in my service of late, and I think I might just be able to ask this of him."

"We cannot let him know about this letter!" Mrs. Spratt hissed. "My daughter could lose her position or worse!"

Eliza shook her head. "I won't mention the letter. I'll think of something else. Please let me try, Mrs. Spratt."

Mrs. Spratt chewed on her lip for a moment, running her fingers tenderly over the letter still clutched in her hand. At last, she nodded. "All right, Eliza. You may approach the Elder, but you must leave both Bette and me out of it. If he thinks I am the one making the request, he will surely never grant it."

"I shall take full responsibility onto myself, Mrs. Spratt," Eliza promised solemnly. "Feign ignorance of the entire matter. I shall tell him I've told you nothing of it yet."

"Thank you, my dear. I truly appreciate you're wanting to help me," Mrs. Spratt said, her voice thick with tears.

"Don't thank me yet, Mrs. Spratt," Eliza said, giving the woman's hand a last squeeze before heading for the door. "I may as yet fail. But at least we will be able to say we tried."

(Letter from Eli to Eliza)

Dear Eliza,

First, I must say how very sorry I am to hear about your friend. You are quite right—there are few who would understand the impact that book might have on a Riftborn orphan better than me. And because of that, I am determined to help you.

The second apology I owe you is for keeping you waiting so long for my reply, but I promise it was not without cause. I wanted to ensure I had a proper answer for you, and some sort of plan of action, and it's taken me a few days to formulate them. I now believe I have. I've even wrangled Jasper into helping us.

I've spoken to an acquaintance of mine who thinks she may be able to help us. A man who works as a guard at Clerkenwell Workhouse frequents her establishment. She thinks it may be quite easy to persuade him to tell us what he knows, if anything, about your friend. It's not a sure bet, by any stretch of the imagination, and will require some patience and improvisation on our part (and perhaps a touch of your Influencer gift), but if we play our cards right, we just might be able to find out what has become of your friend.

Meet me at Sully's house at 8 o'clock on Friday night. Come alone.

Eli

TWENTY

ELIZA LOOKED UP from Eli's letter, relief spreading through her like an antidote to the poison of her fear. He would help her.

Somehow, they would get to the bottom of what happened to Bridie, she just knew it.

"Miss? Are you quite all right?" Colin stared up at her warily as tears of relief splashed their way down her cheeks. It was clear when he had agreed to deliver Eli's reply to her, he had not expected Eliza to react in this manner. But it had been four very long, arduous days that she had waited for this response, and it took her a moment to control herself.

"I am well, Colin, thank you. These are not sorrowful tears," she replied, wiping them hastily from her cheeks.

From Colin's expression, it was clear he did not put much stock in this explanation. He looked terrified as she sniffed again, and offered her a filthy handkerchief from his pocket, which she waved away impatiently. She slipped the letter into her apron and peered out into the grounds, but no one had seen the boy appear in the half-light of evening. Long shadows stretched ghoulishly across the yard, each one a disguise into which the shadow boy could vanish in a trice. He would slip out of Larkspur Manor's sprawling grounds as easily as he had slipped in, of that Eliza was confident.

"What am I to tell him, miss? Do you want to send a reply?" Colin whispered.

"Yes, but you needn't wait for me to write it down. Just tell him that I'll be there, and thank him for me," Eliza said, rummaging in her pocket for a coin she could give the lad. Her fingers closed around a *venia*, and she pressed it into his palm.

"You don't need to pay me, miss," Colin said stoutly, trying to hand it back to her, but Eliza waved off his objections.

"How in the world will you keep up your strength for all these important errands without a bag of roasted chestnuts from the High Street?" she asked with a wink. Colin grinned and pocketed the coin without further protest. Eliza thanked him again and he scampered off toward the nearest shadows nestled beneath a copse of trees, and vanished from sight as only he could.

Eliza went straight to her room and burned the letter to ash in her tiny grate, imagining, as she did so, the way Bridie used to light it for them with just a twinkling of her fingers, coaxing the flames higher and hotter, until they could warm their icy toes delightedly upon the hearth. She wasn't sure how much longer she could stand not knowing what had become of her friend. Luckily, that wait might just be over, if whatever scheme Eli Turner had cooked up actually worked. Normally, she would be sick with worry over the details of the plan, but her fear was curdling into something like recklessness in her stomach. She was starting to think that if Eli Turner's plan had been to lead an angry mob into the Riftwards in search of Bridie, she wouldn't even bat an eye, but pick up her pitchfork and torch and lead the way.

It was this rekindled fire in her belly that finally propelled her out of her room and off through the corridors to Elder Hallewell's study. She had been deliberating all day since she'd seen Mrs. Spratt, agonizing over the best way to approach Elder Hallewell about allowing her to attend her daughter's wedding. Now, however, she knew she would never be more ready—or more determined—than she was at that moment. She knew he was home; she had heard the ringing of the bells echoing through the servants' quarters that announced the arrival of his carriage and had had to flatten herself against the wall as they hurried past her in their rush to attend to him. By this hour, he would have retired to his study for his customary post-dinner drink and perhaps some reading. She'd be unlikely to find him in better humor than sipping on a sherry after one of Mrs. Keats' famous roasts.

When she arrived at his study door, she pressed her ear against it and heard a low hum of voices. She recognized her father's voice at once and hastened to obscure herself in the shadows of the staircase until he emerged. It would not do for him to know what she was about to attempt, or he would surely forbid her from attempting it at all.

212

Braxton was so absorbed in his ledger that he did not so much as glance up as he crossed the polished marble floors of the entrance hall a few minutes later. Eliza waited for him to vanish through one of the doors concealed in the paneling and then approached the study door, knocking briskly before she could doubt her decision.

"Come in," came the deep-voiced reply.

Elder Hallewell was at his desk, poring over a stack of papers. He glanced up and blinked, surprised to see Eliza standing there, and put his pen down upon the desk top. He smiled somewhat indulgently at her, from which she took courage.

"Eliza! I'm glad you're here, I've been meaning to speak with you since we arrived back from the palace."

Eliza's heart, pounding in her chest just a moment before, seemed to stop as she dropped into a curtsy. "Have you, sir?"

"Yes, indeed. I wanted to thank you."

"Th-thank me, sir? Whatever for?" Eliza asked.

"For your assistance with Jessamine. I was nervous about our sojourn to the palace, a feeling I believe I confessed to you in the days before we left."

"Yes, sir, you did."

"I also requested your help in the matter, to ensure that Jessamine continued to cooperate with the arrangement between Reginald Morgan and herself."

Eliza swallowed back a licking flame of anger. "Yes, sir, I recall it well."

"Well, I must say that you have exceeded my expectations, even after seeing what you are capable of at the Presentation. The visit could not have gone more smoothly, and the wedding preparations are already in full swing. Jessamine has not only agreed to the union, but behaved impeccably in every aspect. I would not have gotten where I am today if I did not know how to give credit where credit is due, and I know much of the credit must go to you and your extraordinary faith."

He looked down at Eliza's hands clasped demurely in front of her, and she had to repress a shudder at the nakedly hungry gleam that came into his eyes when he contemplated her Riftmagic. She swallowed convulsively and cleared her throat before replying, "I do thank you sir, but I assure you, Miss Jessamine's dutiful behavior is due much more to her own faithfulness than my Influence."

Elder Hallewell smirked amusedly, and it was clear he thought Eliza was simply being humble. "Regardless, I thank you. You will be rewarded, Eliza, for your commitment to the Path is clear."

Eliza curtsied again and, deciding that no better moment might present itself, she took a deep breath. "I am honored by your words, sir. I wonder if I might beg a favor of you?"

Elder Hallewell's smile broadened and he chuckled. "Ah, eager for that reward already, I see."

"No! It... it isn't a favor for me, sir. It's about Mrs. Spratt."

Elder Hallewell's face fell at once. "Yes? What about her?"

"Well, you see, sir, I met her daughter while I was at the palace," Eliza said. She kept her tone very light.

"Is that so?" Elder Hallewell inquired politely.

"Yes, sir. She works there, you see. She assisted me with the unpacking of the trunks and in the course of our conversation, she revealed that her mother worked at Larkspur Manor."

Elder Hallewell's eyebrows pulled together. Eliza knew she would have to play this very carefully indeed.

"First of all, sir, I think you should know how proud she was. Spoke of her mother's unshakeable commitment to her duty, how she was a paragon of faith, and that she only hopes that she, too, would have a chance to serve in such a way."

Elder Hallewell nodded. "Mrs. Spratt has served us faithfully for many years. That is true."

Eliza smiled. "She then told me she was getting married, sir, in just a fortnight's time, and that she wished her mother could be there to see it. She immediately dismissed the idea, knowing her mother's commitment to her post was absolute, but I wondered if it might not be arranged?"

"Your concern for others is admirable, but I do not see how that would be possible, Eliza. Mrs. Spratt has proven herself invaluable to the peace and safety of our household. She cannot be spared," Elder Hallewell said, smiling indulgently and then turning back to his desk.

But Eliza would not be dismissed so easily. She stepped forward and raised her voice slightly. "Oh, that's what I told her, sir, and I'm sure Mrs. Spratt would say the same thing, if she knew. But then, I wondered if I might not be able to help?"

Elder Hallewell spun back around, one eyebrow quirked with curiosity. "And how do you propose to do that?"

214

Eliza dropped her eyes. "You'll forgive me if I sound boastful, sir, for it is not my intention, but you have yourself but a few moments ago expressed confidence in my abilities as an Influencer. Might it not be possible for me to help out with Mrs. Hallewell, to keep her quiet and content for just a few hours so that Mrs. Spratt might see her only child get married?"

Elder Hallewell hesitated, as though trying to figure out how to deny Eliza's request without sounding like a monster, for she had phrased it very carefully. She met his gaze steadily, solemnly, hands clasped and fairly vibrating with the urge to reach out and work her persuasion on him just as he demanded she use it on his daughter. She let the silence lengthen, and then as he struggled to respond, she dropped her eyes again, letting color flood her cheeks.

"Forgive me, sir. It was not my place. I should not have suggested it. I just thought, when the idea came to me, that it must be the way to illuminate another step along the Path, sir—another way I could make myself useful to the Hallewell family and help another faithful Riftborn as well. But I can see that I have overstepped. I... beg your pardon, sir. I will take my leave."

She turned, praying as she had never prayed in her life. And then, before she had taken more than two steps...

"Wait."

Maintaining rigid control over her expression, she turned. Elder Hallewell was peering thoughtfully at her. She forced herself to breathe slowly and evenly, waiting.

"Eliza, I think you may be right," Elder Hallewell drawled. "You have proven your gifts are more than adequate to maintain control over Mrs. Hallewell in her... condition. I daresay you would prove even more adept at the task than Mrs. Spratt, who, I am sorry to say, has allowed her control to waver on several occasions of late. I have had to speak with her regarding the matter. But," he stroked his chin, contemplating, "perhaps a show of good faith on my part would reinvigorate her commitment to her calling. It is, as you say, only a few hours."

Eliza did not move or speak. She was afraid to break the spell, afraid to say or do anything that might nudge him to change his mind.

"Yes, I shall allow it," he said at last. "I must ask you not to speak to her of the matter. I shall tell her myself, and set the terms of the arrangement. You are quite sure this wedding will not interfere with your commitment to Jessamine?" he added sharply.

"Oh, yes, sir. I considered the matter very carefully in that regard, or I shouldn't have dreamed of bringing it to your attention," Eliza said promptly. "The wedding is this coming Sunday afternoon, at the Riftborn parish on Pentonville Road. Miss Jessamine will be at her charity circle meeting at Elmhurst Hall, sir, and will not arrive home until late in the evening, by which time the ceremony will be long over and Mrs. Spratt returned to her post. Miss Jessamine shall never miss me for a moment, sir, I can promise you that."

Elder Hallewell nodded his satisfaction and turned back to his desk. "Very well. I shall speak to Mrs. Spratt about it. You may go, Eliza."

"Yes, sir. Thank you, sir," Eliza mumbled, bobbing a last curtsy and hurrying toward the door.

"Oh, and Eliza."

Eliza turned obediently on her heel.

"How are you feeling? Shipshape and all that?"

She blinked. "Feeling, sir?"

"Yes. I understand one of the scullery maids has come down with Riftsickness. I was just discussing the matter with your father."

"You mean Bridie!" Eliza blurted out before she could stop herself, her heart careening into a gallop again.

"I think that was her name, yes," Elder Hallewell said, so dismissively that Eliza felt another uncontrolled flame of anger lick at her insides. "I have tasked your father with ensuring that the rest of the staff are seen to. He shall be questioning the lot of you regarding symptoms and warning signs. Shocking that a case of Riftsickness could appear in my household, but every chain has a weak link somewhere, I suppose."

Behind her back, Eliza clenched her hands into fists. "Yes, sir," she managed from between her teeth.

"But you," Elder Hallewell said, smiling at her as though she were a prize horse that had just won him a race, "you aren't such a link, are you, my dear?"

Eliza swallowed back bile as she returned his smile. "No, sir. Weakness is a fault to which I shall endeavor never to succumb," she said, and walked from the room.

The words were a promise to herself, and to Bridie, too. She thought of Eli's letter, no more than ash in the bottom of her grate. She had never felt so recklessly eager to answer one of his summonses.

TWENTY-ONE

E LIZA HURRIED AROUND to the side door where Sully had instructed her to come in the future. She could see the warm cozy light of the kitchen seeping into the little alleyway beside the house as she stepped around the corner. She lifted her hand to knock, but before she could, the door swung open. Eli's face appeared, looking intensely relieved to see her.

"I'm glad you could get away," he whispered. "Come in."

Eliza followed him into the house and stood uncertainly in the doorway as Eli rushed around getting ready. She watched him button his jacket and lace up his boots, before pulling a cap low over his eyes.

"Why did you want me to come here?" Eliza asked. "Wouldn't it have been easier to meet in the Barrens?"

"Yes, but that's not a place you want to be seen in that uniform, not at this time of night," Eli said. "I've got clothes for you to change into."

"You want me to leave my uniform?" Eliza asked, her hand rising automatically to the Larkspur Manor crest upon her cloak.

"Is that a problem?" Eli asked, frowning at her.

"I... no, of course not. I just hadn't thought..." Eliza stammered.

"It was Sully's idea," Eli explained. He tossed a pile of folded clothing to Eliza, who caught it. "She doesn't think it's wise for you to come and go around here or in the Barrens in your uniform. You'll be too easy to identify, and it will attract unwanted attention. If you're going to continue with the Resistance, you've got to try to blend in with the Riftborn in the city."

"You told Sully about our plans?"

"I had to. Surely you don't object?"

"No, I just... I'm surprised she's letting you help me. After all, this isn't exactly Resistance territory, is it, tracking down a manor servant none of you have ever met?"

"Yes, and no," Eli said. "She did disappear just after getting her hands on a book that we produced and distributed. It's worth our time to find out if that book is the reason for her disappearance or not, don't you agree?"

"I do agree! I just wasn't at all sure that Sully would," Eliza admitted.

"Well, she does, and she'll be standing by at the Bell and Flagon tonight to see what we're able to uncover, so we'd best get going. You can change in the pantry, it's just there on the left."

Eliza blushed scarlet and hurried into the pantry. Disguising herself made perfect sense, of course, but she still felt terribly exposed without her uniform. She realized that she had been counting on her status as a manor servant to protect her in some regards, and the thought of traversing the darker corners of the Barrens without it made her feel naked. She caught a glimpse of herself in her borrowed clothes: a rough wool skirt, an ill-fitting blouse, and a gingham-check kerchief wrapped around her hair. How much of her fear came from the acknowledgment that she was no different than the Riftborn she passed in the streets? That beneath the fancy uniform and the sheer luck of her position, she was just another Riftborn, despised for her magic and cast out for the same? She sighed and adjusted the neckline of the blouse. It was far past time to stop deluding herself that a manor crest upon her chest meant she was somehow special. She was always one misstep away from those she used to look down upon, and she'd do bloody well to remember it.

She emerged from the pantry with her uniform draped over her arm. She twirled on the spot. "Well? Will I blend in, do you think?"

Eli smirked. "You're still a bit clean, but you'll do. Let's go."

Eliza wanted to ask if they were going to walk all the way to the Barrens, but she didn't want to sound like she was complaining, so it was with an entirely silent prayer of gratitude that she watched Eli hail a carriage and open the door for her to climb in. She knew the carriage would not bring them all the way to their final destination, but at the very least it would save them the long walk to the edge of the district. Once they were safely ensconced in the rattling carriage, Eliza felt safe to ask more questions.

"Can you tell me any more about this plan of yours? Your letter was rather scant on the details. Who is this man we're going to meet?"

"He works for the Clerkenwell Workhouse, where you thought your friend may have gone. He also happens to be a frequent patron at... well, at an establishment I know of," Eli said, seeming to choose his words carefully. He paused.

"Go on," Eliza urged him.

"He's always there on Friday nights. We've got a plan to get some information out of him, but it might necessitate a little... persuasion. That's why I've asked you to come along."

Eliza blanched. "Do you mean... you want me to use my Riftmagic on him?"

"Only if we have no other choice," Eli said swiftly, an apologetic look on his face. "He's generally rather persuadable by... ah... other means, but we thought it prudent to use all the tools at our disposal."

"And that's what I am? A tool?" Eliza asked, her fear twisting at once into indignation.

"I thought you were a concerned friend who would be willing to do anything if it meant rescuing her friend. Do I have it wrong?" Eli asked, raising an eyebrow.

"No," Eliza sighed. "But I wish you would have warned me."

"If I had warned you, you wouldn't have come," Eli pointed out.

"I most certainly would have come!" Eliza cried.

"My humble apologies, then," Eli said. Eliza narrowed her eyes at him; she was sure that he had just barely managed to suppress a smirk.

"So what's the plan, then?" Eliza asked. "How does my Riftmagic come into it?"

"You'll see when we get there," Eli said. Eliza could not help but think, as they lapsed into silence, that he was avoiding telling her any more.

The carriage trundled over the border into the Barrens and several blocks along the High Street before the driver announced he would go no further. Eli thanked him and pressed some silver into his palm before extending a hand to help Eliza down onto the street. She had to move carefully to keep from tripping over her skirts which were several inches longer than they ought to have been—she guessed they might have belonged to Sully, who, although she did not often wear skirts, was at least six inches taller than Eliza.

Eli and Eliza walked together in silence for a few moments, but now that they were nearing their destination, Eliza had too many questions to allow the silence to continue.

"Where is it we're going, exactly?" Eliza asked, trying to sound as nonchalant as possible.

"It's a business run by a friend of Sully's. Her name is Lavender. Lower level Dignus frequent the place, and we've had success in the past getting information out of them."

"What kind of business is it? A pub?"

"Sort of."

"How can a place be 'sort of' a pub?"

"You'll see."

They were deeper into the Barrens than Eliza had ever been before. Here, it was as though the finer parts of the city did not exist. Eliza tried to imagine a Dignus setting foot here, but she could not fathom it. On a corner, a hoarse-voiced young man was hocking a damp-looking pile of leftover newspapers. Eliza did not need to listen to his cries to know what the headlines would be. Warnings against sin. Calls to worship and service. Reports of all the wonderful things the Illustratum had done for the country that week. Was any of it true, or was it all just a façade? She honestly didn't know what to believe anymore.

They passed under the sputtering light of a gas lamp and arrived at the corner of a crowded and dank little square. Here, Eli stopped so suddenly that Eliza, who had been focused on keeping her hem out of the puddles, nearly bumped into him. His face, as he looked down at her, was wary.

"If this is going to work, you'll have to blend in," Eli muttered.

"Yes, I assume that's why I'm dressed this way," Eliza said, tugging impatiently at the skirt again.

"I'm not just talking about the clothes. You'll need to... pretend not to be shocked."

Eliza blinked. "Shocked?"

Eli hitched a thumb over his shoulder to the bright façade of a building across the road. If Eliza had been looking where they were going rather than at her feet, she would have noticed it at once. Light glowed from every window, turned shocking shades of red and pink by the lacy curtains that had been drawn across them. A raucous blend of jaunty piano music and drunken laughter spilled out through the open door. Inside, women with painted faces and bedraggled dresses in a kaleidoscope of colors were floating around like a riot of summer blooms caught on the wind, laughing and touching and beckoning.

"A brothel!? You've brought me to a brothel?!" The words escaped Eliza in little more than a squeak. She could feel the mortification filling her up, coloring her cheeks, filling her ears with a buzzing sound.

"I told you you wouldn't have come if I'd warned you," Eli pointed out, crossing his arms over his chest as though daring her to contradict him.

She could not. If she'd known this was where they were going, she'd have turned tail and fled without a second thought, though she wasn't about to admit it out loud. Her silence seemed to serve as confirmation enough, however. Eli's mouth turned down at the corners, and he looked at Eliza very seriously.

"Tell me now, Eliza. Can we count on you?"

Eliza hesitated. What was she so afraid of? Getting caught? She had already done enough in the past few weeks to earn a sentence in the Praeteritum, if not a noose on the gallows, and yet she had still gone through with it all. Was she afraid of what she would see in the brothel? What did it matter? She might never have set foot in such an establishment before, but she wasn't so naive not to know that they existed, as well as what went on in them. Was she really going to give up what might be her only chance to find Bridie because she felt... what even did she feel? Embarrassment? Shame? Judgment? She began to wonder, with a pang of horror, if there was a single feeling or opinion inside her that the Illustratum hadn't methodically placed there? A reckless sort of courage rose up in her, a rebellious cutting of the strings. She would no longer be their puppet.

Without answering Eli, she lifted her chin defiantly and began to march toward the door. Eli caught her elbow and she glared at him, but he was grinning.

"I thought you wanted to know if you could count on me?" Eliza demanded, looking down at his hand on her arm. "Well, you can. And so can Bridie. Now let's go."

Eli released her at once with a wary glance at her hands, thinking, perhaps, of her gift. "I appreciate your enthusiasm, but we can't just barge in the place, Eliza. We've got to be discreet."

Eliza stopped in her tracks, momentarily sheepish. "Oh. Right. Well, after you, then."

Eli grinned again, but there was no trace of mockery in the expression. On the contrary, something in it made Eliza want to blush. Surrendering to the fact that she would probably be blushing for the rest of the evening, she heaved a sigh and followed Eli into a narrow alleyway around the side of the building.

As soon as they had been swallowed up by the shadows in the alleyway, (Eliza wished she could wrap herself securely in them and vanish altogether, just like Colin) a door cracked open and Jasper poked his head out. His mouth fell open at the sight of Eliza standing behind Eli.

"You're *joking*," he muttered, just loudly enough that Eliza could hear him.

A second head poked out of the door, and Eliza recognized Zeke. He was grinning.

"What did I tell you? That's five *venia* in my pocket, pay up," Zeke hooted.

Jasper's face twisted into a sour expression as he dug into his pocket and extracted the coins, slapping them into Zeke's palm. "You're buying the drinks, then," he grumbled.

"No one's buying any drinks," Eli snapped, and with a single touch, he shattered the glass in Jasper's hand, showering the ground with ale and causing Jasper to curse as he leaped back in an attempt not to get drenched.

"What the hell did you do that for?" he growled.

"Because we're not here to get pissed. We have work to do, and if you cock it up because you couldn't lay off the ale, Sully's going to do to your sorry arse what I just did to that glass," Eli said through clenched teeth.

Jasper curled his lip, and Zeke laid a restraining hand on his shoulder. "Not to worry, Eli. That's the only one he's had, and he didn't even get to drink it." He chuckled, and Jasper shook off his hand, looking sullen.

"What does he owe you the money for?" Eli asked, still frowning at Jasper as though expecting to have to blow something else up.

"He bet Miss Braxton here wouldn't show up. In fact, I'm willing to bet that's why he agreed to help you in the first place. I told him she had more backbone than that, and I was right. Naturally." Zeke winked at Eliza, whose lips curled into a tentative smile in spite of herself.

224

Well, if the burly, tough-as-nails barkeep thought she had a backbone, perhaps she did. She tried to envision it, standing a little taller and trying to relax the hands currently clenched into anxious balls at her sides. She also avoided Jasper's antagonistic gaze; she knew he would do nothing to bolster her meager supply of courage.

"Is everything still in place?" Eli asked.

Jasper gave up glaring at Eliza and turned his attention back to his brother. "He's just gotten off his shift at the workhouse. He's only just sat down for a pint."

"Excellent. And the girls?" Eli prompted.

"Lavender's set Clarabelle and Penny on him. Poor blighter doesn't stand a chance."

Eli smirked. "Excellent. Well, then, how shall we—"

"Not so fast, lad," Zeke said, holding up a work-roughened hand. "Lavender wants to see you first. Both of you."

Eli's smile faltered. "What for?"

"You think she explained herself to me?" Zeke asked with a snort. "Just go see her, and be quick about it. I don't know how long the girls can distract him before he decides he needs a different kind of distraction." He waggled his eyebrows at Eliza.

Eli grimaced, but beckoned to Eliza to follow him. Jasper and Zeke stepped back inside to let them pass and then closed the door behind them.

Eliza followed Eli down a long, narrow corridor just off of the main tavern room. Eliza kept her eyes focused on the back of Eli's brown wool coat, trying not to interpret the flashes of the rooms beyond that revealed themselves each time they passed a doorway. Once she thought she saw a woman being pulled into a man's lap. The woman was laughing, but also slapping at the man's hands. Someone was sitting at a piano, plunking out a raucous tune, and several voices were now raised in an enthusiastically slurred chorus.

Eli stopped in front of the door at the end of the corridor and knocked. Eliza was too distracted to hear if anyone bade them come in, but a moment later, Eli tugged at her sleeve and pulled her through the door with him.

"Lavender, this is Eliza. Eliza, this is Madam Lavender," Eli said formally, gesturing between Eliza and the grandly dressed woman draped across a velvet chaise lounge. "This is her establishment we've disrupted this evening."

"How do you do?" Eliza said, dropping automatically into a curtsy.

Madam Lavender arched a single, incredulous eyebrow before turning to Eli. "Well, this should be amusing, if nothing else."

"Zeke said you wanted to see us," Eli prompted.

"Yes. And now that I've seen the girl, I'm damn glad I did," Lavender snorted.

Eliza stiffened and glanced at Eli, who smiled encouragingly before turning back to Lavender. "I'm afraid I don't follow."

"Well, I know Sully's not a fool. I knew she wouldn't let the girl come in here in her uniform. But I also know Sully, and well..." her voice trailed off with a smirk as she eyed Eliza's clothes, and it was clear that she believed the thought needed no completion. "I guess we should be glad it's not trousers."

"Did you have something else in mind?" Eli asked, a slight edge of panic to his polite tone.

"She's going to have to blend in with the girls, Eli. No one's going to believe she's here as a customer."

Eli looked at Eliza, his eyes widening. It was clear this wasn't going the way he'd planned. "Can't you... put her behind the bar? Give her a rag and let her wipe down some tables or something?"

Lavender's lips twisted. "Not dressed like that, I can't. Come off it, Eli, you know the standards I set around here. Even the girls who don't service the customers dress like they might take a notion to at any moment." Lavender paused at the look of dawning horror on Eliza's face. "Love, if you hope to get information out of one of my regulars, you're going to have to do better than that." She gestured limply at the ill-fitting blouse and skirt Eliza had been so loath to change into, the ensemble she now clutched to with both hands as though she never wanted to wear anything else again as long as she lived.

"What do you propose then?" Eli asked, the question prying its way through his teeth with difficulty.

"Well, seeing as I anticipated this might be a problem, I've got two of the girls waiting upstairs in my private quarters armed with all the necessaries. A few minutes in their capable hands, and Miss Braxton here will be damn near unrecognizable."

Eliza watched the conversation back and forth between the two of them, comprehension dawning slowly. Before she had had even a

226

moment to process the realization of what was about to happen to her, both Eli and Lavender turned to look expectantly at her.

"Well, what will it be, love?" Lavender sighed. "I ain't got all night here. Tabitha and Edith are needed back out on the floor, and your mark won't wait long once he's had his fill at the bar."

Eli's face was tortured with guilt. "I'm sorry, Eliza. But it may be the only way to—"

"No, it's fine. I'll do it." The words were out of Eliza's mouth before she had decided to say them, and she pressed her lips together as soon as she'd spoken so that she couldn't take them back.

Eli's eyes widened. "Are you sure?"

"Oh, for Creator's sake, Eli, just let me get on with it before I change my mind!" Eliza cried, her voice slightly shrill. She didn't know where this sudden fount of courage was springing from. All she knew was that all she could see in her mind's eye was Bridie's face, looking lost and scared.

Lavender looked as though she couldn't decide whether to laugh or not. Then she caught Eliza's defiant eye and smothered the impulse. It was clear she hadn't expected Eliza to agree.

"Off you get, then, up those stairs, first door on your left."

Eliza turned and marched up the stairs before she could talk herself out of it, Eli close on her heels. Every lecture she'd ever heard about lascivious women and dens of iniquity reared up inside her, each one seeming to come to life in her memory, to rail and shout at her as she climbed upward. She ignored them.

The door at the top of the stairs was closed, but Eliza could hear the tinkling laughter emanating from the room on the other side. She hesitated with her hand on the knob, trying not to hyperventilate.

"Eliza..."

Eliza did not turn to look at Eli. She didn't want to see the guilt or doubt or whatever emotion it was that had made her name sound so heavy in his mouth. She squared her shoulders and cleared her throat.

"Don't, Eli. It may be the only way to find out what happened to Bridie. It's just a bit of paint. I'll survive."

They both knew it was much more than "just a bit of paint," but neither of them said anything else. Eliza turned the knob and pushed the door open.

The first thing Eliza saw was the purple silk dress blooming like a garish flower on a dressing screen in the middle of the floor. And then, like buzzing bees emerging from the petals, two of Lavender's girls revealed themselves, already frowning and clicking their tongues in a disapproving manner as they descended upon her.

"This is her, is it, then?"

"Bloody hell, Eli, you might have brought us a bit more to work with."

Eliza turned to Eli, eyebrows raised. "On a first name basis already, I see," she muttered. Eli grinned a bit sheepishly before turning to the girls.

"Tabitha. Edith. Lovely to see you both."

The one called Tabitha pouted her painted lips. "But not lovely enough to come along with your brother when he pays us a visit," she cooed.

Eli shrugged. "What can I say, girls? I'm a busy man and my pockets are shallow."

Edith had already turned to Eliza and was now walking around her with an appraising eye. After she'd walked all the way around her twice, Edith took Eliza's startled face in both of her hands and turned it forcefully from side to side, examining every angle. Eliza was too shocked at the familiarity to pull away, even when the girl's fingernails bit into her chin.

"Never worn color a day in your life, have you, poppet?" Edith sighed, and there was so much certainty in her tone that Eliza didn't bother to confirm it. "It's almost a shame to cover up such skin, isn't it, Tabby?"

Tabitha snorted. "Pale as a ghost, it's true, but it'll only draw attention to her, and we've been made to understand she needs to blend in." Tabitha turned to Eli, her eyebrows raised, waiting for his confirmation.

"Um, yes, please. As best you... you can," he replied, clearing his throat and avoiding Eliza's eye.

Tabitha nodded, then turned to Eliza. "Well, sit down, love. We've got some work to do."

Eliza sat down and closed her eyes, determined to witness as little of her transformation as possible. If she couldn't see what they'd done to her face, perhaps she could pretend they hadn't done anything at all.

This plan failed swiftly, however, for at each new sound and smell, Eliza's eyes fluttered open, allowing her morbid curiosity to overrule her horror. She watched helplessly as they smeared her with a kind

228

of white paste that dried to a powdery finish and made her look as though she'd been cast from plaster. Next, they attacked her cheeks with a pot of something pink that smelled vaguely of metal. Then they used a small horsehair brush to paint her lips from another pot of color, this one a deeper tone close to red. All the while as they worked, they chatted blithely together about customers and frocks and Madam Lavender's rules.

"Don't see what the harm is for most of us. We know when we've had enough," Edith grumbled as she started pulling the hairpins from Eliza's bun.

"Aye, well, you've got sense, haven't you? Same can't be said for some of the others. Take Paulina. She'll drink as many as they'll buy her, and then what? She can't perform to Lavender's standards if she can't even stand up. Some of the customers have complained."

"Fancy them complaining when they're the ones getting her drunk," Edith declared with a roll of her eyes. "You'd think they want to take her unconscious. Some of them do, you know," she added in a whisper to Eliza, who could feel her skin blushing beneath the thick layers of paint.

"If she can't be on her guard and watch out for herself, a girl's got no business taking a customer," Tabitha announced, and it was clear that she would brook no disagreement on this point.

"True enough, I suppose. Still, a girl should have the right to a stiff drink before facing down some of that lot," Edith muttered. Tabitha laughed darkly and did not argue.

It was not the first time Eliza had to close her mouth after it had popped open in shock at the glibness with which these women discussed their work, and it would not be the last as they moved on to her hair, still bantering on about customers they'd shared and gossip they'd heard about one or another of the other girls.

"Would you look at that head of hair," Tabitha murmured, letting out a low whistle as Eliza's hair swung free at last from the remainder of the hairpins and fell in a shining curtain to her waist. Eliza didn't know what to say. She'd never thought much about her hair, except when she had to drag a comb through it after she'd washed it. She'd never stopped to consider if it was beautiful because she had only ever been taught to hide it as thoroughly as possible. Now, as the two girls remarked upon it, running their fingers through it and declaring it shiny and thick, she wondered if her hair might not be something to be proud of. It was amazing how quickly her mind stamped out the thought, declaring it frivolous vanity.

"We'll have to cover up that Riftmark, too," Tabitha said, eyeing Eliza's wrist. "It's more than Lavender's life's worth to let someone see an Influencer working her customers. She'd be shut down before she could blink, and I know she loves Sully and all that, but she'll not lose everything she's built just for one of Sully's crazy schemes."

"They're not crazy," Eli said quietly.

"If you like," Tabitha replied under her breath. It was clear her mind remained unchanged.

Eliza did not argue now—perhaps because, given everything else terrifying that was happening to her with makeup, dabbing some beige paint and powder on her wrist seemed like the least of her worries. All of the tugging and teasing and rolling and pinning of her hair must finally have resulted in something resembling a finished hairstyle, for Tabitha was now tilting her head from side to side to examine all angles, a satisfied smirk on her face.

"Just like one of the girls. Right, now let's get you into that frock," Edith said.

There was a tall, gilt-framed mirror on the wall, which Eliza pointedly ignored as she stood on trembling legs and walked around the back of the dressing screen. Before she disappeared behind it, she gave Eli a pointed look. He looked at her blankly for a moment, and then comprehension dawned on his face and he excused himself at once to the hallway, his cheeks every bit as red as Eliza's now.

Behind the screen, Tabby and Edith continued their ministrations, not even bothering to ask as they tugged the garments from Eliza's body and tossed them into a heap on the floor. Eliza stood frozen, her hands clutching desperately at her undergarments, trying to fight back the tears welling in her eyes.

Tabitha caught a glimpse of her face and her businesslike expression suddenly softened. "Take a deep breath, love. We ain't gonna hurt you. Just a bit of dress-up is all."

Eliza did not trust herself to answer. She pressed her lips together and nodded.

"Lavender said something about a friend of yours? Gone missing?"

Again, Eliza simply nodded. A tear leaked from her eye and ran down her cheek. She batted it away impatiently.

Both Tabitha and Edith stopped what they were doing, their previously cheerful manner evaporating in a moment. They looked at each other.

"We understand how you feel, love," Tabitha said.

"It's happened here, more times than I care to remember," Edith added.

This unlocked Eliza's lips. She met Edith's gaze and asked, "You have friends who've gone missing?"

Tabitha laughed, but it was a bitter sound, devoid of humor. "Comes with the territory."

"It's one of the reasons you don't see many of the girls venturing out," Edith added.

"Not alone, anyway. Too dangerous."

Eliza looked between the two women. "Venturing out? You mean, around the Barrens?"

"That's right. You might be ready to run screaming out the door, love, but we're safer inside this place than out of it." Tabitha said.

"Don't you... I'm sorry, but isn't your job sort of... well... dangerous?" Eliza asked tentatively.

Edith chuckled. "Not as dangerous as what could happen to us if one of our customers spots us in the wild."

"I don't underst—"

"Here we've got protection. Rules. Everyone who walks in that door knows what would happen if they caused trouble for one of Lavender's girls. Lavender might be a Riftborn, and a woman, but she's a damn powerful one, and she's got weapons none of them want her to use."

"What kinds of weapons?" Eliza breathed, distracted for a moment from her plight.

"Best kind of weapon there is: information," Tabitha said, grinning now. "Just the right fact whispered in just the right ear, and she could bring fully half the men in this city to their knees. It's the reason she's been able to operate this long without getting shut down."

"But outside these walls, there's not much she can do for us, which is why so many of us stay," Edith sighed, examining the beginnings of crow's feet around her eyes in the mirror.

"Men get possessive, see," Tabitha explained, for Eliza was looking perplexed again. "They have their little fantasies, and Creator knows their cold little English wives won't indulge them. So they come here, where the women are a little more... willing."

"But fantasies are expensive," Edith added. "English wives ain't much for fantasies, but they are bloody attentive to where all the money goes, especially if there ain't much of it coming in. And so if a man sees an opportunity to just take what he wants without paying for it..."

"But...*oh*," Eliza gasped as she understood the implications thick in Edith's tone.

"So we know what it means to watch our backs, and each others', too," Tabitha said. "And if that's why you're here, you should know we're happy to help."

Eliza forced a reluctant smile. "Thank you."

Tabitha shrugged. "Ain't all that much trouble. Worth it, to see the look on your face when we've finished with you." Eliza blushed again, and Tabitha laughed heartily. "Now, that corset's not doin' what it ought, for our purposes."

This declaration began a process of grabbing, adjusting, hoisting, pushing, and tightening that left Eliza gasping for air and desperate to crawl into a hole where no one would ever see her. Her corset had never been so tight, and never had her own breasts been thrust so prominently into view. Indeed, she had no idea her breasts could even accomplish such a feat. She closed her eyes again and tried to take slow breaths that could no longer reach deeply enough to calm her. She felt her arms pulled upward, felt the silk of the purple dress slide down over her body, felt the little tugs and jerks that meant that it was being fastened and buttoned into place. The fabric had an almost overwhelming scent of perfume, floral and sickly sweet, making Eliza's head spin. At last, Tabitha and Edith stepped away from her. Edith sighed.

"There you are, love. Just one of the girls."

Before Eliza could reply—not that she had the slightest idea what to say—Madam Lavender's voice boomed out from the other side of the door.

"What's taking so long up here?"

"We've just finished, Lavender. Come have a gander," Tabitha called.

The door swung open and Lavender and another of her girls

stepped through it just as Edith dragged Eliza out from behind the dressing screen. Lavender's eyes boggled.

"Well done, Tabby, Edith. She looks like I could put her to work right now."

"As long as no one looks at the expression on her face," Edith giggled.

"Or her teeth," Tabitha agreed. "Try to keep your mouth closed, love, ain't no girl workin' here what's got teeth as fine as them."

Eliza snapped her mouth closed and tried to ignore the way the women were staring at her. Unfortunately, at that moment, Eli ducked through the door behind Lavender. A spasm of something that might have been amusement flashed across his features, but he controlled it at once, composing himself into an almost detached demeanor. Eliza narrowed her eyes to glare at him.

"There ya go, love," Tabitha said, clapping her hands once. "If you can't look seductive, go on and look angry. The patrons expect the girls around here to have a bit of fire in 'em."

"You'll want to keep your eyes open for wayward hands," Edith said, serious now. "The men who come here will try to get a handful of any girl what walks too close, especially if they can't pay for their own."

"Walk the perimeter of the room," Lavender said. "Keep your back to the wall when possible."

"If you've got to interact with any of them, just laugh at whatever they say and keep moving," Edith said. "We don't want anyone getting 'hold of you long enough to stake a claim."

"But I'll be hangin' around, so if they do, I'll make sure they know you ain't available," Tabitha said.

Eliza tried to swallow, her mouth feeling like it was full of sand. "What do you mean?"

"We've got a few girls here who are special favorites of some of our more prestigious clientele," Lavender said smoothly. "They're... reserved, if you like."

"Not on the menu," Edith added, grinning.

"That's usually warning enough for the riffraff to keep their distance," Lavender said.

"Don't make eye contact."

"Don't smile at anyone."

"Don't approach a table unless another of the girls is there—they've been told to look out for you."

Eliza held up a hand. "All right, I think I understand what I'm *not* supposed to do," she said. "Now Eli, perhaps you could tell me what I *am* supposed to do."

Eli stepped forward, clearing his throat. "Ladies, we are most grateful for your assistance, but the fewer details you have about this, the safer you'll all be."

Far from looking startled at this pronouncement, Tabitha, Edith, and Lavender all nodded their heads and shuffled out of the room at once. Only the girl who had entered the room with Lavender remained. She had said nothing at all since she had appeared, keeping her arms crossed over her chest and looking affronted. Eli noticed Eliza's eyes lingering on her questioningly and turned to make the introduction.

"Penny, this is Eliza. Eliza, meet Penny."

"How do you do?" Eliza asked automatically. Penny merely nodded once, curtly.

Eliza was about to ask why Penny had stayed, while the other women had left, but she was distracted from her question by the look that had now appeared on Eli's face. She could tell he was trying very hard to keep his eyes fixed firmly on her face and not the rest of her ludicrous disguise.

"Oh, I think you should keep the dress, it suits you," he said.

"Shut your mouth, Eli Turner," Eliza snapped.

He tsk-ed. "Now, now, that's not very ladylike."

"You'd better get to the instructions, or I'll show you just how unladylike I can be," Eliza said through clenched teeth.

Eli's mouth twitched, but he composed himself. "All right, then. When you get downstairs, go to the bar. The barkeep, Harry, will give you a tray. Walk the outside of the room and collect any abandoned flagons or plates. Stick to the edges, and don't approach any table with anyone still sitting at it. You'll be safer that way."

"Okay, I can do that," Eliza muttered, mostly to herself. "Go on."

"Patrick Guilford, our mark, is already here. Penny here is going to lure him to a table near the back."

"Does Penny know what we're trying to do?" Eliza asked, flicking her eyes to the girl and then back again.

"Yes, I've told her everything."

234

"Is that safe?"

"Penny is a member of the Resistance. Several of the girls are," Eli said.

"Really?"

Penny's mouth twisted into a defiant expression. "Is that so surprising?" she asked, speaking for the first time. She had a sweet, clear voice completely at odds with the outfit she wore.

"I... no, of course not. I didn't mean—I just didn't realize."

"And I didn't realize that Eli thought me so incompetent at my job that he would need to bring in a manor prude to do it for me," Penny hissed, turning her glare on Eli.

"I don't think you're incompetent at all, Penny," Eli said, closing his eyes for a moment as though searching for patience. "But we only get one shot at this, and might need a bit more persuasion than your natural charms, that's all."

Penny snorted incredulously. "They've never failed me before."

"Well, we've never found ourselves in quite this kind of situation before," Eli said patiently. "This isn't meant to be an insult to your prodigious talents, Penny. She's just here as a bit of insurance. It's her friend that's gone missing, after all."

Penny's mouth twisted. Eli sighed.

"Come on, out with it, Penny. Something's obviously bothering you, and we're running out of time."

"I don't understand why we're taking such a big risk for some manor girl who isn't even part of the Resistance," Penny said, crossing her arms tightly across her chest. "What business is it of ours if she's missing?"

"Because it was most likely one of Sully's books that got her into this mess," Eli said slowly. "And if the Illustratum decides to question her, there's a chance the entire Resistance could be exposed. We want to find her and bring her home before that can happen."

"You think she'd rat us out, and you want to save her anyway?" Penny asked.

"She wouldn't get anyone in trouble on purpose!" Eliza snapped, and Penny looked her in the face for the first time. "I don't know how she got her hands on the book, but I do know that she has no idea what she's caught up in. She's my friend and it's my fault she's in this mess, and so I need to help get her out of it—get us all out of it."

235

"It sounds like we would have been better off never getting the likes of her involved in the first place."

"You sound like Jasper."

"Even Jasper spouts some sense on occasion," Penny said. "I never met a manor girl I could trust. I never met one who didn't look at me like I was a bit of filth she ought to scrub clean with her piousness. And I'm not sure you're any better," she added, looking Eliza up and down.

Eliza stiffened. "I'm not sure I am either," she admitted. "But I assure you, I am trying to be."

Penny blinked in surprise, and then almost smiled as she looked Eliza over one more time. "Well, the disguise is a step in the right direction. Harder to look down on a girl once you've walked in her shoes. And..." she squinted harder at Eliza's feet. "blast it, I think those *are* my shoes! Ugh, when I get my hands on Tabby..."

"Penny, there will be plenty of time to murder Tabby later," Eli cried. "Can we get back to the plan, please? Guilford is waiting for you!"

Penny's expression was still murderous as she looked up from the pilfered shoes, but she nodded grudgingly.

"Keep your eyes on Penny. She'll be working on Guilford, getting his guard down. She'll signal you when Guilford is ready for another drink. You'll bring it over and then stay nearby. Penny is going to move around to the back of him while they're chatting. Once she's behind him, he won't be able to tell whose hand is on him. If all goes well, you'll be able to make contact with him without him being any the wiser, and he'll start telling us everything we need to know."

"And if all doesn't go well?" Eliza asked.

"We'll cross that bridge when we get to it," Eli said, a little too lightly.

"Just follow my lead," Penny said, and though her arms were still crossed tightly over her chest her voice was just a bit softer. "I know Guilford. I know how to distract him. Do what I tell you, and we'll be all right, I reckon."

Eliza nodded. Penny turned on her heel and stomped out of the room without further comment. Eli watched her go, then turned back to Eliza.

"Are you ready?"

"As ready as I'll ever be, which is to say, not at all. After you," Eliza said, gesturing to the door.

TWENTY-TWO

A S THEY DESCENDED the stairs in silence, Eliza felt a strange current running through her. It was more than nervousness—more, even, than fear, though she felt plenty of that. It was... excitement. She could feel her gift buzzing in her fingertips, and she realized that she was eager to use it, for once, in a way that would help someone—*truly* help someone, not just placate them to the Illustratum's will. It was as if her magic had come to understand that it was about to be used for the first time in true service to its owner, and not in service of other shadowy masters to whom it did not and could never belong.

Imagine, it seemed to be whispering to her. *Imagine what we could do.* The whisper inspired terror and elation in equal measure.

The sounds of the main room echoed down the hallway, pulling her forward into a riotous atmosphere where everything was too much—the sounds, the colors, the smells, the heat. She felt like she had landed in the middle of a strange fever dream, and clung to the feeling. If it was all a dream, she would wake up, and none of it would be real. She took a deep breath and walked into the space.

Though she felt so conspicuous that surely everyone would stop and turn to stare at her, she drew not a single curious gaze as she approached the bar. Tabitha and Edith had done their job—she blended seamlessly into the crowd of Lavender's girls. Eli took a seat at the bar and nodded once to the barkeep, who pulled out a wooden tray, tossed a damp rag on it, and handed it wordlessly to Eliza. Eliza held it for a moment, hesitating, then scanned the room until she found another girl with a tray. She tried to imitate the casual way the girl had the tray tucked against her hip, helping to balance the weight of it as she filled it with empty plates and flagons. Once the tray felt secure, she threw one last glance at Eli, who nodded encouragingly, and set off around the room.

She kept her eyes on her task, glancing up only to locate Penny and Mr. Guilford who, as Eli had told her they would be, were cozied away in the far back corner of the room. As she spotted them, Penny threw her head back to laugh, locked eyes with Eliza, and winked at her, cocking her head as though inviting her to join them. Eliza returned the wink nervously and then started to work her way more quickly around the room toward them.

Men were shouting things like, "Come on now, darlin', I don't bite," and "Give a fella a kiss, there's a good lass," but she did not stop to see if any of these comments were directed at her. Suddenly a hand shot out from a nearby table and grabbed her by the wrist. She barely suppressed a scream and looked up to see Zeke grinning at her. He pulled her closer, and though his face looked playful, his words were serious.

"We're right here, lass, if things go south. We'll get you out safe and sound, don't worry," he said.

Then he smiled again, wider this time, as though reminding her, and she hastily smiled back. Then, feeling that she ought to play her part more thoroughly, she put on just enough of a Barren's lilt and replied, "Ain't got time for empty promises, love, unless you want to buy me a drink."

Zeke's grin widened, but she didn't know if that was because she was succeeding or failing at her ruse. Not waiting to find out, she continued her progress around the perimeter of the room until she stood at the table just behind Penny's. She allowed herself to brush against the back of Penny's dress, hoping the gentle swish of silk against silk would be enough to alert the girl to her presence. Without missing a beat, Penny swooped her arm across the table, snatched an empty glass, and turned to plunk it onto Eliza's tray, smiling as she did so.

"Thanks, Violet, love," she said pointedly, and Eliza understood that she was acknowledging her presence. Eliza nodded, afraid to answer out loud, in case her voice shook. She hurried to the bar, where she placed the empty glasses and plates upon the countertop. Before she could ask for it, the barkeep plunked another flagon of mead onto her tray, and Eliza returned to Penny and Guilford's table. Penny reached for the mead, winked surreptitiously at Eliza, and handed the flagon to Guilford, who barely seemed to notice it wasn't the same one. Eliza turned her back on them, pretending to busy herself with wiping down a table that was already perfectly clean. She listened hard as Penny began to expertly steer the conversation.

"You seem tired this week, Patrick. They drivin' you too hard over there at that workhouse?" Penny cooed, running her fingers through the man's sparse hair.

"Ach, that place is a hellhole," Guilford replied with a groan, leaning back in his chair and closing his eyes, clearly enjoying the feeling of Penny's fingers in his hair. As he leaned back, Eliza got her first clear glimpse of his face: bulbous nose, pockmarked skin, and small, watery eyes with eyelashes so fair they were almost invisible. A long scar ran down his left cheek, pink and puckered.

"I certainly never plan to see the inside of one," Penny said.

"With all the money you've gotten off me? Not likely," Guilford said with a laugh like the wheezing of a boiling kettle.

"What's it really like?" Penny asked, her voice alive with vibrant curiosity.

"Ah, come on, Penny, love, I didn't come 'ere to talk about work," Guilford complained.

"But I just find it so fascinating. I mean, working with *mad* people." She whispered the word and affected a little shiver.

"They ain't all mad, love," Guilford said. "Just them in the locked wards, what's overflow from the madhouses."

"Sure, sure, but you must still have quite a time of it. Tell me the maddest thing you've ever seen one of them do."

Guilford smirked now, clearly enjoying the attention. "Had one climb the wall with his bare hands and feet once. Just dug his fingers and toes into the rocks and up he went. Clung there like a cat until we could find a broom to beat him down with."

Penny gasped theatrically, which seemed to please Guilford. For someone who didn't want to talk about work, he certainly seemed to be enjoying the attention it was garnering him. "That ain't even the half of it," he went on. "Had a lunatic try to escape two days ago. I weren't on shift yet, but I heard about it from some of the other lads. Swingin' broken glass at 'em and all sorts. We got a dangerous job."

"I don't know how you're brave enough to work with lunatics,"

Penny practically purred. "I could never do something like that. I'd be too scared. You fancy another mead?"

As she spoke, Penny rose from her chair running her hands along Guilford's shoulders as she stepped around behind him. Eliza's stomach clenched. This was it, the signal Eli had mentioned. She dropped her rag, dried her hands quickly on her dress, and turned to watch. Penny looked pointedly at Eliza and then at her own fingers, drawing slow circles on the back of Guilford's neck. Eliza crept forward, watching the motion for a few moments until she was sure she could replicate it. Then, she reached her trembling fingers forward and touched the skin there just as Penny pulled her fingers away, continuing the same, slow circling movement. Both women held their breath, waiting to see if Guilford would notice the difference.

"That feels good, Penny, love," he murmured instead, closing his eyes and putting his feet up on his table.

Penny looked at Eliza and nodded, looking relieved, before answering Guilford again. "That's right. You deserve to relax. You work too hard."

Guilford snorted. "You mind telling my shrew of a wife that? Actually, on second thought, maybe you ain't the one to tell her." He laughed wheezily again, and Penny echoed him with her tinkling giggle. Eliza could hear the stress in it, but she doubted Guilford could; he still had his eyes closed, his arm lolling over one arm of his chair, looking like he might fall asleep.

That's right, just relax, Eliza thought, and even as she thought it, she felt Guilford's body slump a bit further down in his seat.

Penny watched a moment, then continued in a soft, seductive voice. "Tell me all about it. You look so tired. It must have been such a long week."

Eliza focused on Bridie in her mind, as she might have looked entering Clerkenwell Workhouse, wearing her uniform and her cloak. *This girl,* she thought. *Tell me about this girl.*

Guilford started speaking as though he were half asleep. "There was one nasty incident. Wasn't even one of me own charges. Just some waif what wandered in off the street."

Penny's head shot up, staring at Eliza with her eyes full of questions. Eliza nodded, her heart pounding in her chest. "Off the street, you say? My word, you get all sorts, don't you? Who was she, a beggar?"

"Nah, she were class, for a Riftborn. Manor girl, she was. Right pretty, too."

"Not prettier than me, though," Penny teased.

"Nah, Penny. Ain't no one prettier than you," Guilford mumbled, and his hand groped around for Penny. Eliza only just shifted her lower body out of the way in time for him to close his fingers around Penny's dress rather than her own. Guilford seemed to notice nothing, and reached up under Penny's skirts, stroking at her stockinged leg. Eliza felt the color rushing into her cheeks behind her porcelain face paint, but Penny seemed hardly to notice the man's groping hands, and carried on without so much as a hitch in her voice, her tone honey sweet.

"What happened? What was so nasty about it?"

Tell me everything, tell me what happened to the girl, Eliza thought, feeling the persuasion bleed from her fingertips and disappear into the man's flesh. She wanted to scream the words, to force them right out of the man, but she knew it would only backfire. *Gently,* she reminded herself, *or this will all be for nothing.*

"Well, I don't know what she were even there for, but I think the mistress said she grew up there, before she were taken on as a housemaid. I don't know why she came or what she did to land herself in so much trouble, but by the time I got there, she was already locked up."

Eliza froze in her gentle circling motion. It was only when Penny elbowed her sharply in the ribs that she resumed it, trying to breathe, trying to focus through the fear that had suddenly gripped her.

"They just locked up some girl off the street?" Penny asked, pulling a whiskey off a passing tray and placing it in Guilford's hand. She looked pointedly at Eliza.

Drink it. Eliza willed the order down through her fingertips, and the man slugged back the whiskey in a single go, spluttering slightly and then looking down at the glass as though wondering how it got there. Then he shrugged and plunked the empty glass down on the table with a satisfied belch.

"She were pokin' her nose where it didn't belong. Meddling, like," Guilford said, yawning widely. "We can't have Riftborn filth off the street questioning our establishment. It sets a bad example. The workhouses are run by the Illustratum, after all." The fact that he was stroking and fondling a Riftborn woman as he said this was not lost on Eliza.

"So, what happened, then? After they locked her up?" Penny said. She kept the urgency out of her voice, though her face was troubled.

"What's it matter to you anyway?" Guilford asked, sounding a bit impatient. "I didn't come here to talk, you know."

Penny laughed lightly. "I just find your job fascinating," she said, whispering the last word in his ear and biting gently at his earlobe. "Besides, we've got all night. I'm all yours."

Eliza, sensing an opportunity, sent more soothing thoughts down through her fingertips and then looked up, catching Eli's eye. *Whiskey,* she mouthed to him, and he leaned over to the barman at once. Within seconds, the barkeep had a generous dram poured and Eli handed it off to Tabitha as she passed, who floated across the room in a single, dancelike movement, depositing the glass into Penny's waiting hand, all of it so well choreographed that Eliza thought they must have done it all a hundred times before. Eliza and Penny both watched as Guilford downed the whiskey. It dribbled down his chin, and his words began to slur together as he spoke again, bowing to the pressure of Eliza's constant, silent persuasion. *Tell me about the girl. Tell me more about the girl.*

"You want to hear about fascinating? Just wait till you hear where I brought the nosy little wench."

"Where?" Penny whispered.

"Well, the higher-ups decided she needed to be put away. She ain't mad, but she's trouble. So we put her in the wagon and drove her across the river to Bedlam."

If there was a moment that Eliza might have cried out and lost her focus, this was it. Penny sensed her tension and reached out with her free hand to grip Eliza's upper arm. She shook it, and Eliza looked at her. Penny simply nodded, taking a slow deep breath, which Eliza imitated without conscious thought. *Keep it together,* Penny's eyes seemed to say. *We're almost there.*

Penny affected a shudder of horror and said, "Ooooooooh, Bedlam! I've heard such stories! And you actually went there? Weren't you scared?"

Guilford chuckled and puffed out his chest. "Not on your life. Ain't nothing Bedlam can dish out that I ain't seen before."

"I don't know how you could even set foot there. You're so *brave,*

Patrick." Even as Penny sighed the words into his ear, she looked at Eliza for direction. The question in her eyes was clear: *Have you got what you need?*

Eliza shook her head. *"Who,"* she mouthed. *"Who ordered it?"*

"Who? Who ordered that she be locked up?" Penny whispered, just a hint of a tremor in her voice. She leaned against Guilford, pressing herself into him.

"No one but an Elder can order someone into Bedlam," Guilford said, and then seemed to shake himself a bit. "But I shouldn't be talking about this. Say, what's with all the questions—"

Let it go, it doesn't matter, thought Eliza, just as Penny whispered, "I had no idea you get orders right from the Elders, Patrick. You're quite the catch, aren't you? So powerful."

Their combined efforts worked. Guilford's face, tense and suspicious a moment before, drooped into a satisfied smile. "Yeah, that's right. They need men like me they can rely on. Don't want to get their hands dirty, see? They need me."

"They aren't the only ones," Penny cooed, and nodded her head sharply at Eliza, who pulled her fingertips back from Guilford's neck just as Penny walked back around and threw herself into his lap.

And it was a good thing that Guilford was so suddenly and thoroughly distracted, because Eliza, disoriented from the prolonged use of her gift and the horror of discovering what had happened to Bridie, could not stay on her feet. Before she could find anything to steady herself on, she stumbled sideways right into a man at a neighboring table. He caught her automatically, his surprised expression transforming into a leer.

"What's this now?" he slurred, breathing a foul combination of ale and decay into her face, making her stomach heave.

"I... I'm so sorry, sir. I... lost my balance. Please excuse me," she muttered, desperately trying to find her bearings, but the room just kept spinning.

"Do you hear me complaining?" the man said, pulling her down onto his lap with both hands. "What's your name, then? Don't recall seeing your pretty face here before."

"V-Violet," Eliza gasped, barely able to remember her pseudonym as she grappled with her rising panic.

"And what's a gent got to pay for a tumble with a sweet little flower like you, eh?" the man asked, grasping a fistful of her hair and inhaling deeply.

"Oh, I'm—you can't—" Eliza stammered. She was concentrating so hard on gathering her faculties, preparing to use her magic to force the man to unhand her, that she didn't notice Eli's hand upon her until he had already yanked her from the man's grip.

"Oi!" Eli said. "Hands off, there, mate. She's bought and paid for." Both his voice and his manner were much rougher than she expected—a ruse, she knew, and yet she cringed instinctively away from him, too.

The man laughed. "A girl like that needs a real man to show her how it's done, not some boy barely out of short pants. Maybe I'll have a go when you've had your fun. Shouldn't take too long."

"Don't bet on it, mate," Eli said smoothly.

"Why not let the girl decide, eh?" the man went on, standing up now. Eliza could see his clothing was of much better quality than any of the other men she'd seen hanging about the place, and he carried a silver-topped cane. "What do you say, darling? I reckon I've got deeper pockets. You'll have a better time and get better paid for it."

Eli hesitated, clearly unsure how he should proceed. Eliza thought the man looked like he might be wealthy, one of the more prestigious clients Madam Lavender had warned about. If so, they could not afford to anger him. Imitating Penny's musical giggle, Eliza threw out her hands between the men so that her fingertips touched each of their chests.

"Now, now, gentlemen, let's just calm down," she said, feeling the sentiments bleed out from her fingertips and into both men's bodies. Both of their faces went slack, an almost dazed look coming over them as they struggled to remember what they were angry about. She took advantage of their momentary confusion to defuse the situation. People were staring. What would Penny do? Or one of the other girls?

The answer came to her, and she acted upon it before she could think or talk herself out of it. Still keeping her hand gently on the wealthy man's chest, she turned, wrapped her other arm around Eli's neck, and kissed him.

She was well in control of herself as Eli stood frozen in shock for a moment. But she was not prepared for the feelings that raced through her as he overcame his shock and kissed her back. As he wrapped an arm around her waist, as his lips began to move against hers—first tentatively, then almost urgently—she quite nearly forgot where she was and what she was doing. She only just managed to cling to these new and powerful feelings before they went flooding out of her fingertips and into the mind of the other man, now nearly forgotten, as she kissed a man for the very first time in her life.

It took every ounce of her self control to pull away. Eli stared down at her, his eyes dark with something she could not read. His breath came quickly, and he did not loosen his hold around her waist. Eliza tore her gaze away from him to smile at the second man, who was looking put out.

"I really must honor my commitment to this gentleman, seeing as he's paid in advance," she said, surprised to find that her breathlessness made her voice sound almost seductive. "But I do apologize for my clumsiness, sir, and I assure you that if I find myself unsatisfied with my choice for the evening, I'll come find you at once." She smiled, willing the man to do the same, and he did.

"I reckon I'll see you soon, then," he said, the smile becoming something of a leer, but he sat back down, all confrontation gone from his manner.

"Would you like me to send over some company while you're waiting?" Eliza asked, fingers still lingering on the man's chest, playing with his buttons now as an excuse to maintain contact. "Edith is looking exceptionally lovely tonight."

As though picking up a rehearsed cue, Edith floated over, a drink in hand. "I could fall into your lap too, if you like, but I'd be just as happy to be invited to sit down," she said, her voice caressing each word.

Isn't she lovely? Eliza watched the thought appear in the man's head, watched his expression toward Edith shift subtly, watched the smile spread across his face at the sight of her.

"Far be it from me to deny a lady an invitation," he said, patting his knee. Edith wrapped herself sinuously around him and handed him the drink. She caught Eliza's eye and winked, cocking her head subtly toward the stairs. The meaning was clear: *get the hell out while you can.*

Eliza didn't need telling twice. Entwining her fingers with Eli's she made her way through the tables toward the stairs that led to the rooms upstairs. Eli followed, his arm still wrapped around her waist. Eliza leaned heavily against him, for her fatigue at having used her gift so forcefully had not yet passed. She threw a quick glance over at Guilford's table, afraid she'd blown her cover somehow, but Penny had him well distracted, her lips pressed to his ear. He did not so much as glance at them as they passed.

Together, Eliza and Eli reached the top of the staircase and turned left. The moment they reached the cover of the darkened hallway, Eli pulled his arm back from her waist and shoved his hands into his pockets. He could barely meet her eye.

"I... I'm so sorry. That was exactly the kind of scene I was hoping we could avoid. You, uh... you improvised well."

Eliza was grateful the hallway was so dim, for she was sure not even the inch thick layer of paint she wore would be enough to hide how brightly scarlet she was blushing. "No, I'm sorry. I just... just tried to think of what the other girls would do."

"Yes, well, you uh...I think you played your part very convincingly." His voice was so hard to read, and it was too dim to see his expression. Eliza closed her eyes and wished for a hole to open up in the floor and swallow her whole. How could she have done something so foolish, so... reckless? How he must despise her now, for throwing herself at him like that. How she despised herself for wanting to do it all over again.

"Well?"

Eliza looked up to see Eli staring at her expectantly. She bit her lip. What did he want? An apology? An explanation? She struggled to string together her words, but Eli huffed impatiently.

"Bridie! What did you figure out?"

Eliza gasped. The stress of the confrontation and the intensity of the kiss with Eli had driven Bridie completely from her mind. The terror and the worry for her friend came crashing back into her consciousness now, obliterating everything else.

"She's been locked up, Eli! They've carted her off to Bedlam! Bedlam, of all godforsaken places!" she whispered.

Eli's eyes reflected her horror back to her. "Dear God," he whispered.

"What do we do?" Eliza whispered.

"I... I don't know. I never imagined... Bloody *hell*..."

There was a loud thumping noise from behind a nearby door, making both of them jump. "Come on, let's get you back to

Lavender's rooms so you can change. I'm going to go tell the lads what's happened. They'll be waiting for me downstairs."

Eliza followed Eli down the hallway in silence until they reached the far end, where they were surprised to see Lavender waiting outside her own rooms.

"I'll help the girl. Get yourself down the back staircase and wait for us there," Lavender said.

Eliza felt taken aback, but ducked into the room at once. Lavender closed the door just as Eli looked up and caught Eliza's eye. She could not decipher his expression. She turned from the door to see Lavender smirking at her.

"Well, well, well. I must say I'm impressed. I'd never have believed it of a manor girl, I'll tell you that for free."

Eliza had no idea how to respond, choosing instead to bend over and remove Penny's shoes. Lavender crossed the room in a swish of satin and began unhooking and unbuttoning everything within reach. In a surprisingly short time, Eliza found herself free of the purple gown.

"You can wash the paint off over there. There's a washbasin and a pitcher under the window," Lavender said, gesturing lazily to the corner, where a long set of purple velvet drapes obscured the view of the street below. Eliza wasted no time, attacking her face with the cold water and the washcloth, trying to wash away so much more than the color.

"You did well. Very well. I was watching."

Eliza looked up from her task to find Lavender looking at her thoughtfully. "You were?"

"Does that surprise you so very much?"

Eliza considered it. "No. I imagine you know everything that goes on here."

Lavender smiled. "I'd be a fool if I didn't."

Eliza shrugged. She did not know much of Madam Lavender, but she knew she was no fool. No woman thrived in the Barrens without an unusual amount of savvy and grit.

"You've certainly got that Eli Turner on a string, haven't you?" Lavender chuckled.

Eliza's head shot up again. "I beg your pardon?"

Lavender cocked an eyebrow. "Don't tell me you didn't notice?"

"I don't know what you're talking about," Eliza said, even as her cheeks burned crimson, betraying the lie.

"Don't you? I know manor girls are little models of piety and all that, but I wasn't aware they were also blind."

Eliza did not reply. Madam Lavender was baiting her, and she was not going to fall for it. The last thing she needed was to compound her humiliation about the fact that she had kissed a man. To have been kissed would have been quite bad enough, but knowing that she had initiated it...

"Yes, well, quite aside from kissing hapless boys, you're still quite a dangerous little thing, aren't you?" Lavender murmured.

The response burst from her before Eliza could rein it in. "Excuse me?"

"That gift you have. No wonder they want to keep you under their boot. You could destroy every one of them with a whisper, couldn't you?"

Eliza stiffened. She dried her face with the washcloth and threw it aside, reaching for her other disguise now. "I don't want to destroy anyone."

"What a shame. I can think of a few I'd like to leave in tatters. Couldn't I convince you to talk to a couple of men I have in mind?" Lavender grinned, staring off into the middle distance as though imagining the delicious possibilities presented by such a scenario.

"I'm not interested in being used," Eliza said stiffly.

"You've been used every day of your life," Lavender replied.

"I know that now."

"Better to be used for the common good, don't you think?"

"Better not to be used at all."

Lavender smiled. "That's true enough, however improbable." She tilted her head. "I wonder how many more Elizas there are, sound asleep in the bowels of those manor houses, just waiting to be woken up."

Eliza pressed her lips together. The way Lavender was scrutinizing her made her uncomfortable. She almost wished she could hide behind the paint again. Almost.

"I imagine the girls who work here don't like being used either," Eliza said.

"I'm not using them," Lavender said calmly. "We have an arrangement."

Eliza only just managed to stop herself from making a skeptical sound, but Lavender must have seen the thought flit across Eliza's face because she chuckled again.

"One moment you can't be caught dead near one of my girls, and the next you're ready to jump on a white steed to defend them?" She sighed. "I reckon you've got me cast as some sort of villain in your head, haven't you?"

Eliza didn't reply.

"Every one of these girls is here by choice," Lavender said. "I don't force them to work for me. I take only a small cut of their earnings, and they can leave at any time they choose. The fact that many of them don't is much more a condemnation of how the world treats them than of me and my establishment."

"You think you're giving them the kind of life they deserve?"

"I think I'm giving them the chance to get out of a life they never chose in the first place. I didn't create that place out there." She gestured toward the windows. "It was the workhouses or the gutter for every single one of them. So now they use the very means men created to control them to milk every penny they can from those same men. And that's not all they get from them either."

Eliza raised her eyebrows and Lavender replied.

"Information. I have files on every Dignus who walks in here. Everything they say when they've had too much to drink, every penny they've spent on which girl and when. It's amazing what a man will say when he regards the woman to whom he's speaking as a plaything rather than a person."

"And what do you do with that information?" Eliza asked.

"I use it as leverage. A little blackmail here and there keeps all of us a bit safer in our beds. And of course, I pass everything that might be useful to the Resistance on to Sully."

"Isn't that dangerous? What if these men decide they'd rather just shut you down rather than submit to blackmail?"

Lavender shrugged, looking supremely unconcerned. "If they do, then I'll swing I suppose. But I have yet to meet the man who will choose to be sensible when there's a pretty girl waiting for him to be foolish."

"I still think it sounds like an awful risk."

"Some risks are worth taking."

Eliza straightened up, having laced on the ill-fitting boots, and now struggled to hide her wildly tangled hair back underneath the gingham kerchief.

"You've got your eyes open now, girl, but they're still clouded by the lies they've told you. As things get clearer for you, you'll see that this has only ever been about fear and power. The Illustratum sets rules for others, not for themselves. They impose morality, but they don't abide by it. They demonize what they do not understand and then they use the fear they have created to keep themselves on the throne and us beneath their boots."

Eliza had never heard anyone speak so frankly in opposition to the Illustratum, not even Sully. The ease and surety with which the words fell from Lavender's lips belied the fact that those same words overheard by the wrong person would mean a trip to the gallows. And as Eliza looked at the woman, she suddenly realized that Lavender would have spoken them as frankly to the face of an Elder as she had to Eliza. This was a woman who had lost too much to the Illustratum ever to pretend they were not exactly who she knew them to be.

There was a sharp knock upon the door, and Eli's voice called out from the hallway beyond. "Eliza? Are you ready?"

"Yes," Eliza replied. She hastily tucked the last wayward strands of her hair beneath her kerchief. "Thank you for your help, Madam Lavender. And please thank the other girls for me. Tabby and Edith and... and Penny."

Lavender inclined her head. "At the risk of offending your sensibilities, you are welcome here any time, Eliza."

Eliza's chin thrust out defiantly, but she considered Lavender's words. They both knew what a dangerous path she was on now. They both knew she could very well find herself with nowhere to go. "Thank you. I'll keep that in mind."

Out in the hallway, Eli was bouncing anxiously on the balls of his feet. He heaved a sigh of relief as Eliza joined him. "Are you all right?" he asked her.

"I am perfectly well, thank you," Eliza said. Her voice sounded oddly formal, even in her own ears.

"Jasper and Zeke have gone ahead to gather whoever they can find. We're going to meet them at the Bell and Flagon, unless..."

"Unless what?"

"Unless you, uh... wanted to go home? It's getting very late. I can fill them in on what you found out, if…" He was looking at her as if she might turn tail and flee at any moment.

"I'm coming," she said, in a tone that brooked no opposition. Eli nodded warily and led the way down the back staircase and out through the alleyway into the street.

As they left Madam Lavender's behind them and made their way back toward the High Street, Eliza turned back to gaze at the place one more time. Penny was sitting in one of the upper windows, the sash thrown wide, a cigarette dangling from her hand and a silken robe clutched tightly to her body against the chill. She caught sight of Eliza and looked back at her, her expression almost hollow. She looked at Eliza, and Eliza looked back, wishing that Penny, too, had somewhere else she could go. She wanted to take the girl's hand and run with her as far from this place as her strength would carry her.

Instead, she watched as Penny looked suddenly back over her shoulder, flicked the glowing stub of her cigarette to the ground and, with a musical laugh, drew the crimson curtains closed between them.

TWENTY-THREE

ELI DIDN'T KNOW what to say to the girl.

She hurried along silently beside him, eyes upon the ground, evidently lost in her own thoughts. Each time he cleared his throat and tried to speak, the words shriveled upon his tongue and he swallowed them back, the taste smacking more bitterly of cowardice each time.

Was she angry with him? She certainly ought to be. He had promised to keep her safe and instead he had subjected her to humiliation that had narrowly avoided turning into a violent confrontation.

He had messed up. When the man had put his hands on Eliza, Eli had lost all control over himself, all reason. His vision had blurred instantly, angrily red. It was a miracle no one had noticed the glass he was holding shatter in his grip—not that broken glassware or spilled mead were an uncommon occurrence at an establishment like Lavender's. Still, it could have been very dangerous to draw attention to his Riftmagic in that way, especially with several monied Dignus patronizing the place.

There had already been a plan in place in case a customer had tried to make an advance on Eliza. Edith was standing by, ready to intervene, to explain that Eliza was an exclusive companion of a wealthy client. If Eli had just allowed her to do so, Eliza could have slipped away easily, untouched by any further humiliation.

Instead? He had completely lost his head. Barreled across the room. Confronted the man loudly, surely drawing every eye in the place just as they were trying to be as unobtrusive as possible. And then, when put on the spot, he hesitated, forcing Eliza to kiss him to keep up the charade and get them both out of there safely all while he stood there like a fool, first too angry and then too stunned to act rationally.

The kiss.

The kiss he was trying to feel nothing but guilt about. The kiss which instead was, even now, leaving him almost delirious with feelings he had never grappled with before. Feelings that only compounded his guilt the moment he acknowledged them, until he felt like he would suffocate under the weight of it all.

How dare he think of the kiss in that way, when he had all but forced her to resort to it to save herself? How dare he linger on the details of it—the way her fingers had caught at his hair, the way her lips had parted, the taste of her breath in his mouth—how dare he even think of these things when she must surely be regretting ever having even touching him? He half-wished she could see the thoughts replaying through his head so that she would perhaps give him the slap he knew he deserved.

No doubt someone—Jasper, Zeke, Sully—would offer to land him on his back for endangering all of them with his recklessness. He could only hope so, as he would brook no objection. Jasper would certainly gleefully oblige if Eli suggested it. Jasper, who would surely be gloating even now at the way Eli had messed up, would be so pleased that he could take up the mantle of level-headed brother for once.

Eli was so busy berating himself, he missed the turn off the High Street down to the Bell and Flagon and had to backtrack, muttering an apology as he did so. He chanced another half a glance at Eliza; her face was twisted in misery, and she clutched the borrowed shawl about her shoulders as though it was the only thing preventing her from falling to pieces. At last, he could not help himself.

"Eliza, are you all right?" Eli asked.

She looked up at him with a gaze so fierce he started in surprise. "My best friend has been locked up in Bedlam and it's all my fault! Of course I'm not all right! How could I possibly be all right?"

Feeling like a prize idiot, Eli closed his mouth again. Of course she was thinking about her friend. Here he was, obsessing over a kiss that had clearly been nothing more than a desperately improvised means to an escape, when what he ought to be thinking about was the entire point of the evening's events: the newly discovered whereabouts of

Eliza's friend, Bridie Sloane. He was so disgusted with himself he could hardly stand the sound of his own voice as he tried to reassure her.

"It's not your fault, Eliza," Eli said. "Of all the people involved in this, it's your fault least of all."

Eliza just shook her head. It was clear she did not believe him. He did not try to change her mind. He led her straight through the front room of the Bell and Flagon, which had nearly cleared out due to the lateness of the hour, and behind the bar into the back room where the others had already gathered, grim-faced and quiet. Eli could tell from the look on Sully's face that Jasper and Zeke had already filled her in on what had happened at Lavender's. With nothing but a nod of greeting to the collected company, Eli dropped into a chair, poured himself a drink, and knocked it back in one. Eliza did not sit, choosing instead to hover by the fireplace.

Eli could feel Sully's hard gaze upon him, but by the time he found the courage to look up, Sully was staring at Eliza instead, her lips pressed into a thin line.

"You did well, Eliza. The boys were just telling me. You kept a cool head and got exactly what we needed from Guilford. Well done."

Eliza gave a strange little jerking movement, somewhere between a shrug and a shudder. She did not reply.

"I expect you want to get back into your own clothes. I took the liberty of bringing them over with me," Sully went on, nodding toward a chair by the fire where Eliza's uniform sat in a neat pile.

"Won't I be too conspicuous?" Eliza asked.

"We've got you an escort this time. No one will see your uniform," Sully said. She gestured into the corner where Colin sat, munching on an apple. He waved blithely at Eliza, who managed a shadow of a smile in return. Then she snatched her garments off the chair and disappeared into the little storage room Sully was pointing at. It felt like a very long time before anyone else spoke.

"This is a bloody nightmare," Fergus muttered.

"I told you all that it was a mistake to get manor servants involved," Jasper sighed, though there was no regret in his tone—only poorly concealed gloating.

"What can we do now?" Cora asked the room at large. "She's bound to tell them everything, isn't she? A manor girl in a place like Bedlam? She won't last a day, surely."

"That's just it. She doesn't know everything. We're not even sure *what* she knows," Sully pointed out.

"She knows enough to get herself locked up," Michael said. "They don't throw you in a place like Bedlam unless they need to shut you up."

"Or get you to talk," Cora added. "My God, the thought of even walking through those doors must be enough to loosen anyone's tongue."

"If we just knew what she said to the people at Clerkenwell, we'd have a better idea of how much trouble we're all in," Fergus said.

"That's just it, though, Guilford doesn't know. They'd already detained her by the time he got there. And I don't think we're going to be lucky enough to seduce information out of anyone else on their staff," Zeke said.

"If we only knew how she got the book..."

"She was in the Barrens on Thursday," Eliza said. Everyone jumped at the sound of her voice, for she had emerged silently from the storage room. "She went without me. I was at the High Elder's palace, accompanying my mistress. She was delivering baskets. Someone gave it back to her, I'm sure of it. Someone who understood that the book was dangerous, someone who didn't want to risk being caught with it."

"But she didn't know the books had been distributed in the baskets. You assured us that none of the other maids knew," Jasper said, sounding unnecessarily hostile. Eli glared at him.

"They didn't at the time. I'm quite sure of that," Eliza said, refusing to take the bait. "But maybe when someone tried to return it to her, she got curious."

"But why would a manor maid read a book like that? Why not hand it right over to her master when she realized what it was?"

"Because Bridie was a workhouse orphan. Don't you remember what the book was about? Don't you remember why we worked so hard to distribute the books in the first place?" Eliza asked.

"Well, sure, to exonerate Davies and expose the Illustratum. What's that got to do with—"

Eliza gave a groan of frustration. Were they really so thick? "If you were a workhouse orphan, and you read a book about how the Dignus were killing and abandoning their Riftborn children, what would you think?"

"The same thing I'm thinking," Eli said suddenly. The words came out much more loudly than he intended, and everyone stared at him. "And the same thing Jasper's thinking, even though he won't admit it. She wanted to know where she came from. She thinks there might be a chance she's from a Dignus family, maybe even a powerful one. And she probably thought the workhouse was the right place to start looking for answers."

"Can't see how that would get her into trouble, asking about her parents," Fergus said with a shrug. "So the matron tells her she was a foundling and sends her on her way."

"And what if she didn't go on her way?" Eli asked. "What if she kept pressing the point? What if she actually mentioned the book?"

Cora looked alarmed. "Would she be fool enough to do that?"

"Bridie's not a fool," Eliza snapped. "She would know that book was forbidden to the likes of her. But if she said the wrong thing, or if the matron even suspected what she knew, that might have been enough to detain her."

"The Praesidio sent guards over to collect her things. Could be they were even looking for the book," Eli added.

"And now that we know where she is, it's obvious they lied. She's not in a Riftward at the hospital. They've locked her away in Bedlam, and unless we can get her out, they'll probably torture her for information or otherwise just leave her there to rot!" Eliza stopped speaking, chest heaving, to find every pair of eyes in the room staring at her. No one spoke. No one even moved.

"So, what's the plan, then?" Eliza asked impatiently. "How are we going to get her out?"

Sully shot a glance at Eli. "Get... get her out? Of Bedlam?"

"YES!" Eliza actually stamped her foot in frustration.

Sully looked at Eli again. "You explain, you're the one who brought her into all this."

His heart sinking, Eli turned to Eliza. Her expression was so fierce that it took him a moment to find his voice. "Eliza, maybe you overestimate our resources, or perhaps you just don't know much about Bedlam, but I don't see that there's much we can do."

"What do you mean, there's not much we can do?" Eliza asked, looking from face to face. Everyone was looking anywhere but back at her. "Everything I know about Bedlam is what you yourself told me about the place! You're the ones who told me what they do to people

259

in those places! You know about the experiments with Riftmead! Are you…" she barked an incredulous note of laughter, "…are you telling me you intend to just leave her there?"

"It's not that we *want* to leave her there, but be reasonable, Eliza," Eli began.

"Reasonable? *Reasonable?* My best friend is rotting away in an asylum for the insane because of the books that we distributed! We got her into this mess, and we need to get her out!" Eliza cried.

Still, no one would look at her. It was as though she was doing something shameful and embarrassing, and no one could stomach watching it.

"Someone answer me! How are we getting her out?" she cried, her voice rising shrilly.

Sully stood up from the table, banging her fist upon the wood. "She's not getting out!" she shouted.

Eli watched the color drain from Eliza's face. Her mouth opened and closed wordlessly.

"Eliza, I'm sorry," Sully said, her voice much gentler now. "I wish I had another answer for you. But the Resistance is not what it used to be in the days of the Lamplighters Confederacy. It was badly decimated when Davies was caught. People got scared, and our networks of allies vanished. We've been struggling to build them up again ever since. That's the whole reason it was so important to get the books out there. We needed people to trust us again, to realize that the Illustratum are not what they claim to be, that fighting against them is worth the risk."

"Well, then, haven't the books done that? Can't you go to the people now and ask them to help, to fight?" Eliza asked.

"The Barrens are restless, yes, and the Illustratum has their hands fuller than usual with protests and arrests and defiance, but stirring people up is a long way from organizing them. We simply don't have the resources and connections we need to get into Bedlam, let alone get someone out, and we can't risk the few resources we've built up trying something that's almost guaranteed to fail. I'm sorry, child. We can't help your friend."

Eliza turned to speak directly to Eli now. "I trusted you," she gasped, trying and failing to repress the sobs welling up in her chest. "I risked everything to help you. It's my fault Bridie's in that place because I trusted you!"

"We risk everything every day, love, but there's not a single one of us in this room who's worth the failure of the Resistance," Sully said quietly, answering for Eli who, in any case, could muster no response. "Every one of us is expendable if it means the fight can continue. I'm sorry. It's a brutal lesson to learn, but you've got to learn it or you have no business here."

Eli stood up, desperate to contradict what Sully had said, to find an argument against it. But there was nothing more to say. He gazed furiously at the woman who had raised him and she gazed calmly back, waiting for him to acknowledge what they both knew he must: that Sully was right. That Bridie Sloane was a lost cause—a casualty.

Eli looked away and heard Eliza's sob catch in her throat. He grappled for the right thing to say to her, but she did not wait for his useless platitudes. She marched right for the door, tears streaming down her face, and disappeared. Eli made to follow, but Zeke reached out a hand to stop him.

"Let her go, lad," Zeke muttered. "You can't tell her what she needs to hear, so you best not say anything at all. Let her cry it out, she'll see reason in the morning."

Several heads nodded in silent agreement. Even Jasper, who found amusement in the bleakest of confrontations, looked grim.

"Colin, follow the girl. Make sure she gets home safe," Sully ordered, and Colin was off like a shot after Eliza, leaving a heavy silence in his wake.

"What's the damage, do y' reckon?" Zeke asked after several minutes. "Do you think there's any danger to the Resistance, with that girl locked up?"

Sully shrugged. "There's just no way to know. We know they didn't find the book, so that's something. Incidentally, what did Eliza do with the book?" She tossed this question to Eli.

"She burned it," Eli said, dropping back into his chair in defeat. "It's gone."

Sully nodded. "So, I say we carry on. There seems little chance the book will be traced back to us. I think we just need to plan our next move. We need to capitalize on the unrest in the Barrens before the new infusions of Riftmead douse it out, or everything we've done so far will be for naught."

The assembled company mumbled their agreement, but no one offered up any suggestions to break the silence that followed. Eli couldn't bear it. Without excusing himself, he got up from the table and walked out into the night, his shame and helplessness burning so fiercely that he felt like a torch, lighting up the darkness even as he was consumed by the flames.

TWENTY-FOUR

D ESPITE LAYING IN HER BED staring at the ceiling for what
felt like an interminable period, sleep never carried Jessamine
off to anything resembling restful slumber, leaving her to toss
and turn in a strange limbo between dreaming and waking all night.
She couldn't shake the feeling that she was being watched, and she
knew exactly why. It was no specter haunting her chambers, no
lurking intruder. No, the culprit sat upon her bedside table, nestled in
a cushion of purple silk, each and every facet glimmering with the
promise of a future she had neither imagined nor desired. It had been
nearly a week since Reginald had put that ring on her finger in a
travesty of a proposal; and still, she positively ached with dread at the
thought of having to rise each morning and perform in the well-
choreographed farce that was her social life, smiling and nodding and
preening and graciously accepting congratulations and compliments
when all she wanted to do was pull the blankets back over her head
and vanish, cocooned forever against the knowledge that she would
soon be married to Reginald Morgan.

She tried to imagine it when she was alone like this, in the dark,
with no distractions. She watched it all play out like a performance:
dangling upon his arm at balls and shooting parties, entertaining his
friends at dinners and charitable events, smiling serenely at him as he
took the head of the table—if that was all she had to do, she expected
she would have been able to bear it.

But marriage did not begin and end in the public eye. One could
not shut it off when the guests went home at the end of the day, like
a light in a darkened room. No. She would have no choice but to give
herself over to this man. To allow him to know her as no other man

ever would. To submit to him. To bear him children. To look away when he indulged in his baser tendencies with any woman who caught his eye. To pretend she wasn't humiliated to the marrow of her bones when he came home reeking of spirits and another woman's perfume.

She had no idea how to do any of it. No idea how she would survive it. Surely someone would help her to understand how it was to be borne? Surely she could not be expected to step into that world without a guide, without an inkling of how to cope?

And yet it seemed that was exactly what would happen. She had no elder sisters, not even a married friend she felt close enough to confide in. Only a mother too far adrift on the sea of her grief to even remember her own name. She remembered back to the night of her Presentation only a few weeks ago. She remembered the surety she felt, the security in her future, in what she wanted, in what was waiting for her.

All of that was gone. She was alone. She would have to face it all alone.

A soft creaking and rustling alerted Jessamine to the fact that the maid had come in to tend to her fireplace, a process she usually slept soundly through, only to wake up to a merrily crackling fire that seemed to have appeared entirely on its own. She peeked her face out from beneath her pillows only to see that the traitor sun was splashing its rosy color across the horizon, announcing its arrival. She sighed. It looked like she would have to face the day regardless of her bad humor.

A sound beyond the quiet scrapings and sweepings of the fireplace met her ears then—a very soft, muffled sound, almost more animal than human. Alarmed, Jessamine pulled the pillow from her face and blinked into the dimness. A figure knelt upon the hearth, a bucket of ash in one hand, a small horsehair brush in the other, her head resting upon her knee, her body shaking with nearly silent sobs.

"Bridie? Whatever is wrong?" Jessamine asked.

Her sudden voice in the quiet room made the figure at the hearth gasp and jump.

"Miss Jessamine! I'm so sorry! I didn't mean to wake you."

The voice was not the one she expected, but one that she knew almost as well as her own. "Eliza? Is that you?"

"Yes, miss."

264

"What in heaven's name are you doing kneeling in the fireplace at this time of the morning?"

Eliza stood up, brushing the ash from her apron and the tears from her cheeks. "I'm just helping out, Miss Jessamine."

"Oh." Jessamine yawned widely, stifling it behind her hand. "But why? Where is Bridie? And why are you crying?"

Eliza opened her mouth to answer, froze for a moment, then sank to her knees, sobbing.

"Eliza!" Jessamine gasped, hurriedly extricating herself from her blankets and flying across the room to comfort the girl. The sound was heartbreaking. Jessamine dropped to the floor as well, wrapping her arms around Eliza's shuddering shoulders. She expected the girl to protest, to push her away, but Eliza did neither. Instead, she buried her face in her mistress' neck and redoubled her sobs.

"Shhhh, there, now. It's all right. It's all right," Jessamine murmured, the words rising automatically to her lips.

"Oh! Oh, Miss Jessamine. It's not all right. Nothing will ever be all right again," Eliza moaned into her nightdress, which was growing damp with her tears.

"No, Eliza, it can't be as bad as all that! What's happened? Won't you tell me?"

"It's Bridie. Bridie's gone and she's not coming back and it's all my fault. All, all my fault."

Jessamine rocked the girl like a baby, stroking her hair and rubbing her back, feeling helpless against the onslaught of tears, knowing she'd get nothing else rational out of her until she had cried herself out. At last, the sobs began to slow, the breathing to ease, and Jessamine pulled back to look Eliza in the face.

"I'm so sorry, miss. I never should have... it's not my place to..." Eliza's breath was still hitching too badly to allow her to complete a sentence.

"Eliza, stop apologizing to me! Having a good cry is not a sin, and there is no reason to atone for it. Now, please tell me what's happened to Bridie!"

Eliza did not respond at first. She continued to wipe her streaming eyes on her apron, averting her eyes from Jessamine's penetrating gaze.

"Eliza?" Jessamine hated the authority in her own tone, but she would use it if it was the only way to convince Eliza to help her understand what in the world was going on.

"She's gone, miss. She left to run an errand on last Friday morning and never came back."

"What errand? Is anyone looking for her?" Jessamine asked.

"She… she went to visit the workhouse she'd grown up in. But something… something happened and now she's gone."

Jessamine frowned. She'd taken a tour of a workhouse once with her charity circle and had never forgotten it. Even though the workhouse staff had taken great pains to keep up appearances for the sake of their important guests, Jessamine had been deeply disturbed at the empty, gaunt faces of the children and the hot, crowded conditions of the wards. She still remembered the way her father had responded when she insisted the Illustratum improve the conditions.

"The conditions suit the occupants, Jessamine," he had said, his disapproval severe. "Until they do the very urgent work of bringing their souls closer to the Creator, there can be no hope of bringing their condition closer to his mercy."

"Eliza, what do you mean, something's happened?"

Eliza's hands had dropped to her lap, and she was twisting them anxiously. "Some guards came and took all of her things. They said she had been taken to one of the Riftwards for Riftsickness."

"Bridie has Riftsickness?" Jessamine could not believe it. It was true that her interactions with the girl were very limited, but she could not reconcile the bright, bubbly, pretty young woman who had gushed over the chance to wear her nightdress to the pale, sickly occupants of Riftwards. As with the workhouses, she had toured them before. The memory twisted uncomfortably in the pit of her stomach. Her charitable endeavors were starting to feel less like charity and more like voyeurism into other people's suffering. She cleared her throat.

"I can't believe she's so very sick, Eliza. After all, she was healthy as could be when she helped me get into the Barrens."

"She was healthy as could be on Thursday morning when we left for the palace," Eliza sniffed, her voice turning hard.

"Well, then, it can't be all that dire, can it, now?" Jessamine said soothingly. "I'm sure she'll recover, Eliza. Would you like to go visit her? I can arrange it if you'd like."

Eliza's head shot up, her eyes wide with—unless Jessamine was mistaken—fear. "No!" she cried. "No, I... we... thank you miss, but we can't do that."

Jessamine smiled indulgently. "Eliza, don't be silly, of course we can! All I would need to do is send a letter requesting a visit. I'd be very happy to—"

"Miss Jessamine, that's very kind of you, but—"

"No buts, Eliza. Now let me just get my stationery and—" She stood up and started for the writing desk in the corner.

"Miss Jessamine, stop!" Eliza cried out, her voice shrill and startling in the pre-dawn quiet of the still sleeping house. Jessamine turned to stare at her as she continued. "I appreciate your offer, miss, but it won't do any good. She isn't there. She isn't sick."

Jessamine stood with her hand still outstretched toward her desk, her eyebrows pulled together in confusion. "Eliza what in the world do you—"

"She's not there! It's a lie. She's locked up in Bedlam and she's never getting out and I just... I can't... I don't know what to—" She dropped her face into her hands again and resumed her sobbing.

Jessamine was across the room in a heartbeat. She took Eliza by the shoulders and shook her. "Bedlam?! Eliza! I can't help you if you don't explain to me what is happening!"

But Eliza refused to look at her, shaking her head even as the tears slipped through her fingers. "Don't. You can't help me. I can't let you. Everything is too dangerous and it's all my fault."

"I most certainly can!" Jessamine said, indignant now. "If you don't tell me what's going on, Eliza, I will simply get dressed, get in the carriage, and go find out for myself!"

Eliza was still shaking her head, crying stormily. "No, Miss Jessamine, please. Please leave it alone."

"You seem to think there's nothing you can do, but I assure you, there is plenty I can do. Father will never allow this to stand. I can ask him to—"

"NO!" Eliza's stricken and tear-stained face shot up out of her hands, which clutched instead at the sleeves of Jessamine's nightgown. "No! I beg of you, Miss Jessamine, you mustn't breathe a word to your father! Please, if you've ever harbored even a single pang of affection for me, I beg of you, say nothing to him!"

Jessamine reeled. Did the girl really not know how she felt about her? "A single pang of affection? Eliza, you're the closest thing to a real friend I have in this world. I love you. Surely you know that?"

Eliza's face went slack with shock. "You... love me?"

"Of course I do! You are the one constant in my life, the only person I can count on."

Eliza's face crumpled again. "Oh, Miss Jessamine, I love you, too, truly I do."

The two girls fell into each other's arms, both crying now; the careful distance that usually stood as a solid barrier between them now as insubstantial as smoke.

"You can trust me, Eliza. I give you my word. Please tell me how I can help you," Jessamine whispered, intertwining their fingers and squeezing Eliza's hand. As she watched, waiting, Eliza looked up and met her gaze. There was so much emotion and conflict in those wide grey eyes that Jessamine felt dizzy watching it all swirl around. But she did not look away, and so she saw the very moment when the decision formed in their depths.

"Bridie was a workhouse orphan before she came here to work at the manor. She went back to Clerkenwell Workhouse, where she grew up, in search of information about her parents. Rather than give her that information, they locked her up and then transferred her to Bedlam. Then the Praesidio came here, ransacked our bedroom, took all of her possessions, and told us she had taken suddenly ill and was now confined to a Riftward."

Jessamine stared, her mouth hanging open. "How do you know all of this?"

"I beg of you not to ask me that. Just believe me when I tell you I know it to be true," Eliza said, her voice fervent.

Jessamine considered pressing the point, but let it go, seizing instead upon another, more urgent question. "What in the world could she have said or done at that workhouse to cause her to be locked up like that?"

Eliza bit her lip.

"Eliza! Enough evasiveness! You have to trust me!"

"She had reason to believe that her parents might have been Dignus," Eliza said quietly.

The two girls sat in the stunned silence that followed, each almost afraid to break it. But at last Jessamine's curiosity got the better of her, breaking through her shock and spilling out of her mouth.

268

"A Riftborn child… from a Dignus family? But… how?"

"It has been known to happen," Eliza said.

"I have never heard of such a thing."

"That is the way the Illustratum wants it."

"But why?"

"Because it divides us," Eliza said, and her voice was heavy. "It draws a clear line, between us and you. It's cleaner. Do you understand?"

"I… I think so," Jessamine said, though she was not sure. The thought of it made her want to writhe with discomfort, and she hated herself for it. "Assuming, for a moment, that that's true—"

"It is true."

"Then how did Bridie come to think that she came from a Dignus family?"

"I cannot tell you that."

"Do you not know?"

"I do know. But it is safer if I do not tell you."

"Safer for whom?"

"Both of us."

Jessamine repressed a shiver. Then she looked squarely at Eliza again. "Eliza, are you in trouble?"

Eliza considered this. "No. But Bridie is, and it's my fault that she is. She doesn't deserve to be locked up in that place just for trying to understand the truth about who she is and where she came from. No one deserves punishment in pursuit of the simple truth."

Jessamine nodded. "You are quite right, of course. So, what can we do about it? I know you don't want to get my father involved, and I understand why, but the people who run those workhouses can't just be allowed to pluck people off the street and lock them away!"

"But they aren't allowed," Eliza said, and her voice sounded weary.

"Yes, that's just what I—"

"They are following orders. From the Elders."

Jessamine shook her head, as though she could dispel the words with the motion. "No."

"Yes."

"You don't mean to say that my own father ordered her locked away?" Jessamine asked, her voice rising in a kind of panic.

"I don't know that for sure. I don't know who it was among the

Elders that gave the order. But it seems to me that if his servant was involved, they would have gone directly to him."

Jessamine wanted to deny this, but she could not argue with the logic. In fact, the more she thought about it, the more she was certain it was true.

"I don't want to believe that," she whispered finally.

"Nor do I."

"What... what can we do?" Jessamine asked.

"I don't know. I'm afraid there might be nothing. That's why I'm... I'm just so..." Eliza's voice cracked and broke.

Jessamine reached for her hand again. "Eliza, you keep saying it's your fault. I can't imagine that's true. Why do you keep saying it?"

"Because it is true. I'm the reason she knew about it—about some of the children in the workhouses being from Dignus families."

"You told her?"

"No, not in so many words. But it's still my fault she found out. She's always..." Eliza sighed, and the corner of her mouth turned up in the suggestion of a wistful smile. "She's always yearned for things, things that other girls have. Beautiful dresses, handsome suitors. I think we all do, belowstairs. But for Bridie, it was even more than that. She wanted to belong somewhere, and she never felt that she did. And I think she wanted to know why."

Jessamine bit her lip. "I think we all want that. To belong."

Eliza gave a sad shrug. "I hope it's not too bold to say, but I think we both understand the holes your family can leave inside you. And they are terribly hard to fill."

"It's not too bold," Jessamine whispered. "It's true."

They sat in the ache of those empty places. Then Jessamine stood up suddenly.

"We're going to get her out, Eliza."

Eliza's face was chalk-white. "How? Surely we can't even get into a place like that, let alone get another person out."

"I'm not sure about the second part, but the first is quite easy."

"It is?"

Jessamine smiled grimly and walked over to the bedside table. She plucked her engagement ring out of the ring box, slid it onto her finger and turned back to Eliza, wiggling her fingers so that the diamond cast tiny rainbows onto the walls.

"I think perhaps you forget who I am," she said.

TWENTY-FIVE

E LI TURNER HAD BEEN called many things: a fool, a reckless child, an incompetent leader, a headstrong, stubborn prat.

Well, he thought to himself as he urged his horse closer and closer to the grounds of Larkspur Manor, *I may as well live up to my reputation.*

He still didn't know what in blazes he was doing. He'd never been one for wildly improbable odds or suicide missions—Jasper had always been king of that territory, and long had he reigned unopposed. All Eli knew was that he'd spent the last two nights tossing and turning, tortured by the look on Eliza's face when she'd fled the Resistance meeting, wracked with the kind of guilt he had only felt once before in his short life: when he learned of John Davies' death. Then, there had been nothing he could do—Davies' death was a nightmare from which there had been no waking. But now… now he was not helpless. Now he had a chance, however slim it may be, to right a terrible wrong for which he held himself personally responsible. And blast it all, he was going to take that chance, the rest of the Resistance be damned.

He eased the horse to a stop and jumped down out of the saddle, leading him by the reins into a copse of trees right on the edge of the manor grounds. He tied the horse up and pulled a carrot from his pocket, which the horse munched happily from his hand.

"Stay quiet, now, there's a good chap," Eli murmured to him. "I won't be long."

He had sent the message that morning, but he could not be sure that she had received it, let alone that she would agree to meet him if she did. He would not have blamed her if she'd chucked the letter in the fire and planned to let him wait endlessly until he gave up and rode back into the Commons without having ever laid eyes on her. He would deserve it, he knew that much. And so it was with tangible relief that he arrived at the back of the stables to find Eliza waiting for him, even if her face did resemble a dark cloud prepared to unleash a walloping of a storm. She was hissing at him before he could even cross the threshold into the warm, musky darkness of the stalls.

"Eli, what are you doing here? If someone sees you…"

"No one's going to see me. I realize I'm no Colin, but I assure you, I was very careful."

Eliza crossed her arms over her chest, almost protectively. She held up his letter in one hand. It gave him a modicum of courage to see she hadn't ripped it to shreds. "Why are you here?"

"For two reasons. The first is that I owe you an apology."

Eliza just watched him stonily. He took a deep breath.

"I should have stood up for you. For Bridie. I let the others make the decision—which I felt was the only one we could make at the time. But you were right. You *are* right. We are the reason Bridie is locked away in that place, and we need to acknowledge that, even if we can't fix it. I do not take her situation lightly. I guess I just needed you to know that."

Eliza sniffed and looked away. Her eyes looked brighter, but Eli tried to ignore them. If she didn't want to show him her tears, then he would pretend he had not seen them. He waited for her, giving her space to process his words.

"I… thank you for coming here and saying that. I… didn't know it would be so hard. I didn't think anyone would be hurt. I suppose I sound like a foolish child for admitting that, but it's true. When I agreed to distribute the books, I thought the only person I was endangering was myself. I thought that was the worst that could happen, me being caught. I could laugh at myself now for being so naive." She smiled bitterly.

"There's nothing to laugh about. You were willing to sacrifice yourself. You still are, to help your friend. You aren't naive. You're brave."

The look she gave him was fierce. "I don't feel brave."

"I don't think many brave people do."

She glared at him, then back over her shoulder toward the house. "What was the second reason?"

"Huh?"

"You said you were here for two reasons. What was the second?"

Another deep breath. "I want to help you."

Eliza narrowed her eyes. "Help me what?"

"I want to help you get Bridie out of Bedlam."

Eliza looked at him for so long he wondered if she'd even understood what he'd said. Finally, she blinked. "You told me it was impossible."

"It very well may be. We'd be mad to try it."

"Then why agree to it?"

"Because I finally understand what Jasper's been banging on about for so long. Sully keeps waiting for the perfect moment to start this fight. And I know it's because she wants to win, but she's waiting for a day that will never come. The cost will never be low enough. The risk will always be too great to bear. As much as I hate to say it, Jasper is right. At some point, we will just have to bear it."

"But why would you agree to take the risk for Bridie. I am willing to take it because she's my friend. But she is nothing to you. You've never even met her."

"She is a fellow Riftborn. What has happened to her is wrong. That is enough for me, Eliza."

Eliza's bottom lip began to tremble. "Do you really mean it, Eli? Is the Resistance going to help get Bridie out of Bedlam?"

Eli hesitated. "No. Not the Resistance. Just me. I'm here on my own."

"Does Sully know?"

"No, she doesn't."

"She's going to be so angry with you, Eli."

Eli sighed. "I know. It was only a matter of time."

"I don't want you to fall out with Sully because of me."

"It's not because of you, Eliza. This is my decision."

Eli sat down on the edge of the water barrel. The horse nearest him leaned over the gate of his stall and nudged at him with his nose, looking for food. Eli patted him automatically until the horse, giving him up as a bad job, plunged his nose into the water barrel. Eli jumped up, cursing under his breath as he brushed the water from his clothes.

"I don't understand. What's changed, Eli?"

"I'm sorry?"

"What's changed? You agreed with the others at the meeting on

273

Friday. You said it was impossible. Why would you agree to do this now? To help me?"

Eli bit his lip. He couldn't say what he was thinking, not without scaring her away. "I can't stop thinking about the moment you kissed me" was hardly an appropriate response. Instead, he cleared his throat and tried to sound robustly practical. "Nothing's changed. Or rather the only thing that's changed is my mind. I thought it over. I want to help. Now, do you want my help, or not?"

Eliza stared blankly at him for a moment, then a bark of incredulous laughter burst from her lips. She slapped a hand over her mouth to stifle it, regained control of herself, and lowered the hand again. "You do realize, of course, that getting Bridie out of there without being caught is going to require some kind of direct miracle from on high?"

"I do, indeed."

"And you want to attempt it anyway?"

"That is what I came all this way to tell you."

Eliza laughed again, a laugh that hitched strangely at the end and turned into a sob. Her eyes shone with unshed tears. "Thank you, Eli. I know you aren't just doing this for me, but... thank you all the same."

But I am doing it for you, Eli thought to himself, the thought so loud and insistent inside his head that he thought Eliza must surely be able to hear it as clearly as if he had spoken it aloud.

"Don't thank me yet," he said, with what he hoped was a casual grin. "I said I wanted to help. I didn't say I had any bloody idea how to go about it."

Eliza's face became suddenly sly. "I... may have the beginnings of a plan in place, but I'm not at all sure that you're going to like it."

"Is that so? So after we abandoned you, were you planning on doing this all on your own, then?" Eli asked, trying not to sound as amused as he felt.

Eliza shrugged, blushing. "I had to try. And no, I wasn't going to do it by myself, exactly."

Eli's eyebrows rose in surprise. "I'm intrigued. So what is this mysterious plan?"

Eliza sighed and pointed to the water barrel. "You'd better sit down."

§

"Eli."

Eli sighed. He'd been foolish enough to convince himself he could sneak back into the house from his sojourn to Larkspur Manor without anyone being any the wiser. He should have known better. He knew who had called his name out of the darkened corner of the sitting room, but he was in no humor to answer him, so he stomped his way up the stairs as though he had not heard.

But Jasper had never given up easily in his life, damn him. Eli had barely closed the door to his room before it swung open again.

"I'm perfectly aware that you can hear me, you know," Jasper said as he leaned on the door frame, an insolent look on his face.

"And I was under the impression that knocking was part of your skillset," Eli said through gritted teeth.

"Ah, yes, I've let that particular skill fall by the wayside, haven't I? Ah, well," Jasper sighed, before the mockery fell from his tone and his face. "Where have you been?"

"Nowhere. Out for a walk."

"Well, which is it?"

"Neither. Both. Whatever you please."

"Eli."

Eli sighed, flopping onto his bed and staring up at the ceiling. "Jasper, short of falling asleep right here and now, what subtle device can I use to convince you that I'm not in the mood to talk right now?"

"You've been to see her, haven't you? The Braxton girl." And though he posed it as a question, there was no real question in his voice. And so Eli felt no real need to answer him.

Of course, his silence was answer enough.

"How is she?" Jasper asked.

Eli snorted. "Like you care."

"I care!" Jasper insisted, looking affronted. "Why would you assume I don't care?"

Eli laughed out loud now. "Come off it, Jasper. You've been nothing but terrible to her since you met her."

"That was before I realized you'd fallen for her," Jasper pointed out.

Eli sat bolt upright. "I have not fallen for her!"

Jasper just shrugged, a maddeningly superior look on his face. "If you say so, brother. But I know a besotted fool when I see one."

"You're a tosser."

"And you're a liar. I saw the way you looked when she kissed you."

"I was playing along."

"You're not that good of an actor."

Eli swore under his breath and flopped back onto his pillow. It was no use arguing with Jasper when he got like this, especially since, on this particular occasion, he happened to be right.

"I don't know what you're getting so angry about. I'm not accusing you of anything I haven't done myself on several occasions," Jasper said.

"And what's that?"

"Falling in love with the wrong girl."

"You're wrong Jasper."

"About which bit? That you're in love with her, or that she's the wrong girl?"

"Both."

"As you like," Jasper said with a shrug, but his knowing grin undercut the sentiment. "So, why did you go see her, then? Since you are, as you say, adamantly *not* in love with her?"

"I... it wasn't right, what happened at the meeting. We ought to try to get that girl out of Bedlam, and I told her as much—after I apologized, that is."

Jasper's eyebrows shot up so fast they appeared to have fled his face. "Do mine ears deceive me, or is my careful little brother suddenly game for some danger?"

"I'm not your little brother, and no, I'm not looking for danger. I just... this isn't right, leaving her there."

"Do you think you could convince Sully that getting the girl out could serve the cause?" Jasper asked, sounding uncharacteristically serious as he sat on the edge of Eli's bed.

Eli, noting the change in Jasper's tone, frowned. "No, I don't, which is why I've gone about this on my own. Why do you care? I didn't hear you arguing the point."

"I didn't hear you arguing it either," Jasper pointed out.

Eli sighed, covering his face with his hands. "Yeah, I know. But now..."

276

"Now, you feel like an arse."

"Yes."

"Well, if I'm honest with you, I didn't see the point at the time either," Jasper said, scratching thoughtfully at the stubble on his cheek.

Eli looked over at him. "And now?"

"Now I'm thinking it might not be such a bad idea."

"I beg your pardon?"

"Look, if we were just going in for the girl, that would be one thing," Jasper said, leaning forward eagerly now, a familiar, almost manic glint in his eye, "but what if we could accomplish something else at the same time? Something Sully's been after for ages?"

Eli frowned. "I don't understand where you're going with this. When has Sully ever showed any interest in getting into Bedlam?"

"She hasn't, not in so many words. But she has been desperate for a way to prove that the Riftmead is being used to dull our magic."

Eli propped himself up on his elbows. "Be serious."

"I am being serious. What if we could get in there and find the proof we need? You know they're experimenting on patients. Sully knows it, too. It's time for everyone else to know it."

"But how would we even begin to... we don't even know what we're looking for!" Eli cried.

"But we do! We know from that letter the Braxton girl found."

"Her name's Eliza."

"As you like, then. Eliza," Jasper said, rolling his eyes. "If there's one letter, there must be others—journals, reports, written logs of experiments and their outcomes. Surely, if we could just get into the building..."

"But how? How would we get into the building? I mean, shy of acting a crazy fool in the streets and getting ourselves carted off there as patients?"

"I'm glad you asked," Jasper said, a wide, satisfied smile stretching across his face. "It just so happens I know a girl—"

Eli groaned. "Of course you do."

"Now, now, hear me out," Jasper said, raising a hand. Eli made rather a show of pressing his lips together and gesturing for Jasper to continue. "Her name is Tillie, and she's a washerwoman in the Barrens."

"And I'm assuming she hasn't just been doing your laundry," Eli said dryly.

Jasper laughed but didn't answer. "She does the mending and washing for Bedlam. Well, some of it, anyway."

"And you think she'll be able to sneak us inside in a laundry basket, do you?" Eli asked.

Jasper punched him in the calf, the only bit of him he could reach. "No, but I think she might be able to help us all the same."

Eli narrowed his eyes at Jasper. "Why are you doing this? I know you don't care a whit for Eliza, so what is it? If you're just looking to stir up trouble with Sully—"

"It's not about that," Jasper said, shaking his head. "Sully needs to get out of her own way. She's been too scared for big action ever since the Lamplighters Confederacy fell apart and Davies was arrested. She came so close to being caught—they all did. She knows we need to take bold action, but she's terrified of the casualties."

"She's not wrong. We haven't got the numbers or the resources we used to have," Eli said.

"Yes, but how the bloody hell are we going to get them—the numbers or the resources—if we're too scared to try?" Jasper said.

"She doesn't want us to be reckless," Eli said.

"She doesn't want to lose us."

Eli looked into Jasper's face and fell silent. Sully wasn't an affectionate person. Never in all the years they'd been in her care had she uttered the words "I love you." But she had raised them. Carried them. Bandaged their knees and fed their bellies. Taught them to read and write. Made sure they could defend and protect themselves. It had been a kind of love, hadn't it, to have done all of that for children she shared no blood or connection with, save the fact that they were all of them Riftborn, cast into the dirt and forced to cling to the lowest rungs of society and morality all because of their magic. Perhaps, in her way, Sully did love them. And perhaps that love was holding her back from making the decisions that needed to be made.

"The books weren't enough. The Barrens are going quiet again. The Praesidio patrols have people scared, and now that they're distributing Riftmead like water, they'll all soon be too weak and drugged up to care about a damn thing. We're going to lose our chance if we don't find a way to keep that fire burning," Jasper said.

Eli nodded. Jasper was right. He hated when Jasper was right. It was so much easier when he was transparently a bloody fool.

"Do you think Sully would go for it?" Eli asked.

"Not a chance," Jasper said confidently.

"So, we would be doing this on our own," Eli said, as much to himself as to Jasper.

"I think it's the only way. But if we succeed, Eli—if we bring her what she needs, what the Resistance needs to finally build steam again..."

Eli didn't need Jasper to finish the sentence. He could see it unfolding in his mind's eye—the Riftborn of London, finally rising together in numbers too great to be overcome, snatching their freedom from the grasping fingers of the men who would keep it from them, taking their places in the seat of government, writing new laws, and watching their children rising from the ashes, embracing their magic instead of fearing it. Still, he could not help asking the question:

"And if we fail?"

Eli expected Jasper to laugh it off. He expected him to pull his lips back into a cocky sneer and proclaim that he could not possibly fail. But Jasper surprised him again. He rolled the question around inside his head for a moment—Eli watched as he crumpled his brow with concentration. Finally, he looked up at Eli, no mockery in his features, and a strange clarity in his eyes.

"Then, we fail. But at least we won't have sat by. At least we will have tried."

They held each others' gaze for a long, breathless moment. An understanding passed wordlessly between them, in that almost uncanny way that two people have when they've grown up together, thick as thieves.

"Eliza's been working on a plan to get herself in. She won't tell me all the details. I don't think she's quite got it all figured out yet."

"That's all right. We can fit ourselves in somehow. I mean after all, as long as we can blend in, our options will be far greater," Jasper said, starting to sound properly enthusiastic now that he knew they were going through with it, whatever "it" may be.

"Are you sure? I get the sense there are parts of the plan she's hesitant to share with me. I think she's afraid I won't want to be involved if I know everything," Eli tried to clarify.

But Jasper was in too good a humor to worry about speculation.

"Eli, what are you worried about? That the lady's maid is going to concoct a plan too dangerous for the likes of us?"

A tiny smile tugged the corner of Eli's mouth. He had to admit, it was a humorous thought: prim and proper Eliza, plotting out elaborate escapes full of explosions and danger. Eliza, who had never purposely set foot in a dangerous situation but by pure accident of fate. Eliza, who had been so blindsided by the nature of their plan at Madam Lavender's but had played her part so bravely. Who had even gone so far as to kiss him—*really* kiss him—just to maintain their cover and find her friend. Eliza, who just might be braver than the two of them put together...

His face dropped once more into a grim line, but it was too late: Jasper had already seen the hint of his smile, and the bargain was struck. Eli only hoped that none of them would come to regret it, for there was no going back now.

Proclamation of Prayer, presented to Elder Hallewell and family, 9 June 1871

On behalf of the High Elder and the Elder Council, we issue this official proclamation of prayer for the Hallewell family. All faithful citizens of post-Rift London are asked to lift their voices up in prayer upon the Creator's day this Sunday next at noon, and to recite the following words in reverence:

"Dear Creator, we come to You this day to raise up the Hallewell family in prayer. May You gather them to You and shower them in Your mercy and comfort as they grieve the loss of their son, William Elias Hallewell, so cruelly taken from them in an act of evil born of the curse of Riftmagic. May You take the child to You, Creator, and give him peace everlasting with You in Your kingdom. May his family find comfort in knowing that he is at Your side now. We ask that the vile criminals who have cut his young life short be found swiftly, and that they shall face thunderous retribution at Your hands, and at the hands of Your Elders, to whom You have entrusted the safety of Your people. May they suffer for what they have done, and may their suffering serve as a reminder to all Riftborn of the devastation that results from succumbing to the self-serving temptations of Riftmagic. In Your name we pray. Amen."

TWENTY-SIX

"**E**LIZA, YOU REALLY must be more careful!"

Eliza looked up from the polishing of one of Miss Jessamine's brooches to see her mistress staring at her, her face cocked into an amused smirk. Eliza looked down at the polishing cloth in her hand, examined the gleaming brooch carefully, and then looked at her mistress again, flummoxed.

"Begging your pardon, miss? Careful of what?"

By way of an answer, Jessamine pointed down at the shoes Eliza had laid out for her. They were two different colors.

Eliza groaned and abandoned her polishing to dig out the matching shoe. "I'm so sorry Miss Jessamine. I don't know what's come over me."

"Well, I certainly do. You're distracted. We both are. Yesterday at Sadie Carpenter's quilting circle, I referred to Reginald as 'Ronald' and then forgot half the words to the blessing when we had our tea."

Eliza smiled weakly. "Yes, I'm sure that's it. It's the nerves, miss. I can't stop thinking of Bridie. The waiting is driving me mad."

"Yes, me as well, but we must be cautious. You're very lucky your mistress is in on your scheme, or you'd be getting scolded right and left. I hope you're holding it together better belowstairs than I am in my social circles."

Eliza gave a non-committal shrug. The truth was, she'd been just as scattered in her duties downstairs as she had been with her mistress. The difference was that everyone belowstairs was so worried and distracted and sad about what had happened to Bridie, that Eliza found herself in good company. No one seemed to notice when someone made a mistake or a task slipped their mind. Even Mrs. Keats had stopped yelling at the kitchen staff and had taken to following along behind them, correcting their errors quietly. Millie was constantly red-eyed and sniffly. Liesel was dealing with her feelings by completing tasks no one had even asked her to do, throwing herself into work with such abandon that her body had no choice but to fall into bed at the end of the day and sink into an exhausted slumber. Eliza listened to her snoring through the wall, jealousy seeping through her. She had not slept properly since before their trip to the palace, which now felt like a lifetime ago. Had it really only been a little over a week since she had lain there with Bridie, giggling into their pillows and whispering late into the night?

"Have you heard from your friends? The ones who want to help us?" Jessamine asked, dropping her voice to a whisper.

"Yes. They are hoping to procure staff uniforms that will allow them to move around inside the asylum without being detected."

"Oh, that's an excellent idea. Yes, if we had accomplices disguised as staff, I imagine it would be much easier to find Bridie and perhaps even gain access to where she's being kept. You will let me know if they are successful, won't you?"

"Of course, miss."

"And they still don't know I'm helping you?"

"No. I thought they might back out if they knew I had gotten a Dignus involved," Eliza admitted with a rueful smile.

"I resent that very much, indeed!" Jessamine said, lifting her chin. "You didn't get me involved. I involved myself. In fact, this whole plan was my idea! I involved you!"

"Miss Jessamine, I know that, and you know that, but I don't think it would be a very good idea for them to know that," Eliza said.

"Oh, very well. I suppose I understand why they might hesitate to trust me," she said with a sigh.

"Just leave it to me, miss. We'll find a way to work together," Eliza said. She stood up, having fitted matching slippers onto her mistress' feet. "There we are. Pretty as a picture, and just in time, too. Martin will have the carriage around front for you by now, miss."

Jessamine groaned. "I wish I didn't have to go. Can't I stay here with you? What shall you do while I'm gone?"

"Oh, I'll… I'll find something to occupy myself, I'm sure, miss," Eliza said. She had not told Miss Jessamine about the arrangement she had made to watch over Mrs. Hallewell while Jessamine was at her charity group. It was not that she did not think she could trust her mistress—indeed, she had never trusted her more than she had since she had made the offer to help free Bridie. No, it was simply that she didn't want to cause Miss Jessamine any more pain than she was already coping with, and the mention of her mother would do nothing but deepen her present agony.

"Very well, then. I shall see you when I return," Jessamine leaned forward and planted a quick kiss on Eliza's cheek. "If I send for you while I'm out, be assured it's because I have killed Sadie Carpenter and I need you to help me hide the body."

Eliza burst out laughing. "At your service, in that as in all things, miss."

Jessamine winked and swept across the room to the door. But before she could so much as place her hand upon the handle...

"Miss?"

"Hmm?"

"You've forgotten something."

Eliza held up the engagement ring, a rueful grimace on her face. Jessamine's features twisted as well, but only for a moment. She held out her hand and allowed Eliza to slide the ring onto her finger and, with a cheerless nod of thanks, left the room.

Eliza sighed and glanced at the clock. It was still nearly half an hour before she was due upstairs at Mrs. Hallewell's chambers, but she decided to head up early. The thought of descending into the gloom and sorrow of downstairs was too much to bear. At least she would be sure to be thoroughly occupied if she went up to relieve Mrs. Spratt just a little early.

The face that awaited her on the other side of the door was transformed since last Eliza had seen it. Mrs. Spratt was positively glowing with anticipation, and the light in her eyes took ten years off the rest of her features. She beckoned Eliza inside, and Eliza obliged, slipping quietly into the room in case Mrs. Hallewell was sleeping. Sure enough, she saw the frail frame of the mistress of Larkspur Manor, curled like a small child in her bed, her lashes resting upon her sallow cheeks.

"Eliza, I still can't believe this is happening. I feel as though I must be dreaming," Mrs. Spratt whispered, taking Eliza's hands in hers and squeezing them tightly. Even through her gloves, Eliza could feel the buzzing hum of the woman's Influencer magic as it sparked with her own.

"Well, I'm glad to say that you are very much awake. And as Miss Jessamine has already left for her charity circle, you are free to go as well. I daresay if you leave now, you may arrive in time to visit with your daughter before the ceremony begins!"

A slightly hysterical laugh burst from Mrs. Spratt, and she clapped her hand over her mouth to stifle it. Then she threw one last, anxious glance over her shoulder at Mrs. Hallewell. "Are you quite sure about this?"

"Not a doubt in the world. We shall get along just fine. Odds are she'll sleep until you return, but if she doesn't rest assured I shall keep her as calm and quiet as can be," Eliza said soothingly. "Now, off with you!"

Mrs. Spratt snatched up a handbag, patted at her hair, which was tucked neatly up under her hat, and gave Eliza's hand a last squeeze before departing.

Eliza sighed, and settled herself into Mrs. Spratt's customary chair beside the bed, pushing her feet against the floor and rocking gently. Within minutes, she had removed her cap and pushed her sleeves up past her elbows. The room was stiflingly warm, kept so for the benefit of Mrs. Hallewell, whom, it seemed, chilled easily. Indeed, Eliza could not comprehend piling all those blankets on top of her in a room so warm, but Mrs. Hallewell merely pulled them more tightly about her frame, muttering unintelligibly to herself between soft snores. Eliza stared into the fire where it danced merrily in the grate and cursed herself for not bringing something to occupy her hands—a bit of mending or embroidery or something like that. Without a task, it would be very easy to let her mind wander to the very things she longed to forget—like her debilitating fear that something dreadful would happen to Bridie before they could find and free her.

Bridie would never be able to return to Larkspur Manor, that much was certain. Eli promised that the Resistance would find a place for her, but Eliza had no idea what that would even mean. Would Bridie have to hide in a basement somewhere? Perhaps they would even try to smuggle her out of the country—they had done the same for other Riftborn in the past. It struck Eliza that, even should they be lucky enough to rescue her friend, she'd be very unlikely to see her again. The thought brought a lump into her throat that was very hard to

286

swallow back. She put her head back against the chair and squeezed her eyes shut.

She would not let fear deter her. She would push it down and away, smother it out. She had to remain calm and clear-headed for Bridie's sake. She would take the consequences, whatever they may be, if only she could ensure her friend was safe. She focused all of her energy on picturing Bridie free and happy, giggling over gossip and waxing poetic about gowns and Presentation balls.

A sharp sound, like the snap of a mousetrap, startled Eliza and she opened her eyes, heart hammering. She had thought she had closed her eyes for only a moment, but the embers in the fire told a different story—the fire was burning lower than it had when she'd settled into the chair—perhaps it had been the pop of a log that had roused her from the edge of sleep, for sparks were still floating on wisps of smoky tendrils. She felt a crick in her neck and turned her head to loosen it. It was then that she let her eyes fall upon the bed.

The *empty* bed.

She was on her feet before her brain had even processed what she was looking at. She tore at the mussed blankets, as though Mrs. Hallewell might somehow be discovered beneath them. She turned on the spot, staring frantically into every corner but Mrs. Hallewell was nowhere to be found. Then, Eliza remembered the sound that had awoken her and snapped her head around to look at the door.

It hadn't been a log popping at all. It had been the door, shutting behind Mrs. Hallewell.

Feeling faint with terror, Eliza tore across the room and flung the door open onto the deserted hallway beyond. No, not deserted: she caught a glimpse of the hem of a white nightgown whipping around the corner. Eliza took off as fast as her legs would carry her after her charge, her heart thumping painfully hard against her chest, her breath burning in her lungs. As she ran, she pulled off her gloves. If she could just get a finger on the woman before someone else spotted her, she could compel her back into bed and all would be well.

If not... she shuddered to think of the consequences.

She rounded the corner in time to see Mrs. Hallewell flying down the next hallway like a barefooted specter out of some gothic fever dream. Her dark hair streamed out behind her, her nightgown billowing like a sail. She reached the end of the hallway and turned sharply for the staircase. Eliza willed her legs to move faster. She could not allow Mrs. Hallewell to reach the ground floor. Elder Hallewell was not in the house, but if anyone saw his wife, there would be no keeping it from him that she'd gotten past Eliza.

Mrs. Hallewell did not continue her descent, thank the Creator, but deserted the stairs at the first landing and took off down the hallway into the east wing on the second floor. Eliza let relief wash over her. No one used this wing—it was closed off with the rare exception of dusting off some of the guest quarters for visitors. Eliza had never ventured down this hallway since she was a very small child, not since...

And suddenly Eliza knew which door Mrs. Hallewell would open before she had even reached it, and she made no move to stop her. She held her breath as the woman placed her hand upon the handle, unsure whether the room would be locked after all these years, but the handle turned easily under her grip, and the door swung forward into the dust-cloaked darkness beyond. Eliza slowed to a jog as she approached. She did not want to startle Mrs. Hallewell. It would be much easier to get near her if she took things slowly and gently. She took a deep breath, held it for a moment, and then blew it out. Then she stepped over the threshold.

Were it not for the musty smell and thick layers of dust that coated every surface, Eliza could have believed that she'd stepped back in time into the Hallewell nursery as it had been so many years ago. Ruffled bedding still adorned the little bed and cradle. Long forgotten toys sat upon chairs and windowsills. A rocking horse, its legs stretched out in mid-gallop, looked poised to take off out of the French doors onto the balcony. Porcelain dolls reached out their delicate arms to no one.

Mrs. Hallewell had stopped at the little bed in the corner and was staring down at it, humming to herself. Eliza felt a lump rise in her throat as the lullaby pricked at her memories. She had played in this room. She had been held and sung to beneath this faded fresco of painted cherubs and rainbows, so long ago that it felt like a memory from another girl's life. Her mother had cared for the Hallewell children here, and her along with them. It took every ounce of resolve she had not to flee from the room and the long-drowsing memories it awakened in her.

Instead of turning tail like a coward, Eliza moved further into the room until she was standing only a few feet away from Mrs.

288

Hallewell. She cleared her throat softly, so as to alert the woman to her presence without startling her. Mrs. Hallewell flinched slightly at the sound and turned to face Eliza with such depth of sorrow in her eyes that Eliza, gazing upon it, found she could not breathe.

As she struggled to catch her breath, she watched as the sorrow kindled into something else—first confusion, then recognition, and then a manic kind of desperation.

"Emmeline! Emmeline, you must help me!"

Eliza's insides twisted into a painful knot at the sound of her mother's name. She bit her lip and tried to hold herself together. It wasn't Mrs. Hallewell's fault—she was so terribly confused that she thought she was talking to a younger version of herself when Jessamine made her ill-fated visit to her on the night of the Presentation ball. Eliza knew that she looked very like her mother—her father had remarked upon the resemblance before, always very ruefully. When she was still small, convinced her mother would return, she would scan crowds in the street, hoping to find her own face looking back at her. As she got older, she had stopped searching.

"Mrs. Hallewell, come with me, madam. It's time to return to your room," Eliza said, in what she hoped was a soothing voice. She thought she could hear the tremble in it, but was not sure it was pronounced enough for Mrs. Hallewell to catch it.

"Emmeline, there's no time for that! It's William. Please, you have to help me."

"I am always here to help you, Mrs. Hallewell," Eliza promised. It would be easiest to play along, to answer to her mother's name. "But you have to let me help you. Come along, now. You mustn't torture yourself like this."

But Mrs. Hallewell stumbled toward her, clutching at Eliza's sleeves. Eliza reached up to squeeze the cold, slender fingers, but Mrs. Hallewell's next words froze her like a statue.

"You must take him, Emmeline. You must take him and get him out. He's not safe here, not now that his father knows what he is!"

Eliza's fingers hovered over the woman's hands, not yet making contact. "What do you mean?" she whispered.

"His father knows! I tried to hide it, but he found out!"

"Don't worry, Mrs. Hallewell. William will... will be all right. Let's go."

"No! No, he won't! Don't you understand? Josiah will never let this stand! We cannot have a Riftborn child, it will mean the end of everything for him in the Illustratum!"

Eliza's head was reeling. The Hallewells' eldest child, a Riftborn? Was it possible, or was this simply more raving? "Mrs. Hallewell, I—"

"You are my only hope, Emmeline. You must take him and deliver him to those who can help protect him!"

"Protect him from whom?" Eliza asked, her voice barely more than a hoarse whisper.

"From Josiah! I overheard him and Francis talking. They... they mean to..." The end of Mrs. Hallewell's declaration was swallowed in a sob, and she dropped her face into her hands, moaning.

Eliza, now free of the woman's grasp, reached slowly out and placed a gentle hand on her cheek. She felt her gift flow through her, but she did not seek to calm the woman, not yet. First, she had to know the truth...

"Mrs. Hallewell, tell me what Elder Hallewell said. Tell me why William needs protecting."

Mrs. Hallewell's sobs quieted. She lifted her face and stared at Eliza, who felt she could easily drown in those deep haunted wells of her eyes. Her voice, when she answered, was hollow and broken. "Josiah is going to kill him. Kill him and make it look like the Lamplighters Confederacy kidnapped him."

Eliza swayed on the spot, barely able to keep her legs beneath her. It couldn't be true, and yet she could feel the truth of the words with her magic, knew that they had been dragged up from the depths of this woman by the sheer power of her Influence. She both needed to know and dreaded to know the rest. She looked up to see realization dawning on Mrs. Hallewell's face, like a sleeper waking from a long deep slumber.

"You're not Emmeline," she whispered.

"No. I am Emmeline's daughter, Eliza. You know me. I'm a friend."

She said the words and she also compelled Mrs. Hallewell to believe them.

"You are remembering things that happened a long time ago, Mrs. Hallewell. I know they sometimes feel like they're happening now, but that's all over."

The words washed over Mrs. Hallewell, who seemed to sag with the knowledge. She let her eyes wander around the room, taking in the dust and the gloom for the first time. Her bottom lip trembled.

"Mrs. Hallewell, please. I need to know. Did my mother help you? Is that why Emmeline Braxton disappeared?"

Mrs. Hallewell nodded her head. "She took him because I asked her to. She brought him somewhere—somewhere safe. I had meant to take the baby and meet them, but..."

"But the Lamplighters Confederacy fell before you could arrange it," Eliza whispered.

Mrs. Hallewell nodded. "And then your mother was caught. I swear, I do not know how they discovered what she'd done. I never told a soul. I pretended I had no idea what happened to our son, but Josiah suspected my part in it, and ordered me locked away."

"What happened to my mother?" Eliza asked.

"I don't know. I'm so sorry, but I don't know," Mrs. Hallewell said, her voice shaking and shattering again into tears. "I don't know what they did to her, and I don't know what's become of my sweet boy."

Her grief finally overpowering her, Mrs. Hallewell sank to the floor. Eliza sank with her, wrapping her arms around the woman's thin shoulders and stroking her hair while she let her sob into her uniform. Inside her head, the thoughts whirled like a tornado, making her dizzy with realization.

Her mother had not run off as Eliza had been told. She had not left her only child behind, not on purpose, and certainly not because she had desired to. She had been caught trying to smuggle the Hallewell boy to safety. Did her father know? Surely he did not. The letter her mother had left behind had told another story altogether, a story meant to protect them from the truth. And all this time Eliza had thought her mother had not loved her enough to stay...

But leaving had not been her choice. She had been caught—arrested, most likely. How would they have punished her? Hanging, surely. It did not seem possible that a servant could kidnap the young master of the household and escape with her life. They could have given her a false name, as they had done with Davies, in order to cover up who it was they had really hanged. If that was true, Eliza thought, her mother was just as lost to her as ever she had been.

But what if they hadn't killed her? What if, like Davies, they

291

had sent her to the Praeteritum? Was it possible her mother had been locked up there for all these years? Had Eliza perhaps even glimpsed her as she passed the high fences, just another of the ragged prisoners toiling and wasting away behind the bars?

No. No, she would not allow herself such hope. It was already too much to bear, this new truth of why her mother had vanished. She looked down at the broken woman in her arms and felt the tears slip down her cheeks. She let them come, for her mother, for Mrs. Hallewell, for little William who, if by some miracle he had survived, would never know the hell his mother had gone through to save him.

And beneath the tears? Rage. Rage as she had never known it before, licking like flames at the tenderest parts of her. Was there nothing the Illustratum touched that they did not destroy?

Me, she thought. *They have not destroyed me. And they will come to regret it.*

TWENTY-SEVEN

T HE NIGHT WAS UNUSUALLY WARM and the breeze off
the Thames carried a foul, fishy stench up onto the bank where
Eli and Jasper waited. The moon was full, bright enough to
illuminate the thin clouds that kept slipping by in front of it, bathing
the riverbank in a ghostly glow.

"Are you sure about this, Jasper?" Eli asked, for what he thought
might be the fifth time.

Jasper ground his teeth together. "Would you stop asking me that?
I told you she'll come and she'll come."

"Did she actually *say* she would come?"

"Practically."

Eli groaned.

"I know her," Jasper said confidently. "I know her like the back of
my hand. She'll come."

"It's because you know her like the back of your hand that I'm
afraid she *won't* come."

"Sod off, Eli. Do you want my help or not?"

Eli sighed. He wasn't sure if he did want Jasper's help. He'd
accepted it in a moment of desperation, but he'd come dangerously
close to regretting it approximately every ten minutes since. But for
once he had convinced himself that Jasper would be an asset. After all,
Jasper was usually the most unpredictable element of any plan. But
this plan was so ludicrously unpredictable already, that adding Jasper
into the mix felt almost natural. And, of course, it had been the only
way to keep him from running to Sully like a petulant child.

"Jasper."

Both Eli and Jasper whirled around at the sound of Jasper's name to see a petite woman standing at the top of the stairs, two large baskets of clothing balanced precariously on one hip. She could not have been even five feet tall, but though her stature was small, there could be no mistaking her for a child: no child alive had ever fixed a person with so thunderous an expression as she now levied at Jasper. Eli was surprised Jasper did not cower away in fear—he had taken an unintentional step backward himself.

"All right, Tillie?" Jasper asked, in what he clearly hoped was a charming voice.

"Don't you 'all right' me, you useless lout," Tillie practically spat. She charged down the steps, her red curly hair fanning out around her face in the breeze like flames. Her sleeves were pushed back to reveal muscled, heavily freckled forearms, and her green eyes sparkled like emeralds out of her face. She was, Eli decided on the spot, the fiercest little slip of a thing he'd ever had the misfortune to cross.

"Ah, go on, Tillie, how many times are you going to make me apologize?" Jasper asked with a groan.

"At least once more," Tillie said, arriving upon the shore and setting her baskets down with a thunk.

Jasper hung his head and sighed. Then he raised it again, clasped his hands in front of him, and said, "Tillie, I am endlessly, eternally sorry."

"What the hell did you—" Eli began, but Jasper stepped on his foot and he shut his mouth.

"I have learned the error of my ways. Can you please forgive me?" Jasper finished, not a trace of mockery in his voice.

"No," Tillie said, arms crossed truculently across her chest.

Jasper swore. Eli, recognizing a flagging effort, moved in.

"Tillie, is it?"

She aimed her glare at Eli now, and he did his damnedest not to cringe away from it. It was not easy, like staring down an angry bull. How did someone so tiny manage to inspire such terror? Jasper sure could pick them.

"I don't know what my bumbling idiot of a brother has done to offend you, and frankly, I'm not sure I want to. But he hasn't asked you here as a personal favor. It isn't for him, that is. It's for me. I need help."

Eli couldn't be sure—her eyes were still so fierce—but he thought her lips might have twitched when he spoke the words "bumbling idiot." Jasper must have seen it too, for rather than punching Eli in the arm for the insult as he would normally have done, he jumped eagerly back into the conversation.

"He's telling the truth. I wouldn't be fool enough to ask for a favor, Tillie. I know I don't deserve one."

"Putting aside what you deserve," Tillie hissed, "what am I doing here, then? I've got deliveries to make, and more washing and mending to pick up."

"You're off to Bedlam, aren't you?" Jasper asked. "That's part of your Thursday rounds, isn't it?"

Tillie narrowed her eyes suspiciously. "That's right."

"We need a couple of uniforms. Staff uniforms. With liveries."

Tillie's eyes widened, her contempt for Jasper temporarily forgotten. "Whatever for?"

"I'm not sure you want to know that."

Tillie's face went white beneath her freckles. "I don't do the mending for the staff uniforms. They handle those on the premises. I only do the patient washing and mending."

"But you've seen the uniforms? You could put your hands on them, if you wanted to."

Tillie did not deny it, but she shook her head. "But I don't want to. Why would I risk something like that?"

Jasper looked at Eli now, and the silent question in his eyes was clear: how much do we tell her? Eli sighed.

"Tillie, have... have you ever seen any of the inmates at Bedlam?" Eli asked.

Tillie made a half-hearted movement, something between a nod and a shrug. "Not many. A few from a distance, being taken for walks by the staff. And..."

"And?"

"Well, you can hear 'em, sometimes, even down in the washrooms. Screams." She shuddered.

"What if I told you that some of the inmates aren't mad at all?"

Tillie snorted. "I'd tell you to listen to that screaming. No sane person is going to make that sound."

"But what about a sane person trapped with lunatics against their will? Might a sane person make that sound then?"

In spite of her best efforts, Tillie looked disturbed. "That... that couldn't be. They wouldn't..."

"Ah, come on, Till. You've got a cousin and an uncle in the Praeteritum. You know there's almost nothing they wouldn't do," Jasper said.

No one needed to clarify who "they" were. Tillie gave a rather anxious look around her now, as though she feared they would be overheard.

"Even if that was true," she hedged, though it was clear from her expression that she knew it bloody well could be, "what has that got to do with me? How could my stealing uniforms help any of that?"

"There's a girl," Jasper began, then swiftly, because Tillie's expression instantly hardened, "it's not like that! I haven't even met her. Neither of us has."

Tillie crossed her arms over her chest. "Go on."

"They plucked her right off the street for asking the wrong questions. Locked her up. Claimed Riftsickness and madness. Sound familiar?"

Tillie bit her lip. "Course it does. You think she's the only one?"

"She's a manor girl."

Tillie's eyes widened. Everyone knew the Illustratum mistreated the lowly population of the Barrens. But to hear of the same treatment of manor servants or wealthier residents of the merchant districts was clearly shocking. She set her chin stubbornly. "How do you know she's not a manor girl who simply went mad?"

"Can't you just trust that we know?" Jasper asked, a pleading note in his voice. "Come on, Till. You know your uncle and your cousin don't deserve to be where they are either."

"But you ain't fixin' to free them, are you?" she asked bitterly.

"Not quite yet," Jasper said. His tone made Tillie's eyes widen.

"What are you dragging me into, Jasper?" she whispered.

Jasper shook his head. "Nothing. Two uniforms. Pulled out of a laundry basket. And that's an end to it."

Tillie shifted anxiously from foot to foot. It was clear she was wavering. Jasper opened his mouth to push his point, but Eli laid a restraining hand on his arm. Tillie was considering it, and the wrong word from Jasper could ruin everything. He recognized the very moment the decision crystallized in her eyes.

"Fine. I'll try. I make no promises, and I ain't risking my neck. If I can't get them easily, I'll not go to any great measures, you understand?"

"Of course," Jasper said, relief coloring his voice. "We would never dream of asking anything more."

"You most certainly would," Tillie grumbled. "Wait here. I shouldn't be more than an hour or so." And with one last, vindictive look, she picked up her baskets and stalked back up the steps.

Eli let out a long, low whistle. "That was like trying to negotiate with a banshee."

Jasper's face had fallen back into its familiar lines of arrogant indifference. "Ah, she's always like that. She's harmless, really."

Eli raised an eyebrow. "That woman may be a lot of things, but she was decidedly not harmless. I also suspect that she isn't always like that. Just after an encounter with you."

Jasper laughed. "Nah, she's just got that classic Irish temper. It's the hair, you know. Fiery hair, fiery spirit."

"Yeah, keep telling yourself that," Eli muttered. Jasper just chuckled and started looking for a place to sit down. He settled on a dry patch of grass under a scrawny tree. He leaned himself against it with a groan and closed his eyes.

"Are you going to sleep?" Eli asked, incredulous.

Jasper shrugged but did not open his eyes. "Might as well. Got to do something while we're waiting."

"And you think dozing off next to the Thames at night is a reasonable option?"

"Beats sitting here having to smell it."

Eli snorted. "You're going to get yourself robbed."

"Not with my dear brother here to protect me," Jasper said with a wide, mocking grin.

"Hey, I'm not your brother by choice, you know."

"No one is anyone's brother by choice, you fool. You can't choose who you're born to."

"Not really what family means to the likes of us, though, is it?" Eli said quietly.

The smile slipped from Jasper's face. "No. I suppose it's not."

A small fishing boat chugged past them. Eli watched its progress, cutting a glimmering stripe through the murky water. A single fisherman was visible on the deck, a cigar dangling from his mouth as he mended a net.

"Don't you ever wonder?" Eli asked.

Jasper scratched his nose, eyes still closed. "Not really. I already know what makes you so insufferable."

Eli rolled his eyes. "Come off it, Jasper. I'm serious."

"Well, be more specific then. I'm too tired for riddles."

"Don't you ever wonder about your family? The people who gave you up?"

Eli listened to Jasper's hesitation in the dark. Then...

"No."

"You're lying."

"I'm not."

Eli turned, and though the dark obscured most of Jasper's features, he could tell from the faint gleam that his eyes, at least, were open now. "How is that possible?"

Jasper shrugged. "I used to. I used to wonder about them all the time. I used to wander the market district and watch the parade of Dignus entering Sunday services, looking for faces that would trigger a memory. All I ever felt was angry."

"Surely some part of you still wants to know?" Eli asked, barely keeping the plea out of his voice.

Jasper considered this. "Yes, but not for the same reasons as when I was a child."

"Explain that."

"When I was a child, I wanted to find them so they would take me back. Now I want to find them so I can personally knock them down off whatever pedestal they've built that had no room for me in the first place."

Eli nodded, a humorless chuckle bubbling up in his throat. "Yeah. Yeah, I guess I can see that."

Eli could feel Jasper's razor-sharp gaze on his face. "Is that why you're so hellbent on helping this manor girl?"

"I suppose so, yeah. I understand why she did what she did. I would have done the same, I reckon, if I hadn't spent my whole life well aware of the reason I was abandoned. Sully explained it to me, and so I was never taken by surprise."

Jasper pursed his lips.

"What?"

"Nothing. Forget it."

"Jasper, just spit it out. I know that look. You've got something to say. Out with it."

Jasper sighed. "Sully doesn't always tell us everything we should know."

Eli waited, but Jasper was still silent. "Ah, well, thanks for that, Jasper, that's really cleared things up."

Jasper leaned up on his elbow, his expression uncharacteristically serious. "What do you remember about the day you came to Sully?"

Eli shrugged. "Nothing. I was barely three years old. I can't remember anything before Sully. Sometimes I get flashes—running through the dark street, feeling scared—but otherwise, it's like I had no life before Sully. All my earliest memories are sparring with you and banging around that old house."

"Yeah, I think she's counting on that," Jasper said quietly.

"Jasper, would you stop being so bloody cryptic and just—"

"I remember the night you came to Sully. Well, I remember bits of it."

Eli froze. "You never told me that."

"I know."

"Why didn't you—"

"You know why. When Sully told us to keep our mouths shut, we bloody well shut them. And by the time I let myself think about it again, so much time had passed, I didn't see how it could do any good."

"Well, what do you remember? Tell me!"

Jasper sighed. "Did you ever ask Sully about it?"

Eli considered ignoring the question and forcing Jasper to talk, but sighed instead. "Of course, dozens of times."

"And what did she tell you?"

"That my Dignus family abandoned me, and a member of the Resistance brought me here."

Jasper laughed bitterly. "And never once did she mention that the member of the Resistance who brought you was a manor servant?"

Eli's heart seemed to thud to a standstill in his chest. "A manor servant?"

"Yes. A woman. A woman in a lady's maid uniform."

"How do you know this?" Eli asked, his voice little more than a breathless whisper.

"I saw her. I snuck down to the staircase and watched. Sully told me to stay in my room and hide, but I was too scared something was going to happen to her, so I followed her instead."

299

"What else do you remember? Anything else?" Eli asked.

Jasper shook his head. "Look I only stayed on the stairs for a few moments—just long enough to make sure that whoever it was wasn't going to kill or arrest us all. But I remember the woman pleading with Sully to take you."

"What did she say?"

"Something along the lines of, 'I can't take him back there. You know what they'll do to him.'"

Eli ran a hand over his face. "You know what this means."

"I do. But it doesn't matter."

Eli felt a fit of sudden anger swell inside him. "Doesn't matter?!"

"Eli, consider it," Jasper said, sitting up straight now and looking Eli squarely in the face. "Just... take the emotion out of it, for a minute..."

Eli threw his head back and laughed. "Are you—*you*, of all people—asking me to be reasonable and logical? You can't be serious, Jasper."

"I am serious. Let's say it's true. Let's say that lady's maid took you from a manor house. That makes you the child of an Elder. What does that change?"

Eli's words exploded out of him. "It changes EVERYTHING, Jasper! It means I... that I could... that I might..."

"That you might *what?*" Jasper shouted, before tossing a cursory look around them and lowering his voice again. "That you might walk up to every manor house, knock on the door, and announce that the prodigal son has returned? What makes you think they won't shut every one of those doors in your face? Or worse yet, kill you on the spot before you have a chance to expose them? Don't you understand, Eli? There will never be a place for you there! You could be the son of the High Elder himself and the only thing it will entitle you to is a spot on the gallows!"

Eli's face twisted as though Jasper's words were a bitter medicine he had been forced to swallow. "You still should have told me. I still had the right to know!"

"Yeah, that's right. You had the right to torture yourself day and night with the knowledge that you're supposed to be knocking around one of the wealthiest households in the country, drinking champagne and dancing with beautiful women; but instead, your family probably would have killed you. How dare I try to protect you from that?"

300

Eli was pulled up short. "You were trying to protect me?"

Jasper snorted. "Yes. And what a bloody success I've made of that. What kind of question is that, anyway? Why else would I keep it from you?"

Eli shrugged. "I don't know. Spite? Jealousy?"

"Yeah. That does sound more like me, truth be told," Jasper said with a sigh.

Eli couldn't quite manage a laugh, but he did feel a smile—a genuine one—flash across his face before it fell back into the wrinkles and folds of pensiveness. "Thanks for that."

"That's what brothers are for. Even accidental ones."

An uneasy quiet fell between them, their thoughts rushing beneath it like water under a bridge.

"Is that why you didn't want Eliza to be a part of the Resistance?" Eli asked after a while.

"Why, because she might bring along another brother to annoy me?"

"Because you thought it might drag something up for me? Something I'd forgotten?"

For all his joking, Jasper seemed to seriously consider his answer to the question, for which Eli was grateful. "I don't know if I thought it through that much. I just... the proximity to the Dignus. It poisons everything. It always has. I suppose I just thought it was opening a door that we might not be able to close."

"We're going to have to open all those doors in the end, though, if we want to change anything," Eli pointed out.

"Open them? Pity. I thought we might get to knock them down and light them on fire."

Jasper grinned. Eli grinned back. For a moment it felt easy between them like it had when they were younger. Eli savored the moment, sure it would be fleeting. Sure enough, a moment later, a hissing sound alerted them to Tillie's return. They jumped up from where they had slumped under the tree and stood tensely, poised to run for it; but Tillie was not running, and her two baskets were tucked under her arm. Beside him, Eli heard Jasper let out a sigh of relief.

"Well, I've managed it," Tillie said sourly. She dug her hand under the pile of dingy white fabric and retrieved a bundle, which she thrust at Jasper, who quickly unwrapped it to look inside. Eli caught a glimpse of patches in the Illustratum livery colors. "Two staff uniforms. I grabbed what I could. No idea if they'll actually fit you."

"Do all the staff wear the same uniforms?" Eli asked.

Tillie shook her head. "These are the uniforms the janitors and groundskeepers wear. There are dozens of them who work there, for the place is a shambles, and in constant need of upkeep and cleaning. They're also one of the lowest-paid positions at the hospital, so workers come and go all the time. It's your best bet to blend in without anyone questioning who you are."

Despite her insistence that she didn't care if they were caught, she'd clearly considered their safety when choosing which uniforms to steal, and Jasper grinned as though he knew it. "Thanks, Tillie. I owe you one."

"You owe me several," Tillie snapped. "And don't thank me yet. There's still every chance you'll be caught the moment you walk through the doors. Don't say I didn't warn you. And I'll deny ever seeing you in my life if they question me, do you understand? You found those yourself, on a mending pile when you got inside."

"Of course," Eli said quickly. "No one will ever know you helped us, we swear to it."

Tillie tore her glare from Jasper to give Eli an appraising look. "His word ain't worth the mud on my boots, but yours I'll take," she said grimly. "Now get out of here before someone sees you." And she stalked off, muttering darkly with each stomp of her feet.

Jasper turned to Eli, a triumphant smile on his face. "There you are, see? I told you Tillie would come through!"

"Don't smile just yet," Eli said grimly. "All this means is that we're actually going through with this ludicrously dangerous plan."

"I know," Jasper said, his smile widening into a wicked grin. "That's precisely why I'm smiling."

An excerpt from the remarks of Elder Kiernan Harris upon the public re-opening of Bethlem Hospital, 12 July 1817

"It is my great pleasure to dedicate this institution to our Creator, to whom we offer up all our good works. In His name today, we open to the public a feat of public service and medical achievement. The new Bethlem Hospital at St. George Fields shall serve as the standard against which all other asylums across the civilized world shall be judged, a modern marvel of medical knowledge and research. Here the weakest among us shall be cared for and rehabilitated into useful and faithful members of society. Here our most brilliant doctors shall seek out new medicines and cures, aided by their faith and the mercy and will of the Creator, whom we pray will guide their hands.

I invite you, our honored guests here today, to walk with me through these gates and behold not only the remarkable work that has been done, but the seeds of great work that shall be done—the advancements and achievements yet to come that shall improve the lives of the poor souls who enter through these doors, riddled with Riftsickness and mental decay. I invite you to witness the Creator's mercy in action, and the methods and treatments that shall surely become the envy of the world as the plague of Riftmagic continues to spread, unchecked, outside of our borders. May our example inspire others to take up the cause, to fight this great plague of our modern age, and embrace, at last, the Creator's will. And with that, I invite Dr. Cook to join me as we cut the ribbon…"

TWENTY-EIGHT

"**M**ISS JESSAMINE, there's still time to turn around. If you've changed your mind, I entirely understand," Eliza mumbled as their carriage bumped along the road closer and closer to the Thames.

"Eliza, for Creator's sake, would you please stop trying to talk me out of this?" Jessamine cried, sounding exasperated. "Do you want to find Bridie or not?"

"Of course I do, but..." Eliza bit down on her lip.

"But what?"

"I just feel so awful, miss, mixing you up in this mess. Please don't misunderstand, I am terribly grateful for your help, but—"

"Eliza, for the hundredth time, you are not mixing me up in anything. This was my idea. I am the one who came up with this plan. If anything, I am mixing *you* up in this mess. So please stop speaking as though I am not a grown woman perfectly capable of making my own decisions."

Eliza continued to watch Jessamine's face, guilt eating away at her insides. Ever since the afternoon that Mrs. Hallewell had escaped to the nursery, Eliza had struggled about what to do with the truth she now carried. It was entirely too large a burden to carry on her own, and yet she had not been able to bring herself to share it with anyone—not Mrs. Spratt, who arrived home several hours later with shining eyes and a lighthearted spring in her step. Not Jessamine, who had already had such a burden of her own to bear in the form of her boorish fiancé. And certainly not her father, though she knew he had more of a right to know than anyone. She had considered it. She had gone down to his office later that night after Mrs. Spratt's return and knocked upon the door. But when it came time to open her mouth, the words refused to come. Her mother had gone out of her way to protect them from what she had done, and Eliza didn't feel right stripping that protection away. It was kinder, wasn't it, to allow her father to think that his wife had simply left? Surely it would be a hundred times worse to know that she had been arrested and likely killed for defying the Illustratum. And so Eliza had carried the weight of the knowledge all by herself for days, feeling at times that it might simply crush her under its bulk.

No, she could not focus on that right now. Eliza shoved the thoughts of her mother and little William Hallewell back into the shadowy recesses of her mind. She would have to reckon with it all, and soon, but not today, not when so much was at stake. She must focus all her energy on getting Bridie back—and the plan was certainly going to need every ounce of her concentration if it was to have a prayer of succeeding.

The plan itself was, on its surface, doomed to fail, though that failure would fall squarely on Eli and Jasper's shoulders if it came to pass. The premise was simple. In the back of the carriage were baskets of charitable donations for the patients of Bedlam. As a daughter of an Elder and the future daughter-in-law of the High Elder himself, Jessamine was entitled to request a tour of any property that was run by the Illustratum. She had written to Bedlam to inform them when she would be arriving. Jasper and Eli would meet them outside the gates wearing uniforms of the institution staff and conceal themselves inside the carriage until they were inside the grounds. (Eli had been hesitant to explain how they had managed to procure these uniforms, and Eliza did not press him.) The carriage would take them within the grounds, and Eli and Jasper would carry the baskets in as though they had been instructed to do so, and hopefully, no one would be any the wiser. Then, once inside, Jessamine and Eliza would create a distraction that would allow Eli and Jasper to slip away into the building and find Bridie.

After that, the plan dissolved into a murky fog of unknowns. How would they find her? If they did manage to find her, how would they get her out without getting caught? Eli and Jasper had told Eliza to let them worry about this aspect of the plan, but she could sooner stop breathing than stop worrying about just how they would manage to pull this off. She could not help but think they were keeping their own worries quiet and assuming a confidence they did not feel. Or rather, a confidence that Eli did not feel: Jasper's overconfidence appeared to be a fixed and unchanging state of being, which did not soothe Eliza's worries at all.

The carriage crossed the Thames, clattering noisily over the Lambeth Bridge. The Illustratum loomed over them as though the towers themselves were watching them, leaning over them to catch their every whispered word. It seemed impossible to Eliza that they would be able to defy the Illustratum within its very shadows. They would be able to see it in the distance, even from St. George's Fields, piercing them like a glare. Eliza realized the prisoners in Bedlam must be able to see it, too, a constant reminder of the powers that kept them locked away from the rest of the world.

Many years before Eliza had been born, in the very early days of the Illustratum's rule, the old Bethlem Hospital in Moorfields had been torn down. From the outside, it was all opulence and flower gardens and tree-lined promenades, but within the walls was a different matter. It was, the critics had argued, like biting into a red, rosy apple, all glossy sheen and rounded cheeks, only to find it black and worm-eaten within. The conditions in which the prisoners were kept were so deplorable, so inhumane, that the city grew up in arms about it, particularly the women of the Dignus who, still learning how to wield their status in the newly formed society, rallied around the cause eagerly. The Elders vowed to restore order to the halls of Bedlam, just as they had restored order to the chaos of post-Rift London, and thus the plans for the new Bethlem Hospital began. It had none of the grandeur of the rotting old palace in Moorfields—the new Bethlem was much starker, more sterile looking, with a grim façade surrounded by high walls and metal fencing. A cupola marked the main entrance to the place, with six long white columns that gave the impression of jail bars.

At least, Eliza thought, as the carriage rolled down Lambeth Road toward it, this building had not been constructed as a lie. What went on within its walls was just as stark, cheerless, and grim as the walls that contained them. Her stomach, churning and twisting moments before, seemed to have dropped completely out of her as they reached the gates. She closed her eyes and searched for a shred of courage she could cling to. There was no turning back now.

Jessamine ordered Martin to call at the gates and announce their arrival. The moment he had jumped down and hurried away as he hastened to obey her, Jasper and Eli crept out from around the corner, sprinting like mad for the carriage and jumping inside. Eliza just had time to slide into the seat beside Miss Jessamine before they had crowded in on the other seat, pulling the door carefully closed behind them. Their reaction, when they realized they were in a carriage with the daughter of an Elder, was predictable.

"Bloody hell!" Jasper gasped, his hand on the door handle again at once. Eliza reached out to stop him from flinging himself back out of the carriage.

"Jasper, it's all right! Miss Jessamine is here to help us get in. This whole plan was her idea," Eliza hissed.

Jasper threw a panicked glance at Jessamine before turning to Eli, whose mouth was hanging open as though his jaw had ceased working. "And you think my schemes are mad? We should have just brought along our own nooses and been done with it! Did you know about this?"

Eli shook his head. "I assure you, I did not."

"There is nothing to fear from Miss Jessamine," Eliza hissed, the edge of desperation clear in her voice. "I give you my word, she will not betray our cause."

"And what does she know of our cause?" Eli hissed through tightly clenched teeth.

"That we wish to free Bridie from Bedlam. That, and nothing more," Eliza replied coolly.

Jasper still looked as though he was considering leaping from the carriage. Eli's face was full of indecision. But before either of them could make any further argument, they heard Martin climbing back into his seat and the grating squeal of metal on metal as the gates to Bedlam began to creak open.

An awkward silence hung heavily in the air between them until at last, Miss Jessamine cleared her throat impatiently and said, "Eliza, won't you please introduce me to our compatriots?"

Eliza blushed. "Oh, I... yes, all right. Eli and Jasper, may I present Miss Jessamine Hallewell."

Jessamine did not hesitate a moment, but thrust out her hand. Eli and Jasper stared at each other for a moment, clearly unsure of how to proceed.

"Oh, come now, gentlemen," Jessamine said with a roll of her eyes. "Surely we can dispense with the formalities here? We are, after all, in cahoots."

Jasper let slip an incredulous laugh, and then reached out and shook Jessamine's hand. Eli blinked a few times in surprise, and then followed suit. Jessamine's eyes lingered on him, a small frown creasing the space between her eyebrows.

"You look terribly familiar. Have we met?"

"Most assuredly not, Miss Hallewell," Eli replied, barely able to meet her eye. "I think I would have remembered being introduced to the daughter of one of the most powerful men in England."

Jessamine nodded thoughtfully, and then released his hand, folding her own demurely in her lap again.

"We, uh... we appreciate your assistance in this matter, although we were not expecting it," Eli said.

"And I yours, Mr...?"

"You can call me Eli. It is safer for all of us if we do not divulge too much about ourselves."

"As you say. Eli, then. I can assure you, I care as much about securing Bridie's freedom as you do. Not all Dignus harbor such contempt for the Riftborn, you know. Bridie means a great deal to me. She once did me a great service, and I do not intend to abandon her when she needs me to return the favor."

Eli and Jasper looked at each other, clearly incredulous. Jasper laughed again.

"Is something amusing?" Jessamine asked politely.

Jasper shook his head. "Not at all, Miss Hallewell."

"Then I must ask why it is you continue to laugh at me."

This sobered Jasper up a bit. He tried to compose his face into a more respectful expression. "My apologies. Despite how it may appear, I am not laughing at you. It is merely that I'm not very often surprised, and today I find myself completely and utterly gobsmacked."

Jessamine smirked. "I shall assume you meant that as a compliment, and take it as such."

"As well you should," Jasper said, inclining his head and winking rather roguishly. Eliza would have liked to slap him for his boldness, but she was too relieved that he had not already leaped from the carriage in alarm. If Jessamine was offended, she did not show it. Her own smirk broadened for a moment before she composed her face back into a slightly imperious mask more befitting her relative status within the coach.

Under cover of this exchange, Eli leaned across the carriage and whispered to Eliza, "You might have warned me."

"If I warned you, you wouldn't have come," Eliza said. "And I needed your help."

"Is this payback for the fiasco at Lavender's? That was unexpectedly devious of you, Miss Braxton."

Eliza shrugged. "I did warn you that you wouldn't like the plan."

"You did," Eli admitted.

"Are you angry with me?"

"I'm not sure yet. I'll let you know if we manage to escape with our lives today," Eli said sternly, but his mouth betrayed the beginnings of a smile.

"We can trust her, Eli," Eliza said earnestly. "Please believe me."

"I trust you, Eliza, and so I shall take you at your word, and Miss Hallewell, too, Creator help me," Eli replied.

"I am glad to hear it, for it is time to put our plan into action," Miss Jessamine whispered, jerking her head toward the window.

The carriage was now passing through the gates and making its way around the side of the enormous building. The tall narrow windows flashed past, set into the walls like staring, empty eyes. There was no time to turn back, no time to change their minds. What would come of this ludicrous plan would come, and they would have to face it.

"Have you brought the daguerreotype?" Eli asked, holding out his hand.

"What? Oh! Yes, here it is," Eliza said, reaching into her pocket and extracting the little silver-framed photograph. She dropped it into Eli's hand, and he looked down at it for a moment, studying Bridie's face. Then he dropped it into his own pocket with a curt nod.

"How will you get her out if you find her? I'm not at all sure they allow the patients to simply wander around. Surely she'll be locked up in a cell or something?" Jessamine asked.

Jasper grinned again. "Let's just say locks won't be a problem."

When Jessamine's expression crumpled in confusion, Jasper's grin widened, and he flicked his hand toward the coach door handle. It turned with a squeak, and the door fell open an inch or two before Jasper reached out and caught it.

310

"Oh, I see!" Jessamine said, smiling now herself. "Your Riftmagic! How remarkable!"

Eliza refrained from rolling her eyes with great difficulty. In her opinion, everyone in that carriage was far too enthusiastic about the terrible amount of danger they were about to put themselves in. Jasper and Jessamine were looking at each other like two small children about to steal some sweets from the kitchen. Eli seemed to know what Eliza was thinking. He caught her eye and shook his head in exasperation before turning his attention out the window again.

"For Creator's sake, stop showing off and pay attention, Jasper. It's nearly time."

They fell silent as Eli and Jasper kept watch out of the windows. At last, as the carriage reached the corner of the building and started to turn, Eli nodded his head. Noiselessly, they pushed the door open and jumped down into the courtyard, keeping close to the side of the carriage and jogging along with it until they reached a small copse of scrawny trees, where they darted off to conceal themselves. Eliza held her breath but heard no shouts, no indication that anyone had seen them exit the carriage.

"Don't worry, Eliza, your friends seem more than capable," Jessamine said, her eyes shining with excitement. "Are you ready to play our part in this charade?"

Eliza nodded, her stomach twisting into such knots of anxiety that she was afraid to open her mouth. How had she ever agreed to this? It was madness, utter madness, and the closer they got to the doors of Bedlam, the madder it seemed. But she thought of Bridie and knew they had to go through with it.

And besides, she thought ruefully, *where better to carry out a plan born of madness?*

The carriage rumbled to a halt outside a set of wide wooden doors set into the shadowy side of the building, an entrance intended for workers and deliveries. Important guests such as Miss Jessamine were meant to be received at the hulking front entrance, but the use of this door was crucial to their scheme. Jessamine closed her eyes and took a long, slow breath as Martin hastened down to open her door. Then, assuming an air of commanding self-importance, she stepped onto the gravel and began giving orders.

"Thank you very much, Martin. Please see that the crates are unloaded. I'm sure there are some workers here who can... ah, yes!

You two! Please see that the donations are unloaded and brought into the kitchens. I am sure that is where they ought to be dealt with." She snapped her fingers imperiously at Jasper and Eli, who chose that moment to reveal themselves, and began at once, heads bowed, to assist Martin in unloading the heavy crates.

"Miss Hallewell!"

A portly man in a slightly threadbare suit came hurrying around the corner, puffing and blustering as he went. He carried a gold pocket watch on a chain in his hand, and his face was crumpled into a harried expression. The late afternoon sun glinted off of his bald head, which was shining with droplets of sweat.

"Miss Hallewell, I am so very sorry! I was waiting for you at the front entrance. I am Mr. Brown, the overseer of this fine institution. Did I forget in my letter to instruct you where to meet me?" He was practically falling over himself to take Jessamine's hand as he dipped into a low bow.

"Hello, Mr. Brown," Jessamine said briskly. "Yes, you did say to meet you at the front entrance. Do forgive me, but it seemed quite impractical with all of these boxes."

"B-boxes? What boxes?" Mr. Brown watched in bewilderment as Martin, Eli, and Jasper stacked the wooden crates by the door.

"Why, the donations to the patients, from my charity circle!" Jessamine said, her eyes widening in feigned surprise. "Surely I mentioned that I would be making a sizeable donation of supplies to the hospital?"

"Uh, no. N-no, I'm afraid you didn't," Mr. Brown said, hurrying forward to peer at the crates. Eliza held her breath, but he did not give Eli or Jasper so much as a glance.

"Oh, Mr. Brown, you must forgive me! I feel just dreadful. Did you want me to take them back?" she asked. "Only, I've made sure to include provisions for the staff as well. I can't imagine the toll your jobs must take." The smile that spread over her face was a masterclass in charm as she gestured to a case of fine brandy. Mr. Brown's eyes widened and he barely managed to smother a satisfied expression.

"No, not at all! Please don't apologize, Miss Hallewell! Your donations are most welcome, and your generosity will be sung to the rafters for this act of kindness." Mr. Brown snapped his fingers at Eli and said dismissively, "Lock them into the storage room off the kitchen, but see that *that* crate," he pointed at the case of brandy, "is

312

brought to my quarters." He turned to Jessamine with a long-suffering expression. "I'll have to see to it that the donations to the staff are distributed responsibly. You can understand why I can't leave such a temptation lying around in the kitchens for any kitchen maid to stumble upon."

Jessamine nodded solemnly. "Oh, yes, indeed, Mr. Brown, I quite agree. That would be like letting Eliza here have run of my jewelry collection! I'd never see my diamonds again!"

Jessamine laughed airily and Brown joined in, moving a step closer to her, like they were sharing a private joke. Eliza kept her head down deferentially, watching out of the corner of her eye as Jasper and Eli lifted the crate and went through the door. Eli looked up and gave her a shadow of a smile just as the door closed behind them.

It had been almost too easy, she thought, but her relief dried up almost at once. Getting in, they had all agreed, would be the simple part. From here on out, their plan would come almost entirely down to sheer luck.

"Well, Miss Jessamine, I am sure my staff can attend to your charitable donations. Won't you accompany me for a stroll around to the front entrance, and we can begin our tour?"

"That would be wonderful, Mr. Brown. I thank you," Miss Jessamine said, and she took the man's proffered arm. "Come along, Eliza. I want you with me. Do you mind if I bring my maid along, Mr. Brown? I would not feel right leaving her behind here with lunatics on the premises."

"Certainly, Miss Hallewell," Mr. Brown said, waving a hand over his shoulder at Eliza and sparing her not a glance. "Whatever makes you most comfortable, though I assure you, you are quite safe here. I run a very tight ship."

"I have no doubt of that, Mr. Brown," Miss Jessamine simpered, though as she looked over her shoulder to beckon Eliza along, she gave her a mischievous grin and a wink. Eliza understood the joke.

Given the ease with which two stowaways had just managed to slip aboard, the ship was not quite so tight as Mr. Brown believed it to be.

TWENTY-NINE

W ITH EACH HEAVY WOODEN CRATE they carried inside, Eli held his breath, waiting for the inevitable moment that someone would discover them, but after ten trips back and forth to the carriage without anyone so much as glancing at them, he began to relax just a bit. Their mere presence, it seemed, would not be enough to arouse suspicion. The driver, Martin, was managing the whole business, speaking with the downstairs staff and pointing imperiously where the donations ought to be placed, clearly enjoying the illusion of temporary authority. Once they had set down the last of the boxes, he chanced raising his head to get a better look around the place.

The boxes were being directed into a large pantry off the main kitchen area. The hallway was exceptionally long—so long, in fact, that Eli suspected it might run the entire east wing of the building without obstruction. Doors lined both sides, and people came and went through them like a hive full of bees, carrying stacks of towels, buckets of dirty dishes, and, once, a set of long, thick chains, each of them so intent on their work that they had not a thought to spare for the two young strangers in the janitor uniforms.

"Where do you think we go from here?" Jasper whispered, pulling a handkerchief out of his pocket and wiping his face in an attempt to mask his words.

"I say we find ourselves a couple of mops and buckets and work our way upstairs," Eli replied. "The women's wards are on the east side of the building.

"How in blazes do you know that?" Jasper murmured.

"The bloody great directory on the wall," Eli muttered back, jerking his thumb over his shoulder. Sure enough, there were signs posted at the far end of the hall. The words "Women's Riftwards" were clearly visible, with an arrow pointing up to the staircase on the left.

"Oh. Right. Well, that makes it a bit easier to find the girl, I suppose, but where do you suppose we start looking for proof of the Riftmead poisoning? Doctor's offices? A research laboratory?"

"I'm not sure. Oddly enough, it doesn't say, 'Proof To Incite Rebellion, Third Floor.' We're just going to have to improvise, Jasper. That part of the plan was your idea, after all."

Jasper flashed a quick grin. "I like improvising."

"I know. It's one of the most aggravating things about you." It was also their only chance of finding what they were looking for, but Eli wasn't going to give Jasper the satisfaction of hearing him say it out loud.

"Is that everything?" A middle-aged woman with faded brown hair and the air of a harassed housekeeper was cataloging the donations, counting the contents of the crates and writing them down in a large black ledger. She peeked into a smaller crate, rolling her eyes and tutting. "Silken handkerchiefs. I ask you, why does the woman think lunatics have any use for silken handkerchiefs?" She wrote them down anyway, shaking her head and muttering to herself.

"That's everything that's meant for the patients, yes," Martin replied. He was staring around eagerly, bouncing on the balls of his feet. "Say, are there any lunatics on this floor? Do you suppose I might get a glimpse at 'em?"

The woman looked up from her ledger, sighing. "No, I'm afraid they are quartered upstairs, sir."

Martin sagged a bit with disappointment. It was clear he'd been hoping to gawk at the patients as though they were animals in a zoo.

"You said that was everything meant for the patients. Are there other donations as well?" the woman asked impatiently.

Martin was still staring eagerly down the hallway as though a patient might wander down accidentally. "Huh? Oh, yeah. There's this last crate here, Mr. Brown requested it be taken directly up to his quarters," Martin informed her. She took one look at the box, clearly labeled with its contents, and pursed her lips.

"Yes, I shouldn't be surprised." She sighed, as though she could already see that the contents of the box were going to make her life

316

measurably more trying. "Very well, then, up it goes, Creator help us all." She snapped her fingers at Eli and Jasper who jumped to attention. "Second floor, west wing, first door past the medical offices, and be quick about it. One of the doctors can let you in."

Jasper and Eli looked at each other and hastened to obey. They grasped either end of the heavy crate and began to lug it down the hallway towards the stairs, trying to look like they knew where they were going. They were halfway up the staircase before they dared converse.

"What are the odds? It was as though she heard us and gave us directions!" Jasper whispered excitedly.

"A stroke of luck to be sure, but don't get too excited yet. Plenty of ways yet to get caught and arrested."

"You're so cheerful, Eli."

"That's me, a bloody ray of sunshine."

"So, I guess that's made our decision for us, then," Jasper said. "We'll investigate the medical offices first, and then make our way over to the women's Riftwards and try to find the maid. Should be a lark, eh?"

Eli didn't reply, but merely adjusted his grip on the crate and kept climbing the stairs. He did not have breath to waste, even to tell Jasper he was a fool.

The hallway into which they entered was wide and wood-paneled, with dull bronze plaques upon the doors to designate the purpose of each room. Between the doors, great paintings hung upon the walls, though they did not depict landscapes or portraits, but words: passages from the Book of the Rift, painted upon canvasses in bold black script and bordered in heavy gold frames. Eli paused for a moment and stared at the words on the walls, the words that had taken root in the world and poisoned the minds of an entire nation, relegating him—and those born like him—to a lifetime of servitude and struggle. For one fleeting moment of madness, he wanted to rip them from the walls, pile them up, and set fire to them. If he hadn't had a very important job to do, he mightn't have been able to resist. Jasper seemed to understand his hesitation, for he snorted with disgust and then nudged Eli with his foot.

"Come on. We haven't got time to destroy property, brother. Maybe on our way out the door, eh?"

They hurried along, meeting no one but a harassed-looking nurse who had not a glance to spare for them as she half-ran along the hallway, several medicine bottles clutched in her hands. At last, about halfway down the hallway, they reached the door they had been instructed to find.

"W. F. Brown, Hospital Overseer," Eli read aloud. "Here we are then." He hesitated. "It's locked, surely?"

He tried the handle and found that the door was indeed locked. The woman downstairs had instructed them to find a doctor who could let them in, but they were not about to draw unnecessary attention to themselves, nor interact with anyone whom they did not strictly need to speak to. Instead, Jasper placed his hand upon the handle and screwed up his face in concentration. A moment later, after several loud clicking sounds, the knob turned freely under his fingers. He was about to push it open when a voice rang out sharply behind them.

"Can I help you with something?"

Eli and Jasper whirled around to see an elderly gentleman in a finely cut suit frowning at them. He wore the Illustratum livery across his chest and carried a notebook under one arm. He had just emerged from an office three doors down. A doctor, then.

"What are you doing up here?" he added, an impatient snap in his voice. Clearly, he felt it was beneath him to converse with janitorial staff.

"We was asked to deliver this crate up to Mr. Brown's office, sir," Eli said, putting on a cockney accent and a bit of lisp.

"Indeed," the doctor replied, narrowing his eyes and walking toward them. Eli heard Jasper curse under his breath.

"And how do you propose to open the door without a key?" the doctor asked.

"We... we was told to ask someone on the staff up here to let us in," Eli said. "But we didn't want to disturb anyone."

"I should say not," the doctor replied. He had reached them now, and stood with his heels together, looking down his long, crooked nose at them through a fussy little pince-nez. "Still, since I've seen you."

He heaved a long-suffering sigh and reached into his pocket, pulling out a ring with five keys on it. Then he waved his hand impatiently at them to move out of his way, and they hastened to do so.

The doctor bent over the door and placed his hand upon the

318

handle, which turned under his touch and swung inward, causing him to stumble before he could regain his footing.

"Good Lord. This door is already unlocked!" the doctor cried.

"You don't say, guv? We ain't even tried it yet, did we, Bill?" Eli said.

"Naw. On'y just got here when you spotted us, sir," Jasper chimed in. "Unlocked, you say?"

"Mr. Brown left his office unlocked! That is highly irregular, not to mention dangerous."

"Dangerous, sir?"

The doctor looked incredulous, as though Eli could not have asked a stupider question. "You are well aware of what kind of patients we have here. Imagine them having unfettered access to the files and information in this office!"

"Oh, yeah, I can see how that would be a bit of a problem for you, sir," Jasper replied.

"A *bit* of a problem? It's a security nightmare, that's what it is! I wonder how this could have—"

But his voice trailed off as his eyes fell upon the crate that Eli and Jasper had hefted between them, and his eyes narrowed suspiciously.

"What the devil is that?"

"A donation to this fine institution, sir, from the daughter of one of the Elders—'fraid I didn't catch her name, sir. We was just instructed to take it up to Mr. Brown's office right quick."

Without invitation, the doctor pried up the corner of the lid, revealing the bottles of brandy, nestled in a bed of hay to protect them from shattering. His expression, already disapproving, became a grim mask of anger.

"Well, this explains everything. A case of brandy, indeed. Less a donation than a bribe, I'd be willing to bet. And what man can be trusted to concentrate on security if he's hoarding liquor in his office! I'm going to have no choice but to speak to the board of governors about this. This shall not stand, not while I am a physician at this institution. Our work is too critical, too vital to the security of this fine nation to entrust its management to a drunkard who cannot even be trusted to lock his own door!" He glared back and forth between Eli and Jasper, as though he expected a response. Eli cleared his throat.

"Guv, I understand your predicament, so to speak, but this crate ain't filled with feathers. Would it be all right with you if we set it down now?"

The doctor flared his nostrils. "Yes, but not in there. Follow me, please." And he turned smartly on his heel, walking back toward his own office. Eli and Jasper threw panicked glances at each other and followed him. Of course, it was a stroke of luck to be invited into one of the doctor's offices, but this was hardly the surreptitious trip into the hospital they'd been hoping to make. They had to shake this doctor off, and quickly, or they were in very great danger of being found out.

The doctor stopped in front of the office he had vacated only a few minutes before, muttering angrily to himself and fumbling with his keys to open the door again. The plaque on the door, burnished to a rosy shine, said, "Dr. Francis Blakewell, Head Physician." Dr. Blakewell pushed his way in and snapped impatiently at Eli and Jasper to follow him. They lugged the crate into the office and placed it on the floor by the mantelpiece. Eli tried to get a good look around without drawing attention to himself. The desk was littered with files, sheaves of notes and open books—clearly, Dr. Blakewell had been deep in the middle of research when he had come upon them. Jasper was craning his neck as well, but it was impossible to make sense of the documents without properly examining them. Still, Eli knew that there was a very good possibility that the information they needed was sitting right in front of them on the desk. The question was, how to get their hands on it? They would have to let themselves back in, once the doctor left again.

Dr. Blakewell was muttering angrily to himself as he bustled over behind his desk and extracted a clean sheet of paper from the top drawer. Then he took up his fountain pen and began scribbling furiously, all the while keeping up a steady stream of hissing and mumbling. Eli cocked his head toward the door. Jasper took the hint and the two of them began backing toward it.

"No, don't go yet! Wait right there. I want you to take this letter for me and post it to the chair of the board of governors. I have no intentions of allowing this to go on a moment longer."

"Right you are, sir. We'll wait till you're finished," Eli said, walking around toward the back of the desk. He clasped his hands behind his back and bounced on the balls of his feet, whistling softly a bit, for effect. His eyes, however, were raking the contents of the desktop, scanning what text he could make out. He thought perhaps most of the papers might be individual patient files, but he couldn't get close enough without attracting Dr. Blakewell's attention to know for sure.

Dr. Blakewell signed his name with unnecessary violence and folded up the letter, sealing it and writing the intended address upon it. Then he stood up and handed it to Eli. "You said Mr. Brown ordered the box brought up to his office?"

"That's right, sir."

"Does that mean you've seen him?"

"Yes, sir," Eli replied, touching his cap respectfully. "He was headed for the front doors, sir, with the young lady what donated it. Takin' her on a tour, I think he said. That right, Bill?"

"Aye, that's what I heard. A private tour of the facility," Jasper said with a nod.

"Well, I'm going to have words with him right now," Dr. Blakewell said, storming around the desk and right out the door.

Jasper and Eli stood for a moment, motionless, and then heard the door at the end of the hallway slam. Jasper stuck his head out of the door and then pulled it back in again, grinning. "Can you believe that? Loses his mind over someone forgetting to lock their door and then leaves his wide open. What a prat!"

Eli smiled. "His righteous indignation is our lucky break. Keep an eye on the hallway, and I'll see what we can find here."

Jasper pulled the door nearly closed and stationed himself against it, peering out into the hallway while Eli descended upon the desk and began rifling through the contents. At first, he found nothing of note: the files appeared to be for people who had been admitted for legitimate mental conditions, and the pictures accompanying them painted grim pictures of disturbed individuals. Eli looked at the books and notes on the table. They appeared to be on the same topic: some kind of therapy that involved conducting electricity through patients. What little of the details he scanned were gruesome. He shuddered and dropped to his knees, pulling open the drawers.

"Find anything?" Jasper asked.

"Not yet," Eli replied. The drawer was full of files, each labeled with a patient's name, in alphabetical order. He flipped through them quickly, but there was no Bridie Sloane among them. He shut the drawer and tried another without success. It was not until he opened the third drawer that he struck gold. He extracted a folder with the official Illustratum seal on the front of it and began flipping through the pages, scanning the contents. His eyes widened.

"Jasper! Come look at this!"

Jasper hurried across the room to read over Eli's shoulder. The contents of the folder appeared to be some kind of report. The first page was a letter to the Elders, signed by Dr. Blakewell, followed by page after page of detailed notes and charts on individual patients.

"What does it all mean?" Jasper asked.

"It's an experiment. Look, see these charts? They track dosages and resulting side effects!" Eli cried out eagerly. He flipped through to the bottom of the stack. The very last paper was a concluding recommendation to the Elder Council. Eli read aloud.

"'It is with great confidence I can recommend that two to three dosings a week with Riftmead is safe enough for the general population to subdue the threat of uprising. Any more than that will result in an uptick of Riftsickness in the general population that will be hard to control and even harder to explain away. This should, at present, be avoided in children as we do not yet know the ramifications, though the research is already underway...' Creator help us all. They're experimenting on children, too."

Jasper looked nauseous at the very thought. "Those bastards. But this is it, Eli, isn't it? This is everything Sully needs!"

"Yeah, it is," Eli said, slamming the drawer and standing up. "Now, what can we hide it in to smuggle it out of here?"

"Don't worry, your brother has come prepared," Jasper said, grinning, and began unbuttoning his shirt.

"Jasper, I don't think blinding the staff with your bare chest is going to be enough," Eli said.

"Oh, shut up, I'm not undressing. Look!" And he pulled his shirt open to reveal a kind of fabric sling he had fashioned against his midsection. He reached out for the folder, which Eli handed over to him, and tucked it securely into the sling, buttoning it closed.

"Jasper, I... that was a really good idea," Eli said.

"It was bound to happen eventually," Jasper replied, refastening his uniform over the sling to hide it. "Don't worry, I'll be sure to do something reckless and stupid momentarily, just to balance it out."

Eli and Jasper ran for the door, but before they could reach it, a bell began clanging, echoing through the hallways. Eli and Jasper emerged from the office in time to see doors opening right and left, and people spilling out into the corridor, looking around frantically and then running for the stairs.

"What's goin' on, guv?" Eli asked, grabbing at a man as he ran past.

"Emergency in the patient wards," he called back, wrenching his arm out of Eli's grip and racing down the hall after the other staff members.

Eli turned to look at Jasper, whose face had gone slack. "That sounds bad. What should we do?"

"We'll draw more attention to ourselves if we don't follow the rest of the staff," Jasper whispered, even as another man in a janitor's uniform raced past them. "Let's go see what the trouble is. Maybe we can use it as a diversion."

Eli patted his hand against Jasper's chest. "Look, Jasper, you should get out now. Those papers you've got in there are too important. Backtrack to the kitchens and slip out the same door we came in."

Jasper's mouth fell open. "What? No! I'm not leaving you in here on your own!"

"I'm not on my own. Eliza's still here."

Jasper rolled his eyes. "Oh, yeah, well that makes me feel much better."

"It should. She could compel that Mr. Brown to burn this place to the ground if she wanted to. Get those papers back to Sully, and all of this will be worth it, even if..."

He did not finish the thought, but he didn't need to. Jasper finished it for him.

"Even if you get caught? I don't bloody think so, Eli."

"Look, I'm not going to get caught! Now will you just get out of here?"

Jasper's face twisted. It was clear he didn't like the idea, but Eli's logic was hard to argue with. "All right, I'll smuggle these out. But I'm not going far, and if you're not out in an hour, I'm finding a way back in."

"Fair enough," Eli said, relief flooding through him. "Just make sure you hide those somewhere safe."

"Leave it to me. And Eli?"

"Yeah."

"Don't cock it all up, eh?"

Eli smiled. "Likewise."

Jasper squeezed his arm, which brought a lump of emotion to Eli's throat. Then he jogged off down the hallway in the direction they had come and Eli, whispering a prayer with no fixed destination, took off after the rest of the staff to find himself a diversion.

THIRTY

ELIZA WALKED THROUGH THE HALLS of Bedlam like a
dreamer in a strange dream. Several feet in front of her, Mr.
Brown was walking arm in arm with Jessamine, pointing out the
various points of interest in the architecture of the place in a gloating
voice that suggested he had personally designed and executed every
single one of them. So far, he had paraded them through the front
entrance hall, the kitchen area, the visitor's waiting area, and the
library. They had encountered only two patients so far, an ancient
woman in a wheelchair who was being read to by a white-capped
nurse in the corner of the library, and a young man with bandages over
his eyes being led out the front door on a walk by a barrel-chested
orderly. Eliza began to worry they may not have a chance to look for
Bridie among the patients. Miss Jessamine seemed to be thinking
along the same lines, for she turned to Mr. Brown as they exited the
library and flashed her most winning smile at him.

"Yes, the building is very impressive, of course," she said, "but I
must confess, I'm far more interested in the kind of care you provide
to your charges than in any architectural details."

"Is that so?" Mr. Brown asked, looking quite put out.

"Oh, yes. My charity circle is most interested in how we care for
the most vulnerable among us, as I'm sure you'll understand. It is our
mission as a group, you see, to provide help where it is most needed,
and I could think of no better place than Bethlem. Would you be so
kind as to show me more of the patient spaces?"

Mr. Brown stopped walking, bouncing instead on the balls of his
feet and mopping at his head again. "Your heart is in the right place,
Miss Hallewell. I would of course be delighted to give you a more

intimate look at the patient wards themselves, but I must warn you, what you see may disturb you. I do not want to be the cause of any undue distress."

"Mr. Brown, I assure you, I am stouter of heart than my hat may lead you to believe," Jessamine said, pointing to the silk rose and netting confection perched on her pile of curls. "I have not come all this way to lose heart. I feel it is of the utmost importance to look adversity in the face, even if we do not like what we see. We cannot help if we do not understand."

Mr. Brown pursed his lips, considering. Miss Jessamine held his gaze steadily, waiting. Finally, his shoulders sagged into a simpering bow. "Of course. Your empathy does you credit. And fear not, for I shall be beside you each step of the way. You shall be perfectly safe."

Jessamine took the man's arm again as he positively preened. "I have no doubt about that, Mr. Brown, with such a stalwart protector at my side."

"To ensure that safety, I shall only take you through the women's ward. I'm sure you understand, it would be unconscionable to expose you to the men's ward."

"Of course. I would never dream of asking to see the men's ward. That would be most improper."

It was all Eliza could do not to roll her eyes. The ploy had worked, though, and Mr. Brown began to steer them toward a set of doors which he had to unlock with a key from the ring he kept on his belt. Eliza's heart rate sped up, and perhaps her breathing, too, for Miss Jessamine used Mr. Brown's temporary distraction to turn to her and demonstrate a deep, slow breath. Eliza nodded and tried to do the same, though her lungs did not seem to want to expand.

Mr. Brown pushed the doors open and offered his arm again to Jessamine, who took it with another bewitching smile. Eliza nearly smiled herself; if she didn't know better, she'd have sworn there was Influencer magic in her mistress' expressions, so effective were they in delivering the desired response.

All thoughts of smiles—bewitching or otherwise—melted away at the sight of what met them on the other side of the door.

Mr. Brown was treating Jessamine to what sounded like a prepared speech—Eliza caught the words "moral degradation" and "lack of character" and "power of prayer" mixed up in his rhetoric, but she could not focus for long enough to glean any meaning from them.

326

She was too distracted by the scene of wretchedness laid out before her. Patients were scattered around the room—slumped over in chairs, heads lolling against pillows, or tucked under blankets in wheelchairs. None of them seemed to know where they were, and took no notice of the tour now sweeping through their midst. In one corner, an elderly woman was rocking and cooing to a rag doll. In another, two women sat on either side of a chessboard, staring in bewilderment at the pieces. A few of the patients had restraints clearly visible on their wrists or ankles. Every face was a portrait of misery.

And the *noise*. It sounded like the doors along the walls housed caged animals rather than people. Shrieking, moaning, and grunting provided a constant soundtrack that the staff and other patients seemed completely oblivious to, but which seeped right into Eliza's bones, chilling her from the inside. People were crying out for help, for their mothers. Someone was singing an Illustratum hymn with bawdy, made-up lyrics. Even as she cringed away from the sounds, however, Eliza found herself listening for a voice that might belong to Bridie. It was all she could do to keep her face composed and tears from filling her eyes.

At first glance, Jessamine seemed to be doing a better job of holding herself together. Her expression was calm and her voice was clear and strong as she posed questions to Mr. Brown, but a closer look revealed that her knuckles were white as she clutched at his arm. Eliza could tell she was trying to get as close a look at as many inmates as possible in the hopes of locating Bridie. But they had agreed before they arrived, that they would hide any recognition from the staff—it would not do to let on that they knew one of the patients, especially right before that same patient escaped from the asylum.

"...engage in a number of revolutionary new therapies in the hopes that we can attack the root cause of the madness. Of course, once Riftmagic turns inward, it is very difficult to undo the damage. But with time and attentive care, we find we can make mild improvements," Mr. Brown was droning on, gesturing impressively to the patients who were not locked away, as though their mere presence outside of barred cells was some kind of achievement of which to be proud. Jessamine "ooh-ed" and "aah-ed" appropriately, which kept Mr. Brown in preening distraction so that Eliza could keep searching. After a few minutes, though, she was forced to conclude that Bridie was not in the main recreational area, which meant she must be locked in one of the cells. She wondered how she might communicate this to Miss Jessamine, but it seemed her mistress had already come to the same conclusion.

"Might we venture a bit closer to the cells, Mr. Brown?" Jessamine cooed. She leaned closer to Mr. Brown's ear and added, in a stage whisper, "I hope you won't think less of me for confessing to you that I am fascinated with the idea of madness. I would so love a closer look."

Mr. Brown smiled indulgently and patted her hand. "Not at all, Miss Hallewell. It was my own fascination that led me to this profession, and I see no harm in indulging your curiosity. After all, you shall be perfectly safe. The doors are all locked."

"You will stay close to me, though, won't you?" Jessamine continued, widening her eyes.

Eliza had never seen a face so smug as Mr. Brown's as he replied, "Every moment."

Heavens, but she was devilishly good at this, Eliza thought. She could give Lavender's girls a run for their money.

With that, Mr. Brown walked them to the outer perimeter of the room, where he began a slow promenade along the rows of cells, taking his time so as to allow Jessamine ample time to rise onto her tiptoes and peek into each one. Eliza trailed along behind them and Mr. Brown took no notice of her whatsoever. Jessamine posed a constant stream of questions about what she witnessed in each cell, keeping Mr. Brown so thoroughly engaged that Eliza was able to look into every cell as well. She had only glimpsed a few before she realized that what she was witnessing would haunt her nightmares for the rest of her days.

It was unspeakably sad as view after view presented itself from behind the tiny, barred windows, each one a perfect tiny tableau of human suffering. Chains dangled from walls, attached to restraints that hung around wasted necks and skeletal wrists. One woman's face was obscured by a strange device that seemed part muzzle and part medieval torture device. Buckets of human filth stank in dark corners, and once clean white tunics now hung, soiled and torn, upon the living shells that occupied them. Eliza had to swallow back the urge to vomit more than once, and quickly began to breathe through her mouth to avoid the eye-watering stench. They had walked along the entire north side of the cells without any sign of Bridie, and had just crossed the room to peruse the south side when an angry voice rang out through the space, making several patients shriek in surprise.

"Mr. Brown!"

Their little tour group turned to see a doctor charging toward them, his face thunderous. Mr. Brown's complexion suddenly paled so that it resembled cold porridge and he cleared his throat nervously.

"Ah, Dr. Blakewell. Miss Hallewell, this is Dr. Blakewell, our head doctor here at Bethlem Hospital."

Dr. Blakewell spared a grudging nod in Jessamine's direction before he turned to glare at Mr. Brown again. "I need to speak with you, Brown."

"Can it wait, Dr. Blakewell? I'm in the middle of giving a tour to a very important—"

"No, it most certainly cannot wait, unless you'd like me to go directly to the board of governors."

Mr. Brown gave an uncomfortable chuckle and mopped his shining head once again with his handkerchief. "Please do excuse me for a moment, Miss Hallewell. It seems Dr. Blakewell here has worked himself up into a bit of a state."

"I wouldn't be in this state if you showed even a modicum of competence or professionalism!" Dr. Blakewell shouted, spit flying from his mouth. Mr. Brown stepped back in alarm, placing Jessamine between them. Jessamine recognized the opportunity to escape Mr. Brown's clutches for a moment and extricated herself from between the two men.

"Gentlemen, I can see your business with each other cannot be delayed on my account. I shall wait just over here, Mr. Brown, until it is concluded."

Mr. Brown looked as though he half wanted to ask her to stay, but he pulled himself together and gave a deferential bow. "I do so appreciate your patience, Miss Hallewell. I shall be only a moment."

"You'll be as long as I keep you, and not a moment less. You've got to listen to what I have to say, and I won't be rushed or pushed aside so you can ignore the run of this institution and instead make a fool of yourself over a woman half your age!" Dr. Blakewell shouted.

Jessamine backed away from the men, now arguing over each other, and toward Eliza, who was standing and staring open-mouthed at the confrontation. Jessamine snatched at her hand and pulled her a few steps further away.

"I haven't seen her yet, have you?" Jessamine murmured.

She stepped close to Eliza and patted at her hair. Eliza, taking the cue, began fiddling with the hairpins as a pretext for whispering in her mistress's ear. "Not yet. She must be in one of the cells on the other side, unless... do you suppose there are any other places in the building where they might keep female patients?"

"I shouldn't be surprised. This place is massive. There are probably entire wards that aren't open to the public."

Eliza could feel the despair starting to creep in. How could they have been so foolish as to think they would be able to find her? It had been such a pointless, dangerous gamble, and all for nothing.

"What should we do?" Eliza whispered.

Jessamine looked anxiously over her shoulder where Mr. Brown and Dr. Blakewell were still in a heated discussion that was growing louder and more hostile by the moment. "Let's continue searching along the other side. I don't think Mr. Brown will notice, not at first. It seems he's landed himself in a spot of bother."

"I think *we* landed him in a spot of bother, miss," Eliza replied.

Jessamine shrugged. "From what I've seen of this place, I'd say he rather deserves it, wouldn't you?"

"Oh, most certainly, miss."

"Let's go."

Moving as quietly and unobtrusively as they could, Eliza and Jessamine continued their walk along the south side of the cells, peeking into the tiny barred windows atop each door, but they'd only managed to glance into half a dozen cells when the two men's shouting reached a peak.

"I don't bloody well care where it came from, or who gave it to you!" Dr. Blakewell was shouting. "What kind of example are you setting for the staff, turning your office into your own personal pub?"

"That is a ludicrous accusation!" Mr. Brown blustered. The top of his head was now as shiny and red as a ripe apple. "How dare you insinuate that—"

"Insinuate? Do you suggest there is not a case of brandy sitting up in your office right now? Do you really have the audacity to look me in the eye and tell me this place hasn't suffered because of your drunken incompetence?"

"That crate was brought by our visitor, Miss Hallewell, and was intended as a gift to the staff!" Mr. Brown said, the words hissing through his teeth like steam out of a kettle. "And I really don't think you should be making a scene like this in front of the daughter of an Elder!"

"Oh, I think that might be exactly who I should make a scene in front of," Dr. Blakewell blustered. His voice was getting louder and angrier by the second. "You think I should let this pass just because there's a Hallewell here? Round them all up, the whole lot of Hallewells, and any other Elder family you can get your hands on. In fact, let's get the whole Council down here. I think they'd all like a tour of your incompetence. Doors left unlocked, liquor being hoarded, overcrowded wards, and my reports sitting unread on your desk for weeks on end—"

Noise from the patients rose up all around them in a billowing swell. Eliza grabbed onto Jessamine's arm.

"Miss, I think we're going to have to get out of here. I can feel it in the air—I don't think it's going to be safe much longer to—"

"Miss Jessamine!"

A familiar voice cried out from one of the very last cells. Grimy fingers reached out from between the bars. A single spark popped and cracked from a fingertip.

Eliza's heart stopped cold.

"Bridie."

§

At first, Bridie was sure she had dreamed it. The name Hallewell echoed through her sleep-addled fog, and she sighed with longing. She would do anything to go back to Larkspur Manor, even in her dreams—anything to escape her present reality. She rolled over on her filthy mattress and tried to envision the place, hoping her sleep would carry her there. But then the name sounded again, louder this time, and someone nearby gave an agitated whimper. Bridie peeled her eyes reluctantly open.

Beside her, huddled on the same mattress, was Emmeline. Her eyes were wide and swimming with moisture. Her hands twisted in her lap and her lips were trembling.

"Emmeline?" Bridie's voice was nothing more than a hoarse croak. She cleared her throat. "What is it? What's wrong?"

Emmaline did not speak—she rarely did. But now her mouth was

331

forming a word over and over again, like a silent prayer to ward off evil: "Hallewell. Hallewell."

Bridie hauled herself into a sitting position and rubbed the sleep from her eyes. "You heard it too?" she asked.

Emmeline nodded, the word still falling soundlessly from her lips over and over again. Her eyes were fever-bright with fear.

Bridie reached out and squeezed her hand. "It's all right, Emmeline. He's not here. Don't be afraid."

But Emmeline's face was so stricken with terror that Bridie sighed and hauled herself to her feet, taking a moment to steady herself on shaky legs. "I'll go look. I'm sure it's nothing, all right?" Bridie could not imagine Elder Hallewell debasing himself by stooping to visit such a place, though if he had, she thought, she would not miss the opportunity to plead her case.

She shuffled her way over to the door. The room swam around her, and she had to throw her hands out to the sides to steady herself, as though she was crossing the deck of a storm-tossed boat rather than the cold stone floor of the cell. She leaned against the door for support and stretched onto her tiptoes to peer out into the ward.

At first, she saw nothing out of the ordinary; patients grouped around, a few staff milling about. But then angry voices broke over the usual din, and she spotted Mr. Brown, who ran the place, in a heated argument with one of the doctors. Bridie did not know his name, but he had examined her when she'd first come in. She'd begged him to listen to her, but he'd paid her as little mind as the rest of the staff. And then the name rose again, and Bridie could finally make out what they were saying.

"You think I should let this pass just because there's a Hallewell here? Round them all up, the whole lot of Hallewells, and any other Elder family you can get your hands on. In fact..."

Bridie's stomach clenched and her heart began to race. A Hallewell? Here? Surely she must have misunderstood. Surely...

She gripped the bars as her knees wobbled violently and she began to search the room outside her cell, blinking to try to clear her vision. Some movement in her periphery caught her attention and she craned her neck, pressing her face against the bars to try to see as far to her right as she could. What she saw nearly brought her to her knees with shock.

Miss Jessamine was walking along the row, peering into the cells like a tourist at a zoo. And just behind her…

"Eliza!" Bridie turned back over her shoulder. "Emmeline, I don't believe it! It's Eliza! And Miss Jessamine! What in Creator's name are they doing here?"

Emmeline made a strangled sort of noise in response, but Bridie had already turned back to the door. How could she get their attention without alerting Mr. Brown and the doctor? She threw a terrified glance over at the two men, who were now red-faced and shouting directly into each other's faces.

"…must insist that you leave this ward at once, Dr. Blakewell! You will upset the patients! See how they grow agitated!"

"I will not be told to leave my own hospital! How dare you!"

Surely they would not hear her over their own shouting? All around her, patients' voices were growing louder as they became more and more upset. What was one more voice in all the commotion? She might not get another chance. She decided to risk it. Clearing the sleep from her throat again, Bridie called out as loudly as she dared.

"Eliza!"

Neither Eliza nor Miss Jessamine turned at the sound of her voice. Dr. Brown was right—the patients were getting more agitated by the second as the argument between the two men got louder, and the usual din of wailing and shrieking and muttering was growing louder in response. Already within her own cell, Nellie had stopped singing her constant refrain of "Tom o' Bedlam" and had begun a keening sort of cry instead, pressing her hands to her ears and rocking backward and forward. And under all of the noise, there was a strange sort of buzz in the air—the repressed magic of hundreds of Riftborn, whipped into a frenzy as the room seemed to expand with negative energy. Bridie tried again.

"Miss Jessamine!"

This time, she found enough of her voice to carry over the ruckus. Miss Jessamine's head snapped around in surprise, and Eliza peered around her, both of them searching for the source of the sound. Bridie shoved her hand out through the bars and wiggled her fingers, calling out again. Her pulse raced out of control and, for the first time in days, she felt a flicker of her Riftmagic at the tips of her fingers.

"Miss Jessamine! Eliza! Over here!"

Throwing anxious looks over at the arguing men to ensure they had not noticed, Eliza and Miss Jessamine hurried along the row until they reached Bridie's door. Eliza's face appeared in the window, and her fingers reached out to entwine around Bridie's.

"Bridie! There you are! Thank heavens! I was afraid we'd never find you!"

Eliza's face blurred out of focus as tears filled Bridie's eyes, obscuring everything but the feeling of Eliza's fingers around her own. "What in the world are you doing here?" she sobbed.

"Looking for you, of course!"

"But how did you know I was—"

"Never mind all of that, we have to get you out!"

"But how—"

A shriek rang out from the room beyond, and all three women turned to watch as a patient flew across the room like a vengeful spirit, hair flying, and leaped upon Dr. Blakewell, knocking him to the ground with a scream like a wild banshee. Before anyone could do more than stare at the place where they had fallen to the ground, she began to tear at the man so ferociously that her fingertips were reddened with his blood almost instantly.

All hell broke loose. As though the woman's scream was a battle cry to waiting troops, the other patients leaped into motion. It was all Mr. Brown could do to throw his hands up in front of his face before a patient leaped up from one of the chess tables and launched herself upon him. The staff raced around, panicked, but the hysteria seemed to be spreading faster than they could control it. A deafening bell began to clang, adding to the cacophony. More patients began to panic, and from within every cell, the sounds of running and screaming and banging upon the walls and windows fueled the pandemonium.

"Miss Jessamine, you've got to get out of here! It isn't safe!" Eliza cried as a chair flew through the air and smashed into a wall only a few feet away from where they stood outside Bridie's cell. "Just go, I'll find a way to—"

"I'm not leaving you here!" Jessamine cried, looking scandalized at the very thought. "We leave together or not at all, Eliza. We just have to find a way to open this door!"

Bridie looked down at her hands and cursed the dulling of her own magic, though it seemed unlikely she'd have been able to burn through the door.

"Where are your friends?" Jessamine asked. "They can open locks!"

"What friends?" Bridie asked breathlessly.

"I don't know! I thought they'd have made their way here by now. Perhaps they've been caught!" Eliza's voice broke with fear.

"What in the world is going on, Eliza?" Bridie asked. "Who are you—"

But Eliza had suddenly turned on her heel and was marching toward an orderly in a red uniform who was trying to wrestle a patient to the ground. In one fluid motion, she pulled her glove from her hand, reached out, and placed her hand on the back of the man's neck. At once he released the woman upon the floor and stood up straight. From what Bridie could see from across the scene of pandemonium, Eliza whispered something in the man's ear. A moment later, he turned and walked purposely toward them, Eliza following just behind him, her fingers still pressed to the back of his neck. Though the chaos was still breaking all around them, the man did not even flinch as they made their way through a tangle of shouting and grasping and violence. In fact, he did not so much as take his eyes off of Bridie, who stared back at the man with increasing alarm as he barreled toward her. Bridie stepped back from the door just as the man reached it, and then heard the scraping of the key in the lock and the squeal as the mechanism turned, letting the door swing free.

Bridie froze as the door revealed the orderly standing on the other side of it, his hand still extended, though the ring of keys was still dangling from the door. His expression was completely blank, his eyes dazed. Then, Bridie watched as Eliza leaned over the man's shoulder and whispered in his ear again.

"Forget this. Go hide."

And as obediently as a well-trained animal, the man turned, never looking once at Eliza, and took off into the tumult again, taking refuge underneath a table. All of this happened so swiftly that not a single person in the room seemed to have noticed. Mr. Brown was nowhere to be seen, evidently having fled the room. Dr. Blakewell was still curled up on the floor as several patients descended upon him now, fists flying. A patient had broken a window with a chair and several others were now trying to climb out of it. A blanket in the corner was smoking.

All Bridie could do was stammer at Eliza.

"I... how did you..."

"There's no time. We have to figure out how to get you out of here!" Eliza replied, grasping Bridie by the wrist and pulling her out of the cell. "If we can slip out under cover of the fight..."

"Eliza, no! Wait! We can't go yet!"

Eliza's eyes widened at her. "Bridie, whatever it is, surely it can't be more important than getting you out of here!"

"Yes, it can! Eliza, it's your mother! She's in here with me!"

"My... what did you say?"

"Your mother, Eliza! With me in this cell!"

Eliza's face drained of all color. She could not seem to bear to look anywhere but at Bridie's face. "I... I don't understand—"

"Eliza, just... look! It's her, I swear it!" Bridie's panic and frustration and fear all bubbled up inside her at once. She reached out and dragged Eliza into the cell until she was standing right in front of Emmeline.

And though the fight raged on outside the door as more staff answered the frantic ringing of the bell, everything seemed to stop within the walls of the cell. Eliza stared down at the figure of her mother, gaunt and frail, curled into the corner. She did not speak—she simply stared, shaking her head, her eyes slowly filling with tears.

"It's... it's not possible..." she whispered. "All this time?"

"No, she was in the workhouse, Eliza, in one of the Riftwards. I recognized her—that's why they wouldn't let me leave," Bridie said. She knelt beside Emmeline and smoothed the hair back from her face, which Emmeline had hidden in her arms. "Emmeline, it's time to go. Eliza's here to rescue us. We need to go now."

Emmeline lifted her face from her arms and blinked around, her eyes falling on Eliza. At once she let out a moan and averted her eyes, as though the sight of her daughter was too bright, like looking directly into the sun. Eliza might have turned to stone—she stood rooted to the spot, her eyes brimming, shaking her head in shock.

"Impossible," she whispered again.

Bridie reached out for Eliza's hand, anxious to bring the two women together, but at that moment a scream rang out from the doorway, and they all turned to see Miss Jessamine scurrying into the cell with them, her arms flung over her head.

"What's..."

"The cells! They're all opening!" she gasped.

Bridie jumped to her feet, swaying unsteadily, and ran to the doorway with Eliza. Sure enough, what had begun as a fight had now exploded into unimaginable chaos. Up and down the walls, cell doors were bursting open as a young man in a janitor's uniform ran past them, running his outstretched fingers over them.

"It's Eli!" Eliza cried, her voice rich with relief.

Bridie didn't ask who Eli was and she didn't care. She could not find room for curiosity as adrenaline and sheer terror flooded her veins. Patients spilled out into tumult, adding their shouts and cries to the din. Some simply ran for the doors, but others leaped into the fray like wild animals scenting blood. As she watched, a Catalyst set fire to a long set of curtains. Flames licked their way up the red fabric and smoke began to billow through the room.

"We've got to get out of here!" Bridie gasped, and she raced back to Emmeline and began tugging at her arm to get her up.

At that moment, the man Eliza had called Eli came skidding to a stop in front of the cell door. He took one look inside and his mouth fell open. "Eliza! Miss Hallewell! Is this Bridie?"

"Yes! We've found her! Now, how do we get out of here before we're all burned alive?" Eliza gasped.

"Where's Jasper?" Jessamine asked.

"He's already out. Don't worry about Jasper, he can look after himself. Now, follow me!" Eli shouted.

"Eliza, help me with her!" Bridie cried out, for Emmeline was whimpering and refusing to leave the cell, her wide eyes now fixed on the fire steadily snaking its way across the far wall. Eliza rushed forward and grasped ahold of Emmeline's other arm. Together, they dragged her out of the cell and into the smoke-choked chaos.

"What about the others?" Bridie gasped, gesturing helplessly to Nellie and the other old woman curled in a ball in the corner of their cell.

"There's no time! We have to go, now!" Eli yelled.

Bridie stumbled back into the cell and gave Nellie's arm one last, fruitless tug, but the woman shook her head. Her eyes filling with angry tears, Bridie shouted at the woman. "You must run, Nellie! You must get out!"

But Nellie would not move; she just began placidly humming her song again. Bridie gave a strangled cry of frustration and turned her back on Nellie. There was nothing more she could do. They would be lucky to make it out alive as it was. Half-blinded by tears, she hurried out after Eliza and the others.

They could hardly see which way they were going now, the smoke was so thick. Several times they tripped over bodies or stumbled on overturned furniture. A woman reached out from the floor and snatched at Jessamine's dress. Jessamine shrieked and tugged herself free, a handful of lace petticoat coming away in the woman's claws. Hardly any staff remained now—all had fled for the exits or else were among the feebly stirring bodies upon the floor. Dr. Blakewell lay utterly motionless in a dark puddle of his own pooling blood. A splintered bit of wood protruded from the side of his neck.

They burst through a door at the end of the room into a corridor full of screaming and fleeing people. They flung themselves into the buffeting crowd, allowing it to sweep them along like a current toward the staircase. People were so panicked to escape that they were shoving each other, and several bodies tumbled heavily down the stairs under the trampling feet. Eli had pulled Emmeline onto his shoulders in a fireman's carry rather than continue to drag her along. It was impossible to tell patient from staff, Riftborn from Dignus among the sea of fleeing bodies—all they could do was try not to lose each other and keep on their feet so they wouldn't be trampled.

At last, they burst through the door at the bottom of the staircase and out into the grounds, where the scenes of chaos continued. Patients were scaling the walls and fences and climbing into trees while Praesidio guards swarmed the grounds, some dragging firefighting wagons and ladders, others weapons. People lay all over the neatly manicured lawns, coughing and wiping soot from their blackened faces and hands. The fire had spread rapidly, shattering windows and creeping toward the roof of the building. Desperate screams could be heard from the floors above. Bridie turned back just in time to see a woman fling herself from a window on the top floor. She whimpered and squeezed her eyes shut so that she wouldn't have to see the moment she hit the ground.

Eli led them around the back side of a storage shed, where Bridie's legs gave out beneath her at last and she sank to the grass, the air burning in her lungs as she struggled to catch her breath.

"We've got to split up," Eli wheezed. Emmeline lay limply over his shoulders like a rag doll.

"What? No!" Eliza cried out.

338

"Eliza, we must! If anyone sees us together, we'll all be arrested! You and Miss Jessamine need to blend back into the crowd on the lawn."

"But how will you escape? What will you—"

"Eli!"

They all turned to see a second man in a janitor's uniform waving frantically at them from the top of the nearby wall.

Eli's mouth fell open. "Jasper, what the devil?"

"I've got transport! Now, come on, before we're spotted!" the man called Jasper hissed.

Bridie watched as Eliza bit at her lip, clearly torn about leaving them. Bridie reached out and squeezed her hand.

"It's okay. We'll be okay. I'll take care of her, Eliza."

Eliza's lips trembled and she pressed them together. "You can trust Eli and Jasper. Just do what they tell you to do. Send me word right away, you understand? As soon as you're safe."

"Of... of course," Bridie promised.

Eliza's arm shot out and pulled Bridie right off the ground and into a hug so fierce that it would have knocked the breath from her if she'd had any left in her lungs.

"Thank you. Thank you for coming for me," Bridie gasped.

"I love you, Bridie. Stay safe. All of you," Eliza whispered back.

"We will. I love you, too."

Eliza pulled away and threw one last tortured look at her mother's limp body. Then she grabbed Miss Jessamine by the hand and started back across the lawn toward a knot of Praesidio guards speaking with a frantic-looking Mr. Brown, who was no doubt beside himself wondering what had happened to Miss Jessamine in all the confusion.

"Come on, shift it!" Jasper hissed. Eli started to lower Eliza's mother to the ground, but Bridie reached out a hand to stop him.

"No! She's got to come, too!" Bridie cried.

"It's Bridie, right? Look, Bridie, I appreciate that you're worried about her, but we can't rescue every patient that—"

"No, no, it's not that! She's Eliza's mother!"

Eli's face went slack with shock. "Eliza's..."

"Her mother, yes! And we can't leave her here!" Bridie snapped.

"Oi!"

Jasper snapped his fingers impatiently at them from the top of the wall. Eli hesitated only one more moment, and then hoisted Emmeline more securely onto his shoulders. "Let's go, then."

They made a break for the far wall where Jasper waited for them, not bothering to wait and see if they were being pursued. Jasper reached down and heaved Emmeline up onto the wall beside him, cursing loudly.

"Who the devil is this?"

"I'll explain later, just get her into the carriage," Eli panted. Jasper and Emmeline disappeared over the wall, and Eli scrambled up the stones and pulled himself to the top. Then he reached down a hand and held it out to Bridie.

"Come on, now. I'll pull you up."

Bridie took a deep breath and with all of her remaining strength, reached up and grasped Eli's hand. Bracing her bare feet against the stone, together they managed to haul her up onto the top. She clung there for a moment while Eli jumped down on the other side and then swung her legs over the edge. The pavement swam below her.

"Just jump! I'll catch you!" Eli called to her.

With a whimper, Bridie closed her eyes and let go. She landed hard in Eli's arms, and he set her on the ground, keeping a hand on her while she stumbled to keep her feet. There was no time to rest, however. He tugged her toward the waiting carriage, where Jasper had already heaved Emmeline inside and deposited her onto the seat. Eli and Bridie climbed hastily inside, collapsing onto the seat as Jasper pulled the door shut behind them.

"Jasper, who's driv—" Eli began, but the carriage jolted forward violently, tearing them away from the madness and the flames and the crowds gathering on the street to watch the spectacle of escaped lunatics and a madhouse going up in smoke.

For a few minutes, there was silence but for the jingling of the carriage and the heavy labored breathing as they all fought to catch their breath again. Then, the carriage turned into a narrow alleyway and came to a sudden stop. Bridie felt her stomach clench as she heard a pair of boots hit the pavement and the door swing open.

A wild-haired woman stood there, dressed in a man's suit, hands on her hips and a fierce gleam of anger in her eyes.

"Is one of you going to tell me what in the absolute bloody blazes is going on?" she barked.

Eli turned to Jasper. "You told Sully?!"

Jasper held up his hands in surrender. "Don't look at me, I didn't tell her. She was waiting out here when I scaled the wall with the documents."

"I was tipped off," Sully snapped.

"Tipped off? By who?"

Sully threw a sour look at Jasper. "You ought to take more care than to piss off a woman like Tillie McCleary." Jasper swore.

"Look, Sully—"

I don't want your excuses or your useless apologies, and I'm not getting caught housing an escaped mental patient. She'll have to find somewhere else to... to..."

But at that moment, Emmeline had stirred fretfully and rolled over on the seat, her curtain of blonde hair falling away to reveal her face. The woman named Sully took one look at her and let out a gasp, clapping her hand over her mouth.

"Creator burn it all. Emmeline Braxton."

Eli looked wildly between Sully and Emmeline. "You know this woman?"

Sully dropped her hand from her mouth and nodded. "We met. A long time ago, now."

"But how..."

"There's no time for that. Bloody hell, we're in for it now. Close the shades, and keep them quiet and their heads down."

"But I thought you said you couldn't be caught housing—"

"Never mind what I said! You can't imagine the danger we're in!" She threw a burlap sack full of clothes into the carriage. "Get changed, all of you."

"Sully, you've got to tell me what's going on!" Eli cried.

Sully's face spasmed with some painful emotion. "I will. But not here. We need to get undercover."

And with uncharacteristic gentleness, Sully reached out and laid a hand on Emmeline's forearm. "I took care of him, just as you asked. It looks like we both kept our word," she murmured. Then she glared around at all of them, a finger pressed to her lips, and slammed the carriage door again.

"Who was that woman? What is she talking about?" Bridie whispered as soon as the door had closed.

Eli simply shook his head, pulling the bundle of clothes from the bag. "That's Sully, and the first thing you should know about her is

341

that she won't tell you a blasted thing until she wants to," he said, squeezing the words out between his teeth. "Here, put this on over your shift," he added, tossing a dress and a bonnet into Bridie's lap.

Bridie tugged the dress down over her head and shoved her arms through the sleeves. The carriage juddered away again over the cobblestones. Relief would come, she knew, but not yet. For now, all she could think of were the souls still trapped inside Bedlam as it burned. The last thing she saw before Eli drew the shade down over the window was a single plume of smoke, curling like a snake against the stormy bosom of the sky.

EPILOGUE

J OSIAH STOOD BEFORE THE GOLDEN DOORS, his eyes
closed, his face uplifted. He took the silent air in slowly through
his nose, held it, let it fill him, and then expelled it through his
parted lips. His destiny lay beyond those doors. He had known it since
he was a small child, following his father into the hallowed halls of
the Illustratum, feeling the eyes of Elders past staring down at him.
They whispered to him. The very motes of dust that hung in the air
had vibrated with the surety of this calling. He had spent every day
toiling and building and shaping and scheming, bringing himself inch
by hard-won inch closer to that destiny.

Today he would seize it at last.

And when he had done so—when his name rang out in that
Council room, sealing his position and his power, he would walk
through those golden doors and he would commune with the Rift for
the very first time. His fingers ached with the desire to push those
doors open and finally to understand. Finally not just to believe, but to
know.

The wait was very nearly over.

He touched his hand to his breast pocket, where the speech he
had been toiling over for the last week sat folded and safely tucked
away. It was not until the previous night that he had finally decided
he was satisfied with it. He had not shared a word of it with anyone
but Francis, and he had agreed that it struck all the right notes, not a
single phrase out of tune. There would be many he would never win
over, but he could not focus on that—after all, he was not the only man
who had spent his life standing in front of these doors and dreaming
of the day he could walk through them. But the opposition, though

unquestionably loud, would be small. And with John Morgan there, voicing his support, any contention would quickly fizzle and die. No, Josiah was not worried. He felt more sure of himself than he had in a very long time. He was ready.

He turned his back on the golden doors and walked back toward the Council chambers. He was not the only member who had arrived early. The chamber had been full of dark mutterings and whispered rumors since the sun had barely risen. Josiah had avoided the chamber, choosing to spend the morning in his own office, reviewing his speech and reading through the legislation he planned to prioritize when he had at last taken the highest seat. He would waste no time, he was determined about that. Too many times he had watched as important ideas had languished and died on the chamber floor. Things would be very different when he assumed the mantle. He would engage in none of this sophomoric foolishness. Efficiency, reverence, and authority, in all things, always.

In the Illustratum clock tower, the bell struck the noon hour, sending deep vibrations through the air as he walked the final few steps to the Council chamber doors. It felt as though the air, the halls, the very stones beneath his feet were heralding his rise, singing the rightness of it all deep in his bones. He had never felt more confident as he reached for the handle and pushed the door open.

He thought he was prepared for what would meet him on the other side of that door. He was terribly wrong.

He knew something was amiss the moment he laid eyes on the room. Elders were scurrying from bench to bench, huddled together like gossiping old women. This was to be expected, but the energy was all wrong. This was not political intrigue. Something had happened—something unexpected.

His heart seized up in his chest. The High Elder. Surely he had not...

But no—John Morgan was there, looking ill and gaunt, perhaps, but very much alive. As Josiah watched, a Praesidio guard bent low over him, gesticulating wildly as he spoke. Josiah pushed his way into the room, determined to discover what all the commotion was about, but Francis descended upon him at once and obliged.

"Meeting's been postponed. There's a fire broken out," he said.

"What are you on about? A fire? What's all this?"

Francis lowered his voice. "Josiah, it's Bedlam. Bedlam is burning."

Josiah blinked. Surely he had misunderstood. It couldn't be. Not today.

Francis looked cautiously over his shoulder at the other Elders, many of whom had now paused in their milling about to stare at Josiah. Then he took Josiah by the arm and steered him back out into the hallway. Josiah could feel the eyes burning into his retreating back until the door closed behind them.

"What happened? How did it start?"

"We're still trying to parse out the details. It seems that some sort of fight broke out, and then one of the patients that got free of the staff set fire to the place."

"A Catalyst?"

"No way to know. They oughtn't to have that kind of control over their magic, not with the levels of Riftmead they use to subdue them in that place, but who's to say?"

"And the... the patients? Are they all accounted for?"

Francis shook his head, looking grim. "It was utter chaos. There have likely been escapes, but they won't know for many hours who is accounted for, dead or alive."

Josiah ran a frantic hand through his hair. All trace of his earlier confidence in the rightness of the world was gone, replaced by a gnawing anxiety that ate away at his insides. "How do we confirm it? How do we know if they've still got the maid and the Braxton woman?"

"Only time. It's a bloody disaster over there, Josiah. There's no possible way to know for hours yet, and even then... charred bodies aren't easy to identify."

Josiah swore.

"There's... there's something else I feel I should warn you about," Francis said, his voice heavy with hesitation.

"Well? Out with it, man!"

Francis cleared his throat. "It's your daughter. It's been reported that she was in the place at the time."

It was several seconds before the meaning of Francis's words sunk in. Then Josiah swayed on his feet, and Francis shot out an arm to steady him.

"Steady now. She's all right. It seems she was there for charity work, or something like that."

"She's all right?"

"Shaken but unharmed, according to the information from the Praesidio. She's been seen to and sent home to Larkspur Manor along with her lady's maid," Francis replied, keeping his voice calm and steady.

Josiah closed his eyes, running a hand over his face. He suddenly felt so weary. "What the devil was she doing there, of all places?"

"You know those meddling charity circles. They can't help but stick their noses in the worst hellholes they can find. My Rebecca toured a workhouse last month and took to her bed for two days afterward. These female temperaments. They can't stomach the realities of running a modern society. I'm sure it was a coincidence, Josiah, albeit an unfortunate one."

"Unfortunate? Are you mad? This is a catastrophe! What if she'd been killed? What if she's seen something I can't explain away?"

"You'll have to keep her close to home, Josiah. The wedding is just a month away."

"Well, is the fire under control at least? How bad is it?"

But Francis shook his head. "There won't be a beam left standing. It's going up even as we speak."

Josiah turned on his heel and took off in the direction of his office. He was vaguely aware of Francis calling after him, but he did not stop to listen. He had to see it for himself. He had to know.

He burst through the door and crossed the room at a run, throwing his doors wide and stepping out onto the balcony. He could smell it first, the ever-present stench of the Thames below, now cloaked in the thick, choking scent of smoke. He squinted across the water and spotted it; a great pillar of black smoke rising like an exorcised spirit into the grey London sky. He could hear the screams and shouts carried on the wind, hear the bells of the fire brigade as they fought a battle they could not win against a raging inferno. At last, the façade of Bedlam reflected the madness within.

Josiah reached into his breast pocket and removed his speech—a speech that would now have to wait as he tried to ascertain what damage had been done. He reached for his drawer and then, on second thought, walked over to his fireplace and tossed it, without a second glance, into the sinuously twisting flames.

Let it all burn at once, he thought savagely. If he must rise from the ashes of another scandal, so be it. But rise he would, and Creator have mercy on anyone who dared to stand in his way.

E.E. Holmes is a writer, teacher, and actor living in central Massachusetts with her husband, two children, and a small, but surprisingly loud dog. When not writing, she enjoys performing, watching unhealthy amounts of British television, and reading with her children. Please visit www.eeholmes.com to learn more about E.E. Holmes, *The World of the Gateway*, and *The Riftmagic Saga*.

Made in the USA
Middletown, DE
25 November 2022